ANOTHER LITERARY TRIUMPH

from "The best novelist
of his generation."
—Harper's

John Updike

"ONE ANSWER TO THE QUESTION,
WHO WILL SUCCEED HEMINGWAY
AND FAULKNER?"
—David Boroff
The National Observer

"NATURAL, PERTINENT AND FRESH
. . . SUBTLE, SUPERBLY WRITTEN."
—Newsweek

"ANY BOOK BEARING HIS SIGNA-
TURE IS AN EVENT."
—Washington Post

"ONE OF THE MILESTONES OF
MODERN LETTERS . . . "
—St. Petersburg Times

"A BRILLIANT AND MOVING
NOVEL."
—Baltimore Sun

John Updike

THE CENTAUR

"Heaven is the creation inconceivable to
man, earth the creation conceivable to
him. He himself is the creature on the
boundary between heaven and earth."

KARL BARTH

FAWCETT CREST • **NEW YORK**

THE CENTAUR

Published by Fawcett Crest Books, a unit of CBS Publications, The Consumer Publishing Division of CBS Inc., by arrangement with Alfred A. Knopf, Inc.

Chapter II of this novel, in a somewhat different form, was first printed in *The New Yorker* under the title "On the Way to School."

Chapter VIII, slightly shortened, was first printed in *Esquire* under the title "After the Storm."

The lines by Karl Barth are from his *Dogmatics in Outline*. S. C. M. Press, London; Torch Books (Harper & Row), New York.

ISBN: 0-449-23974-8

Printed in the United States of America

21   20   19   18   17   16   15   14   13

But it was still needful that a life should be given to expiate that ancient sin,—the theft of fire. It happened that Chiron, noblest of all the Centaurs (who are half horses and half men), was wandering the world in agony from a wound that he had received by strange mischance. For, at a certain wedding-feast among the Lapithæ of Thessaly, one of the turbulent Centaurs had attempted to steal away the bride. A fierce struggle followed, and in the general confusion, Chiron, blameless as he was, had been wounded by a poisoned arrow. Ever tormented with the hurt and never to be healed, the immortal Centaur longed for death, and begged that he might be accepted as an atonement for Prometheus. The gods heard his prayer and took away his pain and his immortality. He died like any wearied man, and Zeus set him as a shining archer among the stars.

—*Old Greek Folk Stories Told Anew*
BY JOSEPHINE PRESTON PEABODY, 1897

THE CENTAUR

I

CALDWELL turned and as he turned his ankle received
an arrow. The class burst into laughter. The pain scaled
the slender core of his shin, whirled in the complexities of his
knee, and, swollen broader, more thunderous, mounted into
his bowels. His eyes were forced upward to the blackboard,
where he had chalked the number 5,000,000,000, the prob-
able age in years of the universe. The laughter of the class,
graduating from the first shrill bark of surprise into a deliberately aimed hooting, seemed to crowd against him, to
crush the privacy that he so much desired, a privacy in which
he could be alone with his pain, gauging its strength, estimat-
ing its duration, inspecting its anatomy. The pain extended a
feeler into his head and unfolded its wet wings along the walls
of his thorax, so that he felt, in his sudden scarlet blindness, to
be himself a large bird waking from sleep. The blackboard,
milky slate smeared with the traces of last night's washing,
clung to his consciousness like a membrane. The pain seemed
to be displacing with its own hairy segments his heart and
lungs; as its grip swelled in his throat he felt he was holding
his brain like a morsel on a platter high out of hungry reach.
Several of the boys in their bright shirts all colors of the rainbow had risen upright at their desks, leering and baying at
their teacher, cocking their muddy shoes on the folding seats.
The confusion became unbearable. Caldwell limped to the
door and shut it behind him on the furious festal noise.

Out in the hall, the feather end of the arrow scraped on the
floor with every step. The metallic scratch and stiff rustle
mixed disagreeably. His stomach began to sway with nausea.
The dim, long walls of the ochre hall wavered; the classroom
doors, inset with square numbered panes of frosted glass,
seemed experimental panels immersed in an activated liquid
charged with children's voices chanting French, singing
anthems, discussing problems of Social Science. *Avez-vous
une maison jolie? Oui, j'ai une maison très jolie for amber*

9

*waves of grain, for purple mountain majesties above the
fruited plain throughout our history boys and girls* (this was
the voice of Pholos), *the federal government has grown in
prestige, power, and authority but we must not forget, boys
and girls, that by origin we are a union of sovereign republics,
the* United *God shed his grace on thee, and crown thy good
with brotherhood*—the beautiful song was blindly persisting
in Caldwell's brain. *To shining sea.* The old baloney. He had
heard it first in Passaic. Since then, how strange he had
grown! His top half felt all afloat in a starry firmament of
ideals and young voices singing; the rest of his self was
heavily sunk in a swamp where it must, eventually, drown.
Each time the feathers brushed the floor, the shaft worked in
his wound. He tried to keep that leg from touching the floor,
but the jagged clatter of the three remaining hooves sounded
so loud he was afraid one of the doors would snap open and
another teacher emerge to bar his way. In this crisis his
fellow-teachers seemed herdsmen of terror, threatening to
squeeze him back into the room with the students. His bowels
weakly convulsed; on the glimmering varnished boards, right
in front of the trophy case with its hundred silver eyes, he
deposited, without breaking stride, a steaming dark spreading
cone. His great gray-dappled flanks twitched with distaste, but
like a figurehead on the prow of a foundering ship his head
and torso pressed forward.

The faint watery blur above the side doors drew him on.
Here, at the far end of the hall, through windows exteriorly
screened against vandalism, light from outdoors entered the
school and, unable to spread in the viscid, varnished atmosphere, remained captured, like water in oil, above the entrance. Toward this bluish bubble of light the moth inside
him drove Caldwell's high, handsome, compounded body.
His viscera squirmed; a dusty antenna brushed the roof of
his mouth. Yet also on his palate he eagerly tasted an antici-
pation of fresh air. The air brightened. He bucked the double
doors whose dirty glass was reinforced with chicken wire. In a
tumult of pain, the arrow battering the steel balusters, he
threw himself down the short flight of steps to the concrete
landing. In ascending these steps a child had hastily penciled
FUCK on the darkly lustrous wall. Caldwell gripped the brass
bar and, his mouth thin with determination beneath his
pinched and frightened eyes, he pushed into the open.

His nostrils made two plumes of frost. It was January. The
clear blue of the towering sky seemed forceful yet enigmatic.

The immense level swath of the school's side lawn, pointed at the corners by plantings of pines, was, though this was winter's heart, green; but the color was frozen, paralyzed, vestigial, artificial. Beyond the school grounds, a trolley car, gently clanging, floated up the pike toward Ely. Virtually empty— the time was eleven o'clock, the shoppers were all going the other way, into Alton—it swayed lightly on its tracks and the straw seats showered sparks of gold through the windows. Outdoors, in the face of spatial grandeur, his pain seemed abashed. Dwarfed, it retreated into his ankle, became hard and sullen and contemptible. Caldwell's strange silhouette took on dignity; his shoulders—a little narrow for so large a creature—straightened, and he moved, if not at a prance, yet with such pressured stoic grace that the limp was enrolled in his stride. He took the paved walk between the frozen lawn and the brimming parking lot. Beneath his belly the grimacing grilles flashed in the white winter sun; the scratches in the chrome were iridescent as diamonds. The cold began to shorten his breath. Behind him in the salmon-brick hulk of the high school a buzzer sounded, dismissing the class he had abandoned. With a sluggish digestive rumble, the classes shifted.

Hummel's Garage adjoined the Olinger High School property, a little irregular river of asphalt separating them. Its association with the school was not merely territorial. Hummel had for many years, though not now, served on the school board, and his young red-haired wife, Vera, was the girls' physical education instructor. The garage got much trade from the high school. Boys brought their derelict jalopies here to be fixed, and younger boys pumped up basketballs with the free air. In the front part of the building, in the large room where Hummel kept his accounts and his tattered, blackened library of spare-parts catalogues and where two wooden desks side by side each supported a nibbled foliation of papers and pads and spindles skewering up to the rusted tip fluffy stacks of pink receipts, here a cloudy glass case, its cracked top repaired with a lightning-shaped line of tire tape, kept candy in crackling wrappers waiting for children's pennies. Here, on a brief row of greasy folding chairs overlooking a five-foot cement pit whose floor was flush with the alley outside, the male teachers sometimes—more of old than recently—sat at noon and smoked and ate Fifth Avenues and Reese's Peanut Butter Cups and Essick's Coughdrops and put their tightly laced and polished feet up on the railing and let their martyred nerves uncurl while, in the three-sided pit below, an automobile like an immense metal baby was washed and changed by Hummel's swarthy men.

The main and greater part of the garage was approached on an asphalt ramp as rough, streaked, gouged, flecked, and bubbled as a hardened volcanic flow. In the wide green door opened to admit motored vehicles, there was a little man-sized door with KEEP CLOSED dribblingly dabbed in blue touch-up paint below the latch. Caldwell lifted the latch and entered. His hurt leg cursed the turn needed to close the door behind him.

A deep warm darkness was lit by sparks. The floor of the grotto was waxed black by oil drippings. At the far side of the long workbench, two shapeless men in goggles caressed a great downward-drooping fan of flame broken into dry drops. Another man, staring upward out of round eyesockets white in a black face, rolled by on his back and disappeared beneath the body of a car. His eyes adjusting to the gloom, Caldwell saw heaped about him overturned fragments of automobiles, fragile and phantasmal, fenders like corpses of turtles, bristling engines like disembodied hearts. Hisses and angry thumps lived in the mottled air. Near where Caldwell stood, an old potbellied coal stove bent brilliant pink through its seams. He hesitated to leave its radius of warmth, though the thing in his ankle was thawing, and his stomach assuming an unsettled flutter.

Hummel himself appeared in the doorway of the workshop. As they walked toward each other, Caldwell experienced a mocking sensation of walking toward a mirror, for Hummel also limped. One of his legs was smaller than the other, due to a childhood fall. He looked hunched, pale, weathered; the recent years had diminished the master mechanic. The Esso and Mobilgas chains had both built service stations a few blocks away along the pike, and now that the war was over, and everybody could buy new cars with their war-work money, the demand for repairs had plummeted.

"George! Is it your lunch already?" Hummel's voice, though slight, was expertly pitched to pierce the noise of the shop.

As Caldwell answered, a particularly harsh and rapid series of metallic clashes sprang up in the air and flattened his words; his voice, thin and strained, seemed to hang hushed in his own ears. "No, Jesus, I have a class right now."

"Well what is it then?" Hummel's delicate gray face,

bleached by spots of silver bristle, alerted timidly, as if any-thing unexpected had the power to hurt him. His wife had done that to him, Caldwell knew.

"Lookit," Caldwell said, "what one of the damn kids did to me." He put his injured foot up on a severed fender and lifted his trouser leg.

The mechanic bent over the arrow and touched the feathers tentatively. His knuckles were deeply ingrained with grime, his touch silken with lubricant. "Steel shaft," he said. "You're lucky the tip went clean through." He signalled and a little tripod on wheels came rattling by itself across the bumpy black floor. Hummel took from it a pair of wire cutters, the type that has an elbow hinge on one jaw to give extra leverage. As the string of a helium balloon slips from a child's absentminded fingers, so fear set Caldwell's mind floating free. In his dizzy abstraction he tried to analyze the cutters as a diagram: mechanical advantage equals load over force less friction, length of lever AF (fulcrum = nut) over length FB, B being biting point of gleaming crescent jaw, multiplied by secondary mechanical advantage of accessory fulcrum-lever complex, in turn multiplied by mechanical advantage of Hummel's calm and grimy workman's hand, clenching action of contracting flexors and rigid phalanges five-fold, $MA \times MA \times 5MA$ = titanic. Hummel bent his back so Caldwell could brace himself on his shoulders. Un-certain this was being offered and reluctant to presume, Cald-well remained erect and stared upward. The beaded boards of the garage ceiling had been painted velvet by rising smoke and spider traces. Through his knee Caldwell felt Hummel's back shift with twitches of fitting; he felt metal touch his skin through his sock. The fender shuddered unsteadily. Hummel's shoulders tensed with effort and Caldwell clamped his teeth upon an outcry, for it seemed the cutters were biting not into a metal shaft but into a protruding nerve of his anatomy. The crescent jaws gnashed; in a swift telescopic thrust Cald-well's pain shot upwards; coruscated; and then Hummel's shoulders relaxed. "No good," the mechanic said. "I thought it might be hollow but it isn't. George, you'll have to come over to the bench."

Trembling through the length of his legs, which seemed as thin and rickety as bicycle spokes, Caldwell followed Hum-mel and obediently set his foot up on an old Coca-Cola case the mechanic rummaged out of the sooty rubble beneath the long workbench. Trying to ignore the arrow that like an optical defect in his lower vision followed him everywhere, Caldwell concentrated on a bushel-basket full of discarded fuel pumps. Hummel pulled the chain of a naked electric bulb. The windows were opaquely spattered with paint from the outside; the walls between them were hung with wrenches aligned by size, ballpeen hammers with taped handles, electric drills, screwdrivers a yard long, intricate sprocketed socketed tools whose names and functions he would never know, neat coils of frazzled wire, calipers, pliers, and, stuck and taped here and there in crevices and bare spots, advertisements, toasted and tattered and ancient. One showed a cat holding up a paw and another a giant trying in vain to tear a patented fan belt. A card said SAFETY FIRST and another, taped over a window pane, PROTECT YOUR ◁◎▷ ◁◎▷ YOU WON'T BE GIVEN ANOTHER PAIR.

Like the outpouring of a material hymn to material creation, the top of the bench was strewn with loops of rubber, tubes of copper, cylinders of graphite, threaded elbows of iron, cans of oil, chunks of wood, rags, drops, and dusty scraps of all elements. This tumble, full of tools, was raked by intense flashes of light from the two workmen down the bench. They were fashioning what looked like an ornamented bronze girdle for a woman with a tiny waist and flaring hips. Hummel put an asbestos glove on his left hand and plucked a broad scrap of tin from the heap. With the cutters he sliced into the center and, abruptly deft, cleverly folded the piece into a cupped shield, which he fitted around the arrow at the back of Caldwell's ankle. "So you won't feel the heat so much," he explained, and snapped the fingers of his ungloved hand. "Archy, could I have the torch a minute now?"

The helper, careful to keep his feet from tangling in the trailing wire, brought over the acetylene torch. It was a little black jug spitting white flame edged with green. Where the flame streamed from the spout there was a transparent gap. Caldwell locked his jaw on his panic. The arrow had been revealed to him as a live nerve. He braced for the necessary pain.

There was none. Magically, he found himself at the center of an immense insensible nimbus. The light startled into being sharp triangular shadows all around him, on the bench, on the walls. Holding the tin shield in his gloved hand, Hummel without the protection of goggles squinted into the blazing, purring heart of Caldwell's ankle. His face, dead-pale and drastically foreshortened, glittered fanatically on the points of his two eyes. As Caldwell looked down, a wisp of Hummel's tired gray hair strayed forward, shrivelled, and vanished in a whiff of smoke. The workmen watched mutely. It seemed to be taking too long. Now Caldwell was feeling the heat; the touch of tin began to boil against his leg. But by closing his eyes Caldwell could envision in the top of his skull the arrow bending, melting, its molecules letting go. Something metal and small chinked to the floor. The pressures encircling his foot lifted. He opened his eyes, and the torch went off. The yellow electric light seemed brown.

"Ronnie, could you get me a soaking wet rag?"

Hummel explained to Caldwell, "I don't want to pull it through hot."

"You're a damn good workman," Caldwell said. His voice was fainter than he had expected, his praise empty of blood. He watched Ronnie, a one-eyed boy with shoulders like tummocks, take an oily rag and plunge it into a small bucket of black water standing under a far electric bulb. Reflected light bobbed and leaped in the violated water as if to be free. Ronnie handed the rag to Hummel and Hummel squatted and applied it. Cold wet dribbled into Caldwell's shoe and a faint aromatic hissing rose to his nostrils. "We'll wait now a minute," Hummel said, and remained squatting, carefully holding Caldwell's pants leg up from the wound. Caldwell met the stares of the three workmen—the third had come out from under the car—and smiled self-deprecatingly. Now that relief was at hand he had a margin in which to feel embarrassed. His smile made the helpers frown. To them it was as if an automobile had tried to speak. Caldwell let his eyes go out of focus and thought of far-off things, of green fields, of Chariclo as a lithe young woman, of Peter as a baby, of how he had pushed him on his Kiddy Kar with a long forked stick along the pavements under the horsechestnut trees. They had been too poor to afford a baby carriage; the kid had learned to steer, too early? He worried about the kid when he had the time.

"Now George: hold tight," Hummel said. The arrow slid out backwards with a slick spurt of pain. Hummel stood up, his face pink, scorched by fire or flushed in satisfaction. His three moronic helpers clustered around jostling to see the silver shaft, painted at its unfeathered end with blood. Caldwell's ankle, at last free, felt soft, unbraced; his shoe seemed to be filling with warm slow liquid. The pain had changed color, had shifted into the healing spectrum. The body knew. The ache came now to his heart rhythmically: Nature's breathing.

Hummel bent down and picked something up. He held it to his nose and sniffed. Then he set it in Caldwell's palm still piping hot. It was an arrowhead. Three-sided, so sharply pointed its edges were concave, it seemed too dainty a thing to have caused such a huge dislocation. Caldwell noticed that his palms were mottled with shock and exertion; a film of sweat broke out on his brow. He asked Hummel, "Why did you smell it?"

"Wondering if it was poisoned."

"It wouldn't be, would it?"

"I don't know. These kids today." He added, "I didn't smell anything."

"I don't think they'd do anything like that," Caldwell insisted, thinking of Achilles and Hercules, Jason and Asclepios, those attentive respectful faces.

"Where do the kids get their money? is what I'd like to know," Hummel said, as if kindly trying to draw Caldwell's mind away from a hopeless matter. He held up the headless shaft and wiped the blood off on his glove. "This is good steel," he said. "This is an expensive arrow."

"Their fathers give it to the bastards," Caldwell said, feeling stronger, clearer-headed. His class, he must get back.

"There's too much money around," the old mechanic said with wan spite. "They'll buy any junk Detroit puts out." His face had regained its gray color, its acetylene tan; crinkled and delicate like an often-folded sheet of foil, his face became almost womanly with quiet woe and Caldwell became nervous.

"Al, how much do I owe you? I got to get back. Zimmerman'll have my neck."

"Nothing, George. Forget it. I'm glad I was able to do it." He laughed. "It isn't every day I burn an arrow out of a man's leg."

"I wouldn't feel right. I asked a craftsman to give me the benefit of his craft—" He groped toward his wallet pocket insincerely.

"Forget it, George. It took a minute. Be big enough to accept a favor. Vera says you're one of the few over there who doesn't try to make her life more difficult."

Caldwell felt his face go wooden; he wondered how much

Hummel knew of why Vera's life was difficult. He must get back. "Al, I'm much obliged to you. Believe me." There was never a way, somehow, of really getting gratitude across. You went through life in a town and sometimes loved the people in it and never told them, you were ashamed.

"Here," Hummel said. "Don't you want this?" He held out the arrow's bright shaft. Caldwell had absent-mindedly slipped the point into his side coat pocket.

"No, hell. You keep it."

"No, now what would I do with it? The shop's full of junk as it is. You show it to Zimmerman. A teacher in our public school system shouldn't have to put up with crap like this."

"O.K., Al, you win. Thanks. Thank you very much." The rod of silver was too long; it stuck up out of his side coat pocket like a car aerial.

"A teacher ought to be protected from kids like that. Tell Zimmerman."

"You tell him. Maybe he'll take it from you."

"Well, he might. That's no joke. He just might."

"I didn't mean it as a joke."

"I was on the board, you know, that hired him."

"I know you were, Al."

"I've often regretted it."

"Hell, don't."

"No?"

"He's an intelligent man."

"Yes—yes, but there's something missing."

"Zimmerman understands power; but he doesn't keep discipline." Fresh pain flooded Caldwell's shin and knee. It seemed to him that he had never seen Zimmerman so clearly or expressed himself so well on the subject, but Hummel, annoyingly obtuse, merely repeated his own observation. "There's something missing."

His sense of passing time was working on Caldwell's bowels, making them bind. "I got to get back," he said.

"Good luck. Tell Cassie the town misses her."

"Jesus, she's happy as a lark out there. It's what she's always wanted."

"And Pop Kramer, how's he?"

"Pop's tops. He'll live to be a hundred."

"Do you mind the driving back and forth?"

"No, to tell you the truth I enjoy it. It gives me a chance

to talk to the kid. The kid and I hardly ever saw each other when we lived in town."

"You have a bright boy there. Vera tells me."

"It's his mother's brains. I just pray to God he doesn't inherit my ugly body."

"George, may I tell you something?"

"Sure."

"For your own good."

"Say anything you want, Al. You're my friend."

"You know what your trouble is?"

"I'm stubborn and ignorant."

"Seriously."

My trouble is, Caldwell thought, *my leg is killing me.* "What?"

"You're too modest."

"Al, you've hit the nail on the head," Caldwell said, and moved to turn away.

But Hummel kept pinning him. "Your car's holding up all right?" Until they had moved ten miles out of town, the Caldwells had done without a car. They could walk every-where in Olinger and take the trolley to Alton. But when they bought back the old Kramer place they needed a car. Hummel had put them on to a '36 Buick for only $375.

"Just wonderful. It's a wonderful car. I kick myself every day for smashing up that grille."

"That can't be welded, George. But the car runs all right?"

"Like a dream. I'm grateful to you, Al, don't think I'm not."

"That engine should be all right; the man never drove it over forty. He was an undertaker."

If Hummel had said that once, he had said it a thousand times. The fact seemed to fascinate him. "I'm not scared," Caldwell said, guessing that in Hummel's mind the car was full of ghosts. Actually, it was just an ordinary four-door sedan; there was no room to carry corpses. True, though, it was the blackest car Caldwell had ever seen. They really put the shellac on those old Buicks.

His conversation with Hummel was making Caldwell anx-ious. A clock in his head was ticking on; the school called to him urgently. Disjointed music seemed to be tugging at Hum-mel's exhausted face. Images of loose joints, worn thread, carbon deposits, fatigued metal webbed across Caldwell's apprehension of his old friend: Are we falling apart? In his own mind a gear kept slipping: *Shellac on those old Buicks, shellac, shellac.* "Al," he protested, "I got to high-tail it. You won't take a cent?"

"George: now not another word." And this was the way with all these Olinger aristocrats. They wouldn't take any money but they did take an authoritative tone. They forced a favor on you and that made them gods.

He walked toward the door but Hummel limped along with him. The three Cyclopes gabbled so loud the men turned. Archy, outpouring from his throat a noise like a butchery of birds, pointed to the floor. On the stained cement one shoe had left wet prints. Caldwell examined the injured foot; the shoe was saturated with blood. Black in the brown light, it was leaking out above the heel.

"George, you better get that tended," Hummel said.

"I will at lunch. Let it bleed itself out." The thought of poison haunted him. "Let it flush itself."

He opened the door and a box of cold air encased them. In stepping out, Caldwell put too much weight on the bloody foot and hopped in surprise.

"Tell Zimmerman," Hummel insisted.

"I will."

"No, really, tell him, George."

"He's helpless, Al. The kids today just aren't the old kind; Zimmerman *wants* 'em to chew us up."

Hummel sighed. His gun-colored coveralls seemed deflated; a sprinkle of iron filings fell from his hair. "These are bad days, George."

Caldwell's long drawn face tweaked unusually; he was going to make a joke. He was rarely a formally humorous man. "It's no Golden Age, that's for sure."

Hummel was pathetic, Caldwell decided as he walked away. Lonely devil, couldn't stop talking, he couldn't let you go. No need for mechanics like him any more; everything mass-produced. Waste. If one wears out, get another. Biff. Bang. Smash 'em up. Can only get one-eyed morons to work for him, wife sleeps all around town, Mobilgas moving in and now the rumor was Texaco too, Hummel was dead and depressing. Sniffing the point so matter-of-factly for poison; *brrough.*

But as his hobbled walk toward the school building continued, and the cold flattened his threadbare brown suit against his skin, Caldwell's heart changed tone. The garage had been warm. The man had been good to him. Had always been;

Hummel was Pop Kramer's nephew-in-law. He had been the key influence on the board when Caldwell had got the job, in the depths of the Depression, when all the olive trees died, and Ceres roamed the land mourning her stolen daughter. Where one of her tears fell, grass never grew again. The garland she was wearing turned venomous, and now poison ivy flourished by every barn. Hitherto everything in Nature had been kind to Man. Every species of berry had been gently aphrodisiac, and coming from Pelion at a canter he had spied the young Chariclo gathering watercress.

He drew near the immense orange wall. Classroom sounds like snowflakes drifted down on him. Metal tapped a brittle pane. Pholos appeared at a window, holding a window-pole, and looked down startled upon his fellow-teacher. His oblong, old-fashioned spectacles flashed in surprise beneath the neat cap of centrally parted hair. Pholos had once been a semi-pro shortstop, and the line of the cap still indented the hair above his ears, though his broad forehead was a river of middle-aged wrinkles. Caldwell tersely waved at his friend, and exaggerated his limp, as if that explained his being out of school. Though he bobbed like a ten-cent toy, it was scarcely an exaggeration; the pain in his ankle felt plaintive and forsaken after Hummel's radiant attentions. At every other step, the hot earth climbed higher toward his knee. Caldwell gained the side door and grasped the bronze bar. Before entering, he gasped fresh air and stared sharply upward, as if in answer to a shout. Beyond the edge of the orange wall the adamantine blue zenith pronounced its unceasing monosyllable: I.

Back inside the school, he paused, lightly panting, on the rubber mat of the landing. The lustrous yellow wall still said FUCK. Afraid of having to clatter past Zimmerman's office on the first floor, Caldwell took the subterranean route. He went down the steps, past the boys' locker room. The door was open; clothes were flung around in disarray and some clouds of steam loitered. Caldwell pushed through reinforced glass and entered the great basement study-hall. Through its length and width the children were unnaturally still. Medusa, who kept perfect discipline, was at the head desk. She glanced up, yellow pencils thrusting from her tangled hair. Caldwell avoided looking at her face. Head high, eyes forward, mouth in a prim determined set, he walked along the wall at his right hand. From the other side of the wall, where industrial arts were taught, arose the spurt and

cry *txz! aeiiii,* of wood being tortured. On his left he heard
the children rustle like shingle in a threatening tide. He did
not look around until he had gained the safety of the far
doorway. Here Caldwell turned, to see if he had left tracks.
As he feared: a trail of red crescents, moons from his heel,
marked his path. He pinched his lips in embarrassment; he
would have to explain and apologize to the janitors.

In the cafeteria, the green-gowned women were bustling,
setting out 8¢ cartons of chocolate milk, arranging trays of
sandwiches bound in waxpaper, and stirring the cauldrons of
soup. Tomato today. The sickly plangent odor filled the tiled
volume. Mom Schreuer, a fat soul whose son was a dentist
and whose apron was black beneath her bosom from leaning
against the stoves, waved a wooden paddle at him. Grinning like a greeted boy, Caldwell waved back. He always felt
securer among the people who staffed the school, who fed
its furnaces, the janitors, the cooks. They reminded him of
real people, the people of his boyhood in Passaic, New Jersey,
where his father had been the poor minister of a poor church.
Along the neighborhood street each man had an occupation
that could be simply named—milkman, welder, printer, mason—and each house in the row wore to his eyes, in its individual nicks and curtains and flowerpots, a distinct face. A
modest man, Caldwell was most comfortable in the under-
reaches of the high school. It was warmest there; the steam
pipes sang; the talk made sense.

The great building was symmetrical. He left the cafeteria
by climbing a few steps and passing the girls' locker room.
Forbidden territory; but he knew from the tumble in the
boys' locker room that it was a male gym period, so there
was no danger of blundering into the sacred. The sanctum
was empty. The thick green door was ajar, exposing a strip of
cement floor, a bit of tan bench, a tall segment of shut lockers under high frosted windows.

Hold!

Here it was, his feet frozen to this same spot of scratching
cement, careless in his weariness, his eyes worn by correcting
papers in the boiler room, the building growing dark, the students fled, the clocks ticking in unison throughout the empty
rooms, that, climbing toward his room, he had surprised Vera
Hummel, this same green door ajar, standing in view
wreathed in steam, a blue towel held gracefully away from
her body, her amber pudenda whitened by drops of dew.

"Why should my brother Chiron stand gaping like a satyr? The gods are not strange to him."

"Milady Venus." He bowed his splendid head. "Your beauty for the moment ravished me into forgetfulness of my fraternity."

She laughed and, twisting her amber hair forward over one shoulder, indolently stroked it with the towel. "A fraternity, perhaps, your pride disdains to confess. For Father Kronos, in the shape of a horse, sired you upon Philyra in the fullness of his health; whereas at my begetting he tossed the severed genitals of Uranus like garbage into the foam." Turning her head, she gave the negligent rope of her hair another twist. Sudden wrung water slipped along her collarbone. Her throat showed crystalline in silhouette against a red wet cloud; her near hair held the motion of running horses. With downcast eyes she displayed her profile. The pose overwhelmed Chiron; his guts became a harp. Her profession of sorrow at her barbarous birth, though its insincerity was patent, sent his tongue stammering in search of consolation.

"But my mother was herself a daughter of Oceanus," he said, and instantly knew that, in giving her light self-abuse an answer even so delicately serious, he had presumed.

Her brown eyes blazed with a force that struck from him all consciousness of her body; that shining form became the mere mounting of her angered divinity. "Yes," she said, "and Philyra so loathed the monster she bore that rather than suckle you she prayed to be metamorphosed into a linden tree."

He stiffened; with her narrow woman's mind she had cut through to the truth that would give most hurt. But in recalling to him the unforgivable woman, Venus fortified him against herself. In contemplating the legend wherein on an island so tiny it seemed glimpsed through many refracting layers of water there lay neglected a half-furred and half-membranous squid of fear that was his infant self, in contemplating this story, one among many stories save that an unrecognized image in it bore his name, Chiron had arrived as an adult at a compassionate view, framed in his experience of creatures and his knowledge of history, of Philyra as a daughter of Oceanus and Tethys, more beautiful than bright, set upon by savage Kronos who, surprised by watchful Rhea, transformed himself into a stallion and galloped free to leave his interrupted seed work its garbled growth in the belly of the innocent daughter of the sea. Poor

Philyra! His mother. Wise Chiron could almost reconstruct her face as, huge in tears, it begged a heaven whose very patterns had passed away to release her from the decree, antedating even the Hundred-handed and stretching backward to a time when consciousness was mere pollen drifting in darkness, that appointed the female copulation's field of harvest, begged this cruel heaven to forgive her the ugly fruit of an assault but dimly comprehended and shamefully desired: it was here, on the very lip of her metamorphosis, that Chiron most clearly envisioned his mother; and when as a youth in many moods of sadness and wonder he had gone to examine linden trees, a lusty scholar newly maned, glossily fleshed yet already slightly stiffened by the prudent dignity that he had willed to protect his wound and by the pious resolve that was to make him the guardian of so many motherless, Chiron standing embraced by the tree's wide soft shade had believed himself to discover in the tentative attidues of the low branches and in the quiver of the heart-shaped leaves some protest, some hope of return to human form, even some delight at finding her son fully grown, which, together with his eager and exact researches into the chemistry of the lime-flower's quiet honey, enabled him to augment his vision with the taste, odors, and touch of a pathetic, too-docile personality betrayed by a few hysterical moments into the arboreal benevolence that, had she remained human, would have been his mother's and would have branched into words of nonsense, calm attentions, and gestures of love. Then touching his face to the bark he had spoken her name. Yet, for all his painstaking work of reconciliation, often when he contemplated the fable of his birth an infantile resentment welled up bitterly within his mature reconstruction; the undeserved thirst of his first days poisoned his mouth; and the tiny island, not a hundred yards long, on which he, the first of a race by nature reared in caverns, had lain exposed seemed the image of all womankind: shallow, narrow, and selfish. Selfish. Too easily seduced, too easily repulsed, their wills wept self-indulgently in the web of their nerves and they left their dropped fruit to rot on the shore because of a few horsehairs. So, seen through one side of the prism he had made of the tale, the taunting small-faced goddess before him was to be pitied; and through the other, to be detested. In either case Venus was reduced. In a voice grave with composure he told her, "The linden has many healing properties": a deferential rebuke if she chose to accept it;

otherwise a harmless medical truth. His long survival had not been attained without a courtier's tact.

She studied him as she passed the towel across her body; her skin was transparently beaded everywhere. Her shoulders were lightly freckled. "You don't like women," she said. It seemed to be a discovery that did not excite her.

He made no answer.

She laughed; the brilliance of her eyes, through which a lavish Otherworld had poured, turned to an opaque animal lambency and, jauntily holding the towel about her with an arm crooked at her back, she stepped forward out of the pool and touched his chest with one finger of her free hand. Behind her, the water of the pool retreated in wide rings from her disturbing motion. It lapped low banks lined with reeds and narcissus and phallic, unflowered iris; the earth beneath her narrow, veined feet was a tapestry of moss and fine grass interwoven with violets and pale wood anemones sprung from the blood of Adonis. "Now had it been I," she said, in a voice that curled around the whorls of his mind even as her carefully revolving fingertips intertwined with the bronze fleece of his chest, "I would have been pleased to play nurse to a creature combining the refinement and consideration of a man with"—her lids lowered; her amber lashes flared on her cheeks; the plane of her face demurely shifted, and he felt her gaze include his hindquarters—"the massive potency of a stallion." His nether half, an imperfect servant of his will, preened of itself; his hind hooves cut two fresh crescents into the spongy pondside turf.

"A combination, my lady, often cancels the best of its elements."

For the space of her smirk she seemed a rather common young flirt. "That would be true, brother, if your head and shoulders were those of a horse, and the rest human."

Chiron, one of the few centaurs who habitually conversed with cultivated persons, had heard this jest often before; but her powerful nearness had so expanded him that its humor pierced him afresh. His laugh emerged a shrill whinny, in degrading contrast to the controlled *timbre* he had assumed with the girl, as her senior, and kin. "The gods would forbid such a freak," he stated.

The goddess became pensive. "Your trust in us is touching. What have we done to deserve our worshippers?"

"It is not what the gods do that makes us adore them," he recited. "It is that they are." And to his own surprise he discreetly expanded his chest, so that her hand rested more firmly on his skin. In abrupt vexation she pinched him.

"Oh, Chiron," she said, "If only you knew them as I do. Tell me about the gods. I keep forgetting. Name them to me. Their names are so grand in your mouth."

Obedient to her beauty, enslaved to the hope that she would drop the towel, he intoned, "Zeus, Lord of the Sky; cloud-gathering king of the weather."

"A lecherous muddler."

"His bride Hera, patron of holy marriage."

"The last time I saw her she was beating her servants because Zeus had not spent a night in her bed for a year. You know how Zeus first made love to her? As a cuckoo."

"A hoopoe," Chiron corrected.

"It was a silly cuckoo like in a clock. Tell me some more gods. I think they're so funny."

"Poseidon, master of the many-maned sea."

"A senile old deckhand. His beard stinks of dead fish. He dyes his hair dark blue. He has a chest full of African pornography. His mother was a negress; you can tell by the whites of his eyes. Next."

Chiron knew he should stop; but he secretly relished scandal, and at heart was half a clown. "Bright Apollo," he announced, "who guides the sun and sees all, whose Delphinian prophecies regulate our political life and through whose overarching spirit we attain to art and law."

"That prig. That unctuous prig always talking about himself, his conceit turns my stomach. He's illiterate."

"Come now; this you do exaggerate."

"He *is*. He looks at a scroll but his eyes never move."

"And what of his twin Artemis, the fair huntress beloved by the very prey she dispatches?"

"Ha! She never hits them, that's why. Tittering around the woods with a pack of Vassar freshmen whose so-called virginity not a doctor in Arcadia—"

"Hush, child!" The centaur brought his hand toward her lips and in his extremity of alarm almost did touch them. He had heard faint thunder behind him.

She backed off, startled at his presumption. Then she looked skywards over his shoulder and laughed in recognition; it was a mirthless laugh, a high heated syllable defiantly prolonged; it tightened her face across her skull and sharpened her perfect features cruelly, out of all femininity. Cheeks, brow, and throat flushed, she shouted toward Heaven,

"Yes, Brother: blasphemy! Your gods, listen to them—a prating bluestocking, a filthy crone smelling of corn, a thieving tramp, a drunken queer, a despicable, sad, grimy, grizzled, crippled, cuckolded tinker—"

"Your husband!" Chiron protested, striving to keep himself in the graces of the firmament above him. His position was difficult; he knew that the indulgent Zeus would never harm his young aunt. But he might in annoyance toss his bolt at her innocent auditor, whose Olympian position was precarious and ambiguous. Chiron knew that his own intimacy with men was envied by the god, who never visited the created race except, in feathers and fur, to accomplish a rape. Indeed it was rumored that Zeus thought centaurs a dangerous middle-ground through which the gods might be transmuted into pure irrelevance. But the sky, though it had darkened, remained silent. Gratefully Chiron pursued his tactic, telling Venus, "You fail to appreciate your husband. Hephaestus is dexterous and kind. Though every anvil and potter's wheel serves as an altar to him, he remains humble. The calamity of his fall upon Lemnos purged all dross of arrogance from his heart; though his body is bent, there is not a mean bone in it."

She sighed. "I know. How can I love such a ditherer? Give me that mean bone. Do you think," she asked, with the expectant and subtly condescending face of a not usually curious student, "I'm drawn to cruel men because I have a guilt complex about my father's mutilation? I mean, I blame myself and want to be punished?"

Chiron smiled; he was not of the new school. The sky above had paled. Feeling safe, he dared a touch of impudence. He pointed out, "There is one deity you have exempted from your catalogue." He meant Ares, the most vicious of all.

The girl tossed her head; her orange hair flared into a momentary mane. "I know what you're thinking. That I'm no better than the rest. How would you list me, noble Chiron? 'A compulsive nymphomaniac'? Or, less circumspectly, 'A born whore'?"

"No, no, you misunderstand me. I did not mean yourself."

She paid him no heed, crying, "But it's un*fair!*" She clutched the towel about her emphatically. "Why should we deny ourselves the one pleasure the Fates forgot to take from us? The mortals have the joy of struggle, the satisfaction of compassion, the triumph of courage; but the gods are perfect."

Chiron nodded; the old courtier was familiar with the way these aristocrats blithely extolled the class that in the previous breath they had calumniated. Did the girl imagine that her petty set of jibes went near to the heart of the real case against the gods? He felt a weight of weariness; he would always be less than they.

She corrected herself. "Perfect only in our permanence. I was cruelly robbed of a father. Zeus treats me like a pet cat. His blood love is reserved for Artemis and Athene, his daughters. They have his blessing; they are not driven again and again to clasp into their loins that giant leap that for a moment counterfeits it. What is Priapus but His strength without a father's love? Priapus—my ugliest child; worthy of his conceiving. Dionysos made me perform as if I were another boy." She touched the centaur's chest again, as if to reassure herself that he had not turned to stone. "You knew your father. I envy you. Had I seen Uranus' face, heard his voice—were I not the afterthought of his desecrated corpse—I would be as chaste as Hestia, my aunt, the one god who truly loves me. And now she is demoted from Olympus, reduced to a household trinket." The girl's darting thought took another turn. She said to Chiron, "You know men. Why do they revile me? Why is my name a matter of jokes, why is my caricature gouged into lavatory walls? Who else serves them so well? What other god gives them with the same hand such power and such peace? *Why am I blamed?*"

"Your accusations, my lady, are all from yourself."

Her flood of confession drained, she dryly mocked him. "So prudent. So wise. Good Chiron. Our scholar, our propagandist. So docile. Have you ever wondered, nephew, if your heart belongs to the man or the horse?"

He stiffened and said, "From the waist up, I am told I am fully human."

"Forgive me. You are kind, and I repay you in divine coin." She stooped and plucked an anemone. "Poor Adonis," she said, idly fingering the starlike sepals. "His blood was so pale. Like our ichor."

A gust of remembrance ruffled her hair, in whose feathery crown the moisture had evaporated. She turned her back and in half-secrecy brought the flower to her lips, and her still-damp mane dripped in sympathetic curves down flesh as white and smoothly molded as that fabled powder, the earth of Olympus, snow. Her buttocks were pink and faintly roughened; there was a golden tinge of pollen on the backs of her thighs. She kissed the flower, dropped it, and turned with a new expression—tremulous, flushed, diffuse, shy. "Chiron," she commanded. "Make love to me."

His great heart jarred against his ribs; he waved her back with a trembling hand. "But my lady: below the waist, I am fully animal."

Gay, she stepped forward on violets. The towel fell. Her breasts were already tipped with desire. "Do you think you will rupture me? Do you think us women so negligible? We are weak in the arms; but strong in the thighs. Our thighs must be strong; the world is rooted between them."

"But a goddess, and a centaur—"

"Men are reeds; they no longer fill me. Come, Chiron, don't insult your lady. Disrobe of wisdom; you will be wiser when we rise." She cupped her palms below her breasts and stood on tiptoe against him, so that her nipples thrust against his own, the male's vestigial ornaments. But their chests were of unequal spans; she giggled with the game of making the double opposition, and Chiron even in his distraction saw that the problem might be expressed geometrically.

"Are you afraid?" she whispered. "How do you do it with Chariclo? Do you mount her?"

His voice rose small and parched in his constricted throat. "It would be incest."

"It always is; we all flow from Chaos."

"It is day."

"Good; then the gods are asleep. Is love so hideous it must hide in the dark? Do you disdain me because I'm a trollop? But as a scholar you know how after every bath I am restored to virginity. Come, Chiron, crack my maidenhead; it hampers my walking."

More in weakness than in strength, as one would embrace in despair a fevered child, he put his arms around the wiggling girl; her body was slippery and limp with complaisant dissolution. The hollow of her back felt downy. The crest of an erection grazed his belly; a neigh seethed through his nostrils. Her arms were clenched around his withers, and her thighs, lifting weightlessly, murmured among his forelegs. "Horse," she breathed, "ride me. I'm a mare. Plough me." From her body issued a swift harsh scent of flowers, flowers of all colors crushed and tumbled in the earth of his own equine odor. He closed his eyes and was swimming through a shapeless warm landscape studded with red trees.

But his joints held rigid. He remembered the thunder. Zimmerman might still be in the building; he never went home. The centaur listened for a rumble upstairs, and in that moment of listening everything altered. The girl dropped from around his neck. Without a backwards look, Venus vanished into the underwood. A thousand green petals closed upon her passage. Love has its own ethics, which the deliberating will irrevocably offends. Then as now, Caldwell stood on that spot of cement alone and puzzled, and now, as then, climbed the stairs with a painful, confused sense of having displeased, through ways he could not follow, the God who never rested from watching him.

He climbed the flights of stairs to his room on the second floor. The steps seemed built for the legs of a more supple species; his clumsiness was agonizing. Each wave of pain forced his gaze tight against a section of wall where a ballpoint pen had looped, a varnished newel post whose bevelled cap had been torn from the glue-glazed dowel stump, a corner of the stairs in which a little black drift of dust and grit had hardened, a windowpane filmed in grease and framed in rusty mullions, a dead stretch of yellow wall. The door to his room was shut. He expected to hear turbulence through it; but there was instead an ominous quiet. His skin twitched. Had Zimmerman, detecting noise, come and taken over the class?

This fear proved justified. He pushed open the door, and there, not two yards away, Zimmerman's lopsided face hung like a gigantic emblem of authority, stretching from rim to rim of Caldwell's appalled vision. With a malevolent pulse, it seemed to widen still further. An implacable bolt, springing from the center of the forehead above the two disparately magnifying lenses of the principal's spectacles, leaped space and transfixed the paralyzed victim. The silence as the two men stared at one another was louder than thunder.

Zimmerman turned to the class; it had been tamed into alphabetical rows of combed, frightened children. "Mr. Caldwell has graciously returned to us."

The class obediently snickered.

"I think such devotion to duty should be rewarded with a mild round of applause."

He led the clapping; his cupped palms patted each other daintily. Zimmerman's extremities were queerly small for such a massive head and torso. He wore a sports coat whose padded shoulders and broad checkered pattern emphasized the disproportion. Above the ironical applause a few boys' smirks glinted toward Caldwell. The humiliated teacher licked his lips. They tasted charred.

"Thank you, boys and girls," Zimmerman said. "That is quite enough." The gentle applause abruptly stopped. The principal turned to Caldwell again; the unbalance of his face seemed that of a proud pregnant cloud tugged by a wind high in heaven. Caldwell uttered a nonsensical syllable that was meant to be a shout of praise and adoration.

"We can discuss this later, George. The children are anxious for their lesson."

But Caldwell, frantic to explain, to be absolved, bent and lifted his trouser leg, an unhoped-for indecency that burst the class into loud hilarity. And indeed Caldwell had in his heart asked for some such response.

Zimmerman understood this. He understood everything. Though Caldwell instantly dropped the trouser leg and straightened to attention, Zimmerman continued to gaze down at his ankle, as if it were at an infinite distance from him but his eyes were infinitely percipient. "Your socks don't quite match," he said. "Is this your explanation?"

The class burst again. Immaculately timing himself, Zimmerman waited until he would be audible above the last trickling chuckles. "But George—George—you should not allow your commendable concern with grooming to interfere with another pedagogic need, punctuality."

Caldwell was so notoriously a poor dresser, his clothes were so nakedly shabby, that there was rich humor even in this; though doubtless many of the laughers had been lost among Zimmerman's elegant sarcastic turns.

The principal made a fastidious indicative gesture. "Are you carrying a lightning rod? Remarkably prudent, on a cloudless winter day."

Caldwell groped and felt behind him the cold sleek arrow-shaft jutting from his pocket. He took it out and offered it to Zimmerman while he struggled to find the first words of his story, a story that, once known, would make Zimmerman embrace him for his heroic suffering; tears of compassion would fall from that imperious distended face. "This is it," Caldwell said. "I don't know which kid did it—"

Zimmerman disdained touching the shaft; palms lifted in protest, as if the bright stick were charged with danger, he took a few quick backward steps, his small feet twinkling with the athletic prowess that still lingered in them. Zimmerman's first fame had been as a schoolboy track star. Strong-shouldered, lithe-limbed, he had excelled in all tests of speed and strength—the discus, dashes, endurance runs. "George, I said *later*," he said. "Please teach your class. Since the program of my morning has already been interrupted, I'll sit in the rear of the class and make this my month's visit. Please behave, boys and girls, as if I were not present."

Caldwell lived in dread of the supervising principal's monthly classroom visitations. The brief little typewritten reports that followed them, containing a blurred blend of acid detail and educational jargon, had the effect, if they were good, of exalting Caldwell for days and, if they were bad (as they nearly always seemed to be; even an ambiguous adjective poisoned the cup), of depressing him for weeks. Now a visit had come, when he was addled, in the wrong, in pain, and unprepared.

Slyly pussyfooting, Zimmerman sidled down along the blackboard. His broad checkered back was hunched in a droll pretense of being inconspicuous. He took a seat in the last row, behind the cup ears and blazing acne of Mark Youngerman. No sooner was Zimmerman settled at the end desk than he noticed that level with him, two rows away, in the last seat of the third row, Iris Osgood sat immersed in dull bovine beauty. Zimmerman slid out of his seat into the one next to her and in a little pantomime of whispers asked her for a sheet of tablet paper. The plump girl fussed, tore off a sheet, and as he leaned over to take it the principal with a bold slide of his eyes looked down the top of her loose silk blouse.

Caldwell watched this in an awed daze. He felt the colors of the class stir under him; Zimmerman's presence made them electric. Begin. He forgot who he was, what he taught, why he was here. He went over to his desk, put down the arrowshaft, and picked up a magazine clipping that reminded him. CLEVELAND SCIENTIST CHARTS CREATION-CLOCK. Zimmerman's face seemed huge at the rear of the room. "Behind me on the blackboard," Caldwell began, "is the figure five followed by nine zeros. This is five—what?"

A timid girl's voice broke from the silence, saying, "Trillion." Judith Lengel, that would be. She tried, but didn't have it. Her father was one of those biff-bang real estate salesmen who expected their kids to be May Queen, valedictorian, and Most Popular just because he, old Five Percent Lengel, had made a mint. Poor Judy, the kid just didn't have it upstairs.

"Billion," Caldwell said. "Five billion years. This is, under our present state of knowledge, believed to be the age of the universe. It may be older; it is almost certainly at least this old. Now, who can tell me what a billion is?"

"A thousand thousand?" Judy quavered. Poor little bitch, why didn't somebody get her off the hook? Why didn't one of the bright ones like young Kegerise speak up? Kegerise sat there with his legs all over the aisle doodling on his tablet and smiling to himself. Caldwell looked around for Peter and then remembered the kid wasn't in this section. He came in the seventh period. Zimmerman made a notation and winked over at the Osgood girl, who didn't know what was up. Dumb. Dumb as pure white lead.

"A thousand thousand *thousand,*" Caldwell announced. "A thousand million. That's a billion. There are over two billion people in the world right now," he said, "and it all began around a million years ago when some dumb ape swung down out of a tree and looked around and wondered what he was doing here." The class laughed, and Deifendorf, one of the country boys who came in on the bus, began to scratch his scalp and armpit and make monkey chatter. Caldwell tried to overlook it because the boy was his ace swimmer. "Another place you hear billions is in the national debt," he said. "We owe ourselves about two hundred sixty billion bucks right now. It cost us about three hundred fifty billion to kill Hitler. Another place is with the stars. There are about a hundred billion stars in our own galaxy, which is called—what?"

"The solar system?" Judy offered.

"The Milky Way," Caldwell said. "The solar system has just one star in it—what's it called?"

He pointedly looked toward the rear of the class but in the corner of his eye Judy said "Venus?" anyway. The boys laughed at this; Venus, venereal, V.D. Someone clapped.

"Venus is the brightest planet," Caldwell explained to her. "We call it a star because it looks like one. But of course the only real star we're at all close to is—"

"The Sun," somebody in the class said, and Caldwell never knew who it was, because he was concentrating on Judith Lengel's dull strained face and trying to tell her without words that she mustn't let her old man get her down. Relax, girl, you'll get a mate. You'll get a date and then a mate. And then you'll rate. (It would make a good Valentine—every once in a while Caldwell got an inspiration like this.)

"Right," he said to the class, "the Sun. Now here's a figure." He wrote on the blackboard 6,000,000,000,000,000,-000,000. "How would you say it?" He answered himself, "Six," and, looping back the trios of zeros, "thousand, million, billion, trillion, quadrillion, quintillion, sextillion. Six sextillion. What does it represent?" Mute faces marvelled and mocked. Again he answered himself. "The weight of the earth in tons. Now the sun," he said, "weighs this much more." He wrote 333,000 on the blackboard, saying, half to the class, half to the slate. "Three-three-three oh-oh-oh. Multiply it out, and you get"—skrkk, scrak, the chalk chipped as he carried the ones—"one nine nine eight followed by twenty-four goose eggs." He stepped back and looked; his work sickened him:

$$1,998,000,000,000,000,000,000,000,000,000.$$

The zeros stared back, every one a wound leaking the word "poison." "That's the weight of the Sun," Caldwell said. "Who cares?"

Laughter bobbled about him. Where was he? "Some stars are bigger," he said, stalling, "some are smaller. The next nearest star is Alpha Centauri, four light-years away. Light goes one-eight-six oh-oh-oh miles a second." He wrote it on the blackboard. There was little space left. "That's six trillion miles a year." With his fingertips he erased the 5 in the age of the universe and put in a 6. "Alpha Centauri is twenty-four trillion miles away." The pressure in Caldwell's stomach released a bubble and he bit back a belch. "The Milky Way, which used to be thought of as the path by which the souls of the dead travelled to Heaven, is an optical illusion; you could never reach it. Like fog, it would always thin out around you. It's a mist of stars we make by looking the long way through the galaxy; the galaxy is a spinning discus a hundred thousand light-years wide. I don't know who threw it. Its center is in the direction of the constellation Sagittarius; that means 'archer,' like somebody in the lovely class before yours. And beyond our galaxy are other galaxies, in the universe all told at least a hundred billion, each containing a hundred billion stars. Do these figures mean anything to you?"

Deifendorf said, "No."

Caldwell disarmed his impudence by agreeing. He had been teaching long enough to keep a step or two ahead of the bastards occasionally. "They don't to me either. They remind me of death. The human mind can only take so much. The"—he remembered that Zimmerman was here; the principal's ponderous face lifted alertly—"the heck with 'em. Let's try to reduce five billion years to our size. Let's say the universe is three days old. Today is Thursday, and it is"—he looked at the clock—"twenty minutes to twelve." Twenty minutes to go; he'd have to make this fast. "O.K. Last Monday at noon there was the greatest explosion there ever was. We're still riding on it. When we look out at the other galaxies, they're flying away from us. The farther away they are, the faster they're flying. By computation, they all must have begun at one place about five billion years ago; all the billions and trillions and quadrillions squared and squared again of tons of matter in the universe were compressed into a ball at the maximum possible density, the density within the nucleus of the atom; one cubic centimeter of this primeval egg weighed two hundred and fifty tons."

Caldwell felt as if just such a cubic centimeter had been lodged in his bowels. Astronomy transfixed him; at night sometimes when he lay down in bed exhausted he felt that his ebbing body was fantastically huge and contained in its darkness a billion stars.

Zimmerman was leaning over whispering to the Osgood girl; his percipient eyes fondled the hidden smooth curve of her dugs. His lechery smelled; the kids were catching fire; from the way Becky Davis's shoulders were hunching, Deifendorf behind her was tickling her neck with the eraser of his pencil. Becky was a smutty little tramp from outside Olinger. She had a tiny white triangle of a face set in a frizzy square cushion of flesh-colored hair. Dull. Dull and dirty.

Caldwell struggled on. "The compression was so great the substance was unstable; it exploded in a second—not a second of our imaginary time, but a real second, of real time. Now—are you following me?—in our scale of three days, all Monday afternoon the air of the universe was hot and bright with radiant energy; by evening the dispersal had gone far enough so that darkness fell. The universe became totally dark. And the dark matter—dust, planets, meteors, junk, garbage, old stones—still greatly outweighs the luminous matter. In this first night the expanding flux of universal substance broke up into immense gas clouds, the proto-galaxies, and within these, gravitational attraction condensed balls of gas that under the pressure of their own accumulating mass began to burn. So, sometime before Tuesday's dawn, stars began to shine. Are you with me? And these stars were surrounded by rotating clouds of matter that in turn condensed. One of these was our Earth. It was cold, kids, cold enough to freeze not only water vapor but nitrogen, the carbon oxides, ammonia, and methane; around the dust motes of solid matter these frozen gases crystallized in snowflakes that drew together at first slowly but more and more rapidly; soon they were falling to the growing Earth with velocities sufficient to generate considerable heat. The cosmic snow melted and flew back into space, leaving, here, a molten mass of the mineral elements that are, in the universe itself, a minority of less than one per cent. O.K. That's one day down and two to go. By noon of the second day, a crust had formed. It may have been basalt entirely covered by a primeval ocean; then fissures opened up, spewing liquid granite that became the first continents. Meanwhile liquid iron, heavier than lava, sank to the center, where it makes the molten core. Have any of you ever opened up a golf ball?"

He had felt the class sinking from him, like sluggish iron from the cooling crust. The golf ball woke them up a little, but not enough. A braceleted wrist paused in mid-aisle, passing a note; Deifendorf stopped tickling the Davis girl; Kegerise left off doodling; even Zimmerman looked up. Caldwell may have been imagining it, but he thought the old bull had been stroking the Osgood girl's milky arm. In all the class, nothing annoyed him so much as the smirk on the Davis girl's smutty face; sensual, sly; he looked at her so intensely her purple lipstick uttered, "It's blue," in defense.

"Yes," he said slowly, "a little sac of blue fluid is inside a golf ball, underneath all the rubber bands." He forgot what the point of it was. He glanced at the clock. Twelve minutes left. His stomach kicked. He tried to ease all his weight from the tender leg; the puncture in his ankle was stinging as the blood dried. "For a whole day," he said, "between Tuesday and Wednesday noon, the earth is barren. There is no life on it. Just ugly rocks, stale water, vomiting volcanoes, everything slithering and sliding and maybe freezing now and then as the sun like a dirty old light bulb flickered up there in the sky. By yesterday noon, a little life showed up. Nothing spectacular; just a little bit of slime. All yesterday afternoon, and most of the night, life remained miscroscopic." He turned and wrote on the blackboard,

Corycium enigmaticum
Leptothrix
Volvox.

He tapped the first one and the chalk turned to a large warm wet larva in his hand. He dropped it in disgust and the class tittered. Caldwell pronounced, "Corycium enigmaticum. Carbonic remains of this primitive marine organism were found in rocks in Finland believed to be a billion and a half years old. As the name suggests, this primitive form of life remains enigmatic, but it is believed to be a calcareous blue-green algae of the type that still tints large areas of ocean."

A paper airplane shot into the air, wobbled, and sharply fell; it struck the floor of the middle aisle and became an open-faced white flower whose baby-like yowling continued throughout the remainder of the class. Pale fluid dropped from its injured leaf and Caldwell mentally apologized to the janitors.

"Leptothrix," he said, "is a microscopic fleck of life, whose name in Greek means 'small hair.' This bacteria could extract from ferric salt a granule of pure iron and, fantastic as it seems, existed in such numbers that it laid down all the deposits of iron ore which man presently mines. The Mesabi Range in Minnesota was originally put there by American citizens of which thousands would fit on a pinhead. Then, to win World War Two, we gouged all those battleships and tanks and Jeeps and Coke machines out of it and left the poor old Mesabi Range like an old carcass the jackals had chewed. I feel awful about it. When I was a kid in Passaic they used to talk about the Mesabi Range as if she were a beautiful orange-haired lady lying up there by the Lakes."

Not content with pencil-tickling, Deifendorf had put his hands around the Davis girl's throat and with his thumbs was caressing the underside of her chin. Her face was growing smaller and smaller in sensual ecstasy. "Third," Caldwell

called—the undercurrent of noise in the class was rising
to his lips—"the volvox, of these early citizens in the kingdom of life, interests us because he invented death. There
is no reason intrinsic in the plasmic substance why life
should ever end. Amoebas never die; and those male
sperm cells which enjoy success become the cornerstone of
new life that continues beyond the father. But the volvox, a
rolling sphere of flagellating algae organized into somatic
and reproductive cells, neither plant nor animal—under a
microscope it looks just like a Christmas ball—by pioneering
this new idea of *coöperation*, rolled life into the kingdom of
certain—as opposed to accidental—death. For—hold tight
kids, just seven more minutes of torture—while each cell
is potentially immortal, by volunteering for a specialized
function within an organized society of cells, it enters a compromised environment. The strain eventually wears it out
and kills it. It dies sacrificially, for the good of the whole.
These first cells who got tired of sitting around forever in a
blue-green scum and said, 'Let's get together and make a
volvox,' were the first altruists. The first do-gooders. If I
had a hat on, I'd take it off to 'em."

He pantomimed doffing his cap and the class screamed.
Mark Youngerman jumped up and his acne leaped to the
wall; the paint began to burn, blistering in slowly spreading
blotches above the side blackboard. Fists, claws, cocked elbows blurred in patch-colored panic above the scarred and
varnished desk tops; in the whole mad mass the only still
bodies were those of Zimmerman and Iris Osgood. At
some point, Zimmerman had slipped across the aisle and
sat on the same seat with the girl. He had his arm around
her shoulders and beamed forward proudly. Iris in his hug
was tranquil and inert, her eyes downcast and her dull
cheeks lightly flushed.

Caldwell looked at the clock. Five minutes left, and the
main part of the story all before him. "Around three-thirty
this morning," he said, "while you were still asleep in your
trundle-beds, all the large phyla except the Chordata appear in advanced form. As far as the fossils tell, it happened like *that.*" He snapped his fingers. "Up until dawn,
the most important animal in the world, spreading on the
ocean floor everywhere, was an ugly thing called the trilo-
bite."

A boy over by the windows had sneaked a paper grocery
bag into class and now, nudged by another boy, he tumbled

its contents, a clot of living trilobites, onto the floor. Most were just an inch or two long; a few were over a foot in length. They looked like magnified wood lice, only they were reddish. The bigger ones wore on their ruddy cephalic shields partially unrolled condoms, like rubber party hats. As they scuttered among the scrolling iron desk-legs, their brainless heads and swishing glabellae brushed the ankles of girls who squealed and kicked up their feet so high that white thighs and gray underpants flashed. In terror some of the trilobites curled into segmented balls. As a sport the boys began to drop their heavy textbooks on these primitive arthropods; one of the girls, a huge purple parrot feathered with mud, swiftly ducked her head and plucked a small one up. Its little biramous legs fluttered in upside-down protest. She crunched it in her painted beak and methodically chewed.

Caldwell calculated that this late in the game there was nothing to do but ride the rumpus out to the bell. "By seven o'clock this morning," he explained, and a very few smeared faces seemed to be listening, "the first vertebrate fishes appeared. The Earth's crust buckled. The oceans of the Ordovician Age dwindled." Fats Frymoyer leaned over and shoved little Bill Schupp off his seat; the boy, a frail diabetic, fell to the floor with a bump. When he tried to rise, an anonymous hand appeared on his head and pushed him down again. "At seven-thirty, the first plants began to grow on land. In swampy pools, lungfish learned to breathe and drag themselves across the mud. By eight o'clock, the amphibians were here. The earth was warm. There were marshlands in Antarctica. Lush forests of giant ferns rose and fell and laid down the coal deposits of our own state, for which this age is named. So when you say 'Pennsylvanian," you can mean either a dumb Dutchman or a stretch of Paleozoic time."

Betty Jean Schilling had been chewing bubble-gum; now a ping-pong-ball-sized bubble, a triumph, a prodigy, issued from her tongue and lips. Her eyes crossed strenuously and nearly popped themselves in effortful concentration. But the marvelous bubble collapsed, coating her chin with a strip of pink scum.

"Insects appeared and diversified; some dragonflies had thirty-inch wings. The world grew cold again. Some amphibians went back to the sea; others began to lay their eggs on land. These were reptiles, and for two hours, from nine o'clock to eleven o'clock, as the earth grew warm again, they dominated life. Fifty-foot plesiosaurs roamed the sea, pterosaurs flapped through the air like broken umbrellas. On land, gigantic morons made the earth shake." By prearranged signal all of the boys in the room began to hum. No one's mouth moved; their eyes shifted here and there innocently; but the air was filled with a hovering honey of insolence. Caldwell could only swim on. "The brontosaurus had a thirty-ton body and a two-ounce brain. The anatosaurus had two thousand teeth. Triceratops had a helmet of frilled bone seven feet long. Tyrannosaurus rex had tiny arms and teeth like six-inch razors and it was elected President. It ate everything—dead meat, living meat, old bones—"

The first bell rang. The monitors stampeded out of the class; one of them stepped on the anemone in the aisle and the flower shrilly whimpered. Two boys bumped in the doorway and, thrashing, stabbed each other with pencils. Their teeth gnashed; phlegm poured through their nostrils. Somehow Zimmerman had slipped Iris Osgood's blouse and bra off and her breasts showed above her desk like two calm edible moons rising side by side.

"Two minutes left," Caldwell shouted. His voice had grown higher in pitch, as if a peg in his head were being turned. "Keep your seats. We'll have to take up the extinct mammals and the ice ages next period. To make a long story short, one hour ago, spreading in the wake of the flowering plants and grasses, our faithful friends the mammals took over the Earth, and one minute ago, *one minute ago*—"

Deifendorf had pulled the Davis girl out into the aisle and she was giggling and struggling in his long hair-speckled arms.

"—one minute ago," Caldwell called the third time, and a handful of BBs was flung into his face. He winced and put up his right hand as a shield and thanked God his eyes hadn't been hit. You won't be given another pair. His stomach griped sympathetically with his leg. "—evolved from a tiny tree shrew, his depth-perceptive binocular vision, thumb-opposed grasping hands, and highly elaborated cerebral cortex developed in response to the special conditions of arboreal existence, evolved from a tiny tree shrew such as are presently found in Java—"

The girl's mussed skirt was up around her waist. She was bent face down over the desk and Deifendorf's hooves shuffled in agitation in the narrow aisle. From his sleepy careful grin he was covering her; the whole room smelled like a stable: Caldwell saw red. He picked the shining

arrow-shaft from the top of his desk, strode forward through
the sickening confusion of books being slammed shut, and
once, twice, whipped, *whipped* the bastard beast's bare back.
You broke my grille. Two white stripes glowed across the
meat of Deifendorf's shoulders. As Caldwell in horror
watched, these stripes slowly blushed. There would be welts.
The couple fell apart like a broken blossom. Deifendorf
looked up with small brown eyes shelled in tears; the girl
with pointed composure refluffed her hair. Zimmerman's hand
scribbled furiously in the corner of Caldwell's eye.

The teacher, stunned, returned to the front of the class.
Jesus, he hadn't meant to hit the kid so hard. He placed
the steel shaft in the chalk trough. He turned, and closed
his eyes, and the pain unfolded its wet wings in the red darkness. He opened his mouth; his very blood loathed the story
he had told. "One minute ago, flint-chipping, fire-kindling,
death-foreseeing, a tragic animal appeared—" The buzzer
rasped; halls rumbled throughout the vast building; faintness
swooped at Caldwell but he held himself upright, having
vowed to finish."—called Man."

II

MY FATHER and my mother were talking. I wake
now often to silence, beside you, with a pang of fear,
after dreams that leave a sour wash of atheism in my stomach (last night I dreamt that Hitler, a white-haired crazy
man with a protruding tongue, was found alive in Argentina).
But in those days I always awoke to the sound of my parents
talking, voices which even in agreement were contentious
and full of life. I had been dreaming of a tree, and through
the sound of their words I seemed to twist from an upright
trunk into a boy lying in bed. I was fifteen and it was 1947.
This morning their subject seemed to be new; I could not
make out its form, only feel within myself, as if in my sleep
I had swallowed something living that now woke within me,
its restless weight of dread. "Don't feel bad, Cassie," my
father said. His voice had a shy sound, as if he had
turned his back. "I've been lucky to live this long."

"George, if you're just trying to frighten me, it's not funny," my mother answered. Her voice was so often expressive of what I wanted to hear that my own brain sometimes thought in her voice; indeed, as I grow older, now and then, usually in instances of exclamation, I hear her voice issue from my mouth.

I seemed now to know the subject: my father thought he was ill.

"Cassie," he said, "don't be frightened. I don't want you to be frightened. I'm not frightened." His voice blanched in repetition.

"You *are* frightened," she said. "I wondered why you kept getting out of bed." Her voice was white too.

"I can feel the damn thing," he said. "I can feel it in me like a clot of poison. I can't pass it."

This detail seemed to balk her. "You can't feel such things," she said at last, in a voice abruptly small, like a chastened little girl's.

His voice gathered size. "I can feel it in me like a poison snake wrapped around my bowels. *Brooo!*"

Lying in bed, I pictured my father making this noise—his head shaken so abruptly his jowls wagged, his lips a vehement blur. The picture was so vivid I smiled. Their conversation, as if they knew I had awakened, was closing up; the tone of their voices darkened. The little pale piteous bit, like a snowflake at the center of their marriage, which I had glimpsed, still half a tree, in first light, retreated behind the familiar opacities of clownish quarreling. I turned my head, as sleep's heaviness lifted from it, and looked through the window. A few frost-ferns had sprouted from the lower corners of the upper panes. The early sun lay tan on the stubble of the big field beyond the dirt road. The road was pink. The bare trees took white on their sun side; a curious ruddiness was caught in their twigs. Everything looked frozen; the two strands of telephone wire looked locked into place in the sky's blue ice. It was January and Monday. I began to understand. After every weekend, my father had to gather his nerve to go back to teaching. During the Christmas vacation he became slack and in a fury of screw-turning had to retighten himself. "The long haul," he called the stretch between Christmas and Easter. Last week, the first week of the new year, something had happened that had frightened him. He had struck a boy with Zimmerman in the room: he had told us that much.

"Don't be dramatic, George," my mother said. "What does it feel like?"

"I know where I got it." He had a way of not speaking to her, but performing in front of her, as if there were an invisible audience at her side. "The damn kids. I've caught their damn hate and I feel it like a spider in my big intestine."

"It's not hate, George," she said, "it's love."

"It's hate, Cassie. I face it every day."

"It's love," she insisted. "They want to love each other and you're in their way. Nobody hates you. You're the ideal man."

"They hate my guts. They'd kill me, and now they're doing it. Biff, bang. I'm through. Haul away the garbage."

"George, if you feel this seriously," my mother said, "I'd waste no time seeing Doc Appleton."

Whenever my father received the sympathy he sought, he became brusque and antic. "I don't want to see the bastard. He'll tell me the truth."

My mother must have turned away, because it was my grandfather who spoke. "Truth is ev-er a comfort," he said. "Only the Devil loves lies." His voice, interposed between the two others, seemed vaster but fainter than theirs, as if he were a giant calling from a distance.

"The Devil and me, Pop," my father said. "I love lies. I tell 'em all day. I'm paid to tell 'em."

Footsteps sounded on the uncarpeted kitchen floor. My mother was crossing to the bottom of the stairs, at the corner of the house diagonally opposite my bed. "Peter!" she called. "Are you awake?"

I closed my eyes and relaxed into my warm groove. The blankets my body had heated became soft chains dragging me down; my mouth held a stale ambrosia lulling me to sleep again. The lemon-yellow wallpaper, whose small dark medallions peered out from the pattern with faces like frowning cats, remained printed, negatively in red, on my eyelids. The dream I had been dreaming returned to me. Penny and I had been beside a tree. The top buttons of her blouse were undone, pearl buttons, undone as they had been weeks ago, before Christmas vacation, in the dark Buick on the school parking lot, the heater ticking by our knees. But this was broad day, in a woods of slim trees pierced by light. A blue jay, vivid in every feather, hung in the air motionless, like a hummingbird, but his wings stiffly at his sides, his eye alert like a bead of black glass. When he moved, it was like a stuffed bird being twitched on a string; but he was definitely alive.

"Peter, time to get u-up!"

Her wrist was in my lap, I was stroking the inside of her forearm. Stroking and stroking with a patience drawn thinner and thinner. Her silk sleeve was pushed up from the green-veined skin. The rest of the class seemed gathered about us in the woods, watching; though there was no sense of faces. She leaned forward, my Penny, my little dumb, worried Penny. Suddenly, thickly, I loved her. A wonderful honey gathered in my groin. Her flecked green irises were perfect circles with worry; an inner bit of her lower lip, glimmering with moisture, glittered nervously: the aura was like that when, a month ago in that dark car, I found my hand between her warm thighs which were pressed together; it seemed to dawn on her slowly that my hand was there, for a minute passed before she begged, "Don't," and when I withdrew my hand, she looked at me like that. Only that was in shadow and this was in brilliant light. The pores of her nose showed. She was unnaturally still; something was going wrong.

The back of my left hand felt hot and moist as it had when it was pulled from between her thighs; sap flowed from my extremities toward the fork of my body. I seemed delicately distended in the midst of several processes. When from downstairs a loud bumble came crashing, signalling that my father was going to look at the kitchen clock, I wanted to cry, *No, wait—*

"Hey Cassie, tell the kid it's seven-seventeen. I left a whole mess of papers to correct, I got to be there at eight. Zimmerman'll have my neck."

That was it, yes; and in the dream it didn't even seem strange. She became the tree. I was leaning my face against the tree trunk, certain it was her. The last thing I dreamed was the bark of the tree: the crusty ridges and in the black cracks between them tiny green flecks of lichen. Her. My Lord, it was her: help me. Give her back to me.

"*Peter!* Are you trying to torment your father?"

"No! I'm up. For Heaven's sake."

"Well then *get* up. *Get* up. I mean it, young man. Now."

I stretched and my body widened into the cool margins of the bed. The sap ebbed. The touching thing was, in the dream, she had known the change was overtaking her, she had felt her fingers turning to leaves, had wanted to tell me (her irises so round) but had not, had protected me, had gone under to wood without a word. And there was that in Penny, which now the dream made vivid to me, what I had hardly felt before, a sheltering love, young as she was, recent as our touching was, little as I gave her; she would sacrifice for me. And I exulted through my length even as I wondered why. This was a fresh patch of paint in my life.

"Rise and shine, my little sunbeam!"

My mother had reverted to a cozy approach. I knew the shiny gray paint of my windowsill would be cold as ice if I reached out my hand and touched it. The sun had fractionally climbed higher. The dirt road had become a band of glowing salmon. On this side of the road, our side lawn was a sheet of old sandpaper that had rubbed green paint. It had not snowed yet this winter. Maybe this would be the winter when it would not snow. Was there ever such a one?

"Peter!"

My mother's voice had the true tiger in it, and without thinking I leaped from bed. Careful to keep my skin from touching anything hard, using my fingertips to pull the glass bureau knobs like faceted crystals of frozen ammonia, I set about dressing. The house was a half-improved farmhouse. The upstairs was unheated. I stripped out of my pajamas and stood a moment relishing my martyrdom of nakedness: it seemed a smarting criticism of our moving to this primitive place. It had been my mother's idea. She loved Nature. I stood naked, as if exposing her folly to the world.

Had the world been watching, it would have been startled, for my belly, as if pecked by a great bird, was dotted with red scabs the size of coins. Psoriasis. The very name of the allergy, so foreign, so twisty in the mouth, so apt to prompt stammering, intensified the humiliation. "Humiliation," "allergy"—I never knew what to call it. It was not a disease, because I generated it out of myself. As an allergy, it was sensitive to almost everything: chocolate, potato chips, starch, sugar, frying grease, nervous excitement, dryness, darkness, pressure, enclosure, the temperate climate—allergic, in fact, to life itself. My mother, from whom I had inherited it, sometimes called it a "handicap." I found this insulting. After all, it was her fault; only females transmitted it to their children. Had my father, whose tall body sagged in folds of pure white, been my mother, my skin would have been blameless. "Handicap" savored of subtraction, and this was an addition, something extra added to me. I enjoyed at this age a strange innocence about suffering; I believed it was necessary to men. It seemed to be all about me and there was something menacing in my apparent exception. I had never broken a bone, I was bright, my parents openly loved me. In my conceit I believed myself to be wickedly lucky. So I had come to this conclusion about my psoriasis: it was a curse. God, to make me a man, had blessed me with a rhythmic curse that breathed in and out with His seasons. The summer sun melted my scabs; by September my chest and legs were clear but for a very faint dappling, invisibly pale seeds which the long dry shadow of the fall and winter would bring again to bloom. The curse reached its climax of flower in the spring; but then the strengthening sun promised cure. January was a hopeless time. My elbows and knees, pressure areas of skin, were capped with crust; on my ankles, where the embrace of my socks encouraged the scabs, they angrily ran together in a kind of pink bark. My forearms were mottled enough so that I could not turn my shirt cuffs back, in two natty folds, like other boys. Otherwise, when I was in clothes, my disguise as a normal human being was good. On my face, God had relented; except for traces along the hairline which I let my hair fall forward to cover, my face was clear. Also my hands, except for an unnoticeable stippling of the fingernails. Whereas some of my mother's fingernails were eaten down to the quick by what looked like yellow rot.

Flames of cold flickered across my skin; the little proofs of my sex were contracted into a tense cluster. Whatever in me was normally animal reassured me; I loved the pubic hairs that had at last appeared. Reddish-black, metallic, they curled, too few to make a bush, tight as springs in the lemon-tinted cold. I hated being hairless; I felt defenseless in the locker room when, scurrying to hide my mantle of spots, I saw that my classmates had already donned an armor of fur.

Goosebumps stiffened the backs of my arms; I rubbed them briskly, and then like a miser luxuriously counting his coins I ran my palms across my abdomen. For the innermost secret, the final turn of my shame was that the texture of my psoriasis—delicately raised islands making the surrounding smoothness silver, constellations of roughness whose uneven spacing on my body seemed living intervals of pause and motion—privately pleased me. The delight of feeling

a large flake yield and part from the body under the insistence of a fingernail must be experienced to be forgiven.

Only the medallions watched. I went to the bureau and
found a pair of Jockey shorts that still had life in the elastic.
I put on a T shirt backwards. "You'll outlive me, Pop," my
father downstairs said loudly. "I'm carrying death in my
bowels." His saying this so bluntly affected my own innards,
made them feel slippery and urgent.

"The boy's up, George," my mother said. "You can stop
the performance any time." Her voice had left the bottom
of the stairs.

"Huh? You think I'll upset the kid?"

My father had turned fifty just before Christmas; he had
always said he would never live to be fifty. Breaking the
barrer had unbridled his tongue, as if, being in mathematical
fact dead, nothing he said mattered. His ghostly freedom at
times did frighten me.

I stood before the closet deliberating. Perhaps I foresaw
that I would be wearing for a long time the clothes I chose.
Perhaps the weight of the coming ordeal made me slow.
Scolding my hesitation, a sneeze gathered in the bridge of
my nose and itched. My bladder ached sweetly. I took from
their hanger the gray flannel slacks, though their crease was
poor. I had three pairs of slacks; the brown were at the
cleaners and the blue were disgraced by a faint pallor at the
bottom of the fly. It was a mystery to me, and I always
felt unfairly condemned when they came back from the
cleaners with an insulting printed slip about No Responsibility
For Ineradicable Spots.

As for shirts, today the red seemed the one. I rarely wore
it because its bright shoulders pointed up the white specks
that showered from my scalp like a snow of dandruff. It was
not dandruff, I wanted to tell everybody, as if this exon-
erated me. But I would be safe if I remembered not to
scratch my head, and anyway a generous impulse brushed
the risk aside. I would carry to my classmates on this
bitter day a gift of scarlet, a giant spark, a two-pocketed
emblem of heat. Its wool sleeves felt grateful sliding onto
my arms. It was an eight-dollar shirt; my mother couldn't
understand why I never wore it. She rarely seemed conscious of my "handicap," and when she was, it was with a
too-bold solicitude, as if it were a piece of her. Her own
case, except for her fingernails and scalp, hardly existed

in comparison with mine. I did not resent this: she suffered in other ways.

My father was saying, "No, Cassie. Pop *should* outlive me. He's led a good life. Pop Kramer deserves to live forever."

Without listening for her reply, I knew how my mother would take this—as a jab at her father for living so long, for continuing, year after year, to be a dependent burden. She believed that my father was deliberately trying to heckle the old man into his grave. Was she right? Though many things fitted her theories, I never believed them. They were too neat and too grim.

I knew from the noise at the sink below me that she had turned away without answering. I could picture her, her neck mottled with anger, the wings of her nose white and the skin above them pulsing. I seemed to ride the waves of emotion below me. As I sat on the edge of my bed to put on my socks, the old wooden floor lifted under my foot.

My grandfather said, "We never know when we will be called. The world never knows who is needed above."

"Well I know sure as hell they don't need me," my father said. "If there's anything God doesn't need, it's my ugly face to look at."

"He knows how much *we* need you, George."

"You don't need me, Cassie. You'd be better off with me on the dump. My father died at forty-nine and it was the best thing he ever did for us."

"Your father was a disappointed *man*," my mother told him. "Why should *you* be disappointed? You have a wonderful son, a beautiful farm, an adoring wife—"

"Once the old man was in his grave," my father continued, "my mother really cut loose. Those were the happiest years of her life. She was a super-woman, Pop."

"I think it's so sad," my mother said, "that they don't allow men to marry their mothers."

"Don't kid yourself, Cassie. My mother made life a hell on earth for him. She ate that man raw."

One sock had a hole which I tucked deep into the heel of the loafer. This was Monday, and in my sock drawer there was nothing but orphans and a heavy English wool pair my Aunt Alma had sent me this Christmas from Troy, New York. She was a children's clothes buyer for a department store there. I guessed that these socks she had sent were expensive, but when I put them on they were so bulky they made my toenails feel ingrown, so I never wore them. It was a vanity of mine to have my loafers small, size 10½ instead of 11, which would have been proper. I hated to have big feet; I wanted to have a dancer's quick and subtle hooves.

Tapping heel and toe, I left my room and passed through my parents' room. The covers of their bed were tossed back savagely, exposing a doubly troughed mattress. The top of their scarred bureau was covered with combs, in all sizes and colors of plastic, that my father had scavenged from the high school Lost and Found department. He was always bringing junk like this home, as if he were burlesquing his role of provider.

The country staircase, descending between a plaster wall and a wood partition, was narrow and steep. At the bottom, the steps curved in narrow worn wedges; there should have been a railing. My father was sure that my grandfather with his clouded downward vision was going to fall some day; he kept vowing to put up a bannister. He had even bought the bannister, for a dollar in an Alton junk shop. But it leaned forgotten in the barn. Most of my father's projects around this place were like that. Tripping in grace notes like Fred Astaire, I went downstairs, in my descent stroking the bare plaster on my right. So smooth-skinned, this wall shallowly undulated like the flank of a great calm creature alive with the chill communicated through stone from the outdoors. The walls of this house were thick sandstone uplifted by mythically strong masons a century ago.

"Close the stair door," my mother said. We didn't want heat to escape the downstairs.

I can still see everything. The downstairs was two long rooms, the kitchen and the living-room, connected by two doorways side by side. The kitchen floor was of broad old pine boards, recently sanded and waxed. A hot-air register cut into these boards at the foot of the stairs breathed warmly on my ankles. A newspaper, the Alton *Sun*, that had fallen to the floor kept lifting one corner in the draft, as if begging to be read. Our house was full of newspapers and magazines; they flooded the windowsills and spilled from the sofa. My father brought them home by the bale; they had some connection with the Boy Scout scrap-paper drive, but never seemed to get delivered. Instead they slithered around waiting to be read, and on an evening when he was caught in the house with nowhere to go, my father would disconsolately plough through a whole pile. He could read at terrific speed, and claimed never to learn or remember a thing.

"I hate to get you up, Peter," he called to me. "If there's anything a kid your age needs, it's sleep."

I couldn't see him; he was in the living-room. Through the first doorway I glimpsed three chunks of cherry wood burning in the fireplace, though the new furnace in the basement was running as well. In the narrow space of kitchen wall between the two doorways hung a painting I had done of our back yard in Olinger. My mother's shoulder eclipsed it. In the country she had taken to wearing a heavy-knit man's sweater, though in her youth, and in Olinger, when she was slimmer, and when I first recognized her as my mother, she had been what they called in the county a "fancy dresser." With a click like an unspoken scolding she set a tumbler of orange juice at my place at the table. Between the table and the wall was a kind of corridor she filled. Balked by her body, I stamped my foot. She moved away. I walked past her and past the second doorway, through which I glimpsed my grandfather slumped on the sofa beside a stack of magazines, his head bowed as if in prayer or sleep and his fastidious old hands daintily folded across the belly of his soft gray sweater. I walked past the high mantel where two clocks said 7:30 and 7:23 respectively. The faster clock was red and electric and plastic and had been purchased by my father at a discount. The slower was dark and wooden and ornamented and key-wound and had been inherited from my grandfather's father, a man long dead when I was born. The older clock sat on the mantel; the electric was hung on a nail below. I went past the white slab of the new refrigerator's side and out the doors. There were two; the door and the storm door, a wide sandstone sill compelling a space between them. From between the two, I heard my father saying, "Jesus Pop, when I was a kid, I never had any sleep at all. That's why I'm in agony now."

There was a little cement porch where our pump stood. Though we had electricity, we had no indoor plumbing yet. The ground beyond the porch, damp in summer, had contracted in freezing, so the brittle grass contained crisp caves that snapped shut under my feet. Eddies of frost like paralyzed mist whitened the long grass of the orchard slope. I went behind a forsythia bush too close to the house. My mother often complained about the stink; the country represented purity to her but I couldn't take her seriously. As far as I could see, the land was built on rot and excrement.

I suffered a grotesque vision of my urine freezing in mid-air and becoming attached to me. In fact, it steamed on the mulch intimately flooring the interlaced petticoats of the leafless forsythia bush. Lady in her pen scrabbled out of her house, spilling straw, and pushed her black nostrils through the wire fencing to look at me. "Good morning," I said, gentlemanly. When I went to the pen, she leaped high in the air, and when I thrust my hands through the frosty lattice of metal to stroke her, she kept wiggling and threatening to uncoil into another leap. Her coat was fluffed against the cold and bits and wands of straw clung in it. The texture of her throat was feathery, the top of her head waxen. Under her hair, her bones and muscles felt tepid and slender. From the way she kept hungrily twisting her long skull, as if to seize more of my touch, I was afraid my fingers would slip into her eyes, which protruded so vulnerably; lenses of dark jelly. "How are *you?*" I asked. "Sleep well? Dream of rabbits? *Rabbits!*" It was delicious, the way my voice made her swirl, thrust, wag and whine.

As I squatted, the cold came up behind me and squeezed my back. When I stood, the squares of wire my hands had touched were black, my skin having melted the patina of frost. Lady leaped like a spring released. She came down with a foot on her pan and flipped it over and I expected to see water spill. But the water was ice solid with the pan. For the instant before my brain caught up with my eyes, it seemed a miracle.

Now the air, unflawed by any motion of wind, began to cake around me, and I moved quickly. My toothbrush, glazed rigid, was of a piece with the aluminum holder screwed to the porch post. I snapped it free. The pump dragged dry for four heaves of the handle. The water, on the fifth stroke rising from deep in the stricken earth, smoked faintly as it splashed the grooved brown glacier that had built up in the pump trough. The rusty water purged the brush of its stiff jacket, but when I put it in my mouth it was like a flavorless square lollipop. My molars stung along the edges of their fillings. The toothpaste secreted in the bristles melted into a mint taste. All the time, Lady watched my performance with a wild delight that swelled and twitched her body, and when I spat, she barked in applause, each bark a puff of frost. I replaced the brush and bowed, and had the satisfaction of hearing the applause continue as I retired behind the double curtain, the storm door and the main door.

The clocks now said 7:35 and 7:28. The great wash of warm air within the honey-colored kitchen made my movements lazy, though the clocks jabbed at me. "Why is the dog barking?" my mother asked.

"She's freezing to death," I said. "It's too cold out there; why can't she come in?"

"Cruellest thing you can do to a dog, Peter," my father called, invisible. "Get her used to being in the house she'll die of pneumonia like the last dog we had. Don't take an animal out of nature. Hey Cassie: what time is it?"

"Which clock?"

"My clock."

"A little after seven-thirty. The other has it before."

"We gotta go, kid. We gotta move."

My mother said to me, "Eat up, Peter," and him, "That cheap clock of yours runs ahead of time, George. Grandad's clock says you have five minutes."

"That's not a cheap clock. That clock was thirteen dollars retail, Cassie. It's General Electric. If it says twenty of, I'm late already. Gobble your coffee, kid. Time and tide for no man wait."

"For a man with a spider in his bowel," my mother said, "you're awfully full of pep." To me she said, "Peter, don't you hear your father?"

I had been admiring a section of lavender shadow under the walnut tree in my painting of the old yard. I had loved that tree; when I was a child there had been a swing attached to the limb that was just a scumble of almost-black in the picture. Looking at this streak of black, I relived the very swipe of my palette knife, one second of my life that in a remarkable way had held firm. It was this firmness, I think, this potential fixing of a few passing seconds, that attracted me, at the age of five, to art. For it is at about that age, isn't it, that it sinks in upon us that things do, if not die, certainly change, wiggle, slide, retreat, and, like the dabs of sunlight on the bricks under a grape arbor on a breezy June day, shuffle out of all identity?

"*Peter.*" My mother said it in the voice that had no margin left.

I drank the orange juice in two swigs and said, to worry her, "The poor dog is out there without even anything to drink, she's just licking this big chunk of ice in her pan."

My grandfather stirred in the other room and pronounced, "Now that was a favorite saying of Jake Beam's, who used to be stationmaster at the old Bertha Furnace station, before they discon-tinued the passenger station. 'Time and tide,' he would say, so solemn, 'and the Alton Railroad wait for no man.'"

"Yeah but Pop," my father said, "did you ever stop to think, does any man wait for time and tide?"

At this absurdity my grandfather fell silent, and my mother, carrying a pot of simmering water for my coffee, went into the other room to defend him. "George," she said, "why don't you go out and start the car instead of tormenting everybody with your nonsense?"

"Huh?" he said. "Did I hurt Pop's feelings? Pop, I didn't mean to hurt your feelings. I meant what I said. I've been hearing that time and tide line all my life, and I don't know what it means. What does it mean? You ask anybody, and the bastards won't tell you. But they won't be honest. They won't admit they don't know."

"Why, it means," my mother said, and then hesitated, finding, as I had, that my father's anxious curiosity had quite drained the saying's simple sense away, "it means we can't have the impossible."

"No, now look," my father said, going on in that slightly high voice that forever sought a handhold on sheer surfaces, "I was a minister's son. I was brought up to believe, and I still believe it, that God made Man as the last best thing in His Creation. If that's the case, who are this time and tide that are so almighty superior to us?"

My mother came back into the kitchen, bent over me, and poured the smoking water into my cup. I snickered up at her conspiratorily; my father was often a joke between us. But she kept her eyes on my cup as, holding the handle of the pan with a flowered potholder, she filled it without spilling. The brown powder, Maxwell's Instant, made a tiny terrain on the surface of steaming water, and then dissolved, dyeing the water black. My mother stirred with my spoon and a spiral of tan suds revolved in the cup. "Eat your cereal, Peter," she said.

"I can't," I told her. "I'm too upset. My stomach hurts." I wanted revenge for her snub of my flirting overture. It dismayed me that my father, that silly sad man whom I thought our romance had long since excluded, had this morning stolen the chief place in her mind.

He was saying, "Pop, I didn't mean to hurt your feelings; it's just that those old expressions get me so goddam mad I see red when I hear 'em. They're so damn smug, is what gets my goat. If those old peasants or whoever the hell invented 'em have something to say to me, I wish they'd come right out and say it."

"George, it was *you*," my mother called, "who brought it up in the first place."

He changed the subject. "Hey what time is it?"

The milk was too cold, the coffee too hot. I took a sip and scalded my palate; following this the chill mush of the corn flakes was nauseous. As if to make good my lie, my stomach *did* begin to hurt; the ticking minutes pinched it.

"I'm ready," I shouted, "I'm ready, I'm ready." I was like my father in performing for an unseen audience, but his was far off and needed to be shouted at, whereas mine was just over the footlights. *Boy, clutching stomach comically, crosses stage left.* I went into the living-room to gather up my coat and my books. My pea jacket, crusty, faithful, was hanging behind one door. My father was sitting in a rocking chair turned away from the fire that hissed and danced in the fireplace. He had on his overcoat, a tattered checkered castoff with mismatching buttons, which he had rescued from a church sale, though it was too small and barely reached his knees. On his head he wore a hideous blue knitted cap that he had plucked out of a trash barrel at school. Pulled down over his ears, it made him look like an overgrown dimwit in a comic strip. He had just recently taken to wearing this cap, and I wondered why. He still had a full head of hair, barely touched by gray. Understand that to me my father seemed changeless. In fact he did look younger than his years. When he turned his head toward me, his face was that of a sly street urchin prematurely toughened. He had been a child in an humble neighborhood of Passaic. His face, compounded of shiny lumps and sallow slack folds, to me seemed both tender and brutal, wise and unseeing; it was still dignified by the great distance that in the beginning had lifted it halfway to the sky. Once I had stood beside his knees on the brick walk leading to the grape arbor of our house in Olinger and felt him look level into the tops of the horsechestnut trees and believed that nothing could ever go wrong as long as we stood so.

"Your books are on the windowsill," he said. "Did you eat your cereal?"

I rebuked him sharply. "There isn't *time*, you keep telling me." I gathered up my books. Faded blue Latin, its covers all but unhinged. Smart red algebra, freshly issued this year; every time I turned a page, the paper released a tangy virginal scent. And a weary big gray book, General Science, my father's subject. Its cover was stamped with a triangular design of a dinosaur, an atom blazing like a star, and a microscope. On its side and butts a previous possessor had lettered in blue ink the huge word FIDO. The size of this inscription seemed pathetic and abject, like an abandoned religious monument. Fido Hornbecker had been a football hero when I was in the seventh grade. In the list of names written inside the cover, where my own was last, I had never been able to locate the girl who had loved him. In five years, I was the first boy to be assigned the book. The four names written above mine—

Mary Heffner
Evelyn Mays "Bitsy"
Rhea Furstweiler
Phyllis L. Gerhardt—

had melted in my mind into one nymph with inconstant handwriting. Maybe they had all loved Fido.

"Time stolen from food," my grandfather said, "is time stolen from yourself."

"The kid's like I am, Pop," my father said. "I never had time to eat either. Get your carcass away from the table is all I ever heard. Poverty's a terrible thing."

My grandfather's hands were folding and unfolding gingerly and his hightop button shoes twiddled in agitation. He was an ideal foil for my father because as a very old man he imagined that, if listened to, he could provide all answers and soothe all uncertainties. "I would see Doc Appleton," he pronounced, clearing his throat with extreme delicacy, as if his phlegm were Japanese paper. "I knew his father well. The Appletons have been in the county since the beginning." He was sitting bathed in white winter windowlight and seemed, in comparison with my father's bullet-headed shape bulking black against the flickering fire, a more finely evolved creature.

My father stood up. "All he does, Pop, when I go to him, is brag about himself."

There was a flurry in the kitchen. Doors squeaked and slammed; hot claws scrabbled on the wood floor. The dog came racing into the living-room. Lady seemed to hover on the carpet, crouched low as if whipped by joy. Her feet in a frantic swimming motion scratched one spot on the faded purple carpet that was never so worn it could not release under friction further small rolls of lavender fluff—"mice," my grandmother had called them, when this carpet lay in Olinger and she was alive. Lady was so happy to be let indoors she was a bomb of good news, a furry bustle of vortical ecstasy that in vibrating emitted the scent of a skunk she had killed a week ago. Hunting a god, she started toward my father, veered past my legs, jumped on the sofa, and in frantic gratitude licked my grandfather's face.

Along his long life's walks he had had bitter experiences with dogs and feared them. "Hyar, *hyaar*," he protested, pulling his face away and lifting his shapely dry hands against Lady's white chest. His voice was shocking in its guttural force, as if it arose from a savage darkness none of the rest of us had ever known.

The dog pressed her twittering muzzle into his ear and her rump wagged so wildly the magazines began to slide to the floor. We were all churned into motion; my father rose to the rescue but before he could reach the sofa my grandfather lifted himself to his feet. We all three, while the dog swirled underfoot, pressed into the kitchen.

To my mother we must have looked like an accusing posse; she shouted at us, "I let her in because I couldn't stand to hear her bark." She seemed nearly in tears; I was amazed. My own anxiety for the dog had been pretended. I hadn't heard her continue barking. A glance at my mother's mottled throat told me that she was angry. Suddenly I wanted to get out; she had injected into the confusion a shrill heat that made everything cling. I rarely knew exactly why she was mad; it would come and go like weather. Was it really that my father and grandfather absurdly debating sounded to her like murder? Was it something I had done, my arrogant slowness? Anxious to exempt myself from her rage, I sat down in my stiff pea jacket and tried the coffee again. It was still too hot. A sip seared my sense of taste away.

"Jesus kid," my father said. "It's ten to. I'll lose my job if we don't move."

"That's *your* clock, George," my mother said. Since she was defending me, I could not be the cause of her anger. "Our clock says you have seventeen minutes."

"Your clock's wrong," he told her. "Zimmerman's after my hide."

"Coming, coming," I said, and stood up. The first bell rang at eight-twenty. It took twenty minutes to drive to Olinger. I felt squeezed in the dwindling time. My stomach ground its empty sides together.

My grandfather worked his way over to the refrigerator and from its top took the gaudy loaf of Maier's Bread. He moved with a pronounced and elaborate air of being inconspicuous that made us all watch him. He unfolded the wax paper and removed a slice of white bread, which he then folded once and tidily tucked entire into his mouth. His mouth's elasticity was a marvel; a toothless chasm appeared under his ash-colored mustache to receive the bread in one bite. The calm cannibalism of this trick always infuriated my mother. "Pop," she said, "can't you wait until they're out of the house before you start tormenting the bread?"

I took a last sip of the scalding coffee and pushed toward the door. We were all jammed into the little area of linoleum bounded by the door, the wall where the clocks ticked and hummed, the refrigerator, and the sink. The congestion was intense. My mother struggled to get past her father to the stove. He drew himself in and his dark husk seemed impaled on the refrigerator door. My father stood fast, by far the tallest of us, and over our heads announced to his invisible audience, "Off to the slaughterhouse. Those damn kids have put their hate right into my bowels."

"He rattles at that bread all day until I think I have rats in my brain," my mother protested, and, the psoriatic rim of her hairline flaring red, she squeezed past Grampop and pressed a cold piece of toast and a banana at me. I had to shift my books to take them into my hands. "My poor unfed boy," she said. "My poor only jewel."

"Off to the hate-factory," my father called, to goad me on. Bewildered, anxious to please my mother, I had paused to eat a bite from the cold toast.

"If there's anything *I* hate," my mother said, half to me, half to the ceiling, while my father bent forward and touched her cheek with one of his rare kisses, "it's a man who hates sex."

My grandfather lifted his hands in his squeezed space and in a voice muffled by bread pronounced, "Blessings on thee." He never failed to say it, just as, in the early evening, when he climbed "the wooden hill," he would call down to us, "Pleasant dreams." His hands were daintily lifted in benediction, a gesture also of surrender and, as if tiny angels had been clutched in them, release. His hands were what I knew best of him, for, the one in the family with the youngest eyes, it was my job to remove with my mother's tweezers the microscopic brown thorns that on his weed-pulling walks around our farm would gather in the dry, sensitive, translucently mottled skin of his palms.

"Thanks, Pop, we'll need 'em," my father said, wrenching the door open with a quick undercurrent of splintering. He never turned the knob quite enough, so the catch always resisted. "My goose is cooked," he said, glancing at his clock. My mother's cheek brushed mine as I followed him.

"And if there's anything I *hate* in my *house*," she called after my father, "it's cheap red *clocks*."

Safe on the porch, my father striding around the corner, I looked back, which was a mistake. The toast in my mouth turned salty at the sight. My mother, in the momentum of her last cry, went to the wall and, silent through the glass, tore the electric clock from its nail on the wall and made as if to dash it to the floor but then, instead, hugged it with its trailing cord like a baby to her bosom, her cheeks wetly shining. Helplessly her eyes widened, confronting mine. She had been a beautiful young woman and her eyes had not aged. Each day her plight seemed to startle her afresh. Behind her, her father, his head bowed obsequiously, his elastic jaws munching, shuffled across the floor back to his place in the living-room. I wanted to move my face into some expression of consolation or humorous communication but felt it frozen with fear. Fear for her and of her.

And yet, love, do not think that our life together, for all its mutual frustration, was not good. It was good. We moved, somehow, on a firm stage, resonant with metaphor. When my grandmother lay dying in Olinger, and I was a child, I heard her ask in a feeble voice, "Will I be a little debil?" Then she took a sip of wine and in the morning she was dead. Yes. We lived in God's sight.

My father was striding across the sandpaper lawn. I chased him. The little tummocks raised by moles in warm weather made it buckle in spots. The barn wall was full in the sun, a high dappled pentagon. "Mother almost smashed the clock," I told him when I caught up. I meant this to shame him.

"She's in a funny mood," he said. "Your mother's a real

femme, Peter. If I'd been any kind of man I would have put
her on the burlesque stage when she was young."

"She thinks you tease Grampop."

"Huh? Does she? I'm wild about Pop Kramer. He's the
nicest man I ever knew. I worship that man. "

Words seemed whittled and diminished by the still blue
volumes of cold air that clove our cheeks. Our black Buick,
a '36 fourdoor, waited by the barn, facing downhill. That
car had had a beautiful swanky grille; my father, unexpectedly—for material things meant little to him—had taken
childish pride in those slim parallels of chrome. Last fall, Ray
Deifendorf's muddy old Chevvy had stalled on the high
school lot and my father with his usual impulsive Christianity
had volunteered to push him and, just when they had reached
a good speed, Deifendorf through some stupidity braked, and
our car's grille smashed on Deifendorf's bumper. I wasn't
there. Deifendorf himself told me, laughing, how my father
had rushed around to the front and gathered up all the bits of
broken metal, muttering to himself, "Maybe they can weld it
together, maybe Hummel can weld it together." This hopelessly shattered grille. The way Deifendorf told it I had to
laugh too.

The bright fragments still rode around in the trunk, and
our car's face had jagged front teeth. It was a long, heavy
car, and the cylinders needed to be rebored. Also it needed
a new battery. My father and I got in and he pulled out the
choke and switched on the ignition and listened, head
cocked, to the starter churn the stiff motor. There was frost
on the windshield that made the interior dim. The resurrection
felt impossible. We listened so intently that a common picture
seemed crystallized between our heads, of the dutiful brown
rod straining forward in its mysterious brown cavern, skid-
ding past the zenith of its revolution, and retreating, rejected.
There was not even a ghost of a spark. I closed my eyes to
make a quick prayer and heard my father say, "Jesus kid,
were're in trouble." He got out and frantically scraped at the
windshield frost with his fingernails until he had cleared a
patch for the driver's vision. I got out on my side and, heav-
ing together on opposite doorframes, we pushed. Once. Twice.
An immense third time.

With a faint rending noise the tires came loose from the
frozen earth of the barn ramp. The resistance of the car's
weight diminished; sluggishly we were gliding downhill. We
both hopped in, the doors slammed, and the car picked up

speed on the gravel road that turned and dipped sharply around the barn. The stones crackled like slowly breaking ice under our tires. With a dignified acceleration the car swallowed the steepest part of the incline, my father let the clutch in, the chassis jerked, the motor coughed, caught, *caught*, and we were aloft, winging along the pink straightaway between a pale green meadow and a fallow flat field. Our road was so little travelled that in the center it had a mane of weeds. My father's grim lips half-relaxed. He poured shivering gasoline into the hungry motor. If we stalled now, we would be out of luck, for we were on the level and there would be no more coasting. He pushed the choke halfway in. Our motor purred in a higher key. Through the clear margins of the sheet of frost on our windshield I could see forward; we were approaching the edge of our land. Our meadow ended where the land lifted. Our gallant black hood sailed into the sharp little rise of road, gulped it down, stones and all, and spat it out behind us. On our right, Silas Schoelkopf's mailbox saluted us with a stiff red flag. We had escaped our land. I looked back: our home was a little set of buildings lodged on the fading side of the valley. The barn overhang and the chicken house were gentle red. The stuccoed cube where we had slept released like a last scrap of dreaming a twist of smoke that told blue against the purple woods. The road dipped again, our farm disappeared, and we were unpursued. Schoelkopf had a pond, and ducks the color of old piano keys were walking on the ice. On our left, Jesse Flagler's high whitewashed barn seemed to toss a mouthful of hay in our direction. I glimpsed the round brown eye of a breathing cow.

The dirt road came up to Route 122 at a treacherous grade where it was easy to stall. Here there was a row of mailboxes like a street of birdhouses, a STOP sign riddled with rusty bullet-holes, and a lop-limbed apple tree. My father glanced down the highway and guessed it was empty; without touching the brake he bounced us over the final hurdle of rutted dirt. We were high and safe on firm macadam. He went back into second gear, made the motor roar, shifted to third, and the Buick exulted. It was eleven miles to Olinger. From this point on, the journey felt downhill. I ate half of the toast. The cold crumbs got all over my books and lap. I peeled the banana and ate it all, more to please my mother than to satisfy any hunger, and rolled down the window enough to slip the peel and the rest of the toast into the skimming countryside.

Round and rectangular and octagonal advertisements spoke from the edges of the farmland. One weathered barn's whole side said PONY CUT PLUG. The fields where in summer Amish families in bonnets and black hats harvested tomatoes and where fat men on narrow-nosed scarlet tractors swayed through acres of barley seemed, shorn of crops, painfully exposed; they begged the sky to blanket them with snow. At a curve a two-pump gasoline shack wrapped in tattered soft-drink posters limped into our path and fell away wheeling, reappearing in the rear-view mirror ludicrously shrunk, its splotched flying horse sign illegible and dwindling. A dip in the highway made the door of the glove compartment tingle. We passed through Firetown. The village proper was four sandstone houses; here the old squirearchy of Fire Township had lived. One of these houses for fifty years had been the Ten Mile Inn, and there was still a hitching rail by the porch. The windows were boarded. Beyond this kernel, the village thinned into more recent developments: a cinder-block store where they sold beer by the case; two new houses with high foundations and no front steps, though families lived in both; a rambling hunting hut well back from the road, where on weekends parties of many men and sometimes a few women came and made the lights burn; some pre-war composition-shingled houses, built tall as if in a city and filled, my grandfather maintained, with illegitimate children dying of malnutrition. We passed an orange school bus waddling in the opposite direction, toward the township school. I lived now in this school's district, but my father's teaching at Olinger High saved me from going there. I was frightened of the children in the land around us. My mother had made me join the 4-H Club. My fellow members had slanting oval eyes and smooth dun skins. The dull innocence of some and the viciously detailed knowingness of others struck me as equally savage and remote from my highly civilized aspirations. We met in the church basement, and after an hour of slides illuminating cattle diseases and corn pests, I would sweat with claustrophobia, and swim into the cold air and plunge at home into my book of Vermeer reproductions like a close-to-drowned man clinging to the beach.

The cemetery appeared on our right; tablet-shaped tombstones rode at various tilts the settling tummocks. Then the stout sandstone steeple of the Firetown Lutheran Church leaped higher than the trees and dipped its new cross an instant into the sun. My grandfather had helped build that steeple; he had pushed the great stones in a wheelbarrow up a narrow path of bending planks. He had often described to us, with exquisite indications of his fingers, how those planks had bent beneath his weight.

My father and I began going down Fire Hill, the longer, and less steep, of the two hills on the road to Olinger and Alton. About halfway down, the embankment foliage fell away, and a wonderful view opened up. I saw across a little valley like the background of a Dürer. Lording it over a few acres of knolls and undulations draped with gray fences and dotted with rocks like brown sheep, there was a small house that seemed to have grown from the land. This little house presented to the view from the highway a broad bottle-shaped chimney built up one wall from field stones and newly whitewashed. And out of this broad chimney, very white, its rough bulk linking the flat wall to the curving land, the thinnest trace of smoke declared that someone lived here. I supposed that all this country looked this way when my grandfather helped raise the steeple.

My father pushed the choke all the way in. The needle of the temperature gauge seemed stuck in its bed on the left side of the dial; the heater refused to declare itself. His hands as they controlled the car moved with a pained quickness across the metal and hard rubber. "Where are your gloves?" I asked him.

"In the back, aren't they?"

I turned and looked; on the back seat the leather gloves I had bought him for Christmas lay curled palms up between a rumpled road map and a snarl of baling rope. I had paid nearly nine dollars for them. The money came from a little "art school" account I had started that summer with money earned from my 4-H project, a patch of strawberries. I had spent so much for these gloves I only bought my mother a book and my grandfather a handkerchief; I so wanted my father to care about his clothes and his comfort, like the fathers of my friends. And the gloves had fit. He wore them the first day, and then they rested in the front seat, and then when one day three people crowded into the front seat, they were tossed into the back. "Why don't you ever wear them?" I asked him. My voice with him was almost always accusing.

"They're too good," he said. "They're wonderful gloves,

Peter. I know good leather. You must have paid a fortune for 'em."

"Not that much, but aren't your hands cold?"

"Yeah. Boy, this is a bitter day. We're in Old Man Winter's belly."

"Well don't you want to put the gloves on?"

Roadside scruff in a scratchy stream poured past my father's profile. He emerged from thought to tell me, "When I was a kid, if anybody had given me gloves like that, I would have cried real tears."

These words hurt my stomach, weighted as they were by what I had overheard while awaking. I had gathered only that there was something *in* him, and this thing, which I thought might be the same thing that made him resist wearing my gloves, I hoped I could elicit; though I did suspect that he was too old and too big for me to purge or change completely, even for my mother's sake. I leaned closer and studied the edges of white flesh where his fists gripped the steering-wheel. The wrinkles in his skin seemed fissures; the hairs, bits of captured black grass. The backs of his hands were dappled with dull brown warts. "Doesn't the steering wheel feel like ice?" I asked. My voice sounded like my mother's, when she had said, "You can't feel such things."

"To tell the truth, Peter, my tooth hurts so much I don't notice it."

I was surprised and relieved: a toothache was new; perhaps this mere thing was what was in him. I asked, "Where?"

"In the back." He sucked; his cheek, cut in shaving this morning, wrinkled. The blood of his cut seemed very dark.

"You ought to have it looked at. That's simple."

"I don't know which one it is. All of 'em probably. I ought to have every tooth in my head yanked. Slap a plate in there. Go to one of these butchers in Alton that pulls 'em out and puts 'em in the same day. They push 'em right into your bloody gums."

"Is that really what they do?"

"Sure. They're sadists, Peter. Mongoloid sadists."

"I can't believe it," I said.

The heater, thawed by our run down the hill, came on; brown air baked by rusty pipes breathed onto my ankles. Each morning, this event had the tone of a rescue. Now that a margin of comfort had been promised, I turned on the radio. The little dial, thermometer-shaped, glowed wan orange. When the tubes warmed, cracked and jagged night-time voices sang in the bright blue morning. My scalp tingled and tightened; the voices, negroid and hillbilly, seemed to pick their way along the tune over obstacles that made their voices skip, lift, and stagger; and this jagged terrain seemed my country. It was the U.S.A. the songs conveyed: mountains of pine, oceans of cotton, tan western immensities haunted by disembodied voices cracked by love invaded the Buick's stale space. A commercial delivered with an unctuous irony spoke soothingly of the cities, where I hoped my life would take me, and then a song came like a choo-choo, clicking, irresistible, carrying the singer like a hobo on top of its momentum, and my father and I seemed ourselves irresistible, rolling up and down through the irregularities of our suffering land, warm in the midst of much cold. In those days the radio carried me into my future, where I was strong: my closets were full of beautiful clothes and my skin as smooth as milk as I painted, to the tune of great wealth and fame, pictures heavenly and cool, like those of Vermeer. That Vermeer himself had been obscure and poor I knew. But I reasoned that he had lived in backward times. That my own times were not backward I knew from reading magazines. True, in all of Alton County only my mother and I seemed to know about Vermeer; but in the great cities there must be thousands who knew, all of them rich. Vases and burnished furniture stood upright around me. On a stiff tablecloth a loaf of sugary bread lay sequinned with pointillist dabs of light. Beyond the parapet of my balcony a high city of constant sun named New York glimmered in its million windows. My white walls accepted a soft breeze scented with chalk and whole cloves. In the doorway a woman stood, shadow-mirrored by the polished tiles, and watched me; her lower lip was slightly heavy and slack, like the lower lip of the girl in the blue turban in The Hague. Among these images which the radio songs rapidly brushed in for me the one blank space was the canvas I was so beautifully, debonairly, and preciously covering. I could not visualize my work; but its featureless radiance made the center of everything as I carried my father in the tail of a comet through the expectant space of our singing nation.

After the tiny town of Galilee, gathered, no bigger than Firetown, around the Seven-Mile Tavern and the cinder-block structure of Potteiger's Store, the road like a cat flattening its ears went into a straightaway where my father always speeded. Passing the model barn and outbuildings of the

Clover Leaf Dairy, where conveyor belts removed the cows'
dung, the road then knifed between two high gashed embank-
ments of eroding red earth. Here a hitchhiker waited beside a
little pile of stones. As we rose toward him I noticed, his
silhouette being printed sharply on the slope of clay, that his
shoes were too big, and protruded oddly behind his heels.

My father slammed on the brakes so suddenly it seemed he
recognized the man. The hitchhiker ran after our car, his
shoes flapping. He wore a faded brown suit whose pattern
of vertical chalkstripes seemed incongruously smart. He
clutched to his chest as if for warmth a paper bundle tightly
tied with butcher's cord.

My father leaned across me, rolled open my window, and
shouted, "We're not going all the way into Alton, just to the
bottom of Coughdrop Hill!"

The hitchhiker drooped at our door. His pink eyelids
blinked. A dirty green scarf was tied around his neck, keep-
ing his upturned coat lapels pressed against his throat. He
was older than his lean figure glimpsed at a distance suggested. Some force of misery or weather had scrubbed his
white face down to the veins; broken bits of purple had
hatched on his cheeks like infant snakes. Something dainty in
his swollen lips made me wonder if he were a fairy. I had
once been approached by a shuffling derelict while waiting
for my father in front of the Alton Public Library and his
few mumbled words before I fled had scored me. I felt, as
long as my love of girls remained unconsummated, open on
that side—a three-walled room any burglar could enter. An
unreasoning hate of the hitchhiker suffused me. The window
my father had opened to him admitted cold air that made
my ears ache.

As usual, my father's apologetic courtesy had snagged the
very progress it sought to smooth. The hitchhiker was bewildered. We waited for his brains to thaw enough to absorb
what my father had said. "We're not going all the way into
Alton," my father called again, and in impatience leaned
so far over that his huge head was in front of my face. As he
squinted, a net of brown wrinkles leaped up behind his eye.
The hitchhiker leaned in toward my father and I felt absurdly
pinched between their fumbling old faces. And all the while
the musical choo-choo was clicking forward on the radio; I
yearned to board it.

"How far?" the hitchhiker asked. His lips hardly moved.

His hair was lank and sparse on top and so long uncut it bunched in feathery tufts above his ears.

"Four miles, get in," my father said, suddenly decisive. He pushed at my door and said to me, "Move over, Peter. Let the gentleman up front by the heater."

"I'll get in back," the hitchhiker said, and my hate of him ebbed a little. He did have some vestige of decent manners. But in getting into the back seat, he did not lift his fingers from the sill of my window until with the other arm, awkwardly pinching the bundle against his side, he had worked open the back door. As if we were, my selfless father and my innocent self, a treacherous black animal he was capturing. Once safe in the cavity behind us, he sighed and said, in one of those small ichorous voices that seems always to be retracting in mid-sentence, "What a fucking day. Freeze your sucking balls off."

My father let out the clutch and did a shocking thing: turning his head to talk to the stranger, he turned off my radio. The musical choo-choo with all its freight of dreaming dropped over a cliff. The copious purity of my future shrank to the meagre confusion of my present. "Just as long as it doesn't snow," my father said. "That's all the hell I care about. Every morning I pray: 'Dear Lord, no snow.' "

Unseen behind me the hitchhiker was snuffling and liquidly enlarging like some primeval monster coming to life again out of a glacier. "How about you, boy?" he said, and through the hairs on my neck I could feel him hunch forward. "You don't mind the snow, do ya?"

"The poor kid," my father said, "he never gets a chance to go sledding any more. We took him out of the town where he loved to be and stuck him in the sticks."

"I bet he likes the snow real good," the hitchhiker said. "I bet he likes it fine." Snow seemed to mean something else to him; he certainly was a fairy. I was more angered than frightened; my father was with me.

He, too, seemed disturbed by our guest's obsession. "How about it, Peter?" he asked me. "Does it still mean a lot to you?"

"No," I said.

The hitchhiker snorted moistly. My father called back to him, "Where've you come from, mister?"

"North."

"You heading into Alton."

"Guess so."

"You know Alton?"

"I been there before."

"What's your profession?"

"Annnh—I cook."

"You *cook!* That's a wonderful accomplishment, and I know you're not lying to me. What's your plan? To stay in Alton?"

"*Ihnnn.* Just to get a job enough to get me south."

"You know, mister," my father said, "you're doing what I've always wanted to do. Bum around from place to place. Live like the birds. When the cold weather hits, just flap your wings and go south."

The hitchhiker giggled, puzzled.

My father went on, "I've always wanted to live in Florida, and I never got within smelling distance of it. The furthrest south I ever got in my whole life was the great state of Maryland."

"Nothin' much in Maryland."

"I remember in grammar school back in Passaic," my father said, "how they were always telling us about the white stoops of Baltimore. Every morning, they said, the housewives would get out there with the bucket and scrub-brush and wash these white marble stoops until they shone. Ever see that?"

"I been in Baltimore but I never seen that."

"That's what I thought. They lied to us. Why the hell would anybody spend their life washing a white marble stoop that as soon as you scrub it up some moron with dirty shoes comes along and puts his footprint on it? It never seemed credible to me."

"I never seen it," the hitchhiker said, as if regretting that he had caused such a radical disillusion. My father brought to conversations a cavernous capacity for caring that dismayed strangers. They found themselves involved, willy-nilly, in a futile but urgent search for the truth. This morning my father's search seemed especially urgent, as if time were running out. He virtually shouted his next question. "How'd you get caught up here? If I was in your shoes, mister, I'd be in Florida so fast you wouldn't see my dust."

"I was living with a guy up in Albany," the hitchhiker said reluctantly.

My heart shrivelled to hear my fears confirmed; but my father seemed oblivious of the horrible territory we had entered. "A friend?" he asked.

"Yeah. Kinda."

"What happened? He pull the old double-cross?"

In his delight the hitchhiker lurched forward behind me. "That's right, buddy," he told my father. "That's just what that fucking sucker did. Sorry, boy."

"That's O.K.," my father said. "This poor kid hears more horrible stuff in a day than I have in a lifetime. He gets that from his mother; she sees everything and can't do a thing about it. Thank God I'm half-blind and three-quarters deaf. Heaven protects the ignorant."

I dimly appreciated that my father had conjured up Heaven and my mother as a protection for me, as a dam against the flood of vile confidences with which our guest was brimming; but I vividly resented that he should even speak of me to this man, that he should dip the shadow of my personality into this reservoir of slime. That my existence at one extremity should be tangent to Vermeer and at the other to the hitchhiker seemed an unendurable strain.

But relief was approaching. We came to the crest of Cough-drop Hill, the second, and steeper, of the two hills on the way to Alton. At the bottom, the road to Olinger went off to the left and we would have to let the hitchhiker out.

We began the descent. We passed a trailer truck laboring toward the crest so slowly its peeling paint seemed to have weathered in transit. Well back from the road, Rudy Essick's great brown mansion sluggishly climbed through the down-slipping trees.

Coughdrop Hill took its name from its owner, whose coughdrops ("SICK? Suck an ESSICK!") were congealed by the million in an Alton factory that flavored whole blocks of the city with the smell of menthol. They sold, in their little tangerine-colored boxes, throughout the East: the one time in my life I had been to Manhattan, I had been astonished to find, right in the throat of Paradise, on a counter in Grand Central Station, a homely ruddy row of them. In disbelief I bought a box. Sure enough, on the back, beneath an imposing miniature portrait of the factory, the fine print stated MADE IN ALTON, PA. And the box, opened, released the chill, ectoplasmic smell of Brubaker Street. The two cities of my life, the imaginary and the actual, were superimposed; I had never dreamed that Alton could touch New York. I put a coughdrop into my mouth to complete this delicious confusion and concentric penetration; my teeth sweetened and at the level of my eyes, a hollow mile beneath the ceiling that on an aqua sky displayed the constellations with sallow electric stars, my father's yellow-knuckled hands wrung together nervously through my delay. I ceased to be impatient with him and became as anxious as he to catch the train home. Up to this moment my father had failed me. Throughout our trip, an overnight visit to his sister, he had been frightened and frustrated. The city was bigger than the kind he understood. The money in his pocket dwindled without our buying anything. Though we walked and walked, we never reached any of the museums I had read of. The one called the Frick contained the Vermeer of the man in the big hat and the laughing woman whose lazily upturned palm unconsciously accepts the light, and the one called the Metropolitan contained the girl in the starched headdress bent reverently above the brass jug whose vertical blue gleam was the Holy Ghost of my adolescence. That these paintings, which I had worshipped in reproduction, had a simple physical existence seemed a profound mystery to me: to come within touching distance of their surfaces, to see with my eyes the truth of their color, the tracery of the cracks whereby time had inserted itself like a mystery within a mystery, would have been for me to enter a Real Presence so ultimate I would not be surprised to die in the encounter. My father's blundering blocked it. We never entered the museums; I never saw the paintings. Instead I saw the inside of my father's sister's hotel room. Though suspended twenty stories above the street, it smelled strangely like the lining of my mother's fur-collared winter coat of thick green-plaid cloth. Aunt Alma sipped a yellow drink and dribbled the smoke of Kools from the corners of her very thin red lips. She had white, white skin and her eyes were absolutely transparent with intelligence. Her eyes kept crinkling sadly as she looked at my father; she was three years older than he. They talked all evening of pranks and crises in a vanished Passaic parsonage whose very mention made me sick and giddy, as if I were suspended over a canyon of time. Down on the street, twenty stories below, the taxi lights looped in and out, and that was abstractly interesting. During the day, Aunt Alma, here as an out-of-town children's-clothes buyer, left us to ourselves. The strangers my father stopped on the street resisted entanglement in his earnest, circular questioning. Their rudeness and his ignorance humilated me, and my irritation had been building toward a tantrum that the coughdrop dissolved. I forgave him. In a temple of pale brown marble I forgave him and wanted to thank him for conceiving me to be born in a county that could insert its candy into the throat of Paradise. We took the subway to Pennslyvania Station and caught a train and sat side by side as easy as twins all the way home, and even now, two years later, whenever in our daily journey we went up or down Coughdrop Hill, there was for me an undercurrent of New York and the constellations that seemed to let us soar, free together of the local earth.

Instead of braking, my father by some mistake plunged past the Olinger turnoff. I cried, "Hey!"

"It's O.K., Peter," he said to me softly. "It's too cold." His face was impassive under the cretinous cap of knitted blue. He did not want the hitchhiker to be embarrassed by the fact that we were going out of our way to take him into Alton.

I was so indignant I dared turn and glare. The hitchhiker's face, unfrozen, was terrible—a puddle; it mistook my motive and moved toward me with a smear of a smile and an emanation of muddy emotion. I flinched and rigidly cringed; the details of the dashboard leaped up aglitter. I shut my eyes to prevent any further inwash of that unwelcome unthinkable ichor I had roused. Most horrible in it had been something shy and grateful and girlish.

My father reared back his great head and called, "What have you learned?"

His voice strained under a high pain that bewildered the other. The back seat was silent. My father waited. "I don't follow you," the hitchhiker said.

My father amplified. "What's your verdict? You're a man I admire. You've had the guts to do what I always wanted to do: move around, see the cities. Do you think I've missed out?"

"You ain't missed a thing." The words curled back on themselves like offended feelers.

"Have you done anything you like to remember? I was awake all last night trying to remember something pleasant and I couldn't do it. Misery and horror; that's my memories." This hurt my feelings; he had had me.

The hitchhiker's voice scribbled; maybe it was a laugh. "Last month I killed a goddam dog," he said. "How's that? Damn suckin' dogs come up outa the bushes and try to grab a piece of your leg, so I get myself a hell of a big stick and I was walkin' along this cock jumps out at me and I cracked him right between the eyes. He drops down and I thump him a couple times more good and boy there's one suckin' dog won't be tryin' to grab a piece of your leg just because you ain't got no car to go haulin' your ass around in. Christ right between the eyes the first crack."

My father had listened rather dolefully. "Most dogs won't hurt you," he said now. "They're just like I am, curious. I know just how they think. We have a dog at home I think the world of. My wife just worships that animal."

"Well I fixed that one bastard good I tell ya," the hitch-hiker said, and sucked back spittle. "You like dogs, boy?" he asked me.

"Peter likes everybody," my father said. "I'd give my eyes if I had that boy's good nature. But I see your point, mister, when a dog comes up to you in the dark along a strange road."

"Yeah and then nobody picks ya up any more," the hitchhiker said. "Stand there all day your balls freezin' off and yours was the first car in a hour stopped for me."

"I always pick 'em up," my father said. "If Heaven didn't look after fools I'd be in your shoes. You said you're a cook?"

"*Annh*—I done it."

"My hat's off to you. You're an artist."

I felt within myself like a worm hatching the hitchhiker beginning to wonder if my father were sane. I cringed with the desire to apologize, to grovel before this stranger, to explain. *It's just his way, he loves strange people, he's worried about something.*

"There's nothin' to it except keep the griddle greased." This response came cautiously.

"You're lying, mister," my father shouted. "There's a fine art to cooking for other people. I couldn't learn it if you gave me a million years."

"Buddy, that's horse poop," the hitchhiker said, lurching into intimacy. "Just keep the burgers thin's all the bastards run these suckin' joints give a dick about. Give 'em grease and spare the meat; if I had one of those bastards gimme the word I had a hundred. The great god Dollar's the only one they're looking out for. Christ I wouldn't drink the nigger piss they call coffee."

As the hitchhiker grew more and more expansive I felt myself shrivel and shrink; my skin itched furiously.

"I wanted to be a druggist," my father told him. "But when I got out of college there was no do-re-mi. My old man left us a Bible and a deskful of debts. But I don't blame him, the poor devil tried to do what was right. Some of my kids—I'm a schoolteacher—go off to pharmaceutical school and from what they tell me I just wouldn't have had enough brains for it. A druggist is an intelligent man."

"What are you goin' to be, boy?"

My desire to become a painter embarrassed my father. "That poor kid's as confused as I am," he told the hitch-hiker. "He ought to get out of this part of the country and get down where there's some sun. He has a terrible skin problem."

In effect my father had torn off my clothes and displayed my prickling scabs. In the glare of my anger his profile seemed that of a blind raw rock.

"That right, boy? How so?"

"My skin is blue," I said in a congested voice.

"He's just kidding," my father said. "He's a hell of a good sport about it. Best thing in the world for him would be to go down to Florida; if you were his father instead of me he'd be there."

"I expect to be down in two three weeks," the hitchhiker said.

"Take him along!" my father exclaimed. "If ever a kid deserved a break, it's this kid here. My wad is shot. Time to trade in on a new old man; I'm a walking junk heap."

He took the image from the great Alton dump, which had appeared beside the road. A few fires smoldered here and there across its tattered gay acres. Things revert, through rust and rot, to a hopeful brown, and in their heaps of ash take on fantastic silhouettes, frazzled and feathery as ferns. Like a halted host of banners colored bits of paper were pressed by a constant riverside breeze against upright weed stalks. Beyond, the Running Horse River reflected in its strip of black varnish the cobalt blue silently domed above. Ele-phant-colored gas tanks, mounted to rise and fall in cylindri-cal frames, guarded the city's brick skyline: rose madder Alton, the secret city, lining the lap of its purple-green hills. The evergreen crest of Mt. Alton was a slash of black. My hand twitched, as if a brush were in it. Railroad tracks slipped silver along the highway; factory parking lots flashed full; and the road became a suburban street curving between car agencies, corroded diners, and composition-shingled homes.

My father said to the hitchhiker, "There it is. The grand and glorious city of Alton. If anybody had ever come to me when I was a kid and told me I'd die in Alton, P-A, I would have laughed in his face. I'd never heard of it."

"It's a dirty town," the hitchhiker said.

To me it looked so beautiful.

My father stopped the car at the intersection of 122 and the Lancaster Pike; the light was red. The pike to the right became a concrete bridge, the Running Horse Bridge, on whose other side Alton began in earnest. To the left it was three miles to Olinger and another two miles to Ely. "This is it," my father said. "We got to put you out into the cold."

The hitchhiker opened his door. Since my father had announced my skin, the flirtatious emanations in the car had weakened. Nevertheless, perhaps by accident, the back of my neck was touched. In the open air the hobo hugged the paper tight against his chest. The liquid face turned stiff. "I've enjoyed talking to you," my father called to him.

The hitchhiker sneered. "Nnnnyeah." The door slammed. The light turned green. My heart slowed its beating. We nosed onto the pike and drove against the current of the Alton-bound traffic. Through the dusty rear window I watched our guest, looking like a messenger with his undisclosed bundle, dwindle. The hitchhiker became a brown wisp at the mouth of the bridge, flew upwards, vanished. My father said to me in the most matter-of-fact tone, "That man was a gentleman."

There was a tantrum rich and bristling within me; I coldly intended to berate him all the way to school. "This is really great," I said. "Really great. You're in such a hurry you won't let me eat a rotten bite of breakfast and then you pick up some rotten bum and go three miles out of your way for him and he doesn't even thank you. Now we *will* be late for school. I can just *see* Zimmerman, looking at his watch, stamping up and down in the halls, wondering where you are. *Really*, Daddy, I'd think you'd have more sense once in a while. What do you *see* in these bums? Is it *my* fault I was born so you couldn't be a bum? Florida. And then telling him about my skin. That was very nice, I thank you very much. Whyncha make me take off my shirt while you're at it? Maybe I should have showed him my crusty legs. Whydya keep telling everybody every damn thing there is to tell? Who cares, nobody cares, all that moron cared about was killing dogs and breathing on the back of my neck. The white stoops of Baltimore, for Heaven's sake. Really, Daddy, what do you *think* about when you babble like that?"

But you can't keep scolding when the other person says nothing. For the second mile to Olinger we were silent together. He was pressing, panicked now at being late, passing entire rows of cars and hogging the center of the pike. The steering wheel slithered in his hands when our tires got caught in the trolley tracks. He was lucky; we made good time. As we passed the billboard on which the Lions and Rotary and Kiwanis and Elks all welcomed us to Olinger, my father said, "Don't worry about him knowing about your skin, Peter. He'll forget. That's the one thing you learn in teaching; people forget everything you tell 'em. I look at those dumb blank faces every day and it reminds me of death. You fall through those kids' heads without a trace. I remember, when my old man knew he was dying, he opened his eyes on the bed and looked up at Mom and Alma and me and said, 'Do you think I'll be eternally forgotten?' I often think about that. Eternally forgotten. That was a terrible thing for a minister to say. It scared the living daylights out of me."

The last children were crowding into the doors when we pulled into the high school lot. The bell must just have rung. In turning to get out of the car and scoop up my books, I glanced into the back seat. "Daddy!" I called. "Your gloves are gone!"

He was already some paces away from the car. He turned and swept his wart-freckled hand across his skull and removed his blue cap. His hair stood up with static electricity. "Huh? Did that bastard take 'em?"

"He must have. They're not there. Just the rope and the map."

He spared this revelation the space of a blink. "Well," he said, "he needs 'em more than I did. That poor devil never knew what hit him." And he was on his way again, consuming the cement walk with generous strides. Grappling with my books, I could not catch up, and as I followed at an increasing distance behind him, the loss of the gloves, the way he permitted my expensive and painstakingly deliberated gift to sift through him generated a clumsy weight where my books were clasped against my abdomen. My father provided; he gathered things to himself and let them fall upon the world; my clothes, my food, my luxurious hopes had fallen to me from him, and for the first time his death seemed, even at its immense stellar remove of impossibility, a grave and dreadful threat.

III

CHIRON hurried, a little late, down the corridors of tamarisk, yew, bay, and kermes oak. Beneath the cedars and silver firs, whose hushed heads were shadows permeated with Olympian blue, a vigorous underwood of arbutus, wild pear, cornel, box, and andrachne filled with scents of flower and sap and new twig the middle air of the forest. Branches of bloom here and there dashed color across the shifting caverns of forest space that enclosed the haste of his canter. He slowed. The ragged and muted attendants of air escorting his high head slowed also. These intervals of free space—touched by the arching search of fresh shoots and threaded by the quick dripdrop of birdsong released as if from a laden ceiling rich in elements (some songs were water, some copper, some silver, some burnished rods of wood, some cold and corrugated fire)—were reminiscent for him of caverns and soothed and suited his nature. His student's eyes—for what is a teacher but a student grown old?—retrieved, from their seclusion in the undergrowth, basil, hellebore, feverwort, spurge, polypody, bryony, wolf's-bane, and squill. Ixine, cinquefoil, sweet marjoram and gilliflower he lifted, by the shape of their petals, leaves, stems, and thorns, from their anonymity in indiscriminate green. Recognized, the plants seemed to lift crisply in salute, hailing the passage of a hero. *Black hellebore is fatal to horses. Crocuses thrive for being trod upon.* Without his willing it, Chiron's brain rehearsed his anciently acquired druggist's knowledge. *Of the plants called strykhnos, one induces sleep, the other madness. The root of the former, white when dug, turns blood-red while drying. The other some call thryoron and some peritton; three-twentieths of an ounce make the patient sportive, twice this dose induces delusions, thrice the dose will make him permanently insane. And more will kill him.*

Thyme does not grow where a sea-breeze cannot reach. In cutting some roots one must stand to windward. The old

74

gatherers maintained the peony root must be dug at night, for if a woodpecker observes you, you will suffer *prolapsus ani*. Chiron had scorned this superstition; he had meant to bring men out of the darkness. Apollo and Diana had promised to guide him. *One should draw three circles around mandrake with a sword, and, at the cutting, face west.* Chiron's white lips smiled within the bronze fleece of his beard as he remembered the intricate scruples he had scorned in his quest for actual cures. What mattered about mandrake was that, mixed with meal, it assuaged gout, insomnia, erysipelas, and impotence. *Of wild cucumber the root palliates white leprosy and mange in sheep. Of germander the leaves, pounded in olive oil, dress fractures and spreading sores; the fruit purges bile. Polypody purges downwards; the driver—which retains its virtue for two hundred years— both upwards and downwards. The best drugs come from places that are wintry, face the north, and are dry—in Euboea, the drugs of Aigai and Telethrion have most virtue. All perfumes save iris come from Asia: cassia, cinnamon, cardamon, spikenard, storax, myrrh, dill. The poisons are native: hellebore, hemlock, meadow-saffron, poppy, wolf's- bane. Chamaeleon is fatal to dogs and pigs; and if one wishes to discover whether a man that is sick will live, he should be washed with a paste of chamaeleon mixed with oil and water for three days. If he survives the experience, he will live.*

A bird above him released a swift metallic song that seemed to be a signal. "Chiron! Chiron!": the call sprang up behind him and overtook him and, skimming past his ears, outraced him in its bodiless speed of joy to the ragged cave- mouth of sunstruck air that waited at the end of the forest path. He came into the clearing and his students were already there: Jason, Achilles, Asclepios, his daughter Ocyrhoe, and the dozen other princely children of Olympus abandoned to his care. It had been their voices. Seated in a semi-circle on the warm orchard grass, all hailed him gladly. Achilles looked up from sucking the marrow from the bone of a faun; his chin was smeared with crumbs of wax from a honeycomb. The boy's fine body had in it a hint of fat. Across those broad blond shoulders lay like a transparent mantle a suggestion of feminine roundness that gave his developed mass a slightly passive weight, and weakened his eyes. Their blue was too beryline; their gaze both questioned and evaded. Of all Chi- ron's students, Achilles gave his teacher the most trouble yet seemed most needful of his approval and loved him least bashfully. Jason, less favored, slightly built and younger-appearing than his years, yet had the angular assurance of independence, and his dark eyes declared a calm intention to survive. Asclepios, the best student, was quiet and determinedly composed; in many respects he had already surpassed his master. Torn from the womb of faithless Coronis slain, he too had known an unmothered childhood and the distant protection of a divine father; Chiron treated him less as a pupil than as a colleague, and while the others romped at recess the two of them, old at heart, side by side delved deeper into the arcana of research.

But Chiron's eyes rested most fondly on the reddish-gold hair of his daughter. How rich with life this girl was! Her hair waved and interweaved: herds of horses, seen from above. His life, seen from above. It was in her that his plasm was immortal. His gaze foundered on her head, already a woman's head, wantonly crowned: his own seed—he saw down through her into the stamping, angry child, long-legged, wide-browed, who had arisen from the infant that Chariclo had nursed beside him on the moss, in the days when stars spoke at the mouth of the cave. The girl had been too intelligent to take her childhood easily; her tantrums had grieved their pride in her. More keenly than her father, Ocyrhoe was tormented with prescience, a torment of which not all his drugs, not even all-heal uprooted at midnight of the shortest night from the rocky ground about Psophis, could relieve her; so when she taunted him, however shrilly and cruelly, he felt no rage, and submitted meekly, hoping to earn her forgiveness for his inability to work her cure.

In the chorus of greeting, each child's cry was an individual tint known to him. In sum the polyphony formed a rainbow. His eyes wavered on the warm edge of tears. The children opened each day's session with a hymn to Zeus. When they stood, their bodies, clad lightly, were not yet differentiated into wedges and vases, attacking and containing, tools for Ares and Hestia, but were the same in silhouette, though of various heights: slim pale reeds of a single pipe harmoniously hymning the god of existence pure.

> *"Lord of the sky,*
> *Wielder of weather,*
> *Brightness of brightness,*
> *Zeus, hear our song!*

"Fill us with glory,
Crest of the thunderhead,
Shape us with gradualness,
Source of the rain!"

The light and fitful breeze swayed and scattered the song much as young girls toss scarves.

"Radiance beyond itself,
Sun above Apollo,
Earth below Hades,
Sea upon sea,

"Grant us proportion,
Arc of the firmament,
Curve of the gilliflower:
Zeus, let us thrive!"

The centaur's grave voice, uncertain in song, joined in the final petition:

"Brightness of brightness,
Sky of our mortality,
Home of our hopes,
Height of our fear,

"Send us a sign,
A sign of benevolence,
Show forth thy government:
Answer our song!"

They fell silent and above the treetops on the left of the clearing a black eagle arrowed across the sun. Chiron feared for a moment, then realized that though it was on his left, it was on the children's right. On their right, and ascending: doubly propitious. (But on *his* left). The class sighed in awe and, after the eagle vanished on the irridescent edge of the solar halo, chattered excitedly. Even Ocyrhoe, it pleased her father to see, was impressed. Worry in this interval slid from her brow; her glittering hair merged with her shining eyes and she became any gay, thoughtless girl. By no means instinctively reverent, she claimed to foresee a day when Zeus would be taken by men as a poor toy they had themselves invented, and be terribly taunted, be banished from Olympus, sent scrambling down the shingle, and branded a criminal.

The Arcadian sun was growing warmer. Birdsong encircling the clearing turned sluggish. Chiron felt in his blood the olive trees on the plain rejoice. In the cities, worshippers mounting the white temple steps would feel the marble hot on their unsandalled feet. He took his class for their lesson to the shade of a great chestnut tree that it was said Pelasgus himself had planted. The trunk was as thick around as a shepherd's cottage. The boys arranged themselves swaggeringly among the roots as if among the bodies of slain enemies; the girls more demurely sought postures of ease on areas of moss. Chiron inhaled; air like honey expanded the spaces of his chest; his students completed the centaur. They fleshed his wisdom with expectation. The wintry chaos of information within him, elicited into sunlight, was struck though with the young colors of optimism. Winter turned vernal. "Our subject today," he began, and the faces, scattered in the deep green shade like petals after rain, were unanimously hushed and attentive, "is the Genesis of All Things. In the beginning," the centaur said, "black-winged Night was courted by the wind, and laid a silver egg in the womb of Darkness. From this egg hatched Eros, which means—?"

"Love," a child's voice answered from the grass.

"And Love set the Universe in motion. All things that exist are her children—sun, moon, stars, the earth with its mountains and rivers, its trees, herbs, and living creatures. Now Eros was double-sexed and golden-winged and, having four heads, sometimes roared like a bull or a lion, sometimes hissed like a serpent or bleated like a ram; beneath her rule the world was as harmonious as a beehive. Men lived without cares or labor, eating only acorns, wild fruit, and honey that dripped from trees, drinking the milk of sheep and goats, never growing old, dancing, and laughing much. Death, to them, was no more terrible than sleep. Then her sceptre passed to Uranus . . ."

IV

AFTER SCHOOL I went up to my father's room, Room 204. Two students were in there with him. I glared at them both and in my haughty red shirt crossed to the window and looked toward Alton. I had made a vow during the day to protect my father, and these two students consuming his time were the first enemies I had encountered. One was Deifendorf, the other was Judy Lengel. Deifendorf was speaking.

"I can see shop and typing and like that, Mr. Caldwell," he said, "but for somebody like me who's not going on to college or anything, I don't see the point of memorizing lists of animals that've been dead a million years."

"There is no point," my father said. "You are two hundred per cent right: who cares about dead animals? If they're dead, let 'em lie; that's my motto. They depress the hell out of me. But that's what they give me to teach and I'm going to teach it to you until it kills me. It's either you or me, Deifendorf, and if you don't get rid of those jitters I'll do my best to kill you before you kill me; I'll strangle you with my bare hands if I have to. I'm up here fighting for my life. I have a wife and a kid and an old man to feed. I'm just like you are; I'd rather be out walking the streets. I feel sorry for you; I know how you're suffering."

I laughed by the window; it was my way of attacking Deifendorf. I felt him clinging to my father, sucking the strength from him. That was the way of the cruel children. An hour after they had goaded him to the point of frenzy (flecks of foam would actually appear in the corners of his mouth and his eyes would become like tiny raw diamonds), they would show up in his room, anxious to seek advice, make confessions, be reassured. And the instant they had left his company they would mock him again. I kept my back turned on the sickening duet.

From my father's windows I overlooked the school's side lawn, where in the autumn the band and cheerleaders rehearsed, and the tennis courts and the line of horsechestnut trees marking the poorhouse lane and, beyond everything,

Mt. Alton, a humped blue horizon scarred by a gravel pit. A trolley car stuffed with Alton shoppers came sparking and swaying up the line. Some of the students who lived toward Alton were bunched at the stop, waiting for this trolley's mate to come down the pike. Down on the cement walks leading from the girls' exit along the side of the building— I had to touch my nose to the icy glass to see this sharply down—girls, foreshortened into patches of plaid, fur, books, and wool, walked in pairs and trios home together. Frozen breath flew from their mouths. What they said I could not hear. I looked for Penny among them. I had avoided her all day, because to draw near to her seemed a desertion of my parents, whose need for me had mysteriously, solemnly deepened.

". . . the only one," Deifendorf was saying to my father. His voice scratched. His voice was queerly feeble, disassociated from his emphatic, athletic body. I had often seen Deifendorf naked in the locker room. He had stumpy legs woolly with sandy fur and a huge rubbery torso and sloping shining shoulders and very long arms culminating in red scoop-shaped hands. He was a swimmer.

"That's right, you're not, you're not the only one," my father told him. "But on the whole, Deifendorf, I'd say you're the worst. I'd say you're the itchiest kid I have on my hands this year." He made this estimate dispassionately. There were things—itchiness, intelligence, athletic ability —that his years of teaching had given him absolute pitch in gauging.

No Penny had popped up among the girls below. Behind me, the quality of Deifendorf's silence seemed baffled and even hurt. He had a vulnerable side. He loved my father. It pains me to admit it, but there existed between this obscene animal and my father an actual affection. I resented it. I resented how lavishly my father outpoured himself before the boy, as if somewhere in all this nonsense there might be the healing drop. "The Founding Fathers," he explained, "in their wisdom decided that children were an unnatural strain on parents. So they provided jails called schools, equipped with tortures called an education. School is where you go between when your parents can't take you and industry can't take you. I am a paid keeper of Society's unusables—the lame, the halt, the insane, and the ignorant. The only incentive I can give you, kid, to behave yourself is this: if you don't buckle down and learn something, you'll be as dumb as

I am, and you'll have to teach school to earn a living. When the Depression hit me in '31, I had nothing. I knew nothing. God had taken care of me all my life so I was unemployable. So out of the goodness of his heart my father-in-law's nephew Al Hummel got me a job teaching. I don't wish it on you, kid. Even though you're my worst enemy I don't wish it on you."

I was staring, ears warm, toward Mt. Alton. As if through an imperfection in the glass I looked around a corner of time and foresaw, fantastically, that Deifendorf would teach. And so it was to be. Fourteen years later, I went home and on an Alton side-street met Deifendorf in a saggy brown suit from whose breast pocket the pencils and pens thrust as from my father's pocket in the old forgotten days. Deifendorf had gone fat and his hairline had receded, but it was he. He asked me, dared in all seriousness to ask me, an authentic second-rate abstract expressionist living in an East Twenty-third Street loft with a Negro mistress, *me*, if I was ever going to teach. I told him No. He told me, his pale dull eyes shelled in seriousness, "Pete, I often think of what your Dad used to tell me about teaching. 'It's rough,' he'd say, 'but you can't beat it for the satisfaction you get.' Now I'm teaching myself, I see what he meant. A great man, your Dad. Did you know that?"

And now in his weak and scratchy whine of a voice he began to tell my father something of the sort. "I ain't no enemy, Mr. Caldwell. I like you. All the kids like you."

"That's my trouble, Deifendorf. That's the worst thing can happen to a public school teacher. I don't *want* you to like me. All I want from you is to sit still under me for fifty-five minutes a day five days a week. When you walk into my room, Deifendorf, I want you to be stiff with fear. Caldwell the Kid-Killer; that's how I want you to think of me. *Brrouh!*"

I turned from the window and laughed, determined to interrupt. The two of them, the chipped yellow desk between, hunched toward each other like conspirators. My father looked sallow and nauseated, his temples glazed and hollow; the top of his desk was littered with papers and tin-jawed binders and paperweights like half-metamorphosed toads. Deifendorf had stolen his strength; teaching was sapping him. I saw this helplessly. I saw helplessly in the smirk on Deify's face that from my father's whirl of words he had gathered a sense of superiority, a sense of being, in comparison with this addled and vehement shipwreck of a man, young, clean, sleek, clear-headed, well-coördinated, and invincible.

My father, embarrassed by my angry witnessing, changed the subject. "Be at the Y by 6:30," he told Deifendorf curtly. There was a swimming meet this evening and Deifendorf was on the team.

"We'll dunk 'em for ya, Mr. Caldwell," Deifendorf promised. "They'll be cocky and ripe for an upset." Our swimming team had not won a meet all season: Olinger was a very land kind of town. It had no public pool, and the poorhouse dam's bottom was lined with broken bottles. My father was, by one of those weird strokes whereby Zimmerman kept the faculty in a malleable flux of confusion, the team's coach, though his hernia prevented him from ever going into the water.

"Do your best is all we can do," my father said. "You can't walk on water."

I believe now that my father wanted this last statement to be contradicted, but none of the three others of us in the room saw the need.

Judy Lengel was the third student in the room. My father's view of her was that her father bullied her beyond the limit of her mental abilities. I doubted this; in my opinion Judy was just a girl who being neither pretty nor bright had spitefully developed a petty ambitiousness with which she tormented the gullible teachers like my father. She seized the silence to say, "Mr. Caldwell, I was wondering about that quiz tomorrow—"

"Just a moment, Judy." Deifendorf was attempting to leave, sated. He all but belched as he got up from his chair. My father asked him, "Deify, how are you and cigarettes? If anybody reports you smoking again you're off the team."

The feeble primitive voice whined from the doorway. "I ain't touched a weed since the beginning of season, Mr. Caldwell."

"Don't lie to me, kid. Life's too short to lie. About fifty-seven varieties of people have squealed to me about your smoking and if I'm caught protecting you Zimmerman'll have my neck."

"O.K., Mr. Caldwell. I got you."

"I want the breast stroke and the two-twenty freestyle from you tonight."

"You'll get 'em, Mr. Caldwell."

I shut my eyes. It agonized me to hear my father talk like a coach; it seemed so beneath us. This was unfair; for wasn't it after all what I wanted to hear from him—the confident, ordinary, world-supporting accents of other men? Perhaps it hurt me that Deifendorf had something concrete to give my father—the breast stroke and the two-twenty freestyle—while I had nothing. Unwilling to expose my skin, I had never learned to swim. The world of water was closed to me, so I had fallen in love with the air, which I was able to seize in great thrilling condensations within me that I labelled the Future: it was in this realm that I hoped to reward my father for his suffering.

"Now. Judy," he said.

"I don't understand what the quiz will be about."

"Chapters Eight, Nine, and Ten, as I said today in class."

"But that's so much."

"Skim it, Judy. You're no dope. You know how to study." My father flipped open the book, the gray textbook with the microscope, the atom, and the dinosaur on the cover. "Look for italicized words," he said. "Here. Magma. What is magma?"

"Will that be one of the questions?"

"I can't tell you the questions, Judy. That wouldn't be fair to the others. But for your own information, what is magma?"

"Like comes from volcanoes?"

"I'd accept that. Magma is igneous rock in its molten state. And here. Name the three types of rocks."

"Will you ask that?"

"I can't tell you, Judy. You understand that. But what are they?"

"Sentimentary . . ."

"Igneous, sedimentary, and metamorphic. Give me an example of each."

"Granite, limestone, and marble," I said. Judy looked over at me in fright.

"Or basalt, shale, and slate," my father said. The dull girl looked from me to him to me as if we had ganged up on her. For the moment, we had. There were happy moments when my father and I became a unit, a little two-ply team. "You want to know something interesting, Judy?" my father said. "The richest deposit of slate on the continent is right next door to us in Pennsylvania, in Lehigh and Northampton counties." He tapped with his knuckles the blackboard behind him. "Every blackboard from coast to coast comes from around there," he said.

"We aren't expected to know that, are we?"

"It's not in the book, no. But I thought you'd be interested. Try to get interested. Forget your grades; your father will survive. Don't knock yourself out, Judy; when I was your age, I didn't know what it was like to be young. And I've never learned since. Now Judy. Listen to me. Some have it and some don't. But everybody has something, even if it's just being alive. The good Lord didn't put us here to worry about what we don't have. The man with two talents didn't get sore at the man with five. Look at me and Peter. I have no talents, he has ten; but I'm not mad at him. I like him. He's my son."

She opened her mouth and I expected her to ask "Will that be on the quiz?" but nothing came out. My father ruffled the book. "Name some erosional agents," he said.

She ventured, "Time?"

My father looked up and seemed to have taken a blow. His skin was underbelly-white beneath his eyes and an unnatural ruddy flush scored his cheeks in distinct parallels like the marks of angry fingers. "I'd have to think about that," he told her. "I was thinking of running water, glaciers, and wind."

She wrote these down on her tablet.

"Diastrophism," he said. "Isostasy. Explain them. Sketch a seismograph. What is a batholith?"

"You wouldn't ask all of those, would you?" she asked.

"I might not ask any of them," he said. "Don't think about the quiz. Think about the earth. Don't you love her? Don't you want to know about her? Isostasy is like a great fat woman adjusting her girdle."

Judy's face lacked ease. Her cheeks were packed too tautly against her nose, making the lines there deep and sharp; and there was a third vertical crease at the tip of her nose. Her mouth, too, had this look of too many folds, and when she spoke it worked tightly, up and down, like the mouth of a snapdragon. "Would you ask about the Protozone or whatever those things are?"

"Proterozoic Era. Yes, ma'am. A question might be, List the six geologic eras in order, with rough dates. When was the Cenozoic?"

"A billion years ago?"

"You live in it, girl. We all do. It began seventy million years ago. Or I might do this, list some extinct forms of life, and ask that they be identified, with one point for the identification, one for the era, and one for the period. For instance, Brontops: mammal, Cenozoic, Tertiary. Eocene epoch, but

I wouldn't expect you to know that. It may interest you for your own information that the brontops looked a lot like William Howard Taft, who was President when I was your age."

I saw her write "No Epocks" on her tablet and draw a box around it. As my father talked on, she began to ornament the box with triangles. "Or Lepidodendron," he said. "Giant fern, Paleozoic, Pennsylvanian. Or Eryops. What would that be, Peter?"

I really didn't know. "A reptile," I guessed. "Mesozoic."

"An amphibian," he said. "Earlier. Or Archaeopteryx," he said, his voice quickening, sure we would know it. "What's that, Judy?"

"Archy what?" she asked.

"Archaeopteryx." He sighed. "The first bird. It was about the size of a crow. Its feathers evolved from scales. Study the chart on pages two-oh-three to two-oh-nine. Don't tense up. Study the chart, and memorize what you've written down, and you'll do all right."

"I get so sort of sick and dizzy just trying to keep it straight," she blurted, and it seemed she might cry. Her face was a folded bud, but already in her life it had begun to wilt. She was pale and this pallor for a moment swam around the room whose shades of varnish were like shades of honey gathered in a sweetly rotten forest.

"We all do," my father said, and things became firm again. "Knowledge is a sickening thing. Just do the best you can, Judy, and don't lose any beauty sleep. Don't get buffaloed. After Wednesday you can forget all about it and in no time you'll be married with six kids." And it dawned on me, with some indignation, that my father out of pity had hinted away to her the entire quiz.

When she left the room, he got up and closed the door and said to me, "That poor femme, her father'll have an old maid on his hands." We were alone together.

I stopped leaning against the windowsill and said, "Maybe that's what he wants." I was very conscious of wearing a red shirt; its flicker on the floor of my vision as I moved about the room seemed to instill my words with an enigmatic urbanity.

"Don't you believe it," my father said. "The worst thing in the world is a bitter woman. That's one thing about your mother, she's never been bitter. You won't understand this, Peter, but your mother and I had a lot of fun together."

I doubted this, but the way he said it rendered me silent.

One by one, it seemed to me, my father was saying good-bye to all the things he had known in this world. He took a sheet of blue paper from his desk and handed it to me. "Read it and weep," he said. My first thought was that it was a fatal medical report. My stomach sank. I wondered, How could he have gotten it so soon?

But it was just one of Zimmerman's monthly visitation reports.

OLINGER PUBLIC SCHOOLS
OFFICE OF THE SUPERVISING PRINCIPAL

1/10/47

TEACHER: G. W. Caldwell
CLASS: 10th grade Gen. Sci., sec. C
PERIOD OF VISITATION: 1/9/57 11:05 am.

The teacher arrived in the classroom twelve minutes late. His surprise at finding the supervising principal in charge was evident and was remarked upon by the class. Ignoring his students, the teacher attempted to engage the supervising principal in conversation and was refused. The students and the teacher then discussed the age of the universe, the size of the stars, the origins of the earth, and the outline of organic evolution. No attempt was discernible on the teacher's part to avoid offending religious conceptions on the students' part. The humanistic values implicit in the physical sciences were not elicited. The teacher at one point stopped himself from pronouncing the word "hell." Disorder and noise were present from the beginning and rose in volume. The students did not seem well-prepared and the teacher consequently resorted to the lecture method. A minute before the final bell, he struck one boy on the back with a steel rod. Such physical procedure of course violates Pennsylvania state law and in the event of parental protest could result in dismissal.

However, the teacher's knowledge of his subject matter seemed good and some of his illustrations relating subject matter to his students' everyday lives were effective.

Signed,
Louis M. Zimmerman.

My father was pulling the windowshades and the room had been jerked into dusk as I read. "Well," I said, "he thinks you're effective."

"Isn't that the worst God-damn report was ever written? He must have stayed up all night with that masterpiece. If the school board gets ahold of that, I'm O-U-T out, tenure or no tenure."

"Who was the kid you hit?" I asked.

"Deifendorf. That Davis bitch got the poor bastard all excited."

"What's poor about him? He broke our Buick grille and now he's going to get you fired. And two minutes ago he was in here and you were telling him the story of your life."

"He's dumb, Peter. I feel sorry for him. It takes a rat to love a rat."

I swallowed a taste of envy and said, "Daddy, this isn't such a bad report."

"It couldn't be worse," he said, striding down the aisle with the windowpole. "It's murder. And I deserve it. Fifteen years of teaching, and it's all right there. Fifteen years of hell." He took a rag from the book closet and went out the door. I read the report over again, trying to get some picture of Zimmerman's actual mind. I couldn't. My father came back, having soaked the rag at the drinking fountain in the hall. With long rhythmic swipes shaped like sideways 8's he washed the blackboard. His earnest swishing underlined the silence; high on the wall the clock, controlled by the master clock in Zimmerman's office, clicked, jumping from 4:17 to 4:18.

"What does he mean," I asked, "the humanistic values implicit in the physical sciences?"

"You ask him," my father said. "Maybe he knows. Maybe down deep in the atom there's a little man sitting in a rocking chair reading the evening paper."

"Do you really think the school board will see this?"

"Pray not, kid. It's on file. I have three enemies on that board, one friend, and one I don't know. Mrs. Herzog I don't know if she's heads or tails. They'd love to get me out of there. Get rid of the dead wood. A lot of veterans on this GI Bill and they're all gonna need jobs." He was grunting as he washed.

"Maybe you *should* get out of teaching," I said. My mother and I had often discussed this, but our discussions were cramped, for we kept bumping our heads against the fact that my father's teaching was what sheltered us and let us live.

"Too late, too late," my father said. "Too late, too late." He looked at the clock and said, "Jesus, I'm not kidding— I'm late. I told Doc Appleton I'd be there at 4:30."

My face baked with fear. My father never went to doctors. For the first time, I had proof that his illness was not an illusion; it was spreading outward into the world like a stain. "Really? You're really going?" I was begging him to deny it.

He knew my thoughts, and as we confronted each other through the vibrating shadows of the room a locker slammed, a child whistled, the clock clicked. "I called him this noon," my father said, as if he were confessing a sin to me. "I just want to go and hear him tell how smart he was at med school." He hung the wet rag over the back of his chair to dry and went to the windowsill and untwisted the pencil sharpener case and poured a rosy stream of shavings into the wastebasket. The scent of cedar filled the room like the perfume of an offering.

I asked, "Can I go with you?"

"Don't do that, Peter. Go to the luncheonette and kill the time with your friends. I'll pick you up in an hour and we'll go into Alton."

"No, I'll go with you. I don't have any friends."

He took the sadly short coat from his closet. I followed him out. He closed the door of Room 204 behind us and we went down the stairs and through the first floor hall and past the glinting trophy case. This case depressed me; I first saw it as a tiny child and still had a superstitious sense of each silver urn containing the ashes of a departed spirit. Heller, the head janitor, was sprinkling crumbs of red wax over the floor and sweeping them toward us with a broad broom. "Another day, another dollar," my father called to him.

"Ach, ja," the janitor called back. "Too soon oldt and too late schmardt." Heller was a short dark Dutchman with solidly black hair though he was sixty. He wore rimless glasses that made him look more scholarly than most of the teachers in the building. His voice echoed after my father's down the hollow length of the hall, which looked wet where light from a doorway or window lay on it. I was reassured, believing that nothing as absolute and awesome as death could enter a world where grown men could exchange such banalities. While my father waited, I ran to my locker in the annex hall and got my pea jacket and some books; I thought, wrongly, there might be some space in the coming hours when I could do some homework. As I returned to them I heard my father apologizing to Heller for, apparently, a few marks he had made on the floor. "No," he said, "I hate to make the wonderful work you do any harder for you than it is. Don't think I don't appreciate what a job it is to keep this stockyard clean. It's the Augean stable every day of the week."

"Ah well," Heller said, and shrugged. As I came closer, his black shape stooped, so the handle of the broom seemed to pierce it. He straightened and presented in the palm of his open hand, for my father's and my inspection, a few dry oblongs bigger than ordinary dirt and not readily identifiable. "Seeds," he said.

"What kid would be carrying seeds?" my father asked.

"Maybe from an orange?" Heller suggested.

"One goddam more mystery," my father said, and he seemed to shy, and we went out into the weather.

The afternoon was clear and cold and the sun above the westward section of town made our shadows long before us. We seemed from our shadow to be a prancing one-headed creature with four legs. A trolley car went down the pike, its connective wheel sizzling and sparking on the wire, westward into Alton. This was our ultimate direction; we were for the time being working against the tide. In striding silence, my steps three to his two, we passed the school's side lawn. Some yards back from the pavement, there was a glass-fronted billboard. Miss Schrack's senior art class made the posters for it; the present one displayed a great B painted in the school's colors, maroon and gold, and announced:

B ASKETBALL
TUESDAY
7 o'clock

We crossed the little irregular asphalt alley that separated the school property from Hummel's Garage. Here the pavement was stained with little maps of dropped oil, islands and archipelagos and continents undiscovered on this globe. We passed the pumps, and passed the neat white house beside whose little porch a trellis supported the crucified brown skeleton of a rose-vine; in June this rose-vine bloomed and gave every boy who passed this way ambrosial thoughts of undressing Vera Hummel. Two doors further on was Minor's Luncheonette. It shared a brick building with the Olinger Post Office. There were two plate-glass windows side by side: behind one of them fat Mrs. Passify, the postmistress, surrounded by Wanted posters and lists of postal regulations, doled out stamps and money-orders; behind the other, wreathed in adolescent smoke and laughter, Minor Kretz, also fat, scooped ice cream and concocted lemon Pepsis. The two establishments were symmetrically set up. Minor's butterscotch-marble counter mirrored, through the dividing wall, Mrs. Passify's barred windows and linoleum weighing-counter. As a child, I used to peek through the Local slot into the rear of the post office, seeing racks of sorted letters, stacked gray sacks, and one or two postmen in blue pants, hats and coats off, engaging in an official-seeming clatter. Likewise, to me as a child, the older teenagers in the luncheonette seemed to slump in the back booths behind a screen of smoke whose slots permitted glimpses of a mysterious privacy as utterly forbidden to me as if by federal law. The pinball machine and the cancellation machine were twins of noise; where in the post office there was a small shelf bearing a dirty ruffle-edged blotter, a few splayed pens, and two dried bottles with gimcrack hinged mouths, in the luncheonette there was a small table offering for sale plastic cigarette cases, miniature gilt picture frames containing washed-out photographs of June Allyson and Yvonne de Carlo, playing cards with kittens and Scotties and cottages and lagoons on the back, and depraved 29¢ items like transparently loaded dice, celluloid pop eyes and buck teeth, dribble glasses, and painted plaster dog turds. Here you could buy, 2 for 5¢, sepia postcards of the Olinger Town Hall, the business strip of the Alton Pike decked out with overhead lights and plywood candles for Christmas, the view from Shale Hill, the new water-chlorinating plant way up above Cedar Top, and the town Honor Roll, looking as it did during the war—of wood and always being newly lettered—, before they put up the little stone one bearing only the names of those who had died. Here you could buy these cards, and next door, for a penny more, you could mail them; the symmetry, carried right down to the worn spots of the two floors and the heating pipes running along the opposing walls, was so perfect that as a child I had imagined that Mrs. Passify and Minor Kretz were secretly married. At night, and on Sunday mornings, when their windows were dark, the mirroring membrane between them dissolved and, filling the unified brick shell with one fat shopworn sigh, they meshed.

Here my father halted. In the brittle air his shoes scratched on the cement and his mouth moved like a puppet's. "O.K., Peter," he said. "You go into Minor's and I'll come back and pick you up when Doc Appleton's done with me."

"What do you think he'll tell you?" I was tempted. Penny might be in the luncheonette.

"He'll tell me I'm as healthy as a dumb old horse," my father said, "and he's as wise as a dirty old owl."

"You don't want me to come with you?"

"What can you do, you poor kid? Stay away and don't depress yourself. Go see your friends, whoever the hell they think they are. I never had any friends, so I can't imagine it."

My conscience and my father were rarely on opposite sides; I compromised. "I'll go in here," I said. "For a minute, then I'll catch up."

"Take your time," he said, with a sudden sweeping motion of his hand, as if remembering that unseen audience before which he was an actor. "You got lots of time to kill. At your age I had so much time to kill my hands are still bloody." His talk was unreeling wider and wider; I felt chilled.

Walking off alone, he seemed lightened and looked thinner. Perhaps all men look thinner from the back. I wished that for my sake he would buy a respectable coat. As I watched, he took the knit cap out of his pocket and put it on his head; pierced by embarrassment, I ran up the steps, bucked the door, and plunged into the luncheonette.

It was a maze, Minor's place. So many bodies: yet only a tiny section of the school ever came here. Others had other places; the set at Minor's was the most criminal and it thrilled me to be, however marginally, a part of it. I felt in this clouded interior a powerful secret lurking, whose nostrils exhaled the smoke and whose hide exuded the warmth. The voices jostling in the stable-warmth all seemed to be gossiping about the same thing, some event that had happened in the minute before I arrived; I was haunted at that age by the suspicion that a wholly different world, gaudy and momentous, was enacting its myths just around the corners of my eyes. I pushed my way through the bodies as if through the leaves of a close-set series of gates. I picked my way past one, two, three booths and there, yes, there, she was. She.

Why is it, love, that faces we love look upon each re-meeting so fresh, as if our hearts have in this instant again minted them? How can I describe her to you justly? She was small and not unusual. Her lips were too plump and irksomely self-satisfied; her nose rather cursory and nervous. Her eyelids were vaguely Negroid, heavy, puffy, bluish, and incongruously worldly-wise when taken with the startled grassy innocence of her eyes. I believe it was these incongruities—between lips and nose, eyes and lids—these soft and silent clashes like the reticulating ripples hinting in the flow of a stream of irregular depths, that made her beauty for me; this delicate irresolution of feature held out the possibility of her being worthy of me. And made her seem always a bit unexpected.

She was occupying one side of a booth and there was space beside her. Across the table, two ninth-graders she dimly knew, a girl and a boy, were tugging at each other's buttons, blind to everything. She was gazing at them and did not see me until my body, easing in, pushed hers. "Peter!"

I unbuttoned my pea jacket so the devil-may-care flame of my shirt showed. "Give me a cigarette."

"Where have you been all day?"

"Here and there. I've seen *you*."

Nicely she tapped one of her Luckies from her purple-and-yellow plastic case, which had a little sliding door that opened and shut. She looked at me with flecked green irises whose perfect circles of black seemed dilated. I did not understand my ability to dissolve her composure and in my heart honestly took no credit for it. But her dissolution was welcome to me; it couched a kind of repose I had never known before. As a baby wishes to be put to bed, my hand wished to be between her thighs. I dragged and inhaled. "I had a dream about you last night."

She looked away, as if to give herself space in which to blush, "What did you dream?"

"Not quite what you think," I said. "I dreamed you turned into a tree, and I called 'Penny, Penny, come back!', but you didn't, and I was leaning my face against the bark of a tree."

She took it a bit dryly, saying, "Why how sad."

"It *was* sad. Everything around me is sad these days."

"What else is sad?"

"My father thinks he's sick."

"What does he think he has?"

"I don't know. Cancer?"

"Really?"

My cigarette was stirring in me its mixture of nausea and giddiness; I wanted to put it out but instead, for her sake, inhaled. The booth partition across from us leaped a foot closer and the girl and the boy had fallen to bumping heads, like a pair of doped rams.

"Sweetie," Penny said to me. "Your father's probably all right. He's not very old."

"He's fifty," I said. "He just turned fifty last month. He always said he'd never live to be fifty."

She frowned in thought, my poor dumb little girl, and tried to find some words to comfort me, who was so infinitely ingenious at evading comfort. At last she told me, "Your father's too funny to die." A ninth-grader, she only had him as a teacher in study-hall; but the whole school of course knew my father.

"Everybody dies," I told her.

"Yes, but not for a long time."

"Yes, but at some point that time has to become now." And with this we carried the mystery to the far rim, and could only return.

"Has he seen a doctor?" she asked, and, as impersonally as an act of weather, her thigh under the table had become tangent to mine.

"That's where he is now." I shifted my cigarette to my right hand and casually dropped, as if to scratch an itch, my freed left hand onto my thigh. "I should be with him," I told Penny, wondering if my profile looked as elegant as it felt, jut-lipped under a plume of smoke.

"Why? What could you do?"

"I don't know. Be of some comfort. Just be there." As naturally as water slips from higher to lower my fingers moved to her thigh from my own. Her skirt had a faunish weave.

This touch, though she did not acknowledge it, interrupted the flow of her thought. She brought out jaggedly, "How can you? You're just his child."

"I know," I said, speaking quickly lest she think my touch was more than an accident, an incident of innocent elements. Having gained my place, I expanded it, fanning my fingers, flattening my palm against the yielding solid. "But I'm the only kid he has." My using my father's word "kid" brought him too close; his wrinkling squint, his forward-leaning anxiety seemed to loom in the unquiet air. "I'm the only person in the world he can talk to."

"That can't be," she said very softly, in a voice more intimate than the words. "Your father has hundreds of friends."

"No," I said, "He has *no* friends; they don't help him. He just told me." And with something like the questing fear that made my father, in conversations with strangers, gouge deeper than courtesy found common, my hand, grown enormous, seized the snug wealth of her flesh so completely my fingers probed the crevice between her thighs and my little finger, perhaps, touched through the muffle of faunfeeling cloth the apex where they joined, the silken crotch, sacred.

"Peter, no," she said, still softly, and her cool fingertips took my wrist and replaced my hand on my own leg. I slapped my thigh and sighed, well-satisfied. I had dared more than I had dreamed. So it surprised me as needless and in a shy way whorish when she added in a murmur, "All these people." As if chastity needed an outer explanation; as if, if we were alone, the earth would sweep up and imprison my forearms.

I stubbed out my cigarette and pleaded, "I must go after him." I asked her, "Do you pray?"

"Pray?"

"Yes."

"Yes."

"Will you pray for him? My father."

"All right."

"Thank you. You're good." We both looked back amazed at what we had said. I wondered if I had been guilty of blasphemy, using God as a tool with which to score myself the deeper on this girl's heart. But no, I decided, her promise to pray did genuinely lighten my burden. Rising, I asked her, "Are you coming to the basketball game tomorrow night?"

"I could."

"Shall I save you a seat?"

"If you like."

"Or you save me one."

"All right. Peter."

"Huh?"

"Don't worry so much. Not everything is your fault."

Now the couple opposite us, classmates of Penny's, whose

names were Bonnie Leonard and Richie Lorah, came out of their nudging trance. In a burst of derisive triumph Richie yelled at me, "The Pumpkin Eater!" Bonnie feeble-mindedly laughed, and the air of the place, where I had felt so secure, became dangerous with words aimed at my face. Senior boys sporting adult pockets of shadow under their eyes called to me, "Hey, Eater, how's your old man? How's Georgie Porgie puddin' 'n' pie?" Once a student had had my father, he did not forget it, and the memory seemed to seek shape in mockery. An emotion of fermented guilt and fondness would seek to purge itself upon me, the petty receptacle of a myth. I hated it and yet it did give me importance; being Caldwell's son lifted me from the faceless mass of younger children and made me, on my father's strength alone, exist in the eyes of these Titans. I had only to listen and seem to smile as sweetly cruel memories tumbled from them:

"He used to lie down in the aisle and holler, 'Come on, walk all over me, you will anyway' . . ."

". . . about six of us filled our pockets up with horse-chestnuts . . ."

". . . seven minutes to the hour everybody stood up and stared as if his fly was open . . ."

"Christ, I'll *never* forget . . ."

". . . this girl in the back of the class said she couldn't see the decimal point . . . he went to the window and scooped some snow off the sill and made a ball . . . hard as hell at the fucking blackboard . . ."

" 'Now can you see it?' he said."

"Christ, what a character."

"You got a great father there, Peter."

These ordeals usually ended with some such unctuous benediction. It thrilled me, coming from these tall criminals, who smoked in the lavatories, drank hooch in Alton, and visited Philadelphia whorehouses staffed by Negro women. My obliging laugh stiffly dried on my face and, suddenly contemptuous, they turned their backs. I rethreaded my way to the front of the luncheonette. Someone in the booths was imitating a rooster. In the jukebox Doris Day was singing "Sentimental Journey." From the rear a chorus of cheers rhythmically rose as the pinball machine, gonging in protest, gave up one free game after another. I looked back and through the crush saw that it was Johnny Dedman doing the playing; there was no mistaking those broad, faintly fat shoulders, the turned-up collar of the canary-yellow corduroy shirt, the baroque head of wavy hair crying for a haircut and scooped behind into a wet ducktail. Johnny Dedman was one of my idols. A senior flunked back into a junior, he performed exquisitely all the meaningless deeds of coördination, jitterbugging and playing pinball and tossing salted nuts into his mouth. By an accident of alphabetization he sat next to me in one study hall and taught me a few tricks, how to make a wooden popping noise by pulling my finger from my mouth, for instance—though I could never do it as loudly as he. He was inimitable and no doubt it was foolish to try. He had a rosy babyish face and a feathery mustache of pale unshaven hair and an absolute purity of ambitionlessness: even his misbehavior was carried forward without any urgency or stridence. He did have a criminal record: once in Alton, wild on beer at the age of sixteen, he had struck a policeman. But I felt he had not sought this out but rather fell into it coolly, as he seemed on the dance floor to fall into the steps that answered his partner and made her, hair flying, cheeks glowing, ass switching, swing. The pinball machine never tilted on him; he claimed he could feel the mercury swaying in the Tilt trigger. He played the machines as if he had invented them. Indeed, his one known connection with the world of hard facts was an acknowledged mechanical ability. Outside of Industrial Arts, he consistently got E's. There was something sublime in the letter that took my breath away. In that year, the year I was fifteen, if I had not wanted so badly to be Vermeer, I would have tried to be Johnny Dedman. But of course I had the timid sense to see that you do not will to be Johnny Dedman; you fall into it at birth, ripe from the beginning.

Outdoors I turned the points of my wide jacket collar against my throat and walked up the Alton pike two blocks to Doc Appleton's office. The trolley car released from waiting at the turnout by the trolley that was going westward into Alton as my father and I left the school swayed up the pike, full of gray workers and standing shoppers coming home, going eastward toward Ely, the tiny town at the end of the line. I had lost perhaps ten minutes. I hurried and, having told Penny to pray, prayed *Let him live, let him live, do not let my father be sick*. The prayer was addressed to all who would listen; in concentric circles it widened, first, into the town, and, beyond, into the hemisphere of sky, and, beyond that, into what was beyond. The sky behind the eastward houses already was purple; above, it was still deep daylight blue; and behind me the sky beyond the houses was aflame. The sky's blue was an optical illusion that, though described to me in General Science class by my father himself, my mind could only picture as an accumulation of lightly tinted crystal spheres, as two almost invisibly pink pieces of cellophane will together make rose; add a third, you have red; a fourth, crinkling crimson; and a fifth, such a scarlet as must blaze in the heart of the most ardent furnace. If the blue dome beyond the town was an illusion, how much more, then, of an illusion might be what is beyond that. *Please,* I added to my prayer, like a reminded child.

Doc Appleton's house, which had his office and waiting-room in the front part, was a custard-colored stucco set deep on a raised lawn sustained by a sandstone wall a little less than my height. On either side of the steps up to the lawn there were two stone posts topped by large concrete balls, a device of exterior decoration common in Olinger but rare, I have since discovered, elsewhere. Abruptly, as I raced up the sloping walk toward the doctor's door, all the lamps in the homes of the town began to burn—as in a painting the slight deepening of a shade will make the adjacent color glow. The broad line between day and night in this instant had been crossed.

PLEASE RING AND WALK IN. Since I was not myself a patient, I did not ring. I imagined that somehow if I did, Doc Appleton's accounts would be thrown off, like a checkbook with an uncashed check from it. In the vestibule of his house there was a cocoa mat and an immense stucco umbrella stand ornamented, higgledypiggledy, with chips of colored glass. Above the umbrella stand hung a small dark print, frightful to look at, of some classical scene of violence. The horror of the spectators was so conscientiously drama-tized, the jumble of their flung arms and gaping mouths rendered with such an intensity of scratching, the effect of the whole so depressing and dead, that I could never bring myself to focus on what the central event was—my impression was vaguely of a flogging. In the corner of the print, before I snapped my head away as if from the initial impact of pornography, I glimpsed a thick line—a whip?—snaking about a tiny temple etched with spidery delicacy to indicate distance. That some forgotten artist in an irrevocable se-

quence of hours had labored, doubtless with authentic
craft and love, to produce this ugly, dusty, browned, and
totally ignored representation seemed to contain a message
for me which I did not wish to read. I went into Doc
Appleton's waiting-room on my right. Here old oak furniture padded in cracked black leather lined the walls and
encircled a central table laden with battered copies of *Liberty*
and *The Saturday Evening Post.* A three-legged coat rack like
a gaunt witch glowered in one corner and the shelf above
its shoulder supported a stuffed crow gone gray with dust.
The waiting-room was empty; the door of the consulting-
room was ajar and I heard my father's voice asking, "Could
it be hydra venom?"

"Just a minute, George. Who came in?"

With the broad bald face of a yellowish owl Doc Appleton
peered out of his office. "Peter," he said, and like a ray
of sunlight the old man's kindness and competence pierced
the morbid atmosphere of his house. Though Doc Appleton
delivered me, I first remembered him from a time when I
was in the third grade and, worried about my parents' fights,
bullied by older boys coming back from school, ridiculed at
recess for my skin whose spots under the stress had spread
to my face, I came down with a cold that did not go away.
We were poor and therefore slow to call a doctor. On the
third day of my fever they called him. I remember I was
propped up on two pillows in my parents' great double bed.
The wallpaper and bedposts and picture books on my covers
beside me all wore that benevolent passive flatness that
comes with enough fever; no matter how I wiped and swallowed, my mouth stayed dry and my eyes stayed moist.
Sharp footsteps disciplined the stairs and a fat man wearing
a brown vest and carrying a fat brown bag entered with my
mother. He glanced at me and turned to my mother and in
an acid country voice asked, "What have you been doing to
this child?"

There were two strange facts about Doc Appleton: he
was a twin, and like me he had psoriasis. His twin was
Hester Appleton, who taught Latin and French at the high
school. She was a shy thick-waisted spinster, smaller than
her brother and gray-haired whereas he was bald. But their
brief hook noses were identical and the resemblance was
plain. The idea, when I was a child, of these two stately
elderly people having popped together from the same mother
had an inexhaustible improbability that made them both

seem still, in part, infants. Hester lived with the doctor in this house. He had married but his wife had died or disappeared years ago under dark circumstances. He had had a son, Skippy, years older than I but like me an only child; my father had had him in school and the boy had gone on to become a surgeon somewhere in the Midwest, in Chicago, St. Louis, or Omaha. Across the mysterious fate of Skippy's mother there lay this further shadow: Doc Appleton belonged to no church, neither Reformed nor Lutheran, and believed, they said, in nothing. This third strange fact I had picked out of the air. The second, his psoriasis, my mother had revealed to me; until I was born only he and she in the town had been blighted by it. It had kept him, my mother said, from becoming a surgeon, for when the time came for him to roll up his sleeves, the pink scabs would be revealed and the patient on the table in fright might cry, "Physician, heal thyself!" It was a pity, my mother thought, for in her opinion Doc Appleton's great talent lay in his hands, was manipulative rather than diagnostic. She often described how he had painted and cured a chronic sore throat of hers with one fierce expert swab of a long cotton-tipped stick. She seemed to have thought, at one time in her life, a lot about Doc Appleton.

Now he stooped toward me in the dimness of his waiting-room, his pale round face straining to focus on my brow. He said, "Your skin looks fair."

"It's not too bad yet," I said. "It's worst in March and April."

"Very little on your face," he said. I had thought there was none. He seized my hands—I felt that fierce sureness of touch my mother had felt—and studied my fingernails in the light filtering from the brighter room. "Yes," he said. "Stippled. Your chest?"

"Pretty bad," I said, frightened I would have to show him.

He blinked massively and dropped my hands. He was wearing a vest but not a coat and his shirtsleeves above the elbow were clipped by black elastics like narrow bands of mourning. A gold watch-chain formed a shifting pendulous arc across the brown vest of his belly. He wore a stethoscope around his neck. He switched on a light, and an overhead chandelier of brown and orange glass held together by black leading plunged pools of shine onto the wash of magazines on the central table. "You read, Peter, while I finish with your Dad."

From the consulting-room my father's voice earnestly called, "Let the kid come in, Doc. I want him to hear what you have to tell me. Whatever happens to me, happens to him."

I was shy of entering, for fear of finding my father undressed. But he was fully clothed and sitting on the edge of a small hard chair with stencilled Dutch designs. In this bright room his face looked blanched by shock. His skin looked loose; his little smile had spittle in the corners. "No matter what happens to you in life, kid," he said to me, "I hope you never come up against the sigmoidoscope. *Brrough!*"

"Tcha," Doc Appleton grunted, and lowered his weight into his desk chair, a revolving and pivoting one that seemed to have been contoured for him. His short plump arms with their efficient white hands perched familiarly on the accustomed curve of the carved wooden arms, which culminated in an inner scroll. "Your trouble, George," he said, "is you have never come to terms with your own body." To be out of their way, I sat on a high white metal stool beside a table of surgical tools.

"You're right," my father said. "I hate the damn ugly thing. I don't know how the hell it got me through fifty years."

Doc Appleton removed the stethoscope from around his neck and laid it on his desk, where it writhed and then subsided like a slain rubber serpent. His desk was a wide old rolltop full of bills, pill envelopes, prescription pads, cartoons clipped from magazines, empty phials, a brass letter opener, a blue box of loose cotton, and an omega-shaped silver clamp. His sanctum had two parts: this, the one where his desk, his chairs, his table of surgical tools, his scales, his eye-chart, and his potted plants were situated, and, beyond his desk and a partition of frosted glass, the other, the innermost sanctum, where his medicines were stored on shelves like bottles of wine and jugs of jewels. To here he would retire at the end of a consultation, emerging in time with a little labeled bottle or two, and from here at all times issued a complex medicinal fragrance compounded of candy, menthol, ammonia, and dried herbs. This cloud of healing odor could be sniffed even in the vestibule that contained the mat, the print, and the stucco umbrella stand. The doctor pivoted in his swivel chair and faced us; his bald head was not like Minor Kretz's, which declared in its glittering knobs the plates and furrows of his skull. Doc Appleton's was a smooth luminous rise of skin lightly flecked with a few pinker spots that only I, probably, would have noticed and recognized as psoriasis.

He pointed his thumb at my father. "You see, George," he said, "you believe in the soul. You believe your body is like a horse you get up on and ride for a while and then get off. You ride your body too hard. You show it no love. This is not natural. This builds up nervous tension."

My stool was uncomfortable and Doc Appleton's philosophizing always afflicted me with embarrassment. I deduced that the verdict had already been handed down and from the fact that the doctor felt leisure to be boring I deduced that the verdict had been favorable. Still I remained in some suspense and studied the table of wiggly probes and angled scissors as if they were an alphabet in which I could read the word. AI AI, they said. Among these silver exclamations —needles and arrows and polished clamps—there was that strange hammer for tapping your knee to make your leg jerk. It was a heavy triangle of red rubber fixed in a silver handle made concave to improve the doctor's grip. My very first trips to this office that I could remember centered about that hammer, and the table of instruments took its center from this arrowhead of sullen orange as if from something very ancient. It was the shape of an arrowhead but also of a fulcrum and as I watched it it seemed to sink, sink with its infinitesimal cracks and roundnesses of use and age, sink down through time and to be at the bottom sufficiently simple and ponderous to make there a pivot for everything.

". . . know thyself, George," Doc Appleton was saying. His pink firm palm, round as a child's, lifted in admonition. "Now how long have you been teaching?"

"Fourteen years," my father said. "I was laid off late in '31 and was out of work the whole year the kid was born. In the summer of '33, Al Hummel, who as you know is Pop Kramer's nephew, came up to the house and suggested—"

"Does your father enjoy teaching? Peter."

It took me a second to realize I had been addressed. "I don't know," I said, "at times I suppose." Then I thought and added, "No, I guess he doesn't."

"It'd be O. K.," my father said, "if I thought I was any good at it. But I don't have the gift of discipline. My father, the poor devil, didn't have it either."

"You're not a teacher," Doc Appleton told him. "You're a

learner. This creates tension. Tension creates excess gastric juice. Now George, the symptoms you describe might be merely mucinous colitis. Constant irritation of the digestive track can produce pain and the sensation of anal fullness you describe. Until the X-ray, we'll assume that's what it is."

"I wouldn't mind plugging ahead at something I wasn't any good at," my father said, "if I knew what the hell the point of it all was. I ask, and nobody'll tell me."

"What does Zimmerman say?"

"He doesn't say a thing. He thrives on confusion. Zimmerman has the gift of discipline and us poor devils under him who don't have it, he just laughs at us. I can hear him laughing every time the clock ticks."

"Zimmerman and myself," Doc Appleton said, and sighed, "have never seen eye to eye. I went to school with him, you know."

"I didn't know that."

My father was lying. Even I had known that, Doc Appleton said it so often. Zimmerman was a chafe to him, a life-long sore point. I was furious with my father for being so obsequious, for laying us both open this way to a long and often-chewed story.

"Why, yes," Doc Appleton said, blinking in surprise that my father should be ignorant of such a famous fact. "We went all through the Olinger schools together." He leaned back in the chair that fitted him so exquisitely. "Now when we were born here it wasn't called Olinger, it was called Tilden, in honor of the man who got cheated out of the election. Old Pappy Olinger was still farming all that land to the north of the pike and east of where the cardboard box factory is now. I remember seeing him take his team into Alton, a little old fella not five feet tall with a black hat and a mustache you could have wiped your table silver on. He had three sons: Cot, who went crazy one night and killed two steer with a hand hoe, Brian, who had a child by the Negro woman they had to work in the kitchen, and Guy, the youngest, who sold the land to the real estate developers and died of trying to eat the money up. Cot, Brian, and Guy: they're all beneath the ground now. Now what did I start to say?"

"About you and Mr. Zimmerman," I said.

My impudent impatience was not lost on him; he looked over my father's shoulder at me and his lower lip slid thoughtfully to one side and then to the other. "Ah, yes," he pronounced, and spoke to my father. "Well, Louis and I went through the grades together when they were scattered all over the borough. First and second grade was over by Pebble Creek where they put the parking lot for the new diner; third and fourth grades were in Mrs. Eberhardt's barn that she rented the town for a dollar a year; fifth and sixth were in a stone building on what they used to call the Black Acres, because the loam was so deep, over beyond where the race track used to be. Whenever they'd hold a weekday race, on Tuesdays usually, they used to let us out of class because they needed boys to hold and comb the horses. Then for those that kept on past sixth grade, by the time I was the age they had built the high school at the Elm Street corner. Now didn't that look grand to us then! That's the building, Peter, where you went to elementary school."

"I didn't know that," I said, trying to atone for my rudeness before.

Doc Appleton seemed pleased. He relaxed into his creaking chair so deeply his creased high-top shoes dangled, just touching their toes to the threadbare carpet. "Now Louis M. Zimmerman," he went on, "was a month older than myself, and a great hand with the girls and the old women. Mrs. Metzler, that was our teacher in the first and second grade, a woman not an inch under six feet tall and with legs like the siding slats of a tobacco shed, took a shine to Louis, and for that matter so did Miss Leet and Mrs. Mabry that followed her; all his way through school Louis had the best of attention, while of course nobody thought a second thought about an ugly duckling like Harry Appleton. Louis always had that edge. You see: he was quick."

"You said a mouthful," my father said. "He's always a jump ahead of me, I'll tell you that."

"He never had, you see," Doc Appleton continued, making curious ambiguous motions with his plump scrubbed hands, pressing the palms together, lightly chopping the knuckles of one hand with the edge of the other, "the adversity. He always knew success and never developed the character. So he spreads, you see," and his white fingers crabbed through the air, "like a cancer. He's not a man to trust, though he gives the Bible lesson every Sunday up at the Reformed. *Tcha.* If he was a tumor, George, I'd take a knife"—he shifted his hand and held up his thumb and it did seem very stiff and sharp—"and cut him out." And his thumb, sickle-shaped backwards with pressure, scooped a curt divot out of the air.

"I appreciate your being frank with me, Doc," my father said, "but me and those other poor devils up at the high school are stuck with him forever as far as I can see. Three out of four people in this town swear by him—they worship that man."

"People are foolish," Doc Appleton said, and lurched forward in his chair so that his feet softly plopped on the carpet. "That's one thing you learn in the practice of medicine. People are by and large very foolish." He tapped my father's knee once, twice, three times before continuing. His voice assumed a confidential wheeze. "Now when I went to medical school down at Penn," he said, "they thought, you know, a country boy, dumb. After that first year they weren't saying so dumb any more. It might be I was a little slower than some but I had the character. I took my time and learned the books. When the class graduated, who do you think was at the head? Heh, Peter—you're a bright boy. Who do you think?"

"You," I said. I didn't want to say it but the word was forced from me. That's how those Olinger bigwigs were.

Doc Appleton looked at me without nodding or smiling or in any way showing that he had heard. Then he looked into my father's face, nodded, and said, "I wasn't at the head, but I was up there pretty well. I did all right for a country boy supposed to be dumb. George, have you been listening to what I've been saying?" And without warning, in that strange way monologuists have of ending a conversation as if *their* time has been wasted, he got up and went into his inner sanctum and made tinkling noises out of sight. He returned with a small bottle of cherry-colored fluid that from the way it danced and gleamed seemed more mercurial than liquid. He pressed the bottle into my father's wart-freckled hand and said, "A tablespoon every three hours. Until we have the X-rays we won't know any more than we know now. Get rest and don't think. Without death, now, there couldn't be life. Health," he said with a little smiling roll of his lower lip, "is an animal condition. Now most of our ill-health comes from two places—the brain and the back. We made two mistakes; one was to stand up and the other was to start thinking. It strains the spine and the nerves. It makes tension and the brain makes the body." He angrily strode toward me and roughly pressed my hair back from my forehead and stared intensely at my brow. "You're not as bad on your scalp as your mother," he said, and released me. I flattened my hair forward again, humiliated and dazed.

"Do you hear from Skippy?" my father asked.

All fierceness and shimmer left the doctor; he became a heavy old man in a vest and fastened shirtsleeves. "He's on a staff in St. Louis," he said.

"You're too modest to say it," my father told him, "but I bet you're prouder than hell of him. I know I am; next to my own son he was the best student I ever had and not too much of my thickheadedness seemed to rub off on him, thank God."

"He has his mother's graces," Doc Appleton said after a pause, and a pall had fallen. The waiting-room seemed long deserted and the black leather furniture depressed and dented by the shadows of mourners. Our voices and footsteps felt lost in dust and I felt viewed from thousands of years in the future. My father offered to pay. The doctor waved his dollars aside, saying, "We'll wait till the end of the story."

"You're a straight-shooter and I'm grateful," my father said.

Outside, in the gnashing, black, brilliantly alive cold, my father said to me, "See, Peter? He didn't tell me what I want to know. They never do."

"What happened before I came?"

"He put me through the mill and made an X-ray appointment at Homeopathic in Alton for six o'clock tonight."

"What does that mean?"

"You never know with Doc Appleton what he means. That's how he keeps his reputation."

"He doesn't seem to like Zimmerman but I couldn't make out exactly why."

"The story there, Peter, is that Zimmerman—I guess you're old enough to say this to—Zimmerman's supposed to have made love to Doc Appleton's wife. It happened if it happened at all before you were born. There was even supposed to be some doubt as to who Skippy's father was."

"But where's Mrs. Appleton now?"

"Nobody knows where she went. She's either alive or dead."

"What was her name?"

"Corinna."

Alive or dead, made love, before you were born—these phrases, each rich with mystery, rendered the night brimming around us terribly deep, and from beyond the far rim like an encircling serpent my father's death seemed to tighten its coil. The darkness that above the heads of the houses swept past the stars and enclosed them like flecks of mica in an ocean seemed great enough to contain even this most mighty of impossible events. I chased him, his profile pale and grim in streetlight, and like a ghost he kept always a step ahead of me. He put on his cap and my head was cold.

"What are we going to do?" I called after him.

"We'll drive into Alton," he said. "I'll get my X-ray at the Homeopathic and then I'll go across the street to the Y.M.C.A. I want you to go to the movies. Get in where it's warm and come up to the Y afterwards. That should be about seven-thirty or quarter to eight. The meet should be over by eight. It's about quarter after five now. Do you have enough money for a hamburg?"

"Sure, I guess. Hey. Daddy. How are your aches and pains?"

"Better, Peter. Don't worry about me. One nice thing about having a simple mind, you can only think about one pain at a time."

"There ought to be some way," I said, "to make you healthy."

"Kill me," my father said. The sentence sounded strange, outdoors, in the dark and cold, coming from above, as his face and body hurried forward. "That's the cure-all," he said. "Kill me."

We walked west to where the car had been left on the school parking lot and got into it and drove into Alton. Lights, there were lights on both sides solidly supporting us for the full three miles, except for the void on the right that was the poorhouse corn fields and for the interval in which we crossed the Running Horse River over the bridge where the hitchhiker had seemed to lift into the air on his long-heeled shoes. We cut through the gaudy heart of the city, across Riverside Drive, up Pechawnee Avenue, into Weiser Street and Conrad Weiser Square, up Sixth, across the railroad station parking lot, and down an alley only my father seemed to know about. The alley led us to where the railroad embankment widened into a black shoulder sparkling with cinders, near the Essick's coughdrop plant, which flooded the whole sinister area with its sickly-sweet fumes. The Essick's employees used this leftover sloping bit of railroad property as a parking lot, and so my father used it now. We got out. The slams of our doors echoed. The shape of our car sat on its shadow like a frog looking into a mirror. It was alone on the lot. A blue light overhead kept watch like a cold angel.

My father and I parted by the railroad station. He walked left, toward the hospital. I walked on, to Weiser Street, where five movie theatres advertised their shows. The downtown crowds were streaming home. The matinees were dismissed; the stores, their windows proclaiming January White Sales and drifted deep with cotton sheets, were stringing padlocked chains across their doors; the restaurants were in the lull of setting up the tables for dinner; the old men with the soft-pretzel carts draped them with tarpaulins and pushed them away. The city excited me most at this hour, when my father abandoned me and I, a single cross-current in the tidal exodus, strolled homeless, free to gaze into jewellers' windows, to eavesdrop at the mouths of cigar stores, to inhale the breath of pastry shops where fat ladies in rimless spectacles and white smocks sighed behind bright trays of bearclaws, sticky buns, glazed doughnuts, pecan rolls, and shoo-fly pies. At this hour when the workers and shoppers of the city were hurrying by foot, bus, car, and trolley home to their duties, I was for a time released from mine, not merely permitted but positively instructed by my father to go to a movie and spend two hours out of this world. The world, my world with all its oppressive detail of pain and inconsequence was behind me; I wandered among caskets of jewels which would someday be mine. Frequently at this moment, my luxurious space of freedom all before me, I thought guiltily of my mother, helpless at her distance to control me or protect me, my mother with her farm, her father, her dissatisfaction, her exhausting alternations of recklessness and prudence, wit and obtuseness, transparence and opacity, my mother with her wide tense face and strange innocent scent of earth and cereal, my mother whose blood I was polluting in the gritty inebriation of Alton's downtown. Then I would seem smothered in a rotten brilliance and become very frightened. But my guilt could not be eased, I could not go to her, for of her own will she had placed ten miles between us; and this rejection on her part made me vengeful, proud, and indifferent: an inner Arab.

The five movie palaces of Weiser Street in Alton were Loew's, the Embassy, the Warner, the Astor, and the Ritz. I went to the Warner and saw "Young Man with a Horn," starring Kirk Douglas, Doris Day, and Lauren Bacall. As my father had promised, it was warm inside. My best piece of luck for the day, I came in on the cartoon. The day was the thirteenth of the month so I did not expect it to be lucky. The cartoon was, of course, a Bugs Bunny. Loew's had Tom and Jerry, the Embassy Popeye, the Astor either Disney, the best, or Paul Terry, the worst. I bought a box of popcorn and a box of Jordan Almonds, though both were bad for my skin. The sidelights were soft yellow and time melted. At the end, when the hero, the trumpeter who was based upon Bix Beiderbecke, had finally fought free of the rich woman who with her insinuating crooked smile (Lauren Bacall) had been corrupting his art, and the good artistic woman (Doris Day), her lover restored to her, sang, and behind her own transparent voice Harry James's trumpet pretending to be Kirk Douglas's lifted like a silver fountain higher and higher into "With a Song in My Heart"—only here, on the last note, an absolutely level ecstasy attained, did I remember my father. An urgent sense of *being late* caught me up.

The sidelights turned bright. I fled from my seat. In the floor-to-ceiling mirrors that lined the sloping glaring lobby I saw myself full-length, flushed, pink-eyed, the shoulders of my flaming shirt drenched with the white flakes I had scratched from my scalp in the dark. It was a habit of mine to scratch when unseen. I brushed my shoulders wildly and on the cold street was startled by the real faces, which seemed meagre and phantasmal after the great glowing planetary visions I had been watching slowly collide, merge, part, and recombine. I ran toward the Y.M.C.A. It was two blocks up from Weiser Street, at Perkiomen and Beech. I ran along the railroad tracks. The narrow pavement was lined with small bars and shut barber parlors. The sky was an unsteady yellow above the tenements and even at the zenith paleness drained stars from the night. The smell of coughdrops coming from a distance mocked my panic. The perfect city, the city of the future, seemed remote and irrelevant and conceived in cruelty.

The Y.M.C.A. smelled of sneakers and the floor was scuffed gray. At the center desk a Negro boy sat reading a comic book underneath a bulletin board shingled with obsolete posters and bygone tournament results. Far away down a strangely green hall, green as if lit by bulbs shining through grape arbor leaves, a game of billiards studiously muttered. From the other direction drifted the patient *ga-glokka, ga-glokka* of a ping-pong game. The boy behind the desk looked up from his comic book and frightened me; there were no Negroes in Olinger and I was superstitiously timid of them. They seemed to me wizards, possessing the black secrets of love and song. But his face was all innocence, all innocence and the shade of malted milk. "Hi," I said and, holding my breath, swiftly walked to the passageway that led to the downward flight of concrete that in turn led, through the locker room, to the pool. As I descended, the odors of water and chlorine and a third, as of skin, grew upon me.

In the great tiled chamber where the pool lived, a barking resonance broke everything into fragments. On the little wooden bleachers at the poolside my father sat with a wet and naked boy, Deifendorf. Deifendorf wore only the skimpy black official trunks; the droop of his genitals was limply defined between his spread thighs. Hair flowed down his chest and forearms and legs and a stream of water was running across the wood where his bare feet rested. The curves and flats of his hunched white body were harmonious but for his horny red hands. He and my father greeted me with grins that looked much the same: snaggled, ignorant, conspiratorial. To annoy Deifendorf I asked him, "Ja win the breast stroke and the two-twenty?"

"I won more than you did," he answered.

"He won the breast stroke," my father said. "I'm proud of you, Deify. You kept your promise to the best of your ability. That makes you a man."

"Shit if I'd seen that guy in the far lane I'd've taken the two-twenty too. Bastard he sneaked in on me, I thought I'd won it, I was just gliding in."

"That kid swam a good race," my father said. "He won it honestly. He paced himself. Foley's a good coach. If I was any kind of a coach, Deify, you'd be king of the county; you're a natural. If I was any kind of a coach and you'd give up cigarettes."

"Fuck I can hold my breath eighty seconds as it is," Deifendorf said.

There was in their talk a mutual flattery that annoyed me. I sat on the other side of my father and concentrated on the pool: it was the hero here. It filled its great underground cage with staccato glitter and the eye-flagellating stink of chlorine. The reflection of the bleachers across the pool, where the opposing team and the judges sat, made on the rattled water a figment that for split seconds seemed a bearded face. Shattered again and again, the water yet sought with the quickness of crystalline reaction to recompose itself. Shouts and splashes broken by echoes and countersplashes made in collision new words, words of no language I knew, garbled barks that seemed to be answers to a question I had unknowingly asked. CECROPS! INACHUS! DA! No, it was not me who had asked the question, but my father beside me.

"What does it feel like to win?" he had asked aloud, speaking straight ahead and thus equally to Deifendorf and me. "Jesus, I'll never know."

Flecks and blobs skidded back and forth across the volatile aqua skin. The lines of lane demarcation on the pool bottom looped and wavered, refracted, toward the surface; the bearded face seemed about to constitute itself when, each time, another boy dived. Everything was over but the diving. One of our divers, Danny Horst, a runty senior with a huge mane of black hair that for diving he did up in a hairband like a Greek girl, came forward on the board, muscles swirling, and executed a running forward somersault, knees tucked, toes taut, so perfectly, uncoiling into the water through a soft splash as symmetrical as the handles of a vase, that one of the judges flashed the 10 card.

"In fifteen years," my father said, "I've never seen the ten used before. It's like saying God has come down to earth. There is no such thing as perfection."

"Thatta baby Danny *boy*," Deifendorf yelled, and a patter of applause from both teams greeted the diver as he surfaced, tossed his loosened hair with a proud flick, and swam the few strokes to the pool edge. But on his next dive Danny, aware we were all expecting another miracle, tensed up, lost the rhythm of the approach, came out of the one-and-a-half twist a moment too soon, and slapped the water with his back. One judge gave him a 3. The other two gave him 4s. "Well," my father said, "the poor kid gave it all he had." And when Danny surfaced this time, my father, and only my father, clapped.

The final score of the meet was West Alton 37½, Olinger 18. My father stood at the pool edge and said to his team, "I'm proud of you. You're damn good sports to come out for this at all—you get no glory and you get no pay. For a town without even an outdoor pool, I don't see how you do as well as you do. If the high school had its own pool like West Alton does—and I don't want to take any credit away from them—you'd all be Johnny Weismuellers. In my book, you are

already. Danny, that was one beautiful dive. I don't expect
to see a dive like that again as long as I live."

My father looked strange making this speech, standing so
erect in his suit and necktie among the naked torsos; the vibrating turquoise water and beaded cream tiling framed his
dark and earnest head as I saw it from the bleachers. Across
the listening skin of the shoulders and chests of the team a
nervous flicker now and then passed, swiftly as a gust across
water, or a tic in the flank of a horse. Though they had lost,
the team was boisterous and proud in their flesh, and we left
them in the shower room carousing and lathering like a small
herd joyfully caught in a squall.

"Practice this Wednesday as usual," my father had called
to them in parting. "Don't drink any milkshakes or eat more
than four hamburgers before you show up." Everyone
laughed, and even I smiled, though my father was a heaviness
upon me. In all the events of the night that followed there
was this weight and inertia about him that blocked and
snagged at every turn my simple plan, which was to get him
home, where he would pass out of my care.

As we were walking up the hall from the concrete steps
the West Alton coach Foley caught up with us, and the two
men talked for what seemed an hour. The damp air around
the pool had put their suits out of press, and they seemed
in the dimness of the green hall two shepherds soaked in dew.
"You've done a superhuman job with those boys," my father
told Foley. "If I was one-tenth the coach you are we would
have given you a run for your money. I have a few naturals
this year."

"George now, no crap," Foley replied, a thick sandy man
all courtesy and ginger. "You know as well as me there's no
coaching to it; let the tadpoles swim is all you can do. There's
a fish in every one of us, but you have to soak to get him
out."

"That's good," my father said. "I never heard that before.
Bud, how did you like my big man in the breast stroke?"

"He should have had the two-twenty, too; I hope you
burned his ass for letting up like that."

"He's dumb, Bud. D-U-M-B. The poor devil has no more
brains than I do and I hate to bawl him out."

My throat rasped in sheer pressure of impatience.

"You've met my son, haven't you, Bud? Peter, come over
here and shake this man's hand. This is the kind of man you
should have had for a daddy."

"Why hell I know Peter," Mr. Foley said, and there *was* something deeply agreeable about his handshake, gritty and warm and easy. "The whole county knows Caldwell's boy."

In their twilit world of Y.M.C.A.s and recreational programs and athletic banquets, this sort of wildly congratulatory blarney passed for conversation; I minded it less in Mr. Foley than in my father, whose affectation of it always seemed to me embarrassed.

My father was for all his talk at heart a man of silence. He walked through the events of that night in a mood that has become in my memory silence. Once outside, his mouth made a firm line and his heels gathered in the pavement with a kind of aloof greed. I wonder if any man ever enjoyed walking in the small ugly cities of the East as much as my father. Trenton, Bridgeport, Binghamton, Johnstown, Elmira, Altoona: these were the cities where his work as cable splicer for the telephone company had taken him in the years before and the years just after he married my mother, the years before my birth and Hoover's Depression stalled him in the sticks. He feared Firetown and felt uneasy in Olinger but adored Alton; its asphalt and streetlights and tangent façades spoke to him of the great Middle Atlantic civilization, bounded by New Haven in the north and Hagerstown in the south and Wheeling in the west, which was his home in eternal space. To walk beside my father down Sixth Street was to hear the asphalt sing.

I asked him how his X-ray had gone and in answer he asked me if I were hungry. It occurred to me that indeed I was; the popcorn and the Jordan Almonds had settled into a sour aftertaste. We stopped at the trolley-shaped diner beside the Acme's parking lot. My father conducted himself in the city with a simplicity that was soothing. My mother made too much of a decision of everything, as if she were trying to express herself in a foreign language. Just so, in the country my father was confused in action and circuitous in thought. But here, in Alton at quarter after eight o'clock, he handled himself with the deftness, the expertness that is, after all, most of what we hope for from fathers: the door pushed open, the glare and stares calmly blinked down, the two stools located side by side, the menu knowingly plucked from its place between the napkin dispenser and the catsup bottle, the counterman addressed without stridence or equivocating, the sandwiches—his a Western egg, mine a toasted ham—consumed in manful silence. My father quietly sucked the three central fingers of his right hand and pinched his lower lip with a paper napkin. "First time I've felt like eating in weeks," he said to me. In conclusion we ordered apple pie for me and coffee for him; the check was a stiff green tab cryptically nipped by a triangular punch. He paid it with one of two dollar bills left in the worn hip wallet that had curved through the years to fit his haunch. As we rose my father noncommitally slipped, with a practiced flick of his wart-freckled hand, two dimes beneath his empty cup. And as an afterthought he bought for 65¢ one of the diner's ready-made Italian sandwiches. It was to be a present for my mother. There was a vulgar side to my mother which apparently enjoyed smelly slippery Italian sandwiches and to which my father had, I saw jealously, more access than I. He paid for the sandwich with his last dollar and said, "That cleans me out, kid. You and I are penniless orphans." Swinging the little brown paper bag, he walked us to the car.

The Buick was still alone, brooding on its shadow. Its nose was tipped up the slope, toward the unseen tracks. Menthol like a vaporized moon suffused the icy air. The factory wall was a sheer cliff mixed of brick and black glass. The panes of glass were now and then mysteriously relieved by a pane of cardboard or tin. The brick did not yield its true color to the streetlamp that lit the area but instead showed as a diminution of black, a withdrawn and deadly gray. This same light made the strange gravel here glitter. Compounded of coal chips and cinders, it made a loud and restless earth that never settled, crackling and shifting under-foot as if its destiny were to be perpetually raked. Silence encircled us. Not a window looking at us was lit, though deep in the factory a blue glint kept watch. My father and I could have been murdered in this place and until dawn no one would have known. Our bodies would lie in the puddles near the factory wall and our hands and hair would freeze solid into the ice.

The car was slow to start in the cold. *Unh-uh, unh-uh,* the engine grunted, at first briskly and then more and more slowly, self-discouraged. "Jesus, don't quit on me now," my father breathed in a dancing stream of vapor. "Start one more time and tomorrow I'll get your battery charged."

Unnh-uh, unnnnnh-ah.

My father switched off the ignition and we sat in the dark. He made a loose fist and blew into it. "See," I said, "if you'd worn your gloves you'd have 'em now."

"You must be frozen to death," was his answer. "One more time," he said, and switched the ignition back on and depressed the starter button with his thumb. In the pause, the battery had gathered a little juice. It commenced hopefully. *Ih-huh, Ih-huh, uh-uh, unnh-uh, unnhn-ah, uhhhh.* We scraped the bottom of the battery.

My father pulled the emergency brake a notch tighter, and said to me, "We're in the soup. We'll have to try a desperation measure. You get in behind the wheel, Peter, and I'll get out and push. We have a little slope here but we're pointed the wrong way. Put the car into reverse. When I shout, let the clutch out. Don't ease it out, pop it out."

"Maybe we should get a garageman now, before they close," I said. I was frightened of failing him.

"Let's give this a whirl," he said. "You can do it."

He got out of the car and I slid over, accidentally sitting on my books and the paper bag containing the Italian sandwich for my mother. My father went to the front of the car and as he stooped to put his weight into it his grinning face burned yellow like a gnome's. The light of the headlights cut across his face so sharply his forehead seemed all knobs and it was plain how often his nose had been broken when he played football at college thirty years ago. My stomach clenched coldly as I checked the position of the gear shift and ignition switch and choke. At a nod from my father I released the emergency brake. Only the ovoid of his imbecile blue cap showed above the hood as he pitched his weight into the car. It did move backwards. The crunching of the tires on the gravel lifted in pitch; grinding backwards we struck a little declivity that added a precious bit of momentum; the Buick's inertia for a moment tugged to be free of itself. In a piercing sob my father shouted, "Now!" I popped out the clutch as I had been told to do. The car snapped to a stop jaggedly; but its motion was transferred through crusty knobs and clogged pivots to the engine, which, like a slapped baby, coughed. The motor gasped and shook the frame as its cylinders erratically exploded; I pushed in the choke halfway, trying not to smother it, and jiggled my foot on the accelerator: this was the mistake. Twitched out of tune, the motor missed one, two beats, and died.

We were on the flat. Far away beyond the factory wall the door of a bar opened and a slat of light collapsed into the street.

My father flashed to my door and I lurched over, sickly

ashamed. My body burned all over; I needed to urinate. "Son of a bitch," I said, to distract with my manliness my father from my failure.

"You did O.K., kid," he said, panting with excitement as he resumed his place behind the wheel. "The engine's stiff; that may have loosened it up." Delicately as a safecracker, his black silhouette picked at the dashboard as his foot probed the gas pedal. It had to be on the first try and it was. He found the spark again and nursed it into roaring life. I closed my eyes in thanks and relaxed into the coming motion of the car.

It did not come. Instead, a faint disjointed purr arose from the rear of the chassis, where I imagined the corpses had been carried when the undertaker owned the car. My father's shadow hurriedly tried all the gears; to each the same faint and unmoving purr answered. He tried each gear twice in disbelief. The motor roared but the car did not move. The factory wall echoed back the frantic sustained crescendo of the cylinders and I was afraid men would be called toward us out of the distant bar.

My father put his arms up on the wheel and lowered his head into them. It was a thing I had only ever seen my mother do. At the height of some quarrel or sadness she would crook her arms on the table and lower her head into them; it frightened me more than any rage, for in the rage you could watch her face.

"Daddy?"

My father did not answer. The streetlight touched with a row of steady flecks the curve of his knit cap: the way Vermeer outlined a loaf of bread.

"What do you think's wrong?"

Now it occurred to me he had had an "attack" and the inexplicable behavior of the car was in fact an illusionistic reflection of some breakage in himself. I was about to touch him—I never touched my father—when he looked up with a smile of sorts on his bumpy and battered urchin's face. "This is the kind of thing," he said, "that's been happening to me all my life. I'm sorry you got involved in it. I don't know why the damn car doesn't move. Same reason the swimming team doesn't win, I suppose."

He raced the motor again and peered down past his knees at the clutch pedal as he worked it in and out with his foot.

"Do you hear that little rattling behind?" I asked.

He looked up and laughed. "You poor devil," he said.

"You deserved a winner and you got a loser. Let's go. If I never see this heap of junk again it'll be too soon."

He got out and slammed the door on his side so hard I thought the window might shatter. The black body swayed fastidiously on its obstinate wheels and then sat casting its paper-thin shadow as if it had won some inscrutable point. We walked away. "That's why I never wanted to move to that farm," my father said. "As soon as you do you become dependent upon automobiles. All I've ever wanted is to be able to walk to where I had to go. My ideal is to walk to my own funeral. Once you've sold out your legs, you've sold out your life."

We walked across the railroad station parking lot and then turned left to the Esso station on Boone Street. The pumps were dark but a dim golden light burned in the little office; my father looked in and tapped on the glass. The interior was crowded with raw new tires and spare parts in numbered boxes more or less arranged in a green metal frame. A great upright Coca-Cola dispenser vibrated audibly and trembled and shut off, as if a body trapped inside had made its last effort. The electric Quaker State Oil clock on the wall said 9:06; its second hand swept the full circle as we waited. My father tapped again, and there was still no answer. The only motion within was the second hand sweeping.

I asked, "Isn't the one on Seventh Street an all-night place?"

He asked me, "How are you bearing up, kid? This is a helluva thing, isn't it? I ought to call your mother."

We walked up Boone and across the tracks and past the little porches of the brick row houses and thence up Seventh, across Weiser, which wasn't so gaudy this high up, to where indeed the great garage was open. Its white mouth seemed to be drinking the night. Within, two men in gray coveralls, wearing gloves from which the fingers had been cut, were washing an automobile with pails of sudsy hot water. They worked quickly, for the water tended to freeze in a film of ice on the metal. The garage was open to the street at one end and at the other end faded into indeterminate caverns of parked cars. Along one wall a little booth, like a broader telephone booth or like one of those enclosed sheds in which people used to wait for trolley cars—there still was one in the town of Ely—, seemed to function as the heart of the place. Outside its door, on a little cement curb stenciled with the words STEP UP, a man in a tuxedo and white muffler waited, periodically consulting the black-dialled platinum watch strapped to the inside of his wrist. His motions were so jerky and chronic that when I first spotted him in the corner of my eye I thought he was a lifesize mechanical ad. The car being washed, a pearl-gray Lincoln, was presumably his. My father stood in front of him for an instant and I saw from the quality of the man's pearl-gray gaze that my father was literally invisible to him.

My father went to the door of the booth and opened it. I had to follow him in. Here a thickset man was busily scrambling a table of papers. He was standing; there was a desk chair to sit in but it was heaped to the arms with papers and pamphlets and catalogues. The man held a clipboard and a smoking cigarette in the same hand and was sucking his teeth as he searched through his papers.

My father said, "I beg your pardon, my friend."

The manager said, "Just a minute please, give me a break, will ya?" and, angrily wadding a piece of blue paper in his fist, plunged past us out the door. It was much more than a minute before he returned.

To consume the time and conceal my embarrassment I fed a penny into the chewing-gum-ball machine installed by the Alton Kiwanis. I received, the rarest, the prize, a black ball. I loved licorice. So did my father. The time we went to New York my Aunt Alma had told me that in their childhood the other kids in their block of Passaic had called my father Sticks because he was always eating licorice sticks. "Do you want this?" I asked him.

"Oh God," he said, as if in my palm I was holding out a pill of poison to him. "No thanks, Peter. That would just about finish my teeth on the spot." And he began, in a way I can hardly describe, to rear and toss in the confined space of our cabin, turning to confront now a rack of road maps, now a detailed chart of spare part code numbers, now a calendar displaying a girl posed only in a snowbunny cap with pink pointed ears, mittens and booties of white fur, and a fluffy round tailpiece. Her bottom was pertly pointed outward at us. My father groaned and pressed his forehead against the restraining glass; the man in the tuxedo turned around startled at the bump. The men in the fingerless gloves had climbed inside the Lincoln and were wiping the windows with busy swipes like the blur of bees. My father's freckled fists rummaged blindly among the papers on the table as he strained to see where the manager had disappeared to. Afraid he

would disturb a mysterious order, I said sharply, *"Daddy.*
Control yourself."

"I've got the heebie-jeebies, kid," he answered loudly.
"Biff. Bang. I'm ready to smash something. Time and tide for
no man wait. This reminds me of death."

"*Relax*," I said. "Take off your cap. He probably thinks
you're a panhandler."

He gave no sign of hearing me; his communion was all
with himself. His eyes had turned yellowish; my mother sometimes screamed when that amber gleam began to appear in
his eyes. He looked at me with lifesaver irises lit by a ghost's
radiant gaze. His parched lips moved. "I can take anything
by myself," he told me. "But I've got *you* on my hands."

"I'm all *right*," I snapped back, though in truth the cement
floor of this place felt remarkably cold through the soles of
my pinching loafers.

I could hardly believe it, but in time the manager did return, and he listened politely to my father's tale. He was a
short thickset man with three or four parallel creases furrow-
ing each cheek. He had the air—something about the set of
his neck in his shoulders expressed it—of having once been
an athlete. Now he was wearied and harassed by administra-
tion. His hair in thinning backwards had stranded a forelock, half-gray, which as he talked he kept brushing back
brutally, as if to scrub a new sense of focus into his head. His
name, Mr. Rhodes, was stitched in a fat script of orange
thread on the pocket of his olive coverall. He told us, speaking in hurried puffs between pronounced intakes of breath, "It
doesn't sound good. From what you say, the motor running
and the car not moving, it's in the transmission somewheres,
or the driveshaft. If it was just the engine"—he said "enchine"
and the way he said it it seemed to mean something different,
something pulsing and living and lovable—"I'd send the
Jeep down, but this way, I don't know what we can do. My
tow truck's off after a wreck down on Route 9. Do you have
a garage of your own?" He accented "garage" on the first
syllable: *gar*ritch.

"We use Al Hummel over in Olinger," my father said.

"If you want me to get after your car in the morning," Mr.
Rhodes said, "I will. But I can't do anything before then;
these two"—he indicated the workmen in front of us; they
were flicking chamois pads across the Lincoln's serene gray
skin while the man in the tuxedo rhythmically slapped his
palm with an alligator billfold—"go off at ten and that

leaves just me and the two off in the wrecker down Route 9. So it'd be just as soon for you probably to call your own garage out in Olinger and have them look after it first thing in the morning."

My father said, "In your considered opinion, then, as far as tonight goes, my goose is cooked?"

Mr. Rhodes confessed, "It don't sound good, from how you describe it."

"There's a little rattle in the back," I said, "like two cog wheels spinning and just brushing against each other."

Mr. Rhodes blinked at me and brushed back his forelock. "It might be something in the axle. I'd have to get it up on the rack and take apart the whole rear assembly. Do you live far?"

"Way the hell down in Firetown," my father said.

Mr. Rhodes sighed. "Well, yes. I'm sorry I couldn't be more help." A long scarlet Buick, its paint a swirling cosmos of reflections, nosed in from the street and honked its horn: the blast totally possessed the low concrete cavern and Mr. Rhodes' attention was deflected from us.

My father said hurriedly, "Don't apologize, mister. You've told me what you think is the truth and that's the greatest favor one man can do for another." But outside the garage, again walking in the night, he said to me, "That poor devil didn't know what he was talking about, Peter. I've been a bluffer all my life so I can spot another. He was what they call talking through your hat. I wonder how he got to be manager of an important place like that; I bet he doesn't know himself. He acted just the way I feel half the time."

"Where are we going now?"

"Back to the car."

"But it doesn't go! You know that."

"I know it and yet I don't. I have the feeling it'll go now. It just needed a rest."

"It isn't just the motor being cold, it's something in the body!"

"That's what that man was trying to tell me but I can't get it through my thick head."

"But it's nearly ten o'clock. Shouldn't you call Mother?"

"What can she do? We're on our own, kid. The devil take the hindmost."

"Well I know perfectly well if the car didn't move an hour ago it won't move now. And I'm freezing."

As we walked down Seventh, I hurrying and continually

failing to close that gap of a step which was always between us, a drunk slipped out of a dark doorway and capered along beside us. For an instant I thought he was the hitchhiker, but this man was smaller and further gone in degeneracy. His hair was wild like the mane of a muddy lion and it stood straight out from his head like the rays of the sun. His clothes were preposterously tattered and he wore a frazzled old overcoat around his shoulders in the manner of a cape, so that its empty arms waved and bobbled about him as he pirouetted. He asked my father, "Where are you going with this boy?"

My father obligingly slowed his walk so that the drunk, who had stumbled in skipping sideways, could keep pace with us.

"I beg your pardon, mister," he said. "I didn't hear your question."

The drunk exercised an elaborate, pleased control over his intonation, like an actor marvelling at his own performance. "Oh ho ho," he rumbled softly but distinctly. "You dirty, dirty man." He waved his finger back and forth in front of his nose and peered at us roguishly through this windshield-wiper action. For all his raggedness on this bitter night there was much that was merry about him; his face was flat and hard and bright and his teeth were set in his grin like a row of small seeds.

To me he said, "You go home, boy, home to your mother."

We had to stop or else bump into him. "This is my son," my father said.

The drunk turned from me to him so quickly all his clothes fluffed up like feathers. He seemed to be not so much dressed as shingled in rags, layer on layer of torn multi-textured scraps. His voice was like that, too, hoarse and broken and indefinitely soft. "How can you lie?" he said sadly to my father. "How can you lie about a thing so serious? Now let this boy go home to his mother."

"That's where I'm trying to take him," my father said. "But the damn car won't start."

"He's my father," I said, hoping this would make the drunk go away. But it brought him closer to us. His face under the blue streetlight seemed splashed with purple. "Don't lie for him," he said with exquisite gentleness. "He's not worth it. How much is he giving you? I don't care how much it is, it's never enough. When he gets a new pretty boy he'll throw you out on the street like an old Trojan."

"Daddy, let's go," I said, frightened now, and chilled clear through. The night went in one side of me and came out the other and encountered no obstacle.

My father began to push around him and the drunk lifted his hand and my father in answer lifted his own hand. This made the drunk take a back step and he nearly fell. "Knock me down," the drunk said, smiling so broadly his cheeks gleamed. "Knock me down when I want to save your soul. Are you ready to die?" This made my father jerk still like a halted movie. The drunk, seeing his triumph, repeated, *"Are you ready to die?"*

The drunk nimbly sidestepped to me and put his arm around my waist and gave me a hug. His breath was like the odor the seniors taking chemistry sometimes left in Room 107 before we came in for Thursday study hall—a complex stench both sulphurous and sweet. "Ah," he told me, "you're a good warm body. But you're all skin and bone. Doesn't the old bastard feed you? Hey, you," he called to my father, "what sort of an old lech do you call yourself lifting these poor boys off the street with empty stomachs?"

"I thought I was ready to die," my father said, "but now I wonder if anybody ever is. I wonder now if a ninety-nine-year-old Chinaman with tuberculosis, gonorrhea, syphilis, and toothache is ready to die."

The drunk's fingers began to gouge under my ribs and I jerked out of his grasp. "Daddy, let's *go*."

"No, Peter," my father said, "this gentleman is talking sense. Are *you* ready to die?" he asked the drunk. "What do *you* think the answer is?"

Squinting, shoulders back, chest preening, the drunk with pigeon dignity stepped into my father's tall shadow and, looking up, told him carefully, "I'll be ready to die when you and everybody like you is locked up in jail and they throw away the key. You can't even let these poor kids rest on a night like this." He looked over at me under frowning eyebrows and said, "Shall we call the cops, kid? Let's kill this old nance, huh?" To my father he said, "What about it, chief? How much is it worth to you not to have me call the cops and have you picked up with this flower?" He inflated his chest as if to shout, but the street dwindled northward toward infinity without upholding another visible soul—just the painted brick fronts with the little railed porches characteristic of Alton, the stone stoops now and then bearing an ornamented cement flower-pot, the leafless curbside trees alternating and in the end mixing with the telephone poles. Parked cars lined this street but few passed down it because it met a dead end at the Essick's factory wall two blocks away. We stood beside the long low cement-block back of a brewery warehouse; its corrugated green doors had slammed tight shut and the memory of the clang seemed to make the air here hard. The drunk began to pluck at my father's chest, rubbing his thumb and fingers after each pluck as if disposing of a louse or a piece of lint. "Ten dollars," he said. "Ten dollars and my mouth is"—he pressed three blue fingers against his swollen violet lips and held them there as if testing how long he could hold his breath. At last he lifted them away, exhaled a huge feather of frozen vapor, smiled, and said, "So. Ten dollars buys me, lock, stock, and barrel." He winked at me and asked, "Is that a bargain, kid, or not? What's he paying you?"

"He's my *father*," I insisted, frantic. My father was kneading his spotted hands together under the lamplight and the uprightness of his posture seemed a stiffness, as if he had been poleaxed and in the next instant would fall.

"Five dollars," the drunk quickly said to him, "five lousy dollars," and without waiting for an answer he dropped to, "one. One little bitty dollar bill so I can get myself a drink and stop freezing to death. Come on, chief, give me a break. I'll even tell you a hotel where they don't ask any questions."

"I know all about hotels," my father said. "In the Depression I took a job as night clerk at the old Osiris, before they closed it down. The bedbugs got to be as big as the prostitutes so the customers couldn't tell 'em apart. I guess the Osiris was before your time."

The drunk lost his grin. "I come from Easton originally," he said. It occurred to me with a shock that he was much younger than my father; indeed he was virtually a boy like me.

My father dug into his pocket and brought out some change and gave it to the young man. "I'd like to give you more, my friend, but I just don't have it. This is my last thirty-five cents. I'm a public school teacher and our pay scale is way behind that of industry. I've enjoyed talking to you, though, and I'd like to shake your hand." And he did. "You've clarified my thinking," he told the drunk.

My father turned and walked back the way we had come, and I hurried to follow. The things we had been trying to reach—the black car, the sandstone house, my distant and by now, surely, intensely worried mother—tugged like weights within my skin, which seemed stretched transparent by starlight and madness. Walking this way we met the wind that had arisen, and a glass mask of cold was clipped onto my face. Behind us, the drunk kept calling, like an eagle muffled in a storm, "You're O.K.! You're O.K.!"

"Where are we going?" I asked.

"To a hotel," my father said. "That man brought me to my senses. We gotta get you into where it's warm. You're my pride and joy, kid; we gotta guard the silver. You need sleep."

"We must call Mother," I said.

"Right you are," he said. "Right you are." The repetition left me with the impression that he wouldn't do it.

We turned left into Weiser Street. The wealth of neon there made the air seem warmer. One place was grilling hot dogs in the window. Figures liquid in the light poured past, shoulders hunched, faces hid. But they were people and their existing at all exhilarated me, came to me as a blessing and a permission to live myself. My father turned into a narrow doorway I had never noticed. Inside, up six steps and through a blank double door, a surprisingly high open space contained a desk and an elevator cage and some massive stairs and a few frayed chairs all sunk in on themselves and creased. On the left a kind of screen of potted plants held voices and a systematic clink of glass on glass, like a flat bell ringing. There was an odor I had not smelled since, as a child, I would be sent on a Sunday evening to buy a paper pail of oysters at the place, half-restaurant, half-general store, called Mohnie's. Mohnie was a great sluggish Dutchman in a buttoned black sweater and his place was a whitewashed stone house that had stood here along the pike when the town was called Tilden. A bell rang when you pushed open the door and rang again when it shut behind you. Glum counters of exotic candies and tobaccos ran along one wall and in the rest of the space square tables with oilcloth tablecloths waited for supper customers. In the meantime a few old men sat in the chairs, and I had supposed that the smell of the place was something they brought in with them. There was chewing tobacco in it, and wrinkled shoe leather, and wood cured in dust, and the oysters themselves; carrying the slippery little pail home, its top cleverly folded like a napkin at Sunday dinner, was like stealing a section of Mohnie's air; I used to feel that I was trailing behind me in the bluish evening air a faint brownish trail, a flavor of oysters that made the trees and houses of the pike subaqueous. Now here the smell was again, fresh.

The clerk, a hunchback with papery skin and hands warped and made lump-knuckled by arthritis, put down his copy of *Collier's* and listened, crinkled head cocked, as my father unfolded his wallet, elicited identification cards from it, and explained that he was George W. Caldwell, a teacher at Olinger High School, and that I was his son Peter, and that our home was way the hell over in Firetown, and that we would like a room but did not have any money. A tall red wall stood in the forefront of my skull and at its base I prepared to lie down and weep.

The hunchback waved my father's cards away and said, "I know you. I have a niece, Gloria Davis, goes to you. She thinks the world of Mr. Caldwell."

"Gloria's a hell of a nice girl," my father said limply.

"A little wild, her mother thinks."

"I never noticed that."

"A little too fond of the boys."

"She's always been the perfect lady with me."

The other man turned and selected a key tagged with a great wooden disc. "I'll give you a room up on the third floor so the noise from the bar won't be a bother."

"I certainly appreciate this," my father said. "Can I give you a check now?"

"Why not wait till morning?" the little bent man asked, the dry skin of his face twinkling as he smiled. "I guess we'll all still be here." And he led us up a narrow stairway with a lightly twisted bannister whose varnished surface undulated under my hand like a cat ecstatic at being stroked. The stairs wound around the caged elevator shaft, and vistas of spottily carpeted halls seemed to open at every landing. We went down one hall and our footsteps rattled in the gaps between carpets. At the end of the hall, beside a radiator and a window overlooking Weiser Square, the clerk applied the key to a door and it opened. Here was our destination: all night in ignorance we had been winding toward this room, with its two beds, its one window, its two bureaus, its one naked overhead bulb. The clerk switched the light on. My father shook his hand and told him, "You're a gentleman and a scholar. We were thirsty, and ye gave us drink."

The clerk gestured with a shiny crippled hand. "The bathroom's behind that door," he said. "I think there's a clean glass in there."

"I mean, you're a good Samaritan," my father said. "This poor kid here is ready to drop."

"I'm not at all," I said. Still irritated when the clerk had gone, I asked my father, "What's the name of this awful place?"

"The New Yorker," my father said. "It's a real old-time flea-bag, isn't it?"

Now I had to argue with him on the other side, this seemed so ungrateful. "Well he was awfully nice to let us in when we didn't have any money."

"You never know who your real friends are," he said. "I bet if that Davis bitch knew she did me a good turn she'd be screaming in her sleep."

"Why *don't* we have any money?" I asked.

"I've been asking myself that for fifty years. The worst of it is, when I write them a check it'll bounce because I have twenty-two cents in the bank."

"When do you get paid? Isn't this the middle of the month?"

"The way I'm going," my father said, "I never will get paid. The school board reads that report Zimmerman wrote they'll be asking *me* for money."

"Oh who ever reads his reports?" I snapped, angry because I did not know whether or not to undress in front of him. I was shy with him about my spots, because the sight of them seemed to trouble him so. But then, he was my father, and I draped my coat over a rickety, wired-together chair and began to unbutton my red shirt. He turned and gripped the doorknob. "I gotta get on the move," he said.

"Where are you going now? Why can't you stay still?"

"I gotta call your mother and lock up the car. You go to sleep, Peter. We got you up too early this morning. I hate to do that, I've been trying to catch up on sleep since I was four years old. Can you go to sleep? Should I bring your books back from the car so you can do some homework?"

"*No.*"

He looked at me, and seemed on the verge of apology, confession, or a definite offer. There was a word—I did not know it but believed he did—that waited between us to be pronounced. But he only said, "I guess you can go to sleep. You don't seem to have the jumps like I did when I was your age." Tugging the door a touch impatiently, so that the half-retracted latch raked the wood, he went out.

The walls of an empty room are mirrors that double and

redouble our sense of ourselves. Alone, I felt highly excited, as if abruptly introduced into a company of the brilliant and famous and beautiful. I went to the room's one window and overlooked the radiant tangle of Weiser Square. It was a web, a shuttle, a lake where carlights trickling from all quarters of the city dammed. For two blocks Weiser was the broadest street in the East; Conrad Weiser himself had set the surveyor's sticks, planning in the eighteenth century a city of width, clarity, and ease. Now here headlights swam as if in the waters of a purple lake whose surface came to my sill. The shopfronts and bar signs made green and red grass along the banks. The windows of Foy's, Alton's great department store, were square stars set in six rows; or like crackers made of two grains, the lower half of light yellow wheat and the upper half, where the tan shade was drawn, of barley or rye. Across the way, highest of all, the great neon owl by means of electric machinery winked and unwinked as a wing regularly brought to its beak, in a motion of three successive flashes, an incandescent pretzel. Beneath its feet, polychrome letters alternately proclaimed:

OWL PRETZELS
"None Better"
OWL PRETZELS
"None Better"

This sign and the lesser signs—an arrow, a trumpet, a peanut, a tulip—seemed to possess reflections in mid-air, to shimmer on the transparent plane that extended over the square at the height of my hotel room. Cars, stoplights, twinkling shadows that were people, all merged for me in a visual liquor whose fumes were the future. City. This was city: the room I stood alone in vibrated on its paper walls with the haloes of advertisement. Well back from the window, seeing but unseen, I continued to undress, and the patches of scabbed skin I touched seemed the coarsely mottled outer petals of a delicate, delicious, silvery vegetable-heart I was peeling toward. I stood in my underpants, on the edge of a swim; reeds and mud took the print of my bare feet; Alton seemed herself already bathing in the lake of the night. The windowpane's imperfections rippled the wet lights. A virginal sense of the forbidden welled over me like a wind and I discovered myself a unicorn.

Alton distended. Her arms of white traffic stretched riverward. Her shining hair tanned on the surface of the lake. My sense of myself amplified until, lover and loved, seer and seen, I compounded in several accented expansions my ego, the city, and the future, and during these seconds truly clove to the center of the sphere, and outmuscled time and tide. I would triumph. Yet the city shuffled and winked beyond the window unmoved, transparent to my penetration, and her dismissal dwindled me terribly. Hurrying as if my smallness were so many melting crystals which would vanish altogether if not gathered swiftly, I partially redressed and got into the bed nearest the wall; the cold sheets parted like leaves of marble, and I felt myself a dry seed lost in the folds of earth. *Dear God, forgive me, forgive me, bless my father, my mother, my grandfather, now let me sleep.*

As the sheets warmed, I enlarged to human size, and then, as the dissolution of drowsiness crept toward me, a sensation, both vivid and numb, of enormity entered my cells, and I seemed a giant who included in his fingernail all the galaxies that are. This sensation operated not only in space but in time; it seemed, as literally as one says "a minute," an eternity since I had risen from bed, put on my bright red shirt, stamped my foot at my mother, patted the dog through the frosted metal mesh, and drunk orange juice. These things seemed performed in photographs projected on a mist at the distance of the stars; they mixed with Lauren Bacall and Doris Day and via their faces I was returned to the bracing plane of everyday. I became aware of details: a distant rumble of voices, a spiral of wire holding together the leg of a chair a few feet from my face, the annoying flicker of lights on the walls. I got out of bed and lowered the shade and returned to bed. How warm the room was, compared with my room at Firetown! I thought of my mother and for the first time missed her; I longed to inhale her scent of cereal and to forget myself in watching her plod back and forth in our kitchen. When I saw her again I must tell her I understood why she moved us to the farm and that I did not blame her. And I must show my grandfather more respect and listen when he talks because . . . because . . . he will not always be with us.

My father seemed to come into the room at this moment, so I must have fallen asleep. My lips felt swollen, my bare legs boneless and long. His great shadow cut across the strip of pink light that the lowered shade left standing along the wall

by the corner. I heard him set my books down on our table.
"You asleep, Peter?"

"No. Where have you been?"

"I called your mother and Al Hummel. Your mother tells
me to tell you not to worry about anything, and Al's going
to send his truck in for the car in the morning. He thinks it
sounds like the driveshaft and he'll try to get second-hand
parts for me."

"How do you feel?"

"O.K. I was talking to an awfully nice gentleman downstairs in the lobby; he travels all over the East consulting
with these big stores and companies about their advertising
programs and clears twenty thousand a year with a two-
month vacation. I told him that was the kind of creative
work you were interested in and he said he'd like to meet
you. I thought of coming up to get you but figured you
could probably use the sleep."

"Thanks," I said. His shadow cut back and forth across
the light as he took off his coat, his tie, his shirt.

His voice chuckled. "The hell with him, huh? I guess that's
the attitude to take. A man like that would walk over your
dead body to grab a nickel. That's the kind of bastard I've
done business with all my life; they're too smart for me."

When he got into bed, after his body stopped rustling the
sheets, there was a pause, and he said, "Don't worry about
your old man, Peter. In God we trust."

"I'm not worried," I said. "Good night."

There was another pause, and then the darkness spoke:
"Pleasant dreams, as Pop would say." And his evoking my
grandfather unexpectedly did make this strange room safe
enough to sleep in, though a woman's voice giggled down the
hall, and doors kept slamming above and below us.

My sleep was simple and deep and my dreams scanty.
When I awoke, all I remembered was being in an endless
chemical laboratory, like a multiplication with mirrors of the
basins and test tubes and Bunsen burners in Room 107 at
Olinger High. There was on a table a small Mason jar such
as my grandmother used to put up applesauce in. Its glass was
clouded. I picked it up and put my ear to the lid and heard a
tiny voice, as high in pitch as the voice that calls numbers in
a hearing test, saying with a microscopic distinctness, "I want
to die. I want to die."

My father was already up and dressed. He stood by the
window, its shade raised, and looked down at the city stirring

itself into the gray morning. The sky was not clear; clouds like the undersides of long buns unrolled beyond the brick horizon of the city. He opened a window, to savor Alton, and the air tasted different from yesterday's: milder, preparatory, stirred. Something had moved nearer.

Downstairs, our clerk had been replaced by a younger man, who stood straight and did not smile. "Has the old gentleman gone off duty?" my father asked.

"It's a funny thing," the new clerk said, without smiling at all. "Charlie died last night."

"Huh? How could he do that?"

"I don't know. It happened around two in the morning, they said. I wasn't supposed to come on until eight. He just got up from the desk and went into the men's room and died on the floor. Heart, it must have been. Didn't the ambulance wake you?"

"Was that siren for my friend? I can't believe what you're saying. He was a wonderful Christian to us."

"I didn't know him very well myself." The clerk accepted my father's check only after a long explanation, and with a doubtful grimace.

My father and I scraped together the change in our pockets and found enough for breakfast at a diner. I had one dollar in my wallet but did not tell him, intending it to be a surprise when things got more desperate. The counter of the diner was lined with workmen soft-eyed and gruff from behind half-asleep still. I was relieved to see that the man working the griddle was not our hitchhiker. I ordered pancakes and bacon and it was the best breakfast I had had in months. My father ordered Wheaties, mushed the cereal into the milk, ate a few bites, and pushed it away. He looked at the clock. It said 7:25. He bit back a belch; his face whitened and the skin under his eyes seemed to sink against the socket bone. He saw me studying him in alarm and said, "I know. I look like the devil. I'll shave in the boiler room over at school, Heller has a razor." The pale grizzle, like a morning's frost, of a day-old beard covered his cheeks and chin.

We left the diner and walked south toward the high dull owl of dead tubing. A tenuous winter mist, released by the rise in temperature, licked the damp cement and asphalt. We boarded a trolley at Fifth and Weiser. The interior was gay with the straw of the seats, and warm and nearly empty. Few other people were heading outwards against the pull of the city. Alton thinned; the row houses split like ice breaking; a distant hill was half tranced green and half new pastel houses; and after the long gliding stretch beyond the ice-cream stand crowned by a great plaster replica of a cone, the motley brick houses of Olinger took hold around us. The school grounds and then the salmon-brick school appeared on the left; the boilerhouse smokestack admonished the sky like a steeple. We got out by Hummel's Garage. Our Buick was not there yet. We were not late today; cars were still nosing into their slots. An orange bus racily heaved through a loop and swayed to a stop; students the size of birds, colored in bright patches, no two alike, tumbled from the doors in pairs.

As my father and I strode along the pavement that divided the school side lawn from Hummel's alley, a little whirlwind sprang up before us and led us along. Leaves long dead and brittle as old butterfly wings, an aqua candy wrapper, flecks and dust and seed-sized snips of gutter chaff all hurried in a rustling revolution under our eyes; a distinctly circular invisible presence outlined itself on the walk. It danced from one margin of grass to another and sighed its senseless word; my instinct was to halt but my father kept striding. His pants flapped, something sucked my ankles, I closed my eyes. When I looked behind us, the whirlwind was nowhere to be seen.

In the school we parted. A student, I was held by regulations to this side of the wire-reinforced doors. He pushed through and walked down the long hall, his head held high, his hair fluffed from the removal of his blue knit cap, his heels pounding the varnished boards. Smaller and smaller he grew along their perspective; at the far door he became a shadow, a moth, impaled on the light he pressed against. The door yielded; he disappeared. With a grip of sweat, terror seized me.

V

GEORGE W. CALDWELL, TEACHER, 50. Mr. Caldwell was born December 21st, 1896, on Staten Island, New York City. His father was the Reverend John Wesley Caldwell, a graduate of Princeton University and the Union Theological Seminary, New York. Upon graduation from the latter place he entered the Presbyterian ministry, making his the fifth generation of clergymen supplied by the Caldwell family to this denomination. His wife, née Phyllis Harthorne, was of Southern extraction, hailing from the near environs of Nashville, Tennessee. To their marriage she not only brought her great personal beauty and charm but the energetic piety characteristic of Southern gentlewomen. Countless parishioners were to stand indebted to her example of devotion and Christian testimony; when, at the tragically early age of forty-nine, her husband was called to move "from strength to strength" in the Higher Service, it was she who, in the difficult year of his lingering illness, carried on the work of the church, on several Sundays herself mounting into the pulpit.

The couple was blessed with two offspring, of which George was the second. In March of 1900, when George was three, his father resigned his Staten Island pastorate and accepted the call of the First Presbyterian Church of Passaic, New Jersey, at the corner of Grove Street and Passaic Avenue—a splendid structure of yellow limestone still standing and recently enlarged. It was here that for two decades John Caldwell was destined to shed his learning, wry wit, and firmly held faith upon the upturned faces of his flock. So it was that Passaic, of old called Acquackanonk, a gentle river town whose rural beauties were at that time far from eclipsed by the vigor of its industry, came to be the seat of George Caldwell's rearing.

Many still living in this city remember him as a cheerful boy, adept at all sports and as skilled in retaining friends as at making them. His nickname was "Sticks"—presumably an allusion to an unusual physical thinness. Following his father's intellectual bent, he showed an early interest in formal science, though in later years he claimed, with the joking modesty so intrinsic to the man, that the height of his ambition was to become a druggist. Fortunately for a generation of Olinger students, Fate decreed otherwise.

Mr. Caldwell's young manhood was troubled by the premature death of his father and by America's participation in the First World War. An instinctive and natural patriot, he enlisted in the Headquarters Troop of the Seventy-Eighth Division late in 1917 and narrowly survived, at Fort Dix, the great flu epidemic which was then sweeping the camps. He stood ready, Serial No. 2414792, for overseas duty when the Armistice was declared; George Caldwell would never again come so close to leaving the continental boundaries of the nation he was to enrich as worker, teacher, churchman, civic leader, son, husband, and father.

In the years following his military discharge, George Caldwell, now—with his sister, who had married—his mother's sole support, was engaged at a variety of jobs: as a door-to-door salesman of encyclopedias, as the driver of a sightseeing bus in Atlantic City, as athletic supervisor in the Paterson Y. M. C. A., as a railroad fireman on the New York, Susquehanna, and Western Line, and even as a hotel bellhop and restaurant dishwasher. In 1920 he enrolled in Lake College, near Philadelphia, and, with no financial assistance save that engendered by his own efforts, succeeded in graduating with distinction in 1924, having majored in chemistry. While compiling an excellent academic record and sustaining a demanding schedule of part-time employment, he as well earned an athletic scholarship that reduced his tuition by half. For three years a guard on the Lake football varsity, he suffered a broken nose a total of seventeen times, a severely dislocated kneecap twice, and a leg and a collarbone fracture once each. It was there, on the lovely campus whose central jewel is the shining oak-lined lake deemed sacred by the Lenni Lenape (the "Original People"), that he met and was enchanted by Miss Catherine Kramer, whose family were indigenous to the Fire Township region of Alton County. In 1926 the couple married, in Hagerstown, Maryland, and for the next half-decade travelled widely through the Middle Atlantic States including Ohio and West Virginia, George being employed, as cable splicer, by the Bell Telephone and Telegraph Company.

"Blessings come in strange disguises." In 1931 the national destiny again intruded upon the personal; due to the economic disturbances sweeping the United States, George Caldwell was dropped from the pay rolls of the industrial giant he had so conscientiously served. He and his wife, who was shortly to enlarge George Caldwell's responsibilities by another human soul, came to live with her parents, in Olinger, where Mr. Kramer had several years before purchased the handsome white brick house on Buchanan Road presently occupied by Dr. Potter. In the fall of 1933 Mr. Caldwell took up teaching duties at Olinger High School, duties he was never to put down.

How to express the quality of his teaching? A thorough mastery of his subjects, an inexhaustible sympathy for the scholastic underdog, a unique ability to make unexpected connections and to mix in an always fresh and eye-opening way the stuff of lessons with the stuff of life, an effortless humor, a by no means negligible gift for dramatization, a restless and doubting temperament that urged him forward ceaselessly toward self-improvement in the pedagogic craft— these are only parts of the whole. What endures, perhaps, most indelibly in the minds of his ex-students (of whom this present writer counts himself one) was his more-than-human selflessness, a total concern for the world at large which left him, perhaps, too little margin for self-indulgence and satisfied repose. To sit under Mr. Caldwell was to lift up one's head in aspiration. Though there was sometimes—so strenuous and unpatterned was his involvement with his class— confusion, there was never any confusion that indeed "Here was a man."

In addition to a full load of extra-curricular school activities, including the coaching of our gallant swimming team, the management of all football, basketball, track and baseball tickets, and the supervision of the Communications Club, Mr. Caldwell played a giant's role in the affairs of the community. He was secretary of the Olinger Boosters' Club, Counsellor to Cub Pack 12, member of the Committee to Propose a Borough Park, vice-president of the Lions and chairman of that service club's annual light-bulb-selling campaign for the benefit of blind children. During the recent War he was Block Warden and a willing instrument in many aspects of the Effort. Born a Republican and a Presbyterian, he became a Democrat and a Lutheran, and was a staunch contributor to both causes. For many years a deacon and church-council member of the Redeemer Lutheran Church of Olinger, upon recently moving to a charming rural house in Firetown, his wife's family "homestead," Mr. Caldwell promptly became a deacon and member of the council of the Firetown Evangelical-Lutheran church body. Such a tabulation by its very nature cannot include the countless nameless works of charity and good will by which he, originally an alien to the town of Olinger, wove himself so securely into its fabric of citizenship and fellowship that, him gone, the cloth seems all undone.

He is survived by a sister, Alma Terrio, of Troy, New York; and by his father-in-law, his wife, and his son, all of Firetown.

VI

A S I LAY ON MY ROCK various persons visited me. First came Mr. Phillips, my father's colleague and friend, his hair indented by the memory of a shortstop's cap. He held up his hand for attention and made me play that game which he believed made the mind's hands quick. "Take two," he said rapidly, "add four, multiply by three, subtract six, divide by two, add four, what do you have?"

"Five?" I said, for I had become fascinated by the nimbleness of his lips and so lost track.

"Ten," he said, with a little rebuking shake of his inflexibly combed head. He was a tidy man in all things, and any sign of poor coördination vexed him. "Take six," he said, "divide by three, add ten, multiply by three, add four, divide by four, what do you have?"

"I don't know," I said miserably. My shirt was eating my skin with fire.

"Ten," he said, puckering sadly his rubbery mouth. "Let's get down to business," he said. He taught social science. "Give me the members of Truman's cabinet. Remember the magic mnemonic phrase, ST. WAPNICAL."

"State," I said, "Dean Acheson," and then I could remember no more. "But truly," I called, "tell me, Mr. Phillips, you're his friend. Is it possible? Where can the spirits go?"

"T," he said, "Thanatos. Thanatos the death-demon carries off the dead. Two and three, Billy boy, easy out, easy out." He adroitly sidestepped and stooped and snatched it up in his webbing on the short hop. He braced, pivoted in slow motion, and lobbed it over. It was a volley ball and behind me all the mountaintops began to shout. I strained to bat it back over the net but my wrists were chained with ice and brass. The ball grew eyes and a mane of hair like the cornsilk that flows from the bursting ear. Deifendorf's face moved so close I could smell the tallow on his breath. He was holding his hands so a little lozenge-shaped crevice was

134

formed between the balls of his palms. "What they like, you see," he said, "is to have you in there. No matter who they are, that's all they like, you in there working back and forth."

"It seems so brutal," I said.

"It's disgusting," he agreed. "But there it is. Back and forth, back and forth; nothing else, Peter—kissing, hugging, pretty words—it doesn't touch them. You have to do it." He took a pencil into his mouth and showed me how, bending his face into the conjunction of his palms with the pencil sticking, eraser first, from his tartarish teeth. For this moment of tender attention a whole hushed world seemed conjured in the area of his breathing. Then he straightened up, and broke his palms apart, and stroked the two fatnesses of his left palm. "If there's too much fat here," he said, "along the inside of the thighs, you're blocked—you understand?"

"I think so," I said, furious to scratch my itching arms, where the red shirt was shredding.

"So don't laugh off the lean pieces," Deifendorf admonished me, and the dense seriousness of his face repelled me, for I knew it won my father. "You take a skinny kid like Gloria Davis, or one of these big rangy types like Mrs. Hummel—I mean, when a piece like that takes you, you don't feel so lost. Hey, Peter?"

"What? *What?*"

"Wanna know how to tell if they're passionate?"

"Yes, I do. I really do."

He stroked the ball of his thumb lovingly. "Right in here. The mound of Venus. The more there is, the more they are."

"The more they are what?"

"Don't be dumb." He punched me in the ribs so that I gasped. "And another thing. Why doncha get some pants without a yellow stain on the fly?"

He laughed and behind me I could hear all the Caucasus laughing and snapping their towels and flipping their silvery genitals.

Now the town came to visit me, daubed with Indian paint and vague-faced from idle weeping. "*You* remember us," I said. "How we used to walk up the pike beside the trolley cars, me always hurrying a little to keep up?"

"Remember?" He touched his cheek in confusion, so that dabs of wet clay rubbed off on his fingertips. "There are so many . . ."

"Caldwell," I said. "George and Peter. He taught at the

high school and when the war was over he was Uncle Sam
and led the parade down from the fire hall down the pike,
where the trolley tracks used to be."

"There *was* somebody," he said, his eyelids trembling in
a sleep-walker's concentration, "a stout man . . ."

"No, a *tall* man."

"You all *imag*ine," he said with sudden vexation, "if you're
here for a year or two, that I . . . that I . . . there are thousands. There have been thousands, there will be thousands
. . . First, the People. Then the Welsh, the Quakers, the Germans from the Tulpehocken Valley . . . and all think that I
should remember them. In fact," he said, "my memory is
poor." And with this confession his face was brightened by a
quick smile that, creasing so counter to the earth-colored
markings of paint on his face, made me love him for a second
even in his weakness. "And the older I get," he went on,
"the more they stretch me, the streets up Shale Hill, the new
development toward Alton, the more . . . I don't know. The
less things seem to matter."

"He was in the Lions," I prompted. "But they never made
him president. He was on the committee to get a borough
park. He was always doing good deeds. He loved to walk
up and down the alleys and used to spend a lot of time hanging around Hummel's Garage, on the corner there."

His eyes were closed and, following the pattern of his
lids, his whole face seemed membranous and distended,
flickering with fine veins but rapt as a death-mask is rapt. The
daubs of paint glistened where they had not dried. "When
did they straighten Hummel's Alley?" he murmured to himself. "There had been a woodworking shop there, and that
man blinded by gas in the trenches in that little shack, and
now I see a man coming into the alley . . . His coat pocket
is full of old pens that don't write . . ."

"That's my father!" I cried.

He shook his head crossly and let his lids slowly lift.
"No," he told me, "it's nobody. It's the shadow of a tree."
He grinned and took from his pocket a winged maple seed,
which he expertly split with his thumbnail and glued to his
nose, as we used to when children, so it made a little green
rhinoceros horn there. The effect, in combination with the
ochre paint, was suddenly malevolent, and he stared at me
for the first time directly, his eyes as black as oil or loam.
"You see," he pronounced distinctly, "you moved away.
You shouldn't have moved away."

"It wasn't my fault, my mother—"

The bell rang. It was time for lunch, but no food was brought me. I sat opposite Johnny Dedman and there were two others with us. Johnny dealt us cards. Since I could not pick mine up, he flashed each one in my face, and I saw that they were not ordinary cards. Each of them had instead of central pips a murky photograph.

A ◇ : woman, white, not young, sitting on a chair smiling, naked, legs spread.

J ♡ : female white and male Negro performing that act of mutual adoration vulgarly known as a 69.

10 ♣ : four persons, in rectangular arrangement, female-male alternately, one Negro, three white, performing cunnilingus and fellatio alternately, blurred by the necessary considerable reduction under cheap engraving process, so some details were not as clear as I avidly wished. To cover my confusion I coolly asked, "Where did you get these?"

"Cigar store in Alton," Johnny said. "You have to know the man."

"Are there really fifty-two different ones? It seems fantastic."

"All except this one," he said, and showed me the Ace of Spades. It was simply the Ace of Spades.

"How disappointing."

"But if you look at it upside down," he said; and it was an apple with a thick black stem. I didn't understand.

I begged, "Let me see the other cards."

Johnny looked at me with his wise look, his fuzzy cheeks lightly aflame. "Not so fast, my little teacher's son," he said. "You have to pay. I paid."

"I have no money. Last night we had to stay at a hotel and my father had to give the man a check."

"You have a dollar. You held out on the old bastard. You have a dollar in your wallet in your hip pocket."

"But I can't reach it; my arms are fastened."

"All right then," he said. "Buy your own cards, you little flute." And he put his in the pocket of his shirt, which was forest-green, of a beautifully coarse weave, with the collar turned up so its edge rubbed the nape of his wet-combed hair.

I tried to get at my wallet; my shoulder muscles ached in their frozen sockets; my back seemed welded to the rock. Penny—it was she beside me, giving off a columbine hint of perfume—nuzzled my neck as she tried to reach my wallet for me. "Let it go, Penny," I told her. "It's not important. I need the money because we have to eat in town tonight because of the basketball game."

"Why did you ever move into the country?" she asked. "It sets up all these inconveniences."

"True," I said. "But it also gives me a chance at you."

"You never take advantage of it," she said.

"I did once," I said, blushing in defence.

"Oh, shit, Peter, here," Johnny sighed. "Now don't say I never did you a favor." He ruffled through the deck and showed me the Jack of Hearts again. It seemed very beautiful, a circle completed, a symmetry found, a somber whirlpool of flesh, the faces hidden by the woman's white thighs and the woman's long loose hair. But the beauty of it, like a black pencil rubbed over paper to bring out the buried initials and inscriptions long ago carved on a desk-top, brought up again my sorrow and fear over my father. "What do you think the X-rays will show?" I asked, I hoped casually.

He shrugged and after a little hum of calculation said, "Fifty-fifty. It would go either way."

"Oh my *Lord*," Penny cried, her fingertips darting to her lips. "I forgot to pray for him!"

"That's O.K.," I said. "Forget it. Forget I ever asked you. Just gimme a bite of your hamburger. Just a little bite." All the cigarette smoke was bothering my face; I felt as I opened my mouth I was taking sulphur into myself.

"Easy, easy," Penny said. "This is all I have for lunch."

"You're kind to me," I said. "Why?" It was not really a question, I was just trying to draw her out.

"What do you have next period?" Kegerise asked in his ugly flat voice. He was the fourth.

"Latin. And I haven't done any of the shit-eating work. How could I, I spent the whole screwed-up night gallivanting with my father up and down the streets of Alton."

"Miss Appleton will love to hear *that*," Kegerise said. He envied my brains.

"Oh, I think she'll forgive anything a Caldwell does," Penny said. She had a mood of slyness which I detested; she was not very clever and it did not become her.

"That's an odd thing to say," I said. "Does it mean anything?"

"Haven't you noticed?" Her green eyes went quite round. "The way your father and Hester stand around in the hall talking? She thinks he's wonderful."

"You're mad," I said. "You're really sex-mad."

Meant to be cute, to my surprise it miffed her. "You don't notice anything, do you, Peter? You're just so wrapped up in your own skin you have no idea what other people feel."

"Skin" was a shock; but I was sure she knew nothing about my skin. My face and hands were clear and she had never seen anything else. This troubled me and made her love frightening; for if she loved me we would be driven to make love and there would come this very painful time when I must expose to her my flesh. . . . *Forgive me,* my brain suddenly began murmuring, *forgive me, forgive me.*

Johnny Dedman, irritated at being left out of the conversation—after all, he was a senior and we were sophomores so his being with us was a considerable condescension—riffled through his dirty pack and ostentatiously chuckled. "The one that really kills me," he said, "is the whore of farts. I mean the four of hearts. It's a woman and a bull."

Minor charged over to our booth. Anger flashed from his bald dome and steamed through his flared nostrils. "Here, *hyaar,*" he snorted. "Put those away. Don't come in here again with anything like that."

Dedman looked up at him with a benign flicker of the long curling eyelashes that gave his gaze a starry expectancy. He spoke with his lips hardly moving. "Go chop some horse-meat," he said.

Miss Appleton seemed rather flustered and out of breath, probably from the long climb. "Peter, translate," she said, and then she read aloud with her impeccable quantities,

> *"Dixit, et avertens rosea cervice refulsit,*
> *ambrosiaeque comae divinum vertice odorem*
> *spiravere, pedes vestis defluxit ad imos,*
> *et vera incessu patuit dea."*

As she made these words ring, she wore her Latin face: corners of the lips sternly downdrawn, eyebrows lifted rigidly, her cheeks gray with gravity. In French class, her face was quite different: cheeks like apples, eyebrows dancing, mouth puckered dryly, corners tense naughtily.

"She said," I said.

"She spoke. Thus she spoke," Miss Appleton said.

"She spoke, and . . . and . . . glowed."

"What glowed? Not *she* glowed. *Cervice* glowed."

"She spoke, and, turning, her, uh, rosy crevice—" Laughter from the others. I blushed.

"*No! Cervice, cervice.* Neck. You've heard of the cervix. Surely you've heard of the cervical vertebrae."

"She spoke, and, turning—"

"As she turned."

"As she turned, her rosy neck blushed."

"Very well."

"And, and *coma, coma*—sleep?"

"Hair, Peter, hair. Surely you've heard of the derivative word comose? Think of comb, as a rooster's comb."

"And, uh, turning again—"

"Oh, no. Dear child, no. *Vertice* here is the noun, *vertex, verticis.* Vortex. A vortex, a whirl, a *crown* of hair, of what kind of hair? What agrees?"

"Ambrosial."

"Yes, ambrosial meaning, properly, immortal. Applied most often to the food of the gods, and in that sense descending to us with the meaning of sweet, delicious, honey-like. But the gods also used ambrosia for anointment and perfume." She spoke of the gods with a certain authority, Miss Appleton did.

"And her whirl, her tangle—"

"*Crown*, Peter. The hair of the gods is never tangled."

"And her crown of ambrosial hair breathed out a divine odor."

"Yes. Good. Fragrance, let's say. Odor rather suggests plumbing."

". . . a divine fragrance, her vestment, her robe . . ."

"Yes, a flowing robe. All the goddesses save Diana wore a loose flowing robe. Diana, the heavenly huntress, wore of course a sensible tunic, perhaps with leggings, probably of a heavy green or brown cloth such as what I am wearing. Her robe flowed down—"

"I don't understand *ad imos*."

"*Imus*, a rather archaic word. The superlative of *inferus*, below, down below. *Ad imos*, to the lowest extremity. Here, literally, to the lowest extremity of her feet, which makes little sense in English. It is used as emphasis; the poet is astounded. Some rendering such as 'her robe flowed down, ah, down to her very feet' might be equivalent. The sense is of 'all the way.' She was totally naked. Please proceed, Peter. This is taking much too long."

"Down, down to her feet, and in truth opened—"

"*Was* opened, *was* exposed, made manifest as *vera. Vera dea.*"

"As a true goddess."

"Quite so. What does *incessu* have to do with the sentence?"

"I don't know."

"Really, Peter, this is disappointing. College material like yourself. *Incessu*, in stride, in gait. She was in gait a true goddess. Gait in the sense of carriage, of physical style; there is a *style* to divinity. These lines brim with a sense of that radiance, breaking in upon the unknowing Aeneas. *Ille ubi matrem agnovit;* he recognized his mother. Venus, Venus with her ambrosial fragrance, her swirling hair, her flowing robe, her rosy skin. Yet he sees only as she is *avertens*, as she is turning away. The sense of the passage being that only as she turns to leave him, does he perceive her true glory, her actual worth and her relationship to him. So it is often in life. We love too late. In the next line he cries out to her, most movingly, as she fades away, 'Oh why, why may we never join hand to hand, or hear and give back speech truly?'"

Iris Osgood replaced her; the girl was crying. Tears streamed down her cheeks, soft and bland like the sides of a Guernsey, and she did not have the wit to wipe them away. She was one of those dull plain girls who were totally unfashionable in the class and yet with whom I felt a certain inner dance. That half-shaped fatness of her figure secretly roused the hard seeds in me; I showed it by being quick and bantering of tongue. But today I was tired and wanted only to pillow my head upon her low I. Q. "Why the tears, Iris?"

Through a sob in her throat she brought out, "My blouse: he tore it. It's ruined and what can I tell my mother?"

And now I noticed that indeed the downslipping silver of one breast was exposed to the very verge of its ruddy puckered coin; I could not tear my eyes away, it looked so vulnerable.

"That's all right," I told her, debonair. "Look at *me*. My shirt is totally disintegrated."

And this was true; except for flecks and glutinous threads of red, my chest was bare. My psoriasis was made manifest. A line had formed and, one by one, they walked by, Betty Jean Shilling, Fats Frymoyer, Gloria Davis suppressing a smile, Billy Schupp the diabetic—all my classmates. They had obviously come together in a bus. Each for a moment studied my scabs, and then moved on in silence. A few shook their heads sadly; one girl pressed her lips together and shut her eyes; a few eyes were thick and pink with tears. The wind, the mountaintops, had fallen still behind me. My rock felt padded and there was a tangy chemical smell all but smothered in the artificial perfume of flowers.

Last came Arnie Werner, the president of the senior class and the student council, captain of the football and baseball teams. He was a hollow-eyed boy with the throat of a god and heavy sloping shoulders all shining from the shower. He bent way over and stared at the scabs of my chest and touched one fastidiously with his index finger. "Jesus, kid," he said, "what've you got? Syphilis?"

I tried to explain. "No, it's an allergic condition, not contagious, don't be frightened—"

"Have you had a doctor look at this?"

"You won't believe this, but the doctor himself—"

"Does it bleed?" he asked.

"Only when I scratch too hard," I told him, desperate to ingratiate myself, to earn his forgiveness. "It's kind of relaxing, actually, when you're reading or in a movie—"

"Boy," he said. "This is the ugliest stuff I ever saw." He frowningly sucked his index finger. "Now I've touched it and I'll get it. Where's the Mercurochrome?"

"Honest, cross my heart, it's not contagious—"

"Frankly," he said, and from the solemn-dumb way he said that one word I could see that he was probably a good president of the student council, "I'm surprised they let you bring a thing like that into the school. If it's syphilis, you know, the toilet seats—"

I shouted, "I want my father!"

He came before me and wrote on the blackboard,

$$C_6H_{12}O_6 + 6O_2 = 6CO_2 + 6H_2O + E.$$

It was the last, the seventh period of the day. We were tired. He encircled the E and said, "Energy. That's life. That little extra E is life. We take in sugars and oxygen and burn it, like you burn old newspapers in the trash barrel, and give off carbon dioxide and water and energy. When this process stops"—he Xed through the equation—"*this* stops"—he double-Xed out the E—"and you become what they call dead. You become a worthless log of old chemicals."

"But can't the process ever be reversed?" I asked.

"Thanks for asking that, Peter. Yes. Read the equation

backwards and you have photosynthesis, the life of green plants. They take in moisture and the carbon dioxide we breathe out and the energy of the sunlight, and they produce sugar and oxygen, and then we eat the plants and get the sugar back and that's the way the world goes round." He made a vortex with his fingers in the air. "Round and round, and where it stops, nobody knows."

"But where do they get the energy?" I asked.

"Good question," my father said. "You've got your mother's brains; I hope to hell you don't get my ugly face. The energy needed for photosynthesis comes from the atomic energy of the sun. Every time we think, move, or breathe, we're using up a bit of golden sunshine. When that gives out in five billion years or so, we can all lie down and rest."

"But why do you want to rest?" His face had gone quite bloodless; a film had been interposed between us; my father seemed flattened upon another plane and I strained my voice to reach him. He turned slowly, so slowly, and his forehead wobbled and elongated with refraction. His lips moved and seconds later the sound came to me.

"Huh?" He was not looking at me, he seemed unable to find me.

"Don't rest!" I shouted, glad the tears had come, glad to hear my voice breaking on the spikes of grief; I hurled my words through with a kind of triumph, exulted in the sensations of the tears softly flailing my face like the torn ends of shattered ropes. "Daddy, don't rest! What would you do? Can't you forgive us and keep going?"

The top half of him was bent by some warp in the plane he was caught in; his necktie and shirtfront and coat lapels looped upwards along the curve and his head at the end of the arc was pressed into the angle where the wall met the ceiling above the blackboard, a cobwebby place never touched by a broom. From up here his distorted face gazed down at me mournfully, preoccupied. Yet a microscopic pinch of interest in the corners of his eyes led me to keep calling. "*Wait!* Can't you wait for me?"

"Huh? Am I going too fast?"

"I have something to tell you!"

"Huh?"

His voice was so muffled and far that I willed to be closer to him and found myself swimming upward, with expert strokes, my arms lifting high at the elbow, my feet fluttering like boneless fins. The sensations so excited me I almost forgot to speak. Coming up panting by his side, I told him, "I have hope."

"Do you? That makes me awfully proud to hear that, Peter. I never had any. You must get that from your mother, she's a real femme."

"From *you*," I said.

"Don't worry about me, Peter. Fifty years is a long time; if you don't learn anything in fifty years you never will. My old man never knew what hit him; he left us a Bible and a bucketful of debts."

"Fifty years is *not* a long time," I said. "It's not *enough*."

"You really have hope, huh?"

I closed my eyes; between the voiceless "I" inside my head and the trembling plane of darkness also there, there was a gap, of indeterminate distance but certainly not more than an inch. With a little lie I leaped it. "Yes," I said. "Now stop being silly."

VII

CALDWELL turns and shuts the door behind him. Another day, another dollar. He is weary but does not sigh. The hour is late, after five. He has stayed in his room bringing the basketball books up to date and trying to unravel the tickets; there is a block of tickets missing and in rummaging through his drawers he came across Zimmerman's report and reread it. It depressed him out of all proportion. It was on blue paper and looking at it was like falling upwards into the sky. Also he has corrected the exams he gave the fourth section today. Poor Judy Lengel: she doesn't have it. She tries too hard and maybe that has been his trouble all his life. As he walks toward the stairwell the ache low in his body revives and enwraps him like a folded wing. Some have the five talents, some have the two, some have the one. But whether you've worked in the vineyard all day or just an hour, when they call you in your pay is the same. He hears his father's voice in the memory of these parables and this depresses him further.

"George." A shadow is in the corner of his eye.

"Huh? Oh. You. What are you doing here so late?"

"Fussing. That's what old maids do. Fuss." Hester Appleton stands, arms folded across the ruffles of her virginal blouse, outside her doorway; her room is 202, just down the hall from Room 204. "Harry mentioned that you came to see him yesterday."

"I'm ashamed to admit I did. Did he say anything else? We're waiting for the X-rays to come through or some damn thing."

"Don't be worried." The little step forward in her voice as she blurts this makes Caldwell tilt his long head.

"Why not?"

"It doesn't do any good. Peter's very worried, I could tell today in class."

"The poor kid, he didn't get much sleep last night. Our car broke down in Alton."

Hester tucks a strand of her hair back and with an elegant touch of her middle finger pushes her pencil deeper into her bun. Her hair is glossy and not at all gray in the half-light. She is short, bosomy, broad in the beam and, seen from the front, dumpily thick-waisted. But seen sideways her waist is strikingly small, tucked in by her doughty upright posture; she seems from her stance to be always in the act of inhaling. Her blouse wears a gold clasp shaped like an arrow. "He wasn't," she says, after considering once more in her life the face of the man hulking above her in the gloom of the hall, a strange knobbed face whose mystery, in relation to herself, is permanent, "his usual self."

"He's gonna come down with a cold before I'm through with him," Caldwell says. "I know it and I can't help it. I'm gonna get the kid sick and I can't stop myself."

"He's not such a fragile boy, George." She pauses. "In some ways he's tougher than his father."

Caldwell hears this slightly, enough to bend a bit what he was going to say anyway. "When I was a kid back in Passaic," he says, "I never remember being laid up with a cold. You wiped your nose on a sleeve and if your throat itched you coughed. The first time in my life I went to bed with anything was with the flu in 1918; if *that* wasn't a mess. Brrough!"

Hester feels the pain in the man and she presses her fingers against the gold arrow to hush the disconcerting flutter that has erupted in her chest. She has been in the classroom adjacent to this man for so many years that in her heart it is as if she had often slept with him. It is as if they had been lovers when younger and for reasons never sufficiently examined they had long ago ceased to be.

Caldwell feels this to the extent of being, in her presence, a shade more relaxed than anywhere else. They are both exactly fifty, a trick of birthdays that in their unthinking deeps does oddly matter. He is reluctant to leave her and go down the stairs; his illness, his son, his debts, the painful burden of land his wife has saddled him with—all these problems itch in his brain for expression. Hester wants him; she wants him to tell her everything. Her frame of manners strains to accommodate this desire; as if to empty herself of decades of lonely habit she exhales: sighs. Then says, "Peter's like Cassie. He has that way of getting what he wants."

"I should have put her on the Burly-cue stage, she would have been happier there," Caldwell tells Miss Appleton in a loud earnest rush. "I shouldn't have married her, I should have just been her manager. But I didn't have the guts. I was brought up so that as soon as you saw a woman you half-way liked the only thing you could think of to do was ask her to marry you." This is to say, *I should have married a woman like you. You.*

Though Hester has sought this, now that it arrives it disgusts and alarms her. The man's shadow before her seems about to dilate with anxiety and to overwhelm her physically. It is too late; she is insufficiently elastic now. She laughs as if what he has said were meaningless. The sound of her laughter afflicts the diminishing perspective of green lockers with a look of terror. Their air-slits seem aghast at what they see on the opposite wall: framed pictures of vanished baseball and track teams.

Hester straightens up, inhales, retucks the pencil into her bun, and asks, "What thought have you given to Peter's education?"

"No thought. My only thought is that it's going to take more money than I've got."

"Is he going to attend an art school or a liberal arts college?"

"That's up to him and his mother. They discuss this sort of thing between them; it scares the living daylights out of me. As far as I can tell, the kid knows even less than I did at his age what the score is. If I were to kick off now, he and his mother would sit out there in the sticks and try to eat the flowers off the wallpaper. I can't afford to die."

"It *is* a luxury," Hester says. The Appleton ill-humor has

in her taken the form of an occasional unexpected tartness, or irony. She once again examines the mysterious face above her, frowns at the diseaselike murmur in her breast, and moves to turn, dismissing not so much Caldwell as her own secret.

"Hester."

"What, George?" Her head with its taut round hairdo is caught like a crescent moon half in the light from her room. An unimpassioned observer would conclude, from the light, glad, regretful way she smiles up, that he had once been her lover.

"Thanks for letting me rave on," he says. He adds, "I want to confess something. Tomorrow it may be too late. There've been times in my years here when the kids have got me so down I've stepped out of the classroom and come here by the drinking fountain just to hear you in there pronouncing French. It's been better than a drink of water for me, to hear you pronouncing French. It's never failed to pick me up."

Delicately she asks, "Are you down now?"

"Yep. I'm down. I'm in Old Man Winter's belly."

"Shall I pronounce something?"

"To tell you God's honest truth, Hester, I'd appreciate it."

Her face goes into its Gallic animation—apple-cheeked, prune-lipped—and she pronounces, word by word, savoring the opening diphthong and closing nasal like two liqueurs, "*Dieu est très fin.*"

A second of silence hovers.

"Say it again," Caldwell asks.

"*Dieu - est - très - fin.* It's the sentence I've lived by."

"God is very—very fine?"

"*Oui.* Very fine, very elegant, *very* slender, *very* exquisite. *Dieu est très fin.*"

"That's right. He certainly is. He's a wonderful old gentleman. I don't know where the hell we'd be without Him."

As if by stated consent, both turn away.

Caldwell turns back in time to check her. "You were good enough to recite for me," he says, "I'd like to recite something for you. I don't think I've thought of this for thirty years. It's a poem we used to have to recite back in Passaic; I think I can still do the beginning. Shall I try it?"

"Try it."

"I don't know why the hell I'm bedevilling you like this." Like a schoolchild Caldwell stands to attention, makes fists of concentration at his sides, squints to remember, and an-

nounces, " 'Song of the Passaic,' By John Alleyne MacNab."
He clears his throat.

> *"The great Jehovah wisely planned*
> *All things of Earth, divinely grand;*
> *And, in His way, all nature tends*
> *To laws divine, to serve His ends.*

> *"The rivers run, and none shall know*
> *How long their waters yet may flow;*
> *We read the record of the past,*
> *While time withholds the future cast."*

He thinks, slumps, and smiles. "That's all the further we
go. I thought I'd remember more."

"Very few men would have remembered as much. It's not
a very happy poem, is it?"

"It is for me, isn't that funny? I guess you have to have
been brought up beside the river."

"Mm. I suppose that *is* the way things are. Thank you,
George, for reciting it." And now she does turn back into her
room. The gold arrow on her blouse seems for an instant to
press against her larynx, threatening to smother her. She
brushes vaguely at her brow, swallows, and the sensation
passes.

Caldwell heads for the stairs groggy with woes. Peter. His
education is a riddle to which however it's posed the answer
is money of which there is not enough. Also his skin and his
health. By correcting the exams now Caldwell can give the
kid another ten minutes sleep in the morning tomorrow. He
hates to pull the kid out of bed. It will be eleven before they
get home tonight after the basketball game and this combined
with that weird night in the flea-bag last night will ripen him
up for another cold. A cold a month like clockwork, they say
the skin doesn't have anything to do with it but Caldwell
doubts this. Everything interconnects. With Cassie, he had
never noticed until they were married, just one spot on her
belly, but with the kid it was a plague: arms, legs, chest, even
on his face more than he realized, bits of crust in the ears like
dried soap and the poor kid didn't know it. Ignorance is bliss.
In the Depression when he used to push the kid along on his
Kiddy Kar with the forked stick, he had been frightened, he
had come to the world's cliff-edge, and his son's small face
turning around to look back, the freckles solid under his eyes,

made the world seem solid. Now his son's face, dappled, feminine in the lips and eyelashes, narrow like a hatchet, anxious and sneering, gnaws at Caldwell's heart like a piece of unfinished business.

If he had had any character he would have put on baggy pants and taken her onto the vaudeville stage. But then vaudeville folded just like the telephone company. All things fold. Who would have thought the Buick would give out like that just when they needed it to take them home? Things never fail to fail. On his deathbed his father's religion: "eternally forgotten?"

Nos. 18001 to 18145: these are the basketball tickets missing. Through his closets and his drawers and his papers and the only thing he had found the blue slip of Zimmerman's report, slip of sky, making his stomach bind like a finger in a slammed door. Biff. Bang. Well, he hadn't buried his talent in the ground; he had lifted the bushel from his light and showed everybody what a burnt-out candle looks like.

A thought he had run his mind through in the last minute had pleased him. But what? He picks his way back through the brown pebbles of his brain to locate this jewel. There. Bliss. Ignorance is bliss.

Amen.

The steel mullions of the window of the landing halfway down the stairs, with their little black drifts of dirt by now as solid as steel itself, strike him strangely. As if the wall, in becoming a window, speaks in a loud voice a word of a foreign language. Since, five days ago, Caldwell grasped the possibility that he might die, took it into himself as you might swallow a butterfly, a curiously variable gravity has entered the fabric of things, that now makes all surfaces leadenly thick with heedless permanence and the next instant makes them dance with inconsequence, giddy as scarves. Nevertheless, among disintegrating surfaces he tries to hold his steadfast course.

Hummel.
Call Cassie.
Go to the dentist.   } This is his program.
Be here for game by 6:15.
Get in the car and take Peter home.

He bucks the door of reinforced glass and walks down the empty corridor. See Hummel, call Cassie. At noon Hummel

still hadn't found a second-hand driveshaft to replace the one
that snapped in the little odd-shaped lot between the coughdrop plant and the railroad tracks; he was searching by telephone through the junk yards and auto body shops of Alton
and West Alton. He had estimated the bill would come to between $20-25, he would tell Cassie and she would somehow
make this amount of money matter less, it was just a drop in
the bucket as far as she was concerned, just one more drop
more or less to pour into that thankless land of hers, eighty
acres on his shoulders, land, dead cold land, his blood sunk
like rain into that thankless land. And Pop Kramer can stick
a whole slice of bread into his mouth at one swoop. Call
Cassie. She would be worried; he foresees their worries inter-
twining over the phone like two spliced cables. Was Peter
all right? Has Pop Kramer fallen down the stairs yet? What
did the X-rays show? He doesn't know. He has thought off
and on all day of calling Doc Appleton but something in him
resists giving the old braggart the satisfaction. Ignorance is
bliss. Anyway he has to go to the dentist. Thinking of it
makes him suck the tender tooth. By searching through his
body he can uncover any color and shape of pain he wants:
the saccharine needle of the toothache, the dull comfortable
pinch of his truss, the restless poison shredding in his bowels,
the remote irritation of a turned toenail gnawing the toe
squeezed beside it in the shoe, the little throb above his nose
from having used his eyes too hard in the last hour, and the
associated but different ache along the top of his skull, like
the soreness left by his old leather football helmet after a
battering scrimmage down in the Lake Stadium. Cassie, Peter,
Pop Kramer, Judy Lengel, Deifendorf: he has them all on
his mind. See Hummel, call Cassie, go to the dentist, be here
by 6:15. He foresees himself skinned of chores, purified. One
thing he loved in his life: in splicing cables, the sight of the
copper strands, naked and raw and gleaming and fanning
when suddenly stripped of the dirty old rubber. The cable's
conductive heart. It used to frighten him to bury something
so alive down in the ground. The shadow of the wing tightens
so that his intestines wince: a spider lives there. *Brrough.*
In the shuffle of his thoughts his own death keeps coming
to the top. His face burns. His legs go watery, his heart and
head become enormous with fear. Death that white width for
him? His face is drenched with warmth; a blindness seizes
his body; he silently begs a face to appear in the air. The
long varnished hall, lit by spaced globes of sealed-in light,

shimmers in tints of honey, amber, tallow. So familiar, so familiar it is surprising that his footsteps in fifteen years have not worn a path down these boards, yet it seems freshly strange, as strange as on the day when, a young husband and new father still with that soft New Jersey twang and blur in his voice, he had come in the heat of an Olinger summer afternoon for his first interview with Zimmerman. He had liked him. Caldwell had instantly liked Zimmerman, whose heavy uneasy allusive ways reminded him of a cryptic school friend, a seminary roommate, of his father's who used to come visiting now and then on a Sunday and who always remembered to bring a little bag of licorice for "young Caldwell." Licorice for George, and a hair ribbon for Alma. Always. So that in time the little stencilled casket Alma kept on her bureau overflowed with hair ribbons. He had liked Zimmerman and had felt liked in turn. They had shared a joke about Pop Kramer. He cannot remember the joke but smiles to remember that one was made, fifteen years ago. Caldwell walks with strengthening strides. Like an unpredictable eddy in the weather, a small breeze arises and cools his cheeks with the thought that a dying man would not have it in him to walk so upright.

Cattycorner across from the trophy case with its hundred highlights, Zimmerman's door is shut. As Caldwell strides by, it pops open and Mrs. Herzog steps out at a slant under his nose. She is as startled as he; her eyes widen behind her cockeyed butterscotch hornrims and her peacock-feathered hat sits crooked as if with shock. She is, from Caldwell's height of age, a young woman; her oldest child has just reached the seventh grade. Already, ripples of protective agitation are spreading upwards from this child through the faculty. She got herself elected to the school board to guarantee personally her children's education. From his professional heart, Caldwell despises these meddling mothers; they haven't a clue as to what education is: a jungle, an unholy mess. Arrogantly her mouth in its blurred purplish lipstick refuses to frame a smile of confessed surprise, instead remaining ajar in frank amazement, like a stuck letter slot.

Caldwell breaks the silence. An urchin's impudence, revived from deep in his childhood by the forgotten sensation of nearly having his nose socked, dimples his face as he tells her, Mrs. Herzog of the school board, "Boy, the way you came out of that door reminded me of a cuckoo clock!"

Her air of interrupted dignity, ridiculous in one not yet

out of her thirties and leaning her weight on a doorknob,
freezes the harder at this greeting. With glassied eyes he resumes his walk to the end of the hall. Not until he has
bucked open the wire-reinforced double doors and started
down the steps under the yellow wall where since yesterday
the word FUCK has been scrubbed away, does the fist sink
into his stomach. His goose, cooked. What in hell had the
pushy bitch been doing in there? He had felt Zimmerman's
presence behind her in his office, a dark cloud; he could
feel Zimmerman's atmosphere through a keyhole. She had
shoved open the door like a woman making a point at her
back and not dreaming her front was exposed. Caldwell in
his present state cannot afford another enemy. Tickets 18001
to 18145, Zimmerman's report saying in black and blue that
he hit the kid in class, and now this: bumping into Mim
Herzog with her lipstick smeared. A bubble expands in his
throat and, stepping into the open, he takes in fresh air with
a gasp as sharp as a sob. Blurred crimped clouds have been
lowered tangent to the town's slate roofs. The roofs seem
greasily lustrous with sullen inner knowledge. The atmosphere feels pregnant with a hastening fate. Lifting his head
and sniffing, Caldwell experiences a vivid urge to walk on
faster, to canter right past Hummel's, to romp neighing
through the front door and out the back door of any house
in Olinger that stood in his way, to gallop up the brushy
brown winter-burned flank of Shale Hill and on, on, over
hills that grow smoother and bluer with distance, on and on
on a southeast course cutting diagonally across highways and
rivers frozen solid as highways until at last he drops, his
head in death extended toward Baltimore.

The herd has deserted Minor's. Only three persons in-
habit the luncheonette: Minor himself, Johnny Dedman, and
that atrocious ego Peter Caldwell, the science teacher's son.
All but the shiftless and homeless are at their own tables
at this hour. Five-forty. Next door, the post office has closed.
Mrs. Passify, moving tenderly on worn legs, lowers the grates
on the windows and eases shut the drawers colorful with
stamps and inserts the counted money into the mock-
Corinthian safe. Behind her, the back room seems a battle-
field hospital where gray mail sacks lie unconscious, steeped
in an anesthesia of shadows, prone, misshapen, and disem-
bowelled. She sighs and goes to the window. To a passerby
on the pavement her great round face would seem the

face of a grotesquely swollen child straining to peek out of a tiny port-hole, the goldleaf O at the zenith of the arc of letters spelling POST OFFICE.

Beside her, Minor methodically twists his coarse white cloth into the steaming throat of each Coca-Cola glass before he sets it down on the towel he has spread beside his sink. Each glass continues to give off a few wisps of mist as the cool air licks it. Through his window, which is beginning to fog, the pike is ripe with cars hurrying home—a laden branch whose fruit glows. The luncheonette behind him is all but empty, like a stage. It has been supporting a debate. Within, Minor is a cauldron of rage; his hairy nostrils seem seething vents.

"Minor," Peter calls from his booth, "you're old-fashioned. There's nothing wrong with Communism. In twenty years we'll have it in this country and you'll be happy as a clam."

Minor turns from the window, dome flashing, brain raging. "If old FDR had lived we'd have it," he says, and laughs angrily, so that his nostrils spread under the burst of pressure. "But he went and killed himself, or else he died of syphilis. God's judgement: mark my words."

"Minor, you don't believe that. You couldn't be sane and believe that."

"I believe it," Minor says. "He was rotten in the head when he went to Yalta or we wouldn't be in the fix we are now."

"What fix? What fix, Minor? This country is sitting on top of the world. We got the big bomb and we got the big bombers."

"*Arrrhh.*" Minor turns away.

"What fix? What fix, Minor? What fix?"

He turns back and says, "The Ruskies'll be in France and Italy before the year's over."

"So what? So what, Minor? Communism has to come, one way or another; it's the only way to beat poverty."

Johnny Dedman in a separate booth is smoking his eighth Camel of the hour and is trying to blow one smoke ring through another. Now he cries, without warning, the word "War!" and with his finger rat-tat-tats the big brown button knotted onto the end of the light cord above his head.

Minor comes back in his narrow runway behind the counter the better to address the boys in their dim booths. "We should've kept marching when we hit the Elbe and taken Moscow when we had the chance. They were rotten and ready for us, the Russian soldier is the most cowardly in the world. The peasants would have risen up to greet us. That's what old Churchill wanted us to do, and he was right. He was a crook but clever, clever. He didn't love Old Joe. Nobody in the world loved Old Joe but King Franklin."

Peter says, "Minor, you really are insane. What about Leningrad? They weren't cowardly then."

"They didn't win it. They did not win it. Our equipment won it. Our tanks. Our guns. Sent courtesy free parcel post by your good friend FDR; he robbed the American people to save the Russians who then turn right around and are ready to march this minute over the Alps into Italy."

"He was trying to beat Hitler, Minor. Don't you remember? Adolf H-I-T-L-E-R."

"I love Hitler," Johnny Dedman announces. "He's alive in Argentina."

"Minor loved him too," Peter says, reedy-voiced with fury and hot in all his limbs. "Didn't you, Minor? Didn't you think Hitler was a nice man?"

"I never did," Minor says. "But I'll tell you this. I'd rather have Hitler alive than old Joe Stalin. There is the Devil Incarnate. You mark my words."

"Minor, what do you have against Communism? They wouldn't make you go to work. You're too old. You're too sick."

"Bam. *Bam*," Johnny Dedman cries. "We should've dropped an atom bomb on Moscow, Berlin, Paris, France, Italy, Mexico City, and Africa. Ka-*Pow*. I love that mushroom-shaped cloud."

"Minor," Peter says. "Minor. Why do you exploit us poor teenagers so ruthlessly? Why are you so brutal? You've got the board of the pinball machine tilted so steeply nobody except Dedman can get any free games out of it and he's a genius."

"I am a genius," Dedman says.

"They don't even believe in a Divine Creator," Minor states.

"Well, my God, who does?" Peter exclaims, blushing for himself but unable to halt, so anxious is he to pin this man who with his black Republican stupidity and stubborn animal vigor embodies everything in the world that is killing Peter's father; he has to keep Minor from turning his back, he has to hold, as it were, the world open. "You don't. I don't. Nobody does. Really." Yet in this boast, now that it is issued, Peter perceives an abysmal betrayal of his father. In his mind he sees his father slip into a pit stunned. He waits, so hungrily his mouth feels parched, for Minor's rejoinder, whatever it might be, so that in the twists and detours of argument he can find a way to retract. So much of Peter's energy is spent in wishing he could take back things he has said.

"I believe you," Minor says simply, turning. The way out is sealed.

"In two years," Johnny Dedman estimates aloud, "there'll be a war. I'll be a major. Minor will be a first sergeant. Peter will be peeling potatoes in the back of the kitchen, behind the garbage pails." He softly blows one swelling smoke ring and then, the miracle, makes his mouth as tiny and tight as a keyhole and puffs out a smaller ring which, spinning quickly, passes through the larger. At the moment of interpenetration both blur, and a loose cloud of smoke lengthens like an arm reaching for the light-cord. Dedman sighs, a bored creator.

"Rotten in the head at Yalta," Minor calls from far up the counter, "and Truman at Potsdam as dumb as they come. That man was so dumb his haberdashery store went bankrupt and the next minute he's running the United States of America."

The door bucks open, and the darkness on the porch materializes into a hard figure in a bullet cap. "Peter here?" it asks.

"Mr. Caldwell," Minor says in that basso he reserves for greeting adults. "Yes he is. He was just telling me he's an atheistic Communist."

"He just does that to kid you. You know that. There isn't a man in town he thinks more of than Minor Kretz. You're a father to that boy, and don't think his mother and I don't appreciate it."

"Hey Daddy," Peter calls, embarrassed for him.

Caldwell comes back toward the booths, blinking; he seems unable to find his son. He stops at Dedman's booth. "Who's this? Oh. Dedman. Haven't they got you graduated yet?"

"Hi there George," Dedman says. Caldwell does not expect much from his students but he does expect the dignity of formal address. Of course they sense this. Cruelty is clever where goodness is imbecile. "I hear your swimming team lost again. What does that make it? Eighty in a row?"

"They tried," Caldwell tells him. "If you don't have the cards, you can't manufacture 'em."

"Hey, *I* got some cards," Dedman says, his cheeks glowing ripely, his long lashes curled. "Look at my cards, George." He reaches into the pocket of his forest-green shirt for the pornographic deck.

"Put them away," Minor calls from far up in his runway. Electric light bleaches his skull and strikes cool sparks from the dried Coke glasses.

Caldwell does not seem to hear. He walks on to the booth where his son sits smoking a Kool. Giving no sign of seeing the cigarette, he slides in opposite Peter and says, "Jesus, a funny thing happened to me just now."

"What? How is the car?"

"The car, believe it or not, is fixed. I don't know how Hummel does it; he's what you call a master of his trade. He's treated me swell all my life." A new thought pricks him and he turns his head. "Dedman? You still here?"

Dedman has been holding his cards in his lap and fanning through them. He looks up, eyes bright. "Yeah?"

"Why don't you quit school and get a job with Hummel? As I remember, you're a natural mechanic."

The boy shrugs uncomfortably under this unexpected thrust of concern. He says, "I'm waiting for the war."

"You'll wait until Doomsday, kid," the teacher calls to him. "Don't bury your talent in the ground. Let your light shine. If I had your mechanical talent, this poor kid here would be eating caviar."

"I got a police record."

"So did Bing Crosby. So did St. Paul. They didn't let that stop 'em. Don't use it as a crutch. You talk to Al Hummel. I never had a better friend in this town, and I was in worse shape than you are. You're just eighteen; I was thirty-five."

Agitated, Peter takes a puff made hopelessly awkward by his father's presence and stubs out his Kool half-smoked. He yearns to divert his father from this conversation, which he knows Dedman in retelling will make into a joke. "Daddy, what was the funny thing?" He is overswept, as the smoke soaks his lungs with its mild poison, by a wave of distaste for all this mediocre, fruitless, cloying involvement. Somewhere there is a city where he will be free.

His father speaks so only he can hear. "I was walking through the hall ten minutes ago and Zimmerman's door bumps open and who the hell pops out but Mrs. Herzog."

"Well what's so funny about that? She's on the school board."

"I don't know if I should tell you this, but I guess you're old enough now; she looked loved up."

Peter giggles in surprise. "Loved up?" He laughs again and regrets having stubbed out his cigarette, which now seems priggish.

"There's a look women get. In their faces. She had it, until she saw me."

"But how? Was she wearing all her clothes?"

"Sure, but her hat looked crooked. And her lipstick had been smeared."

"Uh-oh."

"Uh-oh is right. It's something I wasn't meant to see."

"Well it's not your fault, you were just walking down the hall."

"That doesn't matter, it wasn't my fault; if that was the rule nothing is ever anybody's fault. The fact is, kid, I walked right into a nest of trouble, Zimmerman's been playing cat-and-mouse with me for fifteen years and this is the end of the line."

"Oh, Daddy. Your imagination is so fertile. She was probably in there consulting about something, you know Zimmerman makes appointments for all hours."

"You didn't see the look in her eyes when she saw me."

"Well what did you do?"

"I just give her the old sweet smile and keep going. But the cat is out of the bag and she knows it."

"Daddy, now let's be rational. Would she be capable of anything with Zimmerman? She's a middle-aged woman, isn't she?"

Peter wonders why his father smiles. Caldwell says, "She has a kind of name around town. She's a good ten years younger than Herzog; she didn't marry him until he'd made his pot."

"But Daddy, she has a *child* in the seventh grade." Peter is exasperated at his father's inability to see the obvious, that women who run for the school board are beyond sex, that sex is for adolescents. He does not know how to put this to his father delicately. Indeed, the juxtaposition of his father and this subject is so stressful that his tongue feels locked in the bind.

His father kneads his brown-spotted hands together so hard that the knuckles turn yellow. He moans, "I could feel Zimmerman sitting in there like a big heavy raincloud; I can feel him on my chest right now."

"Oh, *Daddy*," Peter snaps. "You're ridiculous. Why do you make such a mountain out of a molehill? Zimmerman doesn't even exist in the way you see him. He's just a slippery old fathead who likes to pat the girls."

His father looks up, cheeks slack, startled. "I wish I had your self-confidence, Peter," he says. "If I had your self-confidence I would've taken your mother onto the Burly-cue stage and you never would have been born." This is as close to a rebuke of his son as he ever came. The boy's cheeks burn. Caldwell says, "I better call her," and heaves himself up out of the booth. "I can't get it out of my head that Pop Kramer is going to fall down those stairs. If I live I'm determined to put up a bannister."

Peter follows him to the front of the luncheonette. "Minor," Caldwell asks, "would it break your heart if I asked you to break a ten-dollar bill?" As Minor takes the bill, Caldwell asks him, "When do you think the Russians will reach Olinger? They're probably getting on the trolley up at Ely now."

"Like son, like father, huh Minor?" Johnny Dedman calls from his booth.

"Is there any special way you want this?" Minor asks, displeased.

"A five, four ones, three quarters, two dimes, and a nickel." Caldwell goes on, "I hope they do come. It would be the best thing that happened to this town since the Indians left. They'd line us up against the wall of the post office and put us out of our misery, old bucks like you and me."

Minor doesn't want to hear it. He snorts so angrily that Caldwell asks in a high pained voice, his searching voice, "Well what do *you* think the answer is? We're all too dumb to die by ourselves."

As usual, he receives no answer. He accepts the change in silence and gives Peter the five.

"What's this for?"

"To eat on. Man is a mammal that must eat. We can't ask Minor to feed you for free, though he's gentleman enough to do it, I know he is."

"But where did you get it?"

"It's O. K."

By this Peter understands that his father has again borrowed from the school athletic funds that are placed in his trust. Peter understands nothing of his father's financial involvements except that they are confused and dangerous.

Once as a child, four years ago, he had a dream in which his father was called to account. Face ashen, his father, clad in only a cardboard grocery box beneath which his naked legs showed spindly and yellowish, staggered down the steps of the town hall while a crowd of Olingerites cursed and laughed and threw pulpy dark objects that struck the box with a deadened thump. In that way we have in dreams, where we are both author and character, God and Adam, Peter understood that inside the town hall there had been a trial. His father had been found guilty, stripped of everything he owned, flogged, and sent forth into the world lower than the hoboes. From his pallor plainly the disgrace would kill him. In his dream Peter shouted, "No! You don't understand! Wait!" The words came out in a child's voice. He tried to explain aloud to the angry townspeople how innocent his father was, how overworked, worried, conscientious, and anxious; but the legs of the crowd shoved and smothered him and he could not make his voice heard. He woke up with nothing explained. So now, in the luncheonette, it feels to him as if he is accepting a piece of his father's flayed skin and inserting it into his wallet to be spent on hamburgers, lemon Pepsis, the pinball machine, and Reese's Peanut Butter Cups whose chocolate is terrible for his psoriasis.

The pay phone is attached to the wall behind the comic book rack. With a nickel and a dime Caldwell places the call to Firetown. "Cassie? We're in the luncheonette . . . It's fixed. It was the driveshaft . . . He thinks about twenty bucks, he hadn't figured out the labor yet. Tell Pop Al asked about him. Pop hasn't fallen down the stairs yet, has he? . . . You know I didn't mean that, I hope he doesn't too . . . No, no I haven't, I haven't had a second, I gotta be at the dentist in five minutes . . . To tell the truth, Cassie, I'm scared to hear what he has to say . . . I know that . . . I know that . . . I'd guess around eleven. Have you run out of bread? I bought you an Italian sandwich last night and it's still sitting in the car . . . Hugh? He looks O. K., I just gave him five bucks so he can eat . . . I'll put him on."

Caldwell holds the receiver out to Peter. "Your mother wants to talk to you."

Peter resents that she should invade this way the luncheonette that was the center of his life apart from her. Her voice sounds tiny and stern, as if, in pinching her into this metal box, the telephone company has offended her feelings. The magnetic pull she exerts over him is transmitted through the wires, so that he too feels reduced in size.

"Hi," he says.

"How does he look to you, Peter?"

"Who?"

"*Who?* Why Daddy. Who else?"

"Kind of tired and excited, I can't tell. You know what a puzzle he is."

"Are you as worried as I am?"

"I guess so, sure."

"Why hasn't he called Doc Appleton back?"

"Maybe he doesn't think the X-rays are developed yet." Peter looks toward his father as if to be confirmed. The man is engaging in some elaborate apologetic exchange with Minor: ". . . didn't mean to be sarcastic a minute ago about the Communists, I hate 'em as much as you do, Minor . . ."

The telephone overhears and asks, "Who's he talking to?"

"Minor Kretz."

"He's just fascinated by that kind of man, isn't he?" the miniature female voice bitterly remarks in Peter's ear.

"They're talking about the Russians."

A kind of cough ticks in the receiver and Peter knows his mother has started crying. His stomach sinks. He casts about for something to say, and his eye like a fly lights on one of the trick turds of painted plaster among the novelties. "How's the dog?" he asks.

His mother's breathing struggles for self-control. In the intervals of her crying jags her voice becomes oddly composed and stony. "She was in the house all this morning and I finally let her run after lunch. When she came back she had been after another skunk. Pop's so mad at me he won't come out of his room. With no bread in the house, his temper is running short."

"Do you think Lady killed the skunk?"

"I think so. She was laughing."

"Daddy says he's going to the dentist."

"Yes. Now that it's too late." Another wave of silent tears spreads into Peter's ear; his brain is flooded with the image of how his mother's eyes would be, red-rimmed and ponderous with water. A faint grainy smell, of grass or corn, affects his nose.

"I don't think it's necessarily too late," he says. It is pompous and insincere but he is compelled to say something. All the telephone numbers teenagers have pencilled on the wall above the phone begin to swap and swirl under his eyes.

His mother sighs. "Yes, I suppose. Peter."

"Yeah?"

"Take care of your father now."

"I'll try. It's hard though."

"Isn't it? But he loves you so."

"O.K., I'll try. Do you want him back?"

"No." She pauses, and then, with that theatrical talent for holding the stage that perhaps is the germ of sense in his father's fantasy about putting her in vaudeville, she repeats with tremulous import, "No."

"O.K., we'll see you around eleven then." His mother's mind, shorn of her comforting body, is keenly exhausting to Peter. She senses this, and sounds even more hurt, more remote, more miniature and stony. "The weatherman wants snow."

"Yeah, the air kind of feels like it."

"All right. All right, Peter. Hang up on your poor old mother. You're a good boy. Don't worry about anything."

"O.K., don't you either. You're a good woman." What a thing to say to your own mother! He hangs up, amazed at himself. It makes his scabs itch, the peculiarity of talking to her over the phone, where she becomes, incestuously, a simply female voice with whom he has shared secrets.

"Did she sound upset?" his father asks him.

"A little. I think Pop's throwing an atmosphere."

"That man can throw 'em, too." Caldwell turns and explains to Minor. "This is my father-in-law. He's eighty-four and he can throw an atmosphere that knocks you out of your shoes. He can throw an atmosphere right through a keyhole in a door. That man has more power in his little finger than you and I have from our bellies up."

"Arrh," Minor grunts softly, setting on the counter a suds-topped glass of milk. Caldwell drains it in two gulps, puts it down, winces, turns a shade paler, and bites back a belch. "Boy," he said, "that milk took a wrong turn down there somewhere." He still tends to pronounce "milk" "melk," New Jersey style. He runs his tongue back and forth across his front teeth as if to clean them. "Now I'm off to Dr. Yankem."

Peter asks, "Shall I go with you?" The dentist's real name is Kenneth Schreuer and his office is two blocks down the pike, beyond the high school on the other side, opposite the tennis courts. Schreuer always has a soap opera going on the radio, from nine in the morning to six at night. On Wednesdays and Sundays from spring to fall he walks across the trolley tracks in white ducks and becomes one of the county's better tennis players. He is a better tennis player than he is a dentist. His mother works in the school cafeteria.

"No, hell," Caldwell says. "What can you do, Peter? The damage is done. Don't worry about this old heap of junk. Stay here where it's warm and you have friends."

So Peter's first piece of work in carrying out his mother's injunction to take care of his father is to watch the suffering man, his coat unbuttoned and too short and his knit bullet cap pulled down over his ears, head out the dark door alone into one more doom.

Johnny Dedman calls from his booth, sincerely, "Hey Peter. With you and your father standing up there against the light for a second I couldn't tell which was which."

"He's taller," Peter says curtly. Dedman as a sincere good boy doesn't interest him. He feels in himself with the coming of night great sweet stores of wickedness ripen. He turns, pivoting on the weight of the five dollars at his hip, and tells Minor triumphantly, "Two hamburgers. No ketchup. And a glass of your watered milk and five nickels for your rigged pinball machine." He goes back to his booth and relights the Kool he had stubbed out half-smoked. Polar ice thrills his proud throat; he preens on the empty stage of Minor's place positive that all the eyes in the world are watching. The stretch of necessarily idle time ahead of him, a child's dream of freedom, so exalts his heart it beats twice as fast and threatens to burst, tinting the dim air rose. *Forgive me.*

"Darling. Wait?"

"Mm?"

"Isn't there some better place than your office?"

"No. Not in winter."

"But we've been seen."

"You've been seen."

"But he knew. I could tell by his face that he knew. He looked as frightened as I felt."

"Caldwell knows and yet he doesn't know."

"But do you trust him?"

"The matter of trust has never come up between us."

"But now?"

"I trust him."

"I don't think you should. Couldn't we fire him?"

He laughs richly, disconcerting her. She is customarily slow to see her own humor. He says, "You overestimate my omnipotence. This man has been teaching for fifteen years. He has friends. He has tenure."

"But he really *is* incompetent, isn't he?"

It disagrees with him, makes an uncongenial texture, when she turns argumentative and inquisitive in his embrace. The stupidity of women has a wonderfully fresh power to disappoint him.

"Is he? Competence is not so easy to define. He stays in the room with them, which is the most important thing. Furthermore, he's faithful to me. He's faithful."

"Why are you sticking up for him? He could destroy us both now."

He laughs again. "Come, come, my little bird. Human beings are harder to destroy than that." Though her turns of anxiety are sometimes disagreeable, her physical presence profoundly relaxes him, and in his condition of innermost rest words seem to slip from him without trouble of thought, as liquid slips from high to low, as gas spins into the void.

She becomes vehement and angular in his arms. "I don't like that man. I don't like his smirky childish look."

"His face makes you feel guilty."

This surprising remark turns her inquisitiveness tender. "Should we feel guilty?" The question is actually shy.

"Absolutely. Afterwards."

This makes her smile, and her smiling makes her mouth soft, and in kissing her he feels he is coming at last to a small sip after an interminable thirst. That the kissing does not quench the thirst, but quickens it, so that each kiss demands a more intense successor and involves him thereby in a vortex of mounting and widening appetite—that such is the case does not seem to him a cruel but, rather, a typically generous and compelling providence of Nature.

A tree of pain takes root in his jaw. Wait, wait! Kenny should have waited a few minutes more on the Novocain. But this is the end of the day, the boy is tired and hurried. Kenny had been one of Caldwell's first students, back in the Thirties. Now this same boy, badly balding, braces one knee against the arm of the chair to win more leverage for the pliers which are grinding around the tooth and crushing it like chalk even as they try to twist it free. Caldwell's fear is that the tooth will crumble between the pliers and remain in his

head as a stripped and scraped nerve. Truly, the pain is
unprecedented: an entire tree rich with bloom, each bloom
showering into the livid blue air a coruscation of lucid lime-
green sparks. He opens his eyes in disbelief that this could go
on and on, and his horizon is filled with the dim pink of the
dentist's determined mouth, odorous of cloves, the lips
pressed together a bit lopsidedly: a weak mouth. The kid had
tried to become an M.D. but hadn't had the I.Q. so he had
settled on being a butcher. Caldwell recognizes the pain
branching in his head as a consequence of some failing in
his own teaching, a failure somewhere to inculcate in this
struggling soul consideration and patience; and accepts it as
such. The tree becomes ideally dense; its branches and
blooms compound into one silver plume, cone, column of
pain, a column whose height towers heavenward from a base
in which Caldwell's skull is embedded. It is pure shrill silver
with not a breath, not a jot, speck, fleck of alloy in it.

"There." Kenneth Schreuer exhales with relief. His hands
are trembling, his back is damp. He displays to Caldwell
their prize in his pliers. As if emerging swollen from a dream,
Caldwell with difficulty focuses. It is a little dull crumb of
ivory, dappled brown and black, mounted on soft pink bow
legs. It seems preposterously trivial to have resisted removal
so furiously.

"Spit," the dentist says.

Obediently Caldwell bends his face to the yellow basin,
and a gush of blood joins the filmy swirl of clear water spinning there. The blood seems orangish and muddied with
spittle. The sense of his head being pure silver yields to an
airy giddiness. Fright and pressure flee through the gap in his
gum. Abruptly he feels absurdly grateful for all created
things, for the clean gleaming rounded lip of the circular
enamel basin, for the bright little bent pipe shooting water
into it, for the little comet-tail-shaped smear of rust this
miniature Charybdis had worn down the section of the vortex where its momentum expires; grateful for the delicate
dental smells, for the sounds of Kenny restoring his tools
to the sterilizer bath, for the radio on the shelf filtering a
shudder of organ music through its static. The announcer in-
tones, "I-Love-a-Mystery!" and the organ swirls forward
again, ecstatic.

"It's a shame," Kenny says, "the caps of your teeth aren't
as strong as the roots."

"That's the story of my life," Caldwell says. "Big feet,

weak head." His tongue in enunciating encounters a bubbly softness. He spits again. Strange to say, he finds the sight of his blood cheering.

With a steel tool Kenny picks at the pulled tooth, now severed forever from its earthly connection and somewhat starlike held high above the floor. Kenny gouges out a chip of black filling and puts the pick to his nostrils and sniffs. "Mm," he says, "yes. Hopeless. This must have been giving you a good deal of pain."

"Only when I noticed it."

On the radio, the announcer explains, "We last left Doc and Reggie trapped in the great subterranean metropolis of monkeys [*sound of monkeys chattering, yipping, cooing sadly*] and now Doc turns to [*fade*] Reggie and says . . ." *Doc:* "We gotta get out of here! The Princess is waiting!" *Cheepy cheep. Birrup, birrrooo.*

Kenny gives Caldwell two tablets of Anacin in a cellophane jacket. "There may be some discomfort," he says, "when the Novocain wears off." *It never wore on,* Caldwell thinks. Preparing to leave, he spits for the last time into the basin. Already the flow of his blood is slowing and thinning and yellowing. He timidly touches his tongue to the place where a slippery crater now is. A vague numb sense of loss afflicts him. Another day, another molar. (He should be writing Valentines.)

Here comes Heller down the annex hall! Twiddle, piddle; piddle, pat!! How the man does love his own broad broom!!!

Past the girl's lavatory he painstakingly goes, strewing red wax and sweeping up the same in the shimmer of varnish, past Room 113 where Art the visible mirror of God's invisible glory is held up by Miss Schrack, past 111 where typewriters lurk under tattered black shrouds through which here and there a space bar thrusts an eerie silver hand, past 109 with its great brittle ochre map of the old trade routes whereby spice, amber, fur, and slaves were transported across Carolingian Europe, past 107 smelling of sulphur dioxide and hydrogen sulphide, 105, 103, doors all shut, glass frosted, facing green lockers that dwindle to an insane perspective of zero, Heller goes, gathering under the methodical push of his broom buttons, fluff, pennies, lint, tinfoil, hairpins, cellophane, hair, thread, tangerine seeds, comb teeth, Peter Caldwell's psoriasis scratchings, and all the undignifiable flecks and flakes and bits and motes and whatnot dust that go to make up a universe: he harvests these. He hums inaudibly an old tune to himself. He is happy. The school is his. Clocks all over the wooden acres tick in unison 6:10. In its subterranean mansion one of the vast boilers makes an irrevocable decision and swallows in a single draft a quarter-ton of hard pea coal: Pennsylvania anthracite, old Lepidodendra, pure compressed time. The furnace heart burns with a white heat that must be viewed through a mica peephole.

Heller hugs to his rusty heart the underside of this high school. It was the promotion of his life when he was lifted from the custodial staff of the elementary building, where the little children, ticklish-tummied as lambs, daily made a puddle or two of rancid vomit to wipe up and perfume with sal ammoniac. Here there was no such indignity; only the words on the walls and now and then a malicious excremental mess in one of the male lavatories.

The memory of people and people's clothes touches the halls with a dry perfume. The drinking fountains wait to spurt. The radiators purr. The side door slams; a member of the JV basketball team has entered with his gym bag and gone down to the locker room. At the front entrance, Mr. Caldwell and Mr. Phillips meet on the steps and enact, one tall and one short, an Alphonse and Gaston routine as to who is to go in the door first. Heller stoops and sweeps into his broad pan his gray mountain of dust and fluff, enlivened by a few paper scraps. He transfers this dirt to the great cardboard can waiting at this corner. Then, setting himself behind the broom, he pushes off and disappears behind the corner, piddle, pat.

There he goes!!!!

"George, I hear you haven't been feeling too well," Phillips says to the other teacher. In the light of the hall in front of the trophy case he is startled to observe a trickle of blood leaking from the corner of Caldwell's mouth. There is usually some imperfection or oversight of grooming about the other man that secretly distresses him.

"Sometimes up, sometimes down," Caldwell says. "Phil, a strip of missing tickets has been preying on my mind. Numbers 18001 to 18145."

Phillips thinks and as he thinks takes—his habit—a jerky sidestep, as if smoothing the infield. "Well, it's just paper," he says.

"So's money," Caldwell says.

He looks so sick in saying it that Phillips asks, "Have you been taking anything?"

Caldwell makes his pinched stoic mouth. "I'll be O.K., Phil. I went to the doctor yesterday and an X-ray's been taken."

Phillips sidesteps the other way. "Show anything?" he asks, looking at his shoes, as if to check the laces.

As if to drown out the implications of Phillips' extraordinary softness of voice, Caldwell virtually bellows, "I haven't found out yet. I've been on the go steadily."

' George. May I speak as a friend?"

"Go ahead, I've never heard you speak any other way."

"There's one thing you haven't learned, and that's how to take care of yourself. You know now, we're not as young as we were before the war; we mustn't act like young men."

"Phil, I don't know any other way to act. I'll have to act childish until they put the half-dollars over my eyes."

Phillips' laugh is a shade nervous. He had been a year on the faculty when Caldwell joined it, and though they have been through much together Phillips has never quite shaken his sense of being the other man's senior and guide. At the same time he cannot rid himself of an obscure expectation that Caldwell out of his more chaotic and mischievous resources would produce a marvel, or at least say the strange thing that had to be said. He asks, "Did you hear about Ache?"—pronounced Ockey. A bright and respectful and athletic and handsome student from the late Thirties, the kind that does a teacher's heart good, a kind once plentiful in Olinger but in the universal decay of virtue growing rare.

"Killed," Caldwell says. "But I don't understand how."

"Over Nevada," Phillips tells him, shifting his armload of papers and books to the other arm. "He was a flight instructor, and his student made a mistake. Both killed."

"Isn't that funny? To go all through the war without a scratch and then get nailed in peacetime."

Phillips' eyes have a morbid trick—little men are more emotional—of going red in the middle of a conversation if the subject were even remotely melancholy. "I hate it when they die young," he blurts. He loves the well-coördinated among his students like sons, his own son being clumsy and stubborn.

Caldwell becomes interested; his friend's neat centrally

parted cap of hair suddenly seems the lid of a casket in which might be locked the nugget of information he so needs. He asks earnestly, "Do you think it makes a difference? Are they less ready? Do you feel ready?"

Phillips tries to direct his mind to the question but it is like trying to press the like poles of two magnets together. They push away. "I don't know," he admits. "They say there's a time for everything," he adds.

"Not for me," Caldwell says. "I'm not ready and it scares the hell out of me. What's the answer?"

There is silence between the two men while Heller passes with his broom. The janitor nods and smiles and passes them by this time.

Again, Phillips cannot bring his mind to touch the issue squarely; it keeps shying gratefully into side issues. He stares intently at the center of Caldwell's chest, as if a curious transition is taking place here. "Have you spoken to Zimmerman?" he asks. "Perhaps a sabbatical is the answer."

"I can't afford a sabbatical. What would the kid do? He couldn't even get to high school. He'd have to go to school in the sticks with a lot of clodhoppers on the bus."

"He'd survive, George."

"I doubt it like hell. He needs me to keep him going, the poor kid doesn't have a clue yet. I can't fade out before he has the clue. You're lucky, your kid has the clue."

This is a sad piece of flattery that makes Phillips shake his head. The rims of his eyes deepen in tint. Ronnie Phillips, now a freshman at Penn State, is brilliant in electronics. But even while in the high school he openly ridiculed his father's love of baseball. He bitterly felt that too many of the precious hours of his childhood had been wasted playing cat and three-stops-or-a-catch under his father's urging.

Phillips says weakly, "Ronnie seems to know what he wants."

"More power to him," Caldwell shouts. "My poor kid, what he wants is the whole world in a candy box."

"I thought he wanted to paint."

"Ooh." Caldwell grunts; the poison has wormed an inch deeper into his bowels. Sons are a heavy subject for these two.

Caldwell changes the subject. "Coming out of my room today I had a kind of revelation; it's taken me fifteen years of teaching to see it."

Phillips asks quickly "What?", eager to know, for all the times he has been fooled.

"Ignorance is bliss," Caldwell states. Seeing no light of welcome dawn on his friend's hopefully wrinkled face, he repeats it louder, so it echoes down the empty diminishing hall. "Ignorance is bliss. That's the lesson I've gotten out of life."

"God help us, you may be right," Phillips fussily exclaims, and makes as if to move toward his room. But for a minute longer the two teachers stand together in the hall, finding a measure of repose in familiar company, and some ambiguous warmth in the sense of having failed each other without blaming each other. So two steeds in the same pen huddle through a storm. If men were horses, Caldwell would have been the drudging dappled type, somewhat anonymous but not necessarily ill-bred, known as a "big gray," and Phillips a gallant little Morgan, chestnut, with a prissy tail and nicely polished hooves—practically a pony.

Caldwell has a last thought. "My old man went and died before he was my age," he says, "and I didn't want to doublecross my own kid like that." With a yank that makes the legs chatter and screech, he pulls a small oak table, much gnawed, from its place against the wall; from off this table basketball tickets are to be sold.

A panicked shout wells in the auditorium and lifts dust in the most remote rooms of the extensive school even while paying customers still stream through the entrance and down the glaring hall. Adolescent boys as hideous and various as gargoyles, the lobes of their ears purple with the cold, press, eyes popping, mouths flapping, under the glowing overhead globes. Girls, rosy-cheeked, glad, motley and mostly ill-made, like vases turned by a preoccupied potter, are embedded, plaid-swaddled, in the hot push. Menacing, odorous, blind, the throng gives off a muted shuffling thunder, a flickeringly articulate tinkle: the voices of the young.

"So I said, 'That's *your* tough luck, buddy boy.' "

"♪ I hear you knockin' but you can't come in ♪"

"I thought it was real doggy."

"The bitch rolled over and, no shit, said, 'Again.' "

"Use common sense. How can one infinity be larger than another?"

"Who says he says, that's what I'd like to know."

"You can tell with her, because there's this little birthmark on the side of her neck that gets red."

"He's his own best lover if you ask me."

"Box lunch—*sluurrp!*"

"I'll put it this way to you: infinity equals infinity. Right?"

"So then I heard that *she* said, so I said to him, 'I don't know what's going on, I guess.'"

"If he can't stop it, he shouldn't have started it."

"His mouth just dropped. Literally dropped."

"When did it all happen, ages ago?"

"But if you take only every *odd* number that exists and add them up, you still get infinity, don't you? Do you follow *that* much?"

"Was this at the one in Pottsville?"

"♪ I'm in my nightie and it's awful thi-in ♪"

"'Tough *luck?*' he said, and I said, 'Yes. Yours.'"

"Finally," Peter calls to Penny as she comes down the auditorium aisle and sees him. She is alone, he has a girl, she is alone, his girl has come to him alone: through the circuit of such simple thoughts his heart spins. He calls to her, "I saved you a seat." He sits in the middle of the row; the seat he has saved for her is piled high with other students' coats and scarves. Herolike, she swims the strait between them, pursing her complacent mouth impatiently, making others rise from their seats to let her by, laughing as she nearly tumbles on an obtruded foot. While the coats are removed from her seat, Peter and Penny are pressed together, he having half-risen. Their knees interlock awkwardly; he playfully blows and the hair above her ears lifts. She seems, the skin of her face and throat a luminous stillness in the midst of hubbub and thumping, delicious to him, edible, succulent. Her smallness makes this succulence. She is small enough for him to lift: this thought makes him himself lift, in secrecy. The last coat is removed and they settle side by side in the happy heat and chaos.

The players, exulting in all the space reserved for them, gallop back and forth on their plain of varnished boards. The ball arches high but not so high as the caged bulbs burning on the auditorium ceiling. A whistle blows. The clock stops. The cheerleaders rush out, the maroon O's on their yellow sweaters bobbling, and form a locomotive. "*O*," they call, seven brazen sirens, their linked forearms forming a single piston.

"Ohh," moans back Echo, stricken.

"*L*."

"Hell," is the answer, deliberately aitched, a school tradition.

"*I.*"

"Aaiii," a cry from the depths. Peter's scalp goes cold and under the cover of a certain actual ecstasy he grips his girl's arm.

"Hi," she says, pleased, her skin still chilly from the out-of-doors.

"*N.*"

The response comes faster, "Enn," and the cheer whirls faster and faster, a vortex between the crowd and the cheerleaders, until at its climax it seems they are all sucked down into another kingdom, "Olinger! *Olinger!* OLINGER!" The girls scamper back, play resumes, and the auditorium, big as it is, subsides into a living-room where everybody knows everybody else. Peter and Penny chat.

"I'm so glad you came," he says. "It surprises me, how glad I am."

"Why thank you," Penny says dryly. "How's your father?"

"Frantic. We didn't even get home last night. The car broke down."

"Poor Peter."

"No, I kind of enjoyed it."

"Do you shave?"

"No. Should I? Am I ready?"

"No; but it looks like a bit of dried shaving cream in your ear."

"You know what that is?"

"What? Is it something?"

"It's my secret. You didn't know I had a secret."

"Everybody has secrets."

"But mine is very special."

"What is it?"

"I can't tell you. I'll have to show you."

"Peter, aren't you funny?"

"Would you rather I didn't? Are you frightened?"

"No. You don't frighten me."

"Good. You don't frighten me, either."

She laughs. "Nobody frightens you."

"Now there you're wrong. Everybody frightens me."

"Your father even?"

"Oh, he's very frightening."

"When will you show me your secret?"

"Maybe I won't. It's too horrible."

"Peter, please do. Please."

"Listen."

"What?"

"I like you." He cannot quite say "love"; it might prove unfair.

"I like you."

"You won't."

"Yes I will. Are you just being silly?"

"Partly. I'll show you at the half. If I keep my nerve."

"You *do* frighten me now."

"Don't let me. Hey. You have such beautiful skin."

"You always say that. Why? It's just skin." He can't answer and she pulls her arm away from being stroked. "Let's watch the game. Who's ahead?"

He looks up at the new combination clock and electric scoreboard, Gift of the Class of 1936. "They are."

She shouts, a regular lipsticked little fury suddenly, "Come *on.*" The JVs, five in Olinger's maroon and gold and five in West Alton's blue and white, looked dazed and alert at once, glued by the soles of their sneakers to tinted echoes of themselves inverted in floorshine. Every shoelace, every hair, every grimace of concentration, seems unnaturally sharp, like the details of stuffed animals in a large lit case. Indeed there is a psychological pane of glass between the basketball floor and the ramp of seats; though a player can look up and spot in the crowd a girl he entered last night (her whimper, the dryness in the mouth afterwards), she is infinitely remote from him, and the event in the parked car quite possibly was imagined. Mark Youngerman with his fuzzy forearm blots sweat from his eyebrows, sees the ball sailing toward him, lifts cupped hands and cushions the tense seamed globe against his chest, flicks his head deceptively, drives in past the West Alton defender, and in a rapt moment of flight drops the peeper. The score is tied. Such a shout goes up as suggests every soul here hangs on the edge of terror.

Caldwell is tidying up the ticket receipts as Phillips tiptoes to him and says, "George. You mentioned a missing strip."

"One eight oh oh one to eight one four five."

"I think I've placed their whereabouts."

"Jesus, that would be a load off my mind if you had."

"I believe Louis has them."

"Zimmerman? What in hell is he stealing tickets for?"

"Shh." Phillips glances with an eloquent twist of his mouth

in the direction of the supervising principal's office. In him, conspiracy becomes a species of dandyism. "You know he's the older boys' teacher up at the Reformed Sunday School."

"Sure. They swear by him up there."

"And did you notice Reverend March coming in tonight?"

"Yeah, I waved him through. I wouldn't take his money."

"That was right. The reason he's here, about forty of the Sunday School were given free tickets and came to the game in a group. I went up to him and suggested he sit on the stage, but he said no he thought he'd be better off standing at the rear of the auditorium and keep an eye out; about half the boys come from up in Ely, where they don't have a Reformed Church."

Vera Hummel, hey, comes through the entrance. Her long yellow coat swings unbuttoned, her bun of red hair is breaking loose from its pins; has she been running? She smiles at Caldwell and nods at Phillips; Phillips is one little biddy she could never warm to. Caldwell is another matter; he brings out what might be, for all she knows, her maternal instinct. Any tall man is automatically on her good side; she is that simple. Contrariwise a man shorter than herself seems to her to be offensive. Caldwell amiably lifts one of his wart-freckled hands in greeting; the sight of her does him no harm. As long as Mrs. Hummel is on the premises he feels the school is not entirely given over to animals. She has a mature tomboy's figure: shallow-breasted, long-legged, with something expressive and even anxious about the narrow length of her freckled wrists and forearms. The primeval female massiveness is limited to her hips and thighs; these thighs, swinging oval and alabaster from a blue gym-suit, show to fair advantage among her girls. There is a bloom that succeeds the first bloom, and then a bloom upon that. Human biology, up to a point, is not impatient. Still she remains childless. The small triangular forehead framed between two copper wings seems vexed; her nose is a fraction long and a touch pointed; there is a bit of the ferret about her face, and when she grins, gums engagingly slip into sight.

Caldwell calls to her, "Did you have a game today?" She coaches the girls' basketball team.

"Just got back," she says, not entirely halting. "We were humiliated. I just gave Al his supper and I thought I'd come see what the boys could do."

She is gone up the hall, toward the rear of the auditorium. "That woman certainly loves basketball," Caldwell says.

"Al works too long hours," Phillips says, more darkly. "She gets bored."

"She's cheerful-looking, though, and when you get to my state, that's all that matters."

"George, your health worries me."

"The Lord loves a cheerful corpse," Caldwell says, rudely exuberant, and asks boldly, "Now what's the secret about these tickets?"

"It's not an actual secret. Reverend March told me that Louis suggested that as an incentive to regular Sunday-school attendance a half-way prize be given, for perfect attendance up to the first of the year."

"So he sneaks in and swipes my basketball tickets."

"Not so loud. They're not your tickets, George. They're the school's tickets."

"Well I'm the poor horse's neck who has to account for them."

"It's just paper, look at it that way. Mark it 'Charity' in your books. I'll back you up if it's ever questioned."

"Did you ask Zimmerman what happened to the other hundred? You said forty kids came. He can't give away the other hundred, next thing every four-year-old in the Reformed nursery will come crawling through that door with a free ticket."

"George, I know you're upset. But there's nothing to be gained in exaggeration. I haven't spoken to him and I don't see that anything would be gained. Make a note for charity and we'll consider the matter closed. Louis tends to be high-handed, I know; but it's for a good cause."

Secure in his knowledge that his friend's prudent advice must be taken, Caldwell indulges in a final verbal expenditure. "Those tickets represent ninety dollars of theoretical money; I resent like hell handing them over to the dear old Reformed Sunday School." He means it. Olinger is, except for a few marginal sects like the Jehovah's Witnesses and the Baptists and the Roman Catholics, divided in friendly rivalry between the Lutherans and the Reformeds, the Lutherans having an advantage of numbers and the Reformeds an advantage of wealth. Born a Presbyterian, Caldwell became in the Depression a Lutheran like his wife, and, surprisingly in one so tolerant, sincerely distrusts the Reformeds, whom he associates with Zimmerman and Calvin, whom he associates with everything murky and oppressive and arbitrary in the universal kingdom.

Vera enters the back of the auditorium by one of the broad doors that are propped open on little rubber-footed legs which unhinge at a kick from snug brass fittings. She sees that Reverend March is over toward the corner, leaning against the stack of folding chairs that for assemblies and stage plays and P.T.A. meetings are unfolded and arranged on the flat area which is now the basketball court. Several boys, legs dangling in dungarees, perch illegally on top of this stack, and through this back area men and boys and one or two girls are standing, craning to see over one another's shoulders, some standing on chairs set between the open doors. Two men in their middle twenties greet Vera shyly and stand aside to make room for her. She is known to them but they are forgotten by her. They are ex-heroes of the type who, for many years, until a wife or ritual drunkenness or distant employment carries them off, continue to appear at high school athletic events, like dogs tormented by a site where they imagine they have buried something precious. Increasingly old and slack, the apparition of them persists, conjured by that phantasmal procession—indoors and outdoors, fall, winter, and spring—of increasingly young and unknown high school athletes who themselves, imperceptibly, filter in behind them to watch also. Their bearing, hushed and hurt, contrasts decisively with that of the students in the slope of seats; here skins and hair and ribbons and flashy clothes make a single fabric, a billowing, twinkling human pennant. Vera squints and the crowd dissolves into oscillating atoms of color. Apparently polarized by the jiggling event before them, in fact these dots agitate sideways, toward one another, aimed by secret arrow-shaped seeds. Sensing this makes Vera proud and serene and competent. For a long time she does not deign a hint of a sideways glance in the direction of Reverend March, who for his part has been rendered rapt by the gold and copper bits of her that glitter through the intervening jostle of bodies and arrive, chinking, at his eyes.

This minister is a tall and handsome man with a bony brown face and a crisp black mustache fastidiously shaped. The war made him. In 1939 he was a tender, small-boned graduate, not quite twenty-five, of a coal regions seminary. He felt effeminate and enfeebled by doubts. Theology had given his doubts shape and depth. In retrospect the religiosity that had prompted his vocation seemed, insofar as it was not sheerly his mother's will, a sickly phosphorescence exuded by sexual uncertainty. His tinny voice mocked his prevaricating sermons with squeakings. He feared his deacons and despised his message. In 1941 war rescued him. He enlisted, not as a chaplain but as a fighting man. By this path he hoped to escape questions he could not answer. So it proved. He crossed water and the furies could not follow. They made him a lieutenant. In North Africa he kept himself and five others alive on three canteens of water for seven days. At Anzio a shell blasted a crater eight feet wide on the spot he had darted from thirty seconds before. In the hills above Rome, they made him a captain. Peace found him unscratched. His voice alone had resisted tempering. He returned, absurdly, to his mild vocation. Was it absurd? No! He discovered, scraping away the rubble, his mother's faith, baked by the heat to an enduring hardness, strange of shape but undeniable, like a splash of cooled slag. He was alive. Life is a hell but a glorious hell. Give God this glory. Though March's voice is still small his silences are grand. His eyes are black as coals set in the sharp brown cheekbones; he carries like a scar the mustache which he left of the beard of battle. With his sense of uniform he retains the Roman collar whenever he appears in public. To Vera, approaching secretly through the hall beyond the open doors, his backwards collar seems so romantic her breath is suspended: a knife of pure white, a slice of the absolute is dangerously poised at his throat.

"Your prayers were not with me this afternoon," she breathes, breathless.

"Hello! Were your girls beaten?"

"Mm." Already she pretends, and indeed slightly feels, some boredom. She gazes toward the game and makes the golden leaves of her coat swirl with her hands in the pockets.

"Do you always attend boys' games?"

"Shouldn't I? To learn things? Did you play basketball?"

"No, I was extremely inept as an adolescent. I was always picked last."

"It's hard to believe."

"That's the mark of a great truth."

She winces at this edge of evangelism in him, and sighs heavily, explaining, as if in response to an impatient insistence of his, "the fact is, if you teach here a while you get so you can't stay out of the building. It's an occupational disease. If the school is lit, you wander over."

"You live so close."

"Mm." His voice disappoints her. She wonders if it is a natural law, that men the proper size must have inadequate voices. Must she always, in some tiny facet of every encounter, be disappointed? In revenge, she teases him with, "You've changed since you were always picked last."

He laughs curtly, baring his quick tobaccoish teeth in an instant, as if a longer laugh would betray his position: a captain's laugh. "The last shall be first," he says.

This a little bewilders her, ignorant of the allusion yet aware, from the satisfied tension of his tan chiselled lips, that it is one. She gazes past his shoulder and, as always when threatened by the possibility that she is stupid, lets her eyes go out of focus, knowing that this renders more profound their sable beauty. "Why—?" She stops her lips. "I won't ask."

"Ask what?"

"Never mind. I forgot who I was talking to."

"No, please. Ask, and ye shall receive." He hopes that by sprinkling the salt of blasphemy on her tail he can hold her here, this golden dove, this sandy sparrow. He suspects she was going to ask him why he had not married. A difficult question; he has sometimes searched for the answer. Perhaps it was that war displays women unflatteringly. Their price goes down, and it is discovered that they will sell for any price—a candy bar, a night's sleep. Their value is not present to themselves, but is given to them by men. Having been forced to perceive this makes one slow to buy. But this would not be an answer that could be spoken.

In truth this was the question on her mind. Was he some kind of nance? She distrusts all ministers and men too well groomed. He is both. She asks, "Why are you here tonight? I've never seen you at a game before, you only ever come here to bless an assembly."

"I came," he answers, "to shepherd forty pagan brutes from my Sunday school. For some reason I never understood, Zimmerman showered basketball tickets like manna all over them last Sunday."

She laughs. "But why?" Anything that diminishes Zimmerman makes her heart gush gratefully.

"Why?" His raven eyebrows lift in two shapely arcs above his rounded eyes whose irises, full in the light, are not black but a fleckish dark gray, as if the jelly were veiling gunpowder. This sense of danger, of dreadful things he has seen, excites her. Her breasts seem to float on her ribs warmly; she suppresses an instinct to bring her hands to them. Her wet lips are framed to release laughter even before his jokes, indignant questions, are out. "Why does anything like this happen to me?" he sternly asks, slightly pop-eyed. "Why do all the ladies of my parish bake cupcakes once a month and sell them to each other? Why does the town drunk keep calling me on the telephone? Why do these people keep showing up in fancy hats on Sunday morning to hear me prattle about an old book?" Successful beyond his expectations, the warm swirl of her laughter lifting him deliciously, he goes on and on in this vein, much as a foolhardy full-blooded Sioux in his outfit used to war-dance around the spot where a land mine had been marked as buried. Though his faith is intact and as infrangible as metal, it is also like metal dead. Though he can go and pick it up and test its weight whenever he wishes, it has no arms with which to reach and restrain him. He mocks it.

And Vera for her part is delighted to have elicited this; it seems like an accelerated sequence in an old silent movie, this sketch he draws of the church as an empty house where people keep calling and nodding politely and saying "Thank you" as if the host were there. The bubbles tumble from her stomach to her lungs and explode, iridescent, in her glad throat; truly, this is all she asks of a man, all she requires, that he have the power to make her laugh. In laughter her girlhood, her virginity is reborn. Her mouth, outlined in the cerise rim of lipstick that has not rubbed off, stretches to let her gladness out; her gums show, her face, flushed, becomes numbingly vivid, a Gorgon's head of beauty, of life. A dungareed boy on top of the stack, riding on this rickety raft the ocean of tumult, looks over the edge to find the source of this new noise. He sees below him a head of red hair like a monstrous orange fish sink with a loose twist of one shimmering coil against the horizontal slats of stained wood. Weak with laughter, Vera has lurched and leans her limp weight back. The minister's flecked eyes melt and his crisp lips pucker bashfully, puzzled. He leans back to join her; an irregularity in the stack makes a ledge the height of a mantel where with a remnant of his captain's composure he props his elbows. His body thus shields her from the mass of the crowd; a bower has been made.

. . . *and he upon thy lap oft flings himself back, conquered by the eternal wound of love; and then pillowing his shapely neck* (tereti cervice) *upon thee and looking up he feeds with love his greedy eyes, gazing wistfully towards thee* (inhians

in te, dea), *while, as he lies back, his breath hangs upon
thy lips.*

The JV game is over. Though Mark Youngerman's face is
purple, his panting painful, and his body as slippery as an amphibian's, Olinger lost. The buzz of the crowd changes pitch.
Many leave their seats. Those who step outside discover that
it is snowing. This discovery is ever surprising, that Heaven
can so prettily condescend. Snow puts us with Jupiter Pluvius
among the clouds. What a crowd! What a crowd of tiny flakes
sputters downward in the sallow realm of the light above the
entrance door! Atoms and atoms and atoms and atoms. A
furry inch already carpets the steps. The cars on the pike
travel slower, windshield wipers flapping, headlight beams
nipped and spangled in the ceaseless flurry. The snow seems
only to exist where light strikes it. A trolley car gliding
toward Alton appears to trail behind it a following of slowly
falling fireflies. What an eloquent silence reigns! Olinger
under the vast violet dome of the stormstruck night sky becomes yet one more Bethlehem. Behind a glowing window
the infant God squalls. Out of zero all has come to birth.
The panes, tinted by the straw of the crib within, hush its
cries. The world goes on unhearing. The town of white roofs
seems a colony of deserted temples; they feather together
with distance and go gray, melt. Shale Hill is invisible. A
yellowness broods low in the sky; above Alton in the west
a ruby glow seeps upward. From the zenith a lavender
luminosity hangs pulseless, as if the particular brilliance of the
moon and stars had been dissolved and the solution shot
through with a low electric voltage. The effect, of tenuous
weight, of menace, is exhilarating. The air presses downward
with an unstressed sibilance, a pedal note, the base C of the
universal storm. The streetlights strung along the pike make a
forestage of brightness where the snowfall, compressed and
expanded by the faintest of winds, like an actor postures—
pausing, plunging. Upward countercurrents suspend snow
which then with the haste of love flies downward to gravity's
embrace; the alternations of density conjure an impression
of striding legs stretching upward into infinity. The storm
walks. The storm walks but does not move on.
Those who remain inside the school are ignorant of the
weather and yet like fish taken up by a swifter ocean current
they sense some change. The atmosphere of the auditorium
accelerates. Things are not merely seen but burst into vision.

Voices carry further. Hearts wax bold. Peter leads Penny back up the aisle and into the hall. His head pounds with the promise he has made but she seems to have forgotten it. He is too young to know those points, those invisible intersections, on a woman's face wherein expectation and permission may be detected. He buys her a Coke and himself a lemon-lime at the bin which the Student Council operates in the main hall. Its vicinity is busy; the couple is pushed to the wall. Here hang framed photographs of bygone track teams in a long chronological row. Penny tips the bottle with her little finger extended and licks her lips in the wake of the sip and looks at him with eyes whose green seems newly minted.

Secret knowledge of his spots obsesses him; should he tell her? Would it, by making her share the shame, wed them inextricably; make her, by bondage of pity, his slave? Can he, so young, afford a slave? On fire with such cruel calculations, he turns his red back on the crowd shoving and sluggishly interweaving around the soft-drink bin. When an iron hand seizes his arm above the elbow and brutally squeezes, it might be one of a hundred idiots.

But it is Mr. Zimmerman, the Supervising Principal. Simultaneously he has seized Penny's arm, and he stands there smiling between them, not letting go. "Two prize students," he says, as if of two netted birds.

Peter angrily tugs his arm away from the grip. The grip tightens. "He begins to look like his father's son," Zimmerman says to Penny, and to Peter's horror Penny echoes the principal's smirk. Zimmerman is shorter than Peter but taller than Penny. Up close, his head, asymmetric, half-bald, and nodding, seems immense. His nose is bulbous, his eyes watery. An absolute rage against this fool wells up in the boy.

"Mr. Zimmerman," he says, "I've been meaning to ask you something."

"Full of questions like his father," Zimmerman says to Penny, and drops his hold on Peter's arm but not hers. She is wearing a pink angora sweater from whose very short sleeves her bare arms thrust like legs out of underpants. The old man's broad fingers indent the cool fat; his thumb wanders back and forth across an inch of flesh.

"I wanted to ask you," Peter says, "what are the humanist values implicit in the sciences?"

Penny titters nervously, her face gone purely stupid. Zimmerman asks, "Where did you hear such a phrase?"

Peter has overreached. He blushes in consciousness of betrayal but in the momentum of pride cannot stop. "I saw it in a report you wrote on my father."

"He shows you those? Do you think he should?"

"I don't know. What affects him affects me."

"I am wondering if it doesn't place too great a responsibility on you. Peter, I value your father enormously. But he does have, as of course you can see—you're an intelligent boy— a tendency to be irresponsible."

Of all possible charges this seems to Peter the least applicable. His father, that blind blanched figure staggering down the steps in a debtor's cardboard box . . .

"It places," Zimmerman goes on gently, "a greater responsibility on those around him."

"I think he's awfully responsible," Peter says, hypnotized by the meditative caressing action of Zimmerman's thumb on Penny's arm. She submits to it; this is a revelation. To think he was about to confide in this whore, this doll, his precious spots.

Zimmerman's smile stretches. "Of course, you see him from a different angle than I do. I saw my own father in the same way."

They see many things the same way, these two; they both see other people as an arena for self-assertion. There is a ground of kinship which makes their grappling possible. Peter feels this, feels a comradeship intertwined with antagonism and a confidence in the midst of his fear. The principal has blundered in seeking intimacy; distance and silence are always most powerful. Peter stares him in the face and, an instant short of irrevocable rudeness, glances away. He feels the side of his neck blushing in the manner of his mother. "He's *terribly* responsible," he says of his father. "He's just had to have stomach X-rays but what he's more worried about is a little strip of basketball tickets he can't find."

Zimmerman quickly blurts, "Tickets?" To Peter's surprise this seems to have scored. The principal's wrinkles are shadowed forth at the new tilt of his head; he seems old. Triumphantly Peter feels descend upon him, his father's avenger, this advantage over the antagonist: he has more years to live. Ignorant and impotent here and now, in the dimension of the future he is mighty. Zimmerman murmurs, seems in his mind to stumble. "I'll have to speak to him about this," he says, half to himself.

Overreached. The possibility of a truly disastrous betrayal makes Peter's stomach grovel as it used to when he was a child and running tardy down the pike to elementary school. "Must you?" His voice thins in pleading, becomes infantile. "I mean, I don't want to have gotten him into any trouble."

Again, the strengths have shifted. Zimmerman's hand leaves Penny's arm and, finger braced against the thumb to flick, comes toward Peter's eye. It is a nightmare second; Peter blinks, his mind blank. He feels the breath being crushed from him. The hand glides past his face and softly snaps a face in the framed picture by Peter's shoulder on the wall. "This is me," Zimmerman says.

It is a photograph of the O.H.S. track team in 1919. They are all wearing old-fashioned black undershirts and the manager wears white ducks and a straw hat. Even the trees in the background—which are the trees of the Poorhouse Lane, only smaller than they are now—look old-fashioned, like pressed flowers. A brownness hangs unsteadily beneath the surface of the photograph. Zimmerman's finger, which with its glazed nail and crinkled knuckle is solid and luminous in the *now,* holds firm under the tiny face of *then.* Peter and Penny have to look. Though as a trackman he was slimmer and had a full head of black hair, Zimmerman is curiously recognizable. The heavy nose set at an uneasy angle to the gently twisted mouth whose plane is not strictly parallel to the line of the eyebrows gave his young face that air of muddled weight, of unfathomable expectation and reluctant cruelty, which renders him in his prime of age so irresistible a disciplinarian even to those who think they have found it within themselves to be defiant and mock. "It *is* you," Peter says weakly.

"We never lost a meet." The finger, dense with existence, everpresent, drops away. Without another word to the young couple Zimmerman moves off down the hall, huge-backed. Students jostle to clear him a path.

The hall is emptying, the varsity game beginning. The pressure of Zimmerman's fingers have left yellow ovals in Penny's naked arm. She rubs the arm briskly and grimaces in disgust. "I feel I should take a bath," she says. Peter realizes he does love her really. They had been equally helpless in Zimmerman's grip. He takes her down the hall, as if to return to the auditorium; but at the hall's end he bucks the double doors and leads her up the dark stairs. This is forbidden. Often at night functions a padlock is placed on these doors but this time the janitors forgot. Peter glances behind them nervously; all who might cry "Halt" have hastened to see the game commence.

On the halfway landing they are out of sight. The bulb burning over the girls' entrance below the steel-mullioned window here casts upward in distorted rhomboids enough light to see by. There must be light enough for her to see. Her naked arms seem silver, her crimson lips black. His own shirt seems black. He unbuttons one sleeve. "Now this is a very sad secret," he says. "But because I love you you should know it."

"Wait."

"What?" He listens to learn if she has heard someone coming.

"Do you know what you're saying? What do you love about me?"

Into the hush the roar of the crowd penetrates like an encircling ocean. Here on this landing he feels dry and cool. He shivers, afraid, now, of what he has begun to do. "I love you," he tells her, "because in the dream I told you about when you turned into a tree I wanted to cry and pray."

"Maybe you just love me in dreams."

"When is that?" He touches her face. Silver. Her mouth and eyes are black and still and terrible like the holes of a mask.

She says gently, "You think I'm stupid."

"I've thought so. But you don't seem so now."

"I'm not beautiful."

"You are now."

"Don't kiss me. The lipstick will smear."

"I'll kiss your hand." He does, and then slips her hand inside his open sleeve. "Does my arm feel funny?"

"It feels warm."

"No. Rough in spots. Concentrate."

"Yes . . . a little. What is it?"

"It's this." Peter pulls back the sleeve and shows her the underside of his arm; the spots look lavender in the cold diffused light. There are less of them than he had expected.

Penny asks, "What is it? Hives?"

"It's a thing called psoriasis I've had all my life. It's horrible, I hate it."

"Peter!" Her hands lift up his head from the gesture of sobbing. His eyes are dry and yet the gesture did release something real.

"It's on my arms and legs and it's worst on my chest. Do you want to see it there?"

"I don't care."

"You hate me now, don't you? You're disgusted. I'm worse than Zimmerman grabbing you."

"Peter, don't just say things to hear me contradict them. Show me your chest."

"Must I?"

"Yes. Come on. I'm curious."

He lifts his shirt and T-shirt underneath and stands in the half-light half-skinned. He feels like a slave ready for flogging, or like that statue of the Dying Captive which Michelangelo did not fully release from the stone. Penny bends to look. Her fingers brush his chilled skin. "Isn't that strange?" she says. "They go in little groups."

"In the summer it pretty well goes away," he tells her, pulling down his shirts. "When I grow up I'm going to spend the winters in Florida and then I won't have it."

"Is this what your secret was?"

"Yes. I'm sorry."

"I expected something much worse."

"What could be worse? In a full light it's really ugly, and I can't do a thing about it except apologize."

She laughs, a glimpse of silver in his ears. "Aren't you silly? I knew you had a skin thing. It shows on your face."

"My God, does it? Badly?"

"No. It's not noticeable at all."

He knows she is lying, yet does not attempt to make her tell the truth. Instead he asks, "Then you don't mind it?"

"Of course not. You can't help it. It's part of you."

"Is that really how you feel?"

"If you knew what love was, you wouldn't even ask."

"Aren't you good?" In accepting her forgiveness he sinks to his knees, there in the corner of the halfway landing, and presses his face against her cloth belly. His knees ache in a minute; in relieving them of pressure his face slides lower. And his hands of themselves slide up silver and confirm what his face has found through the cloth of her skirt, a fact monstrous and lovely: where her legs meet there is nothing. Nothing but silk and a faint dampness and a curve. This then is the secret the world holds at its center, this innocence, this absence, this intimate curve subtly springy in its sheath of silk. Through the wool of her skirt he kisses his own fingertips. "No, please," Penny says, her hand seeking to pull him up by his hair. He hides from her in her, fitting his face tighter against that concave calm; yet even here, his face held in the final privacy, the blunt probing thought of his father's death visits him. Thus he betrays her. When Penny, pinned off balance, repeats "Please," the honest fear in her voice gives him an excuse to relent. Rising, he looks away from her through the window beside them and observes, wonder following wonder, "It's snowing."

In the lavatory Caldwell is puzzled by the word BOOK gouged in square capitals in the wall above the urinal. Close examination reveals that this word has been laid over another; the F had been extended and closed to make a B, the U and C closed into O's, the K left as was. Willing to learn, even by the last flash of light before annihilation, he absorbs the fact, totally new to him, that every FUCK could be made into a BOOK. But who would do such a thing? The psychology of the boy (it must have been a boy) who altered the original word, who desecrated the desecration, is a mystery to him. The mystery depresses him; leaving the lavatory, he tries to enter that mind, to picture that hand, and as he walks down the hall the heaviest weight yet seems laid upon his heart by that unimaginable boy's hand. Could his son have done it?

Zimmerman apparently has been waiting for him. The hall is all but empty; Zimmerman sidles from the stage entrance to the auditorium. "George."

He knows.

"George, have you been worried about some tickets?"

"I'm not worried, it's been explained to me. I marked them Charity in the books."

"I thought I had spoken to you about it. Apparently I was wrong."

"I shouldn't have gotten the wind up. Mental confusion, is what they call it."

"I've had an interesting talk with your son Peter."

"Huh? What did the kid tell you?"

"He told me many things."

Mim Herzog, he knows I know, the goose is cooked, it's out in the open and can never be put back. Never ever, it's a one-way street we're on, ignorance is bliss. The tall teacher feels whiteness fill his body from his toes to his scalp. A weariness, a hollowness and conviction of futility beyond anything he has known before seizes him. A film too thick to be sweat makes pasty his palms and brow as his skin struggles to reject this seizure. "He didn't mean to cause me any trouble, the poor kid doesn't have a clue," Caldwell tells the principal. The pain, the tireless pain, itself seems weary.

Zimmerman sees as if through a rift in clouds that Caldwell's glimpse of Mrs. Herzog is at the bottom of his fear and his mind exults, fairly dances in the security of being on top and able to maneuver. Expertly he skims, like a butterfly teasing a field, above the surface of the dread in the knobbed drained face opposite him. "I was struck," he says glidingly, "by Peter's concern for you. I think he believes that teaching is too great a strain on your health."

Here comes the ax, praise be to God for little blessings, the suspense is over. Caldwell wonders if the dismissal slip will be yellow, as it was with the telephone company. "Is that what the kid thinks, huh?"

"He may be right. He's a perceptive boy."

"He gets that from his mother. I wish to hell he had inherited my weak head and her beautiful body."

"George, I'd like to speak to you frankly."

"Shoot. That's your job." A wave of dizziness simultaneous with an immense restlessness overtakes the teacher; he yearns to swing his arms, twirl around, collapse on the floor and have a nap, anything but stand here and take it, take it from this smug bastard who knows it all.

Zimmerman has risen to his most masterly professional self. His sympathy, his cadences of tact, his comprehensive consideration are exquisite. His body almost aromatically exudes his right and competence to supervise. "If at any time," he says in gentle measured syllables, "you feel unable to go on, please come to me and tell me. It would be a disservice to yourself and to your students to continue. A sabbatical could be arranged easily. You think of it as a disgrace; you shouldn't. A year of thought and study is a very common thing for a teacher in the middle of his career. Remember, you are only fifty. The school would survive; with so many of these veterans returning, the teacher shortage is not what it was during the war."

Dust, lint, spittle, poverty, stuck-together stuff in gutters— all the trash and chaos behind the made world pours through the rent opened by this last subtle prick. Caldwell says, "Christ, the only place I can go if I leave this school is the junkyard. I'm no good for anything else. I never was. I never studied. I never thought. I've always been scared to. My father studied and thought and on his deathbed he lost his religion."

Zimmerman lifts a benevolent palm. "If my last visitation

report is bothering you, remember that it is my duty to tell the truth. But I tell the truth, to quote St. Paul, in love."

"I know that. You've been damn good to me these years; I don't know why you've babied me along, but you have." He bites back the urge to tell a lie, to blurt out that he didn't see Mim Herzog coming out of his office mussed. But that would be nonsense. He did see her. He'd be God-damned if he'd beg. The least you can do is walk in front of the firing squad on your own two legs.

"You've received no favors," Zimmerman says. "You're a good teacher." On this amazing statement Zimmerman turns and walks away, with not a word about Mim or dismissal. Caldwell can't believe his ears. Did he miss something? He wonders if the ax fell and was so sharp he didn't feel it, if the bullets just passed right through him like a ghost. What *had* Zimmerman, underneath it all, *said?*

The man turns back. "Oh, and George."

Now here it comes. Cat and mouse.

"About the tickets."

"Yeah."

"You needn't mention it to Phillips." Zimmerman crookedly winks. "You know how fussy he is."

"O.K. I got your meaning."

Zimmerman's office door closes, the frosted glass opaque. Caldwell doesn't know if it is relief or a symptom of disease that is making his kneecaps tingle and his hands feel numb. The time has arrived for him to use his legs again and they are slow to obey. His torso swims down the hall. Rounding the corner, the teacher surprises Gloria Davis the hopped-up bitch leaning against the wall allowing young Kegerise to rub his knee between her legs. With his I.Q. he ought to know better. Caldwell ignores them and pushes into the auditorium past some Olinger High grads, Jackson is one of them and he can't recall the other's name, standing there with their mouths open looking down at the game. Living corpses, they didn't even have the sense to stay out once they got out. He remembers Jackson always coming to him after class whining about special projects and his love of astronomy and making his own telescope out of mailing tubes and magnifying glass lenses and now the poor bohunk was a plumber's apprentice at 75¢ an hour and sopping it up in beer. What in hell are you supposed to do to keep them from ending like that? He shies away from these his old students, the hunch in their shoulders reminds him of the great whole skinned

carcasses hung on hooks in the freezer of a big Atlantic City
hotel he once worked for. Dead meat. In veering away Caldwell comes face to face with old Kenny Klagle the auxiliary
cop with his white brushed hair and baffled pale eyes and
tender grandmotherly smile, solemnly tricked out in a blue
uniform and paid five dollars a night to be on the premises;
he stands beside a bronze fire extinguisher and they are two
of a kind, in an emergency both would probably just sputter.
Klagle's wife left him years ago and he never knew what hit
him. Never even knew enough to drop dead.

Waste, rot, hollowness, noise, stench, death: in fleeing the
many visages which this central thing wears Caldwell as if by
God's grace comes upon, over in the corner, leaning against
the stacked folding chairs beside Vera Hummel, Reverend
March in his clerical black and backwards collar.

"I don't know if you know me," Caldwell says. "My name
is George Caldwell and I teach general science here in the
school."

March has to leave off laughing with Vera to take the offered hand and say, his smile pointedly patient under the curt
mustache, "I don't believe we *have* met, but of course I've
heard of you and know you by sight."

"I'm a Lutheran so I guess I'm out of your flock," Caldwell
explains. "I hope I'm not interrupting you and Vera here;
the fact is I'm badly troubled in my mind."

With a nervous glance at Vera, who has turned her head
and might slip from his side, March asks, "Oh. What about?"

"Everything. The works. I can't make it add up and I'd
be grateful for your viewpoint."

Now March's glance travels everywhere but into the face
opposite him as he looks through the crowd for some rescue
from this tousled tall maniac. "Our viewpoint does not essen-
tially differ from the Lutheran," he says. "It's my hope that
someday all the children of the Reformation will be reunited."

"Correct me if I'm wrong, Reverend," Caldwell says, "but
as I understand it the difference is the Lutherans say Jesus
Christ is the only answer and the Calvinists say whatever happens to you, happens to you, is the answer."

In his anxiety and anger and embarrassment March reaches
sideways and almost seizes Vera bodily to keep her with him
during this preposterous interruption. "That's ridiculous," he
says. "Orthodox Calvinism—and I count myself more orthodox than not—is fully as Christocentric as the Lutheran doc-

trines. Perhaps more so, since we exclude the saints and any substantive Eucharistic transformation."

"I'm a minister's son," Caldwell explains. "My old man was a Presbyterian, and as I understand it from him there are the elect and the non-elect, the ones that have it and the ones that don't, and the ones that don't have it are never going to get it. What I could never ram through my thick skull was why the ones that don't have it were created in the first place. The only reason I could figure out was that God had to have somebody to fry down in Hell."

The Olinger High basketball team forges into the lead and March has to raise his voice furiously to make himself heard. "The doctrine of predestination," he shouts, "must be understood as counterbalanced by the doctrine of God's infinite mercy." The crowd noise subsides.

"That's my problem, I guess," Caldwell says. "I can't see how it's infinite if it never changes anything at all. Maybe it's infinite but at an infinite distance—that's the only way I can picture it."

March's gray eyes are exploding with pain and irritation as the danger of Vera's leaving him grows. "This is burlesque!" he shouts. "A basketball game is no place to discuss such matters. Why don't you come and visit me in my study sometime, Mr.—?"

"Caldwell. George Caldwell. Vera here knows me."

Vera turns back with a wide smile. "Somebody invoke my name? I don't understand a thing about theology."

"Our discussion of it has just been concluded," Reverend March tells her. "Your friend Mr. Caldwell has some very singular adverse notions about poor abused John Calvin."

"I don't know a thing about him," Caldwell protests, his voice becoming plaintive and high and unpleasant. "I'm trying to learn."

"Come to my study any morning but Wednesdays," March tells him. "I'll lend you some excellent books." He firmly restores his attention to Vera, presenting to Caldwell a profile as handsome and final as if stamped onto an imperial coin.

Make Nero look tame, small town aristocrats, Caldwell thinks, retreating. Heavy and giddy with his own death, sluggish and diaphanous like some transparent predator who trails his poisoned tentacles through the adamantine pressures of the oceanic depths, he moves along behind the backs of spectators and searches the crowd for the sight of his son. At last he spots Peter's narrow head in a row on the right near

the front. *Poor kid, needs a haircut.* Caldwell's work tonight
is done and he wants to go down and get Peter and go home.
Humanity, which has so long entranced him, disgusts him
packed and tangled like germs in this overheated auditorium. Even Cassie's empty land by contrast would look good.
And the snow is piling up outside. And the kid could use the
sleep.

But beside Peter's head there is a small round blondness.
Caldwell recognizes the ninth-grade Fogleman girl. He had
had her brother two years ago, the Foglemans were the kind
who would eat your heart and then wash the rest down the
sink. Brutal Germans, *brrr.* It dawns upon him that she and
Peter are not sitting next to each other by accident. With that
kid's brains, can it be? Now Caldwell remembers seeing Peter
and Penny paired here and there in the halls. By the drinking
fountain giggling. Against the annex lockers leaning broodily.
Framed, blotted together into one silhouette, against the
milky light of a far doorway. He had seen these things but
they hadn't sunk in before. Now they do. The sadness of the
abandoned wells up. A great shout arises as Olinger's lead
expands, and the powerful panic of it licks with four hundred
tongues the lining of the teacher's strained innards.

Olinger wins.

Peter rarely takes his eyes from the game but hardly sees
it, so possessed is his inner eye by the remembrance of pressing his face into the poignant absence between Penny's
thighs. Who would have thought even an instant's access
would be granted him, so young? Who would have thought
thunder would not peal and punishing spirits flap awake?
Who of all those pressed into this bright auditorium would
dream what brimming darkness he had, kiss-lipped, sipped?
The memory of it is a warm mask upon his face, and he
does not dare turn his face to his love for fear she will see
herself there, a ghostly beard, and cry out in horror and
shame, every pore on her nose vivid.

And when he and his father at last leave the school and go
into the snow the multitude of flakes seems to have been released by his profanation. In the pervasive descent an eddy of
air now and then angrily flings a tinkling icy handful upward
into his warm face. Peter had forgotten what snow is. It is
an immense whispering whose throat seems to be now here,
now there. He looks at the sky and it answers his eyes with a
mauve, a lilac, a muffled yellow-pearl. Only after some mo-

ments of focusing does the downflow visually materialize for him, as an edge of a wing, and then an entire broadening wing of infinitesimal feathers, broadening into the realization that this wing is all about them and crowds the air to four hidden horizons and beyond. Wherever he looks, now that his eyes are attuned to its frequency, there is this vibration. The town and all its houses are besieged by a murmuring multitude.

Peter pauses under the high light that guards the near corner of the parking lot. What he sees at his feet puzzles him. On the whiteness that has already fallen small dark spots are swarming like gnats. They dart this way and that and then vanish. There seems to be a center where they vanish. As his eyes travel outward he sees dots speeding toward this center; the further away they are, the faster they speed inward. He traces a few: all vanish. The phenomenon seems totally ghostly. Then the constriction of his heart eases as the rational explanation comes to him. These are the shadows of snowflakes cast by the light above him. Directly under the light, the wavering fall of the particles is projected as an erratic oscillation, but away from the center, where the light rays strike obliquely, the projection parabolically magnifies the speed of the shadow as it hastens forward to meet its flake. The shadows stream out of infinity, slow, and, each darkly sharp in its last instant, vanish as their originals kiss the white plane. It fascinates him; he feels the universe in all its plastic and endlessly variable beauty pinned, stretched, crucified like a butterfly upon a frame of unvarying geometrical truth. As the hypotenuse approaches the vertical the lateral leg diminishes less and less rapidly: always. The busy snowflake shadows seem ants scurrying on the floor of a high castle made all of stone. He turns scientist and dispassionately tries to locate in the cosmography his father has taught him an analogy between the phenomenon he has observed and the "red shift" whereby the stars appear to be retreating at a speed proportional to their distance from us. Perhaps this is a kindred illusion, perhaps—he struggles to picture it—the stars are in fact falling gently through a cone of observation of which our earthly telescopes are the apex. In truth everything hangs like dust in a forsaken attic. Passing on a few yards, to where the lamplight merges with the general agitated dimness, Peter does seem to arrive at a kind of edge where the speed of the shadows is infinite and a small universe both ends and does not end. His feet begin to hurt with being cold and wet and cosmic thoughts turn sickly in his mind. As if leaving a cramped room he restores his focus to the breadth of the town, where large travelling eddies sway and stride from the sky with a sort of ultimate health.

He crawls into the cave of the car with his father and slips off his soaked loafers and tucks his damp stockinged feet under him. Hurriedly his father backs out of the lot and heads up the alley toward Buchanan Road. At first he over-accelerates, so that on the slightest rise the back tires spin. "Boy," Caldwell says, "this is duck soup."

Revelations have skinned Peter's nerves and left him highly irritable. "Well why didn't we start for home two hours ago?" he asks. "We'll never get up Coughdrop Hill. What were you doing at the game so long after the tickets were taken?"

"I talked to Zimmerman tonight," Caldwell tells his son slowly, wondering how not to seem to scold the boy. "He said he'd had a talk with you."

Guilt makes Peter's voice shrill. "I *had* to, he grabbed me in the hall."

"You told him about the missing tickets."

"I just mentioned it. I didn't tell him anything."

"Jesus kid, I don't want to cramp your freedom, but I wish you hadn't told him."

"What *harm* did it do?—it's the truth. Don't you want me to tell the truth? Do you want me to lie all my life?"

"Did you—now it doesn't matter, but did you tell him about my seeing Mrs. Herzog come out of his office?"

"Of course not. I've forgotten all about it. Everybody's forgotten about it except you. You seem to think the whole world's some sort of conspiracy."

"I've never gotten to the bottom of Zimmerman, is I guess my trouble."

"There's no bottom to get to! He's just a befuddled old lech who doesn't know what he's doing. Everybody sees that except you. Daddy, why are you so—" He was going to say "stupid" but a vestige of the fourth commandment checks his tongue. "—superstitious? You make everything mean something it isn't. Why? Why can't you *relax*? It's so ex*haus*ting!" In his fury the boy kicks one foot against the dashboard, making the glove compartment tingle. His father's head is a considering shadow pinched into the pinheaded cap that is for Peter the essence of everything obsequious and absurd, careless and stubborn about his father.

The man sighs and says, "I don't know, Peter. I guess it's part heredity, part environment." From the weariness of his voice, it seems his final effort of explanation.

I'm killing my father, Peter thinks, amazed.

The snow thickens around them. As it dashes into their headlights it flares like a spatter of sparks, swoops upward, vanishes, and is replaced by another spatter of sparks. The onrush is continuously abundant. They meet few other cars on the road now. The lights of homes, thinning beyond the poorhouse, are blurred in the blizzard. The heater comes on and its warmth serves to emphasize their isolation. The arc of the windshield wipers narrows with every swipe, until they stare into the storm through two mottled slits of cleared glass. The purr of the motor is drawing them forward into a closing trap.

Going down the hill beside the Jewish Cemetery, where Abe Cohn, Alton's famous Prohibition gangster, lies buried, they skid. Caldwell fights the wheel as the chassis slithers. They slip safely to the bottom, where Buchanan Road ends at Route 122. On their right, Coughdrop Hill dissolves upwards. A trailer truck like a fleeing house pours down past them and on into Alton, the rapidfire clunk of its chains panicked. When its taillights wink out of sight they are alone on the highway.

The gradient of the hill increases toward the top. Caldwell pulls out in first and remains in this gear until the wheels begin to spin, and then shifts into second. The car plows upward some more dozens of yards; when the wheels start spinning again he shifts desperately into third. The motor stalls. Caldwell yanks out the emergency brake to hold them here on the hill. They are more than half-way up. The storm sinks sighing into the silence of the motor. The motor restarts but the rear tires cannot grip the snow; rather, the weighty old Buick tends to slip backwards toward the low cable fence that guards the edge of the highway embankment. In the end there is nothing for Caldwell to do but to open his door and, leaning out, using the pink glow of his taillights as his only guide, to back all the way down. He backs beyond the Olinger turnoff onto the flat straightaway between Coughdrop Hill and the next little rise on the road to Alton.

Yet, though the momentum gathered here carries them more briskly into the lower part of the hill, they spin to a halt a little short of where they were stopped the first time. Their previous tracks are dark ruts in their headlights.

Suddenly their heads cast shadows forward. A car behind them is coming up the hill. Its lights dilate, blaze like a shout, and sway outward around them; it is a green Dodge, a '47. Its chains slogging, it continues past them, takes the steepest part of the hill, and, gathering speed, vanishes over the crest. Their own stalled headlights pick out the stamp of the cross-links in its tracks. The sparkle of the falling snow is steady.

"We'll have to put on chains like that guy," Peter tells his father. "If we can just get up the next twenty yards we can make it to our road. Fire Hill isn't so steep."

"Did you notice the way that bastard didn't offer to give us a push?"

"How could you expect him to? He just about made it himself."

"I would have, in his shoes."

"But there's nobody else like you, Daddy. There's nobody else like you in the world." He is shouting because his father has clenched his fists on the steering wheel and is resting his forehead on their backs. It frightens Peter to see his father's silhouette go out of shape this way. He wishes to call him to himself but the syllable sticks in his throat, unknown. At last he asks shyly, "Do we have chains?"

His father straightens up and says, "One thing, we can't put 'em on here, the car's likely to slip off the jack. We gotta get down on the level again."

A second time, then, he opens his door and leans out and guides the car backwards down the hill, the snow dyed rose by his taillights. A few flakes swirl in through the open door and prick Peter on the face and hands. He thrusts his hands into the pockets of his pea jacket.

Back at the bottom of the hill, they both get out. They open the trunk and try to jack up the rear of the car. They have no flashlight and nothing is easy. The snow at the side of the road is six inches deep and in trying to lift their tires clear of it they jack the rear too high and the car topples sideways and throws the jack upright, with shocking velocity, into the center of the road. "Jesus," Caldwell says, "this is a way to get killed." He makes no motion to retrieve the upright so Peter goes and gets it. Holding the notched bar in one hand, he looks along the side of the road for a rock to block the front tires but the snow conceals all such details of earth.

His father stands staring at the tops of pines that hover

like dark angels high above them in the storm. Caldwell's thought seems to his son to be describing wide circles, like a scouting buzzard, in the opaque mauve of the heaven above them. Now his thought returns to the problem underfoot and together the father and son prop the jack under the bumper and this time it holds. They discover then that they are unable to fasten the chains. In the dark and cold it is too late for their blind eyes and numb fingers to learn how. For many minutes Peter watches his father squat and grovel in the snow around the tire. In this time no car passes. Route 122 has ceased to bear traffic. His father seems on the verge of clipping the chain fast when it all slips forward into his hands. With a sob or curse blurred by the sound of the storm Caldwell stands erect and with both hands hurls the tangled web of iron links into the soft snow. The hole it makes suggests a fallen bird.

"You should fasten the catch on the inside of the wheel first," Peter says. He digs up the chains and goes onto his knees and crawls underneath the car. He imagines his father telling his mother, "I was at my wits' end and the kid just takes the chains and gets under the car and fastens 'em neat as a pin. I don't know where the kid gets his mechanical ability from." The wheel slips. Several times as he drapes the cumbersome jacket of links around the tire, the tire lazily turns and shucks its coat of mail like a girl undressing. His father holds the wheel still and Peter tries once more. In the underworld beneath the car the muted stink of rubber and the parched smells of rust and gas and grease seem breathed syllables of menace. Peter remembers how the car toppled from the jack, imagines how the springs and axle would crush his skull. One comfort, there is no wind or snowfall here.

There is a little catch that holds the clue to fastening the chains. He finds this catch and, reading with his fingertips, deduces how it operates. Almost he succeeds in snapping it. Only a tiny gap remains to close. He applies a pressure that makes the prostrate length of his body tremble; his kidneys ache sweetly; the metal bites deep into his fingers. He prays; and is appalled to discover that, even when a microscopic concession would involve no apparent sacrifice of principle, matter is obdurate. The catch does not close. He squeals in agony, *"No!"*

His father calls to him, "The hell with it. Get out from under."

Peter obeys, stands, shakes the snow from his jacket. He and his father stare at each other in disbelief. "I can't do it," he says, as if it could be denied.

His father says, "You did a damn sight better than I did. Get into the car, we'll go into Alton for the night. Once a loser, twice a loser."

They put the chains into the trunk and try to lower the car on the jack. But even this piece of retreat proves impossible. The small lever supposed to reverse the jack's direction swings loose and useless. Each shove on the handle lifts the car a notch higher. The fluttering snow pesters their faces; the whine of wind distends their eardrums; the burden on their tempers becomes unendurable. The whole soughing shifting weight of the storm seems hinged on this minute mechanical refusal.

"I'll fix the bastard," Caldwell announces. "Stand clear, kid." He climbs into the car, starts the motor, and drives forward. For a moment the jack upright is caught in the tension of a bow and Peter expects to see it go flying like an arrow into the storm. But the metal of the bumper itself yields under this instant of stress, and the next instant drops the car onto its springs with a sound like icicles snapping. A lip-shaped dent along the lower edge of the rear bumper will always remember this night. Peter gathers up the jack parts and throws them into the trunk and gets into the front seat beside his father.

Aided by the tendency of the rear wheels to slither, Caldwell turns the Buick around and points it toward Alton. But in the hour since they came onto this road another inch of snow has fallen and the packing action of traffic has utterly ceased. The little rise that takes the road out of the trough at the bottom of Coughdrop Hill, a rise so slight that on a fair day it whips by beneath the wheels unnoticed, proves too steep to negotiate. The rear tires never cease slithering. The slits of vision in their windshield go furry and close; the heavenly bin from which the snow has been sifted now bursts its sides. Three times the Buick sloughs forward up the shallow slant to have its motion smothered. The third time, Caldwell grinds his foot into the accelerator and the crying tires swing the rear of the car into the untouched snow at the side of the road. There is a small depression just off the shoulder. Caldwell shifts down to first gear and tries to lift out, but the snow holds them fast in its phantom grip. His lips make a quick silver bubble. Crazed, he shoves the shift into reverse and rams the car backwards so they are hopelessly stuck. He switches off the motor.

A certain peace settles upon their predicament. A delicate friction, like sand being swept up, moves across the top of the car. The overheated motor ticks tranquilly under the hood.

"We'll have to walk," Caldwell says. "We'll walk back to Olinger and stay the night at the Hummels'. It's less than three miles, can you make it?"

"I'll *have* to," Peter says.

"Jesus, you don't have any galoshes on or anything."

"Well neither do you."

"Yeah, but I'm all shot anyway." After a pause, he explains, "We can't stay here."

"Gah-dammit," Peter says, "I *know* it. I know it, stop telling me. Stop telling me things all the time. Let's go."

"A father who was half a man would have gotten you up that hill."

"Then we'd have got stuck someplace else. It's not your fault. It's nobody's fault; it's God's fault. *Please*. Let's stop talking."

Peter gets out of the car and for a time, of the two, is the leader. They walk in their own ruts up the Jewish Cemetery hill. Peter finds it difficult to put one foot directly ahead of the other, as the Indians were said to have done. The wind keeps tipping him. There is a screen of pines here and though the wind is not powerful it yet has an insistence that penetrates the hair on his head and fingers the bone underneath. The cemetery land is held back from the road by a retaining wall of gray stone; each protruding stone wears a beard of white. Somewhere deep in the opaque smoke Abe Cohn lies snug in his pillared mausoleum. Peter draws comfort from this knowledge. He glimpses an analogy with the way his own ego is sheltered under the mineral dome of his skull.

On the flat beyond the cemetery the pines fade away and the wind blows as if minded to pierce his body through and through. He becomes transparent: a skeleton of thoughts. Detached, amused, he watches his feet like blinded cattle slog dutifully through the drifted snow; the disparity between the length of their strides and the immense distance to Olinger is so great that a kind of infinity seems posited in which he enjoys enormous leisure. He employs this leisure to meditate upon the phenomenon of extreme physical discomfort. There is an excising simplicity in it. First, all thoughts of past and future are eliminated, and then any extension via the senses

of yourself into the created world. Then, as further conserva-
tion, the extremities of the body are disposed of—the feet, the
legs, the fingers. If the discomfort persists, if a nagging
memory of some more desirable condition lingers, then the
tip of the nose, the chin, and the scalp itself are removed from
consideration, not entirely anesthetized but deported, as it
were, to a realm foreign to the very limited concerns of the
irreducible locus, remarkably compact and aloof, which alone
remains of the once farflung and ambitious kingdoms of the
self. The sensations seem to arrive from a great distance
outside himself when his father, now walking beside him and
using his body as a shield against the wind for his son, pulls
down upon Peter's freezing head the knitted wool cap he has
taken from his own head.

VIII

MY LOVE, listen. Or are you asleep? It doesn't matter.
In West Alton there was the Alton Museum, set
among magnificent flowering grounds where every tree was
labelled. Black swans drifted preening in pairs upon the surface of the opaque lake created by damming the small shal-
low-bedded stream here called Lenape. In Olinger it was
called Tilden Creek, but it was the same stream. My mother
and I on a Sunday would now again walk to the museum,
the only treasury of culture accessible to us, along the lazy
shady road that kept the creek company and connected the
two towns. This mile or so, then, was a rural interspace, a
remainder of the county's earlier life. We would pass the old
race track, abandoned and gone under to grass, and several
sandstone farmhouses each accompanied, like a mother with
a son, by a whitewashed springhouse of the same stone.
Quickly crossing the harsh width of a three-lane highway,
we would enter on a narrow path the museum grounds, and
an even older world, Arcadian, would envelop us. Ducks and
frogs mixed flat throaty exultations in the scummy marsh half-
hidden by the planted lines of cherry, linden, locust, and
crabapple trees. My mother knew the names of every plant
and bird, would name them for me, and I would forget, as

we walked along the gravel path that widened here and there
into little circlets with a birdbath and benches where, often
as not, a linked pair of humans would break apart and study
our passing with darkened, rounded eyes. Once when I asked
my mother what they had been doing, she replied with a
curious complacence, "They were nesting."

Now the coolness of air off the dammed lake and the
swans' vulgar brackish cries would touch us, and up high
through a gap in a mythic black-leaved beech a pale ochre
cornice of the museum would show, and a sunstruck section
of the raised skylight with its pistachio-green leading. We
would pass through the parking lot that made me covetous
and ashamed, for at that time we had no car; pass along the
gravel pedestrian path among children bringing bags of
breadcrumbs to feed the swans; pass up the wide stairs where
a few people in clean summer clothes would be snapping
cameras and unwrapping sandwiches from waxpaper; and
pass into the high religious hall of the museum itself. Admis-
sion was free. In the basement, indeed, free classes in "nature
appreciation" were held in the summer months. At my
mother's suggestion I once enrolled. The first lesson was to
watch a snake in a glass cage swallow a chattering field
mouse whole. I did not go for the second lesson. The main
floor was given over to scientific exhibits for the benefit of
schoolchildren, stiff stuffed creatures and Eskimo and Chinese
and Polynesian artifacts, case after case, categorized, dust-
proof. There was a noseless mummy, with always a small
crowd around him. As a child this floor filled me with dread.
So much death; who would dream there could be such a
quantity of death? The second floor was devoted to art,
mostly local paintings that, however clumsy and quaint and
mistaken, nevertheless radiated the innocence and hope, the
hope of seizing something and holding it fast, that enters
whenever a brush touches canvas. There were also bronze
statuettes of Indians and deities, and in the center of the
large oval room at the head of the stairs a naked green lady,
life size, stood in the center of a circular black-lipped pool.
She was a fountain. She held to her lips a scallop shell of
bronze and her fine face was pursed to drink, but the mechanics of the fountain dictated that water should spill forever from the edge of the shell away from her lips. Eternally
expectant—with slight breasts, a loosely swirled cast glory of
verdigrant hair, and one foot lightly resting on its toes—she
held the shell an inch away from the face that seemed with

its lowered lids and parted lips asleep. As a child I was troubled by her imagined thirst, and I would place myself so I could see the enduring inch that held her mouth from contact with the water. The water fell as a thin varying ribbon, pearlish green, spiralling as it left the scalloped edge, splaying before it struck the surface of the pond with a ceaseless gentle impact whose splash was sometimes flung by the subtle variations of accident as far away as the rim of the pond, deckling with a tiny cold prick, like the touch of a snowflake, my hand resting there on the black marble. The patience of her wait, the mildness of its denial, seemed unbearable to me then, and I told myself that when darkness came, and the mummy and the Polynesian masks and the glass-eyed eagles below were sealed in shadow, then her slim bronze hand made the very little motion needed, and she drank. In this great oval room, which I conceived as lit by the moon through the skylight above, the fall of water would for a moment cease. In that sense, then—in the sense that the coming of night enwrapped the luminous ribbon of downfalling water and staunched its flow—my story is coming to its close.

The irritable traffic pecks soothingly at the windows of our loft, those windows whose thin glass has so long needed dusting that their delicate grapitic grayness seems internal, a shade of cathedral glass. The cafeteria neon two stories below rhythmically stains them rose. My vast canvases—so oddly expensive as raw materials, so oddly worthless transmuted into art—with sharp rectangular shoulders hulk into silhouette against the light. Your breathing keeps time with the slow rose. Your solemn mouth has relaxed in sleep and the upper lip displays the little extra racial button of fat like a bruise blister. Your sleep contains innocence as the night contains dew. Listen: I love you, love your prim bruised mouth whose corners compress morally when you are awake and scolding me, love your burnt skin ceaselessly forgiving mine, love the centuries of being humbled held in the lilac patina of your palms. I love the tulip-stem stance of your throat. When you stand before the stove you make, all unconscious, undulant motions with the upper half of your body like a drinking hen. When you walk naked toward the bed your feet toe in as if your ankles were manacled to those of someone behind you. When we make love sometimes you sigh my name and I feel radically confirmed. I am glad I have met you, glad, proud, glad; I miss only, and then only a little,

in the late afternoons, the sudden white laughter that like
heat lightning bursts in an atmosphere where souls are trying
to serve the impossible. My father for all his mourning moved
in the atmosphere of such laughter. He would have puzzled
you. He puzzled me. His upper half was hidden from me,
I knew best his legs.

Hey. Listen. Listen to me, lady. I love you, I want to
be a Negro for you, I want to have a wised-up shoe-polish
face taut as a drum at the cheekbones and wear great opaque
anonymous-making sunglasses at three a.m. in a dim lavender cellar and forget everything but the crooning behind my
ribs. But I cannot, quite. I cannot quite make that scene. A
final membrane restrains me. I am my father's son. In the
late afternoons while the day hangs in distending light waiting
to be punctured by the darkness that in arrows of shadow
rides out from the tall buildings across the grid of streets, I
remember my father and even picture—eyes milky with
doubts, mustache indecisive and pale—his father before him,
whom I never knew. Priest, teacher, artist: the classic de-
generation.

Forgive me, for I do love you, we fit. Like a Tibetan lama
I rise out of myself above the bed and see how we make, yin
and yang, a person between us. But at the hour in the afternoon when my father and I would be heading home in the
car, I glance around at the nest we have made, at the floor-
boards polished by our bare feet, at the continents of stain on
the ceiling like an old and all-wrong discoverer's map, at the
earnestly bloated canvases I conscientiously cover with great
streaks straining to say what even I am beginning to suspect
is the unsayable thing, and I grow frightened. I consider the
life we have made together, with its days spent without relation to the days the sun keeps and its baroque arabesques of
increasingly attenuated emotion and its furnishings like a
scattering of worn-out Braques and its rather wistful half-
Freudian half-Oriental sex-mysticism, and I wonder, *Was it
for this that my father gave up his life?*

Lying awake beside you in the rose-touched dark, I wake
on a morning long ago, in Vera Hummel's guest bedroom.
Her room shone in the aftermath of the storm. My dreams
had been a bent extension, like that of a stick thrust into
water, of the last waking events—the final mile staggering
through the unwinding storm; my father's beating at the door
of the dark house, knocking and whinnying and rubbing his
hands together in desperation yet his importunity no longer

seeming absurd or berserk to me but necessary, absolutely in
my blind numbness necessary; then Vera Hummel yawning
and blinking in the bleaching glare of her kitchen, her un-
bound hair fanning over the shoulders of her blue bathrobe
and her hands tucked in the sleeves and her arms hugging
herself as she yawned; and the limping clump of her husband
descending the stairs to receive my father's outpour of explanation and gratitude. They put us in their guest bedroom,
in a postered sway-backed bed inherited from Mr. Hummel's
mother, my grandfather's sister Hannah. It smelled of feathers
and starch and was so like a hammock that my father and I,
in underclothes, had to cling to the edges to keep from sliding
together in the middle. For some minutes I kept tense. I
seemed stuffed with the jiggling atoms of the storm. Then I
heard the first rasp of my father's snuffly little snore. Then
the wind outside the room sighed mightily, and this thrust of
sound and motion beyond me seemed to explain everything,
and I relaxed.

The room was radiant. Beyond the white mullions and the
curtains of dotted Swiss pinned back with metal flowers
painted white, the sky was undiluted blue. I thought, *This
morning has never occurred before,* and I jubilantly felt myself to be on the prow of a ship cleaving the skyey ocean of
time. I looked around the room for my father; he was gone.
I had sunk into the center of the bed. I looked for a clock;
there was none. I looked to my left to see how the sun lay on
the road and field and mailbox, and my gaze met instead a
window giving on the luncheonette's brick wall. Next to the
window, its chipping veneer somehow grimacing, was an old-
fashioned bureau with fluted glass knobs, a wavy-faced top
drawer, and ponderous scroll feet like the toeless feet of a
cartoon bear. The radiance beyond the house picked out the
silver glints in the stems and leaves of the wallpaper. I closed
my eyes to listen for voices, heard a vacuum cleaner hum-
ming at some distance, and must have slipped back into sleep.

When I awoke again the strangeness of it all—the house,
the day so fair and sane in the wake of madness, the silence,
inside and out (why had I not been wakened? what had
happened to the school? wasn't it Wednesday?)—held me
from falling back, and I arose and dressed as much as I
could. My shoes and socks, set to dry on a radiator in the
room, were still damp. The strange walls and hallways, demanding thought and courage at every turn, seemed to suck
strength from my limbs. I located the bathroom and splashed

cold water on my face and ran my wet finger back and forth across my teeth. In bare feet I went down the Hummels' stairs. They were carpeted with a fresh-napped beige strip held in place by a brass rod at the base of each riser. This was the kind of Olinger home, solid and square and orthodox, that I wished my family lived in. I felt dirty and unworthy in my weary red shirt and three-day underwear.

Mrs. Hummel came in from the front room wearing a pinned-up bandana and an apron patterned with starlike anemones. She held a dainty straw wastebasket in her hand and, grinning so her gums flashed, hailed me with, "Good morning, Peter Caldwell!" Her pronouncing my name in full somehow made me completely welcome. She led me into the kitchen and in walking behind her I felt myself, to my surprise, her height, or even an inch taller. She was tall as local women went and I still thought of her as the goddess-size she had appeared to me when I first arrived at the high school, a runty seventh-grader, my waist no higher than the blackboard chalk-troughs. Now I seemed to fill her eyes. I sat at the little porcelain-topped kitchen table and she served me like a wife. She set before me a thick tumbler of orange juice whose translucence cast on the porcelain in sunlight an orange shadow like a thin slice of the anticipated taste. It was delicious for me to sit and sip and watch her move. She glided in blue slippers from cupboard to refrigerator to sink as if these intervals had been laid out after measuring her strides; her whole spacious and amply equipped kitchen contrasted with the cramped and improvised corner where my mother made our meals. I wondered why some people could solve at least the mechanical problems of living while others, my people, seemed destined for lifetimes of malfunctioning cars and underheated toiletless homes. In Olinger, we had never had a refrigerator, but instead a humiliating old walnut icebox, and my grandmother never sat down with us at the table but ate standing up, off the stove with her fingers, her face wincing in the steam. Haste and improvidence had always marked our domestic details. The reason, it came to me, was that our family's central member, my father, had never rid himself of the idea that he might soon be moving on. This fear, or hope, dominated our home.

"Where's my father?" I asked.

"I don't know exactly, Peter," she said. "Which would you prefer—Wheaties or Rice Krispies or an egg some way?"

"Rice Krispies." An oval ivory-colored clock below the

lacquered cabinets said 11:10. I asked, "What happened to school?"

"Have you looked outdoors?"

"Sort of. It's stopped."

"Sixteen inches, the radio said. All the schools in the county have cancelled. Even the parochial schools in Alton."

"I wonder if they're going to have swimming practice tonight."

"I'm sure not. You must be dying to get to your home."

"I suppose so. It seems forever since I *was* home."

"Your father was very funny this morning, telling us your adventures. Do you want a banana with the cereal?"

"Oh, gee. Sure, if you have it." That surely was the difference between these Olinger homes and my own; they were able to keep bananas on hand. In Firetown, on the rare times my father thought to buy them, they went from green to rotten without a skip. The banana she set beside my bowl was perfect. Its golden skin was flecked evenly all over just as in the four-color magazine ads. As I sliced it with my spoon, each segment in dropping into the cereal displayed that ideal little star of seeds at the center.

"Do you drink coffee?"

"I try to every morning but there's never any time. I'm being an awful lot of trouble."

"Hush. You sound like your father."

Her "hush," emerging from an intimacy that someone else had created for me, evoked a curious sense of past time, of the few mysterious hours ago when, while I was sound asleep in my great-aunt Hannah's bed, my father had told of his adventures and they had listened to the radio. I wondered if Mr. Hummel had been here also; I wondered what event had spread through the house this aftermath of peaceful, reconciled radiance.

I made bold to ask, "Where is Mr. Hummel?"

"He's out with the plow. Poor Al, he's been up since five. He has a contract with the town to help clear the streets after a storm."

"Oh. I wonder how our poor car is. We abandoned it last night at the bottom of Coughdrop Hill."

"Your father said. When Al comes home, he'll drive you out in the truck to it."

"These Rice Krispies are awfully good."

She looked around from the sink in surprise and smiled. "They're just the ones that come out of the box." Her kitchen seemed to bring out a Dutchness in her intonation. I had always vaguely associated Mrs. Hummel with sophistication, New York, and the rest of it, she shone to such advantage among the other teachers, and sometimes wore mascara. But in her house she was, plainly, of this county.

"How did you like the game last night?" I asked her. I felt awkwardly constrained to keep a conversation up. My father's absence challenged me to put into practice my notions of civilized behavior, which he customarily frustrated. I kept tugging up the wrists of my shirt to keep spots from showing. She brought me two slices of glinting toast and a dopple of amber crabapple jelly on a black plate.

"I didn't pay that much attention." She laughed in memory. "Really, that Reverend March amuses me so. He's half a boy and half an old man and you never know which you're talking to."

"He has some medals, doesn't he?"

"I suppose. He went all up through Italy."

"It's interesting, I think, that after all that he could return to the ministry."

Her eyebrows arched. Did she pluck them? Seeing them close, I doubted it. They were naturally fine. "I think it's good; don't you?"

"Oh, it's good, sure. I mean, after all the horrors he must have seen."

"Well—they say there's some fighting even in the Bible."

Not knowing what she wanted, I laughed nevertheless. It seemed to please her. She asked me playfully, "How much attention did *you* pay to the game? Didn't I see you sitting with the little Fogleman girl?"

I shrugged. "I had to sit next to somebody."

"Now, Peter, you watch out. She has the look in her eye."

"Ha. I doubt if I'm much of a catch."

She held up a finger, gay-making in the county fashion. "Ahhh. You have the possibilities."

The interposed "the" was so like my grandfather's manner of speech that I blushed as if blessed. I spread the bright jelly on my toast and she continued about the business of the house.

The next two hours were unlike any previous in my life. I shared a house with a woman, a woman tall in time, so tall I could not estimate her height in years, which at the least was twice mine. A woman of overarching fame; legends concerning her lovelife circulated like dirty coins in the student underworld. A woman fully grown and extended in

terms of property and authority; her presence branched into
every corner of the house. Her touch on the thermostat
stirred the furnace under me. Her footsteps above me tripped
the vacuum cleaner into a throaty, swarming hum. Here and
there in the house she laughed to herself, or made a piece of
furniture cry as she moved it; sounds of her flitted across the
upstairs floor as a bird flits unseen and sporadic through the
high reaches of a forest. Intimations of Vera Hummel moved
toward me from every corner of her house, every shadow,
every curve of polished wood; she was a glimmer in the
mirrors, a breath moving the curtains, a pollen on the nap of
the arms of the chair I was rooted in.

I heavily sat in the dark front parlor reading from a little
varnished rack *Reader's Digests* one after another. I read until
I felt sick from reading. I eagerly discovered and consumed
two articles side by side in the table of contents: "Miracle
Cure For Cancer?" and "Ten Proofs That There Is a God." I
read them and was disappointed, more than disappointed,
overwhelmed—for the pang of hope roused fears that had
been lulled. The demons of dread injected their iron into my
blood. It was clear, clear for all the smart rattle of the
prose and the encyclopedic pretense of the trim double col-
umns, that there were no proofs, there was no miracle cure.
In my terror of words I experienced a panicked hunger for
things and I took up, from the center of the lace doily on the
small table by my elbow, and squeezed in my hand a
painted china figurine of a smiling elf with chunky polka-
dot wings. The quick blue slippers sounded on the carpeted
stairs and Mrs. Hummel made lunch for the two of us. In the
brightness of the kitchen I was embarrassed for my com-
plexion. I wondered if it would be manners to offer to leave,
but I had no strength to leave this house, felt unable even to
look out the window; and if I did leave, where would I look,
and for what? My father's mysterious absence from me
seemed permanent. I was lost. The woman talked to me; her
words were trivial but they served to make horror habitable.
Into the shining plane of the table-top between our faces I
surfaced; I made her laugh. She had taken off her bandana
and clipped her hair into a horsetail. As I helped her clear
the table and took the dishes to the sink, our bodies once or
twice brushed. And so, half-sunk in fear and half alive and
alight with love, I passed the two hours of time.

My father returned a little after one. Mrs. Hummel and I
were still in the kitchen. We had been talking about a

wing, an L with a screened porch, which she wanted to have
built onto the back of her house; here in the summers she
could sit overlooking her yard away from the traffic and noise
of the pike. It would be a bower and I believed I would share
it with her.

My father looked in his bullet-head cap and snow-drenched
overcoat like a man just shot from a cannon. "Boy," he told
us, "Old Man Winter made up for lost time."

"Where have you *been?*" I asked. My voice ignobly stumbled on a threat of tears.

He looked at me as if he had forgotten I existed. "Out and
around," he said. "Over at the school. I would have gotten
you up, Peter, but I figured you needed the sleep. You were
beginning to look drawn as hell. Did my snoring keep you
awake?"

"*No.*" The snow on his coat and pants and shoes, testimony of adventure, made me jealous. Mrs. Hummel's attention had shifted all to him; she was laughing without his
even saying anything. His bumpy face was ruddy. He whipped
his cap off like a boy and stamped his feet on the cocoa mat
inside the door. I yearned to torment him; I became shrill.
"What did you *do* at the school? How could you be so *long?*"

"Jesus, I love that building when there aren't any kids in
it." He was speaking not to me but to Mrs. Hummel. "What
they ought to do with that brick barn, Vera, is turn the kids
out on the street and let us teachers live there alone; it's the
only place I've ever been in my life where I didn't feel like
somebody was sitting on the back of my neck all the time."

She laughed and said, "They'd have to put in beds."

"An old Army cot is all I'd need," he told her. "Two
feet wide and six feet long; whenever I get in bed with somebody they take all the covers. I don't mean you, Peter. Tired
as I was last night I probably took 'em from you. In answer
to your question, what was I doing over there, I brought all
my books up to date. For the first time since last marking
period everything is apple pie; I feel like they lifted a concrete block out of my belly. If I don't show up tomorrow, the
new teacher can step right in and take over, poor devil.
Biff, bang; move over, buddy, next stop, the dump."

I had to laugh.

Mrs. Hummel moved to her refrigerator asking, "George,
have you had lunch? Can I give you a roast beef sandwich?"

"Vera, that's kind as hell of you. To tell you the truth,
I couldn't chew a roast beef sandwich, I had a back tooth

pulled last night. I feel a hundred per cent better but it's like
the lost Atlantis in there. I had a bowl of oyster stew up at
Mohnie's. To be perfectly honest with you though, if you
and the kid were having coffee, I'd take a cup. I forget if the
kid drinks coffee."

"How can you forget it?" I asked. "I try to drink it every
morning at home but there's never any *time*."

"Jesus, that reminds me. I tried to get through to your
mother but the lines are out. She doesn't have a scrap of
food in the house and if I know Pop Kramer he'll be trying to
eat the dog. Provided he hasn't fallen down the stairs. That
would be just my luck; no doctor can get in there."

"Well when are *we* going to get there?"

"Any minute, kid, any minute. Time and tide for no
man wait." He called to Mrs. Hummel, "Never take a boy
away from his mother." Then he pinched his lips in; I knew
he was wondering if this had been tactless because she, for
reasons that were dark to me, had no children herself. With
the pointed quiet of a servant she set the smoking coffee on
the counter near him. A coil of hair came loose and trailed
across her cheek like a comment. He tried to subdue the excitement in his voice and told her, "I saw Al over by Spruce
Street and he's on his way home. He and that truck have been
performing miracles out there; this borough does a bang-up
job when the chips are down. Traffic's moving on everything
but the alleys and the section around Shale Hill. Boy, if I
was running this town we'd all be on snowshoes for a
month." He clenched and unclenched his hands happily as he
gazed into this vision of confusion. "They say a trolley was de-
railed over in West Alton late last night."

Mrs. Hummel tucked back her hair and asked, "Was anybody hurt?"

"Nobody. It jumped the rails but stayed on its feet. Our
own trolleys didn't get through to Ely until around noon.
Half the stores in Alton are shut." I marvelled at all this information and imagined him gathering it, wading through snow-
banks, halting snowplows to question the drivers, running up
and down raggedly heaped mounds in his too-small overcoat
like an overgrown urchin. He must have circled the town
while I was asleep.

I finished my coffee and the odd torpor that my nerves had
been holding at bay now was permitted to invade. I ceased to
listen as my father told Mrs. Hummel of his further adventures. Mr. Hummel came in the door, gray with fatigue, and

shook snow from his hair. His wife fed him lunch; when it was over he looked at me and winked. "Do you want to go home, Peter?"

I went and put on my coat and socks and wrinkled clammy shoes and came back to the kitchen. My father took his empty cup to the sink and restored his cap to his head. "This is awfully white of you, Al; the kid and I really appreciate it." To Mrs. Hummel he said, "Thanks a lot, Vera, you've treated us like princes," and then, love, the strangest of all the strange things I have told, my father bent forward and kissed the woman on the cheek. I averted my eyes in shock and saw on the spatter-pattern linoleum floor her narrow feet in their blue slippers go up on their toes as she willingly received the kiss.

Then her heels returned to the floor and she was holding my father's wart-freckled hands in her own. "I'm glad you came to us," she told him, as if they were alone. "It filled up the house for a little while."

When my turn to thank her came I didn't dare a kiss and pulled my face back to indicate I was not going to give one. She smiled as she took my offered hand and then put her other hand over it. "Are your hands always so warm, Peter?"

Outside their door, the twigs of a lilac bush had become antlers. Hummel's truck was waiting between the pumps and the air hose; it was a middle-sized rust-splotched Chevrolet pick-up with a flaring orange plow coupled to the front bumper. When it went into gear ten different colors of rattle seemed to spring into being around us. I sat between my father and Al Hummel; there was no heater in the front and I was glad to be between the men. We drove out Buchanan Road. Our old house looked like Old Man Winter's palace, crowned with snow and sunning itself on the broad white side where I used to bounce a tennis ball when I was a child. Along the street children in passing had shaken the snow loose from the hedges and now and then above us a loosened batch poured down in a shuffling quick cascade through the branches of a horsechestnut tree. As the houses thinned, the snow reigned undisturbed over the curved fields beyond the steady ridge, as high as a man, of stained snow heaped by the plow. In the far distance the wooded hills still showed as blue and brown, but the tints were weak, as in the prints of an etching taken to clean the plate.

The weariness I felt overtakes me in the telling. I sat in the cab of the truck while, framed in the windshield like the blurred comics of an old silent movie, my father and Hummel shovelled out our Buick, which the plows in clearing Route 122 had buried up to the windows. I was bothered by an itching that had spread from my nose through my throat and that I felt to have some connection with the clammy chill of my shoes. The shoulder of the hill threw its shadow over us and a little wind ignited. The sunlight grew long, golden, and vanished from all but the tips of the trees. Expertly Hummel started the motor, backed the rear tires onto the chains, and made them fast with a plier-like tool. Little better than blurs now in the bluish twilight, the men enacted a pantomime with a wallet whose conclusion I did not comprehend. They both gestured widely and then hugged each other farewell. Hummel opened the door of the cab, cold air swept over me, and I transferred my brittle body to our hearse.

As we drove home, the days since I had last seen this road sealed shut like a neat scar. Here was the crest of Coughdrop Hill, here was the curve and clay embankment where we had picked up the hitchhiker, here was the Clover Leaf Dairy where conveyor belts removed the cow dung and all the silver chimneys on the barn roof were smoking against the salmon flush of the sky; here was the straightaway where we had once killed a confused oriole, here was Galilee and, beside the site of the old Seven-Mile Inn, Potteiger's Store, where we stopped for food. Item by item, as if he were a druggist filling a prescription, my father went around the shelves gathering bread and sliced peaches and Ritz crackers and Shredded Wheat, piling them up on the counter in front of Charlie Potteiger, who had been a farmer and had come back from the Pacific to sell his farm to developers and set up this store. He kept our debt in a little brown five-cent notebook and, though it ran as high as sixty dollars between paydays, never forgave us so much as an odd penny. "And a loop of that pork sausage my father-in-law loves so much and a half-pound of Lebanon baloney for the kid to nibble," my father told him. An extravagance had entered his shopping, which was customarily niggardly, a day's food at a time, as if the next day there might be fewer mouths to feed. He even bought a bunch of fresh bananas. As Potteiger with his pencil stub effortfully toted up the bill my father looked at me and asked, "Did you get a soft drink?"

I usually did, as a last sip of civilization before we descended into that rural darkness that by some mistake had become our home. "No," I told him. "I have no appetite. Let's go."

"This poor son of mine," my father announced loudly to the little pack of loafers in red hunting caps who even on this day of storm had showed up to stand around and chew in here, "he hasn't been home for two nights and he wants to see his mamma."

Furious, I pushed through the door into the air. The lake across the road, rimmed in snow, looked black as the back of a mirror. It was that twilight in which some cars have turned on their headlights, some their parking lights, and some no lights at all. My father drove as fast as if the road were bare. In some parts the road had been scraped clean and on these patches our chains changed tune. Halfway up Fire Hill (above us, the church and its tiny cross were inked onto an indigo sky), a link snapped. It racketed against the rear right fender for the remaining mile. The few houses of Firetown patched the dusk with downstairs windows glowing dimly as embers. The Ten Mile Inn was dark and boarded shut.

Our road had not been plowed. Our road was actually two roads, one which went in through the Amish fields and another which led off from that, down past our property, to rejoin the highway by Silas Schoelkopf's pond and barn. We had left by this, the lower road; we returned by the upper. My father rammed the Buick through the heaped snow and it sagged to a stop perhaps ten feet off the highway. The motor stalled. He turned off the ignition and snapped off the lights. "How will we get out tomorrow?" I asked.

"One thing at a time," he said. "I want to get you home. Can you walk it?"

"What *else* can I do?"

The unplowed road showed as a long stretch of shimmering gray set in perspective by two scribbled lines of young trees. Not a houselight showed from here. Above us, in a sky still too bright a blue to support stars, sparse pale clouds like giant flakes of marble drifted westward so stilly their motion seemed lent by the earth's revolution. The snow overwhelmed my ankles and inundated my shoes. I tried to walk in my father's footsteps but his strides were too great. As the sound of traffic on the highway faded behind us, a powerful silence strengthened. There was a star before us, one, low in the sky and so brilliant its white light seemed warm.

I asked my father, "What's that star?"

"Venus."

"Is it always the first to come out?"

"No. Sometimes it's the last to go. Sometimes when I get up the sun is coming up through the woods and Venus is still hanging over the Amishman's hill."

"Can you steer by it?"

"I don't know. I've never tried. It's an interesting question."

I told him, "I can never find the North Star. I always expect it to be bigger than it is."

"That's right. I don't know why the hell they made it so small."

His shape before me was made less human by the bag of groceries he was carrying and it seemed, my legs having ceased to convey the sensations of walking, that his was the shape of the neck and head of a horse I was riding. I looked straight up and the cobalt dome was swept clean of marble flakes and a few faint stars were wearing through. The branches of the young trees we walked between fell away to disclose the long low hump, sullenly lustrous, of our upper field.

"Peter?"

My father's voice startled me, I felt so alone. "What?"

"Nothing. I just wanted to make sure you were still behind me."

"Well where else would I be?"

"You got me there."

"Shall I carry the bag for a while?"

"No, it's clumsy but it's not heavy."

"Why'd you buy all those bananas if you knew we were going to have to lug everything half a mile?"

"Insanity," he answered. "Hereditary insanity." It was a favorite concept of his.

Lady, hearing our voices, began to bark behind the field. The quick dim doublets of sound like butterflies winged toward us close to the earth, skimming the feathery crust rather than risking a plunge upward into the steep smooth dome that capped a space of Pennsylvania a hundred miles wide. From the spot where the lower road led off from the upper we could see on a clear day to the first blue beginnings of the Alleghenies. We walked downward into the shelter of our hillside. The trees of our orchard came first into view, then our barn, and through the crotches and tangled barren branches of the orchard our house. Our downstairs light was on, yet as we moved across the silent yard I became convinced that the light was an illusion, that the people inside had died and left the light burning. My father beside me moaned, "Jesus I know Pop's tumbled down those damn stairs."

But footsteps had beaten a path around the corner of the house ahead of us, and on the porch there were plentiful signs that the pump had been used. Lady, free, raced out of the darkness with the whir of a growl in her throat and then, recognizing us, leaped like a fish from the splashing snow, jabbing her muzzle at our faces, her throat stuck fast on a weak agonized note of whimpering love. She battered and bustled through the double kitchen door with us and in the warm indoors released an unmistakable tang of skunk.

Here was the kitchen, honey-colored, lit; here were the two clocks, the red electric thrown all out of right time by the power failure but running gamely nevertheless; here was my mother, coming forward with large arms and a happy girlish face to take the bundle from my father and welcome us home. "My heroes," she said.

My father explained, "I tried to call you this morning, Cassie, but the lines were down. Have you had a rough time? There's an Italian sandwich in the bag."

"We've had a *won*derful time," my mother said. "Dad's been sawing wood and this evening I made some of that dried-beef soup with apples Grammy used to make when we ran out of food." An ambrosial smell of warm apples did breathe from the stove, and a fire was dancing in the fireplace.

"Huh?" It seemed to daze my father that the world had gone on without him. "Pop's O. K.? Where in hell is he?"

Even as he spoke he walked into the other room and there, sitting in his accustomed place on the sofa, was my grandfather, his shapely hands folded across his chest, his little worn Bible, shut, balanced on one knee.

"Did you cut some wood, Pop?" my father asked loudly. "You're a walking miracle. At some point in your life you must have done something right."

"George, now I don't wish to be ac-qui-si-tive, but by any chance did you remember to bring the *Sun?*" The mailman of course hadn't gotten through, a sore deprivation for my grandfather, who wouldn't believe it had snowed until he read it in the newspaper.

"Hell, no, Pop," my father bellowed. "I forgot. I don't know why, it was insanity."

My mother and the dog came into the living-room with us. Lady, unable to keep the good news of our return to herself any longer, jumped up on the sofa and with a snap of her body thrust her nose into my grandfather's ear.

"Hyar, *yaar*," he said, and stood up, rescuing the Bible from his knee in the same motion.

"Doc Appleton called," my mother said to my father.

"Huh? I thought the lines were out."

"They came on this afternoon, after the electricity. I called Hummel's and Vera said you had gone. She sounded more pleasant to me than I've ever heard her over the phone."

"What did Appleton say?" my father asked, crossing the room and looking down at my globe of the Earth.

"He said the X-rays showed nothing."

"Huh? Is that what he said? Do you think he's lying, Cassie?"

"You know he never lies. Your X-rays are clear. He said it's all in your nerves; he thinks you have a mild case of, now I forget—I wrote it down." My mother passed to the telephone and read from a slip of paper she had left on top of the directory, *"Mucinous colitis.* We had a nice talk; but Doc sounds older."

Abruptly I felt exhausted, empty; still in my jacket, I sat down on the sofa and leaned back into its cushions. It seemed imperative to do this. The dog rested her head on my lap and wriggled her ice-cold nose into place beneath my hand. Her fur felt stuffed fluffy with chill outdoor air. My parents looked enormous and dramatic above me.

My father turned, his great face tense, as if refusing to undo the last clamp on hope. "Is that what he said?"

"He did think, though, you need a rest. He thinks teaching is a strain for you and wondered if there was something else you could do."

"Huh? Hell, it's all I'm good for, Cassie. It's my one talent. I can't quit."

"Well, that's what he and I thought you'd say."

"Do you think he can read X-rays, Cassie? Do you think the old bluffer knows what he's talking about?"

I had closed my eyes by way of giving thanks. Now a large cool dry hand came and cupped itself over my forehead. My mother's voice said, "George. What have you done with this child? He has a roaring fever."

Muffled somewhat by the wooden wall of the staircase, my grandfather's voice called down to us, "Pleasant dreams."

My father strode across the vibrating kitchen floor and called up the stairs after him, "Don't be sore about the *Sun,*

Pop. I'll get you one tomorrow. Nothing'll happen until then, I promise you. The Russians are still in Moscow and Truman's still king."

My mother asked me, "How long has this been?"

"I don't know," I told her. "I've felt sort of weak and unreal all afternoon."

"Do you want some soup?"

"Maybe a little, not much. Isn't it a relief about Daddy? His not having cancer."

"Yes," she said. "Now he'll have to think up some new way of getting sympathy." A quick bitter frown came and went in the soothing oval of her face.

I tried to get back into the little intricate world my mother and I had made, where my father was a fond strange joke, by agreeing, "He *is* good at that. Maybe that's his talent."

He came back into the room and announced to us, "Boy, that man has a temper! He is really and truly sore about my not bringing home a newspaper. He's a powerhouse, Cassie; at his age I'll be dead for twenty years."

Though I was too dizzy and sleepy for calculations, this sounded like an upward revision in his expectations.

My parents fed me and put me to bed and took a blanket off their own bed so I would be warm. My teeth had begun to chatter and I made no attempt to repress this odd skeletal vibration, which both released swarms of chill spirits within me and brought down from my mother warm helpless fluttery gusts of concern. My father stood by kneading his knuckles.

"Poor kid he's too ambitious," he moaned aloud.

"My little sunbeam," my mother seemed to say.

To the tune of their retreating voices I fell asleep. My dreams did not embody them or Penny or Mrs. Hummel or Mr. Zimmerman or Deifendorf or Minor Kretz or Mr. Phillips but seemed to take place in a sluggish whirling world that preceded them all and where only my grandmother's face, flashing by on the periphery with the startled fearful expression with which she used to call me down from a tree I was climbing, kept me company in the shifting rootless flux of unidentifiable things. My own voice seemed throughout to be raised in protest and when I awoke, with an urgent need to urinate, my parents' voices below me seemed a grappling extension of my own. Morning light the tone of lemon filled the frame of my window. I remembered that in the middle of the night I had almost surfaced from my exitless nightmare at the touch of hands on my face and the sound of my father's voice in a corner of my room saying, "Poor kid, I wish I could give him my mulish body."

Now he was saying downstairs in the high strained pitch he used like a whip on my mother, "I tell you, Cassie, I have it licked. Kill or be killed, that's my motto. Those bastards don't give me any quarter and I don't give them any."

"Well that's certainly a very poor attitude for a teacher to have. No wonder your insides are all mixed up."

"It's the *only* attitude, Cassie. Any other attitude is suicide. If I can just hang in there for ten more years, I'll get my twenty-five years' pension and have it licked. If Zimmerman and that Herzog bitch don't have me canned, that is."

"Because you saw her come out of a door? George, why do you exaggerate so? To drive us all wild? What good will it do you when we *are* wild?"

"I'm not exaggerating, Cassie. She knows I know and Zimmerman knows I know she knows."

"It must be *ter*rible to know so much."

A pause.

"It is," my father said. "It's hell."

Another pause.

"I think the doctor's right," my mother said. "You should quit."

"Don't be a femme, Cassie. That's just Doc Appleton baloney, he has to say something. What else could I do? I'm an unemployable."

"Couldn't you quit and, if you can't find other work, farm this place with me?" Her voice had become shy and girlishly small; my throat contracted with grief for her. "It's a good farm," she said. "We could do like my parents, they were happy before they left this place. Weren't you, Pop?"

My grandfather did not answer. My mother hurried nervous little jokes into the gap. "Work with your hands, George. Get close to Nature. It would make a whole man of you."

My father's voice in turn had become grave. "Cassie, I want to be frank with you, because you're my wife. I hate Nature. It reminds me of death. All Nature means to me is garbage and confusion and the stink of skunk—*brrool*"

"Nature," my grandfather pronounced in his stately way, after clearing his throat vehemently, "is like a mother; she com-forts and chas-tises with the same hand."

An invisible membranous tension spread through the house and I knew that my mother had begun to cry. Her tears were half my own yet I was glad she had been defeated, for the thought of my father as farmer frightened me. It would sink me too into the soil.

They had left a potty by the bed and, kneeling humbly, I used it. Only the medallions of my wallpaper watched. Like a flayed hide stiff with blood my red shirt lay crumpled on the floor against the baseboard. The action of getting out of bed threw into relief my condition. I was weak-legged and headachy and my throat felt glazed with dry glass. But my nose had begun to run and I could scrape together a small cough. As I resettled myself in bed I relaxed into the comfortable foreknowledge of the familiar cycle of a cold: the loosening cough, the clogging nose, the subsiding fever, the sure three days in bed. It was during these convalescences that my future seemed closest to me, that the thought of painting excited me most and sprang the most hopeful conceptions. Lying in bed sick I marshalled vast phantoms of pigment, and the world seemed to exist as the occasion of my dreams.

My father had heard me get out of bed and he came upstairs. He was dressed in his too-short coat and his imbecile knit cap. He was ready to go, and today my sleepiness wouldn't hold him back. His face wore a gaiety. "How is it, kid? Boy, I gave you a rough three days."

"It wasn't your fault. I'm glad it worked out."

"Huh? You mean about the X-rays? Yeah, I've always been lucky. God takes care of you if you let Him."

"Are you sure there's school today?"

"Yep, the radio says they're all ready to go. The monsters are ready to learn."

"Hey. Daddy."

"Huh?"

"If you want to quit or take a sabbatical or something, don't not do it on my account."

"Don't you worry about that. Don't you worry about your old man, you got enough on your mind. I never made a decision in my life that wasn't one hundred per cent selfish."

I turned my face away and looked through the window. In time my father appeared in this window, an erect figure dark against the snow. His posture made no concession to the pull underfoot; upright he waded out through our yard and past the mailbox and up the hill until he was lost to my sight behind the trees of our orchard. The trees took white on their sun side. The two telephone wires diagonally cut the blank

blue of the sky. The stone bare wall was a scumble of umber;
my father's footsteps thumbs of white in white. I knew what
this scene was—a patch of Pennsylvania in 1947—and yet I
did not know, was in my softly fevered state mindlessly
soaked in a rectangle of colored light. I burned to paint it,
just like that, in its puzzle of glory; it came upon me that I
must go to Nature disarmed of perspective and stretch myself
like a large transparent canvas upon her in the hope that, my
submission being perfect, the imprint of a beautiful and useful
truth would be taken.

Then—as if by permitting this inchoate excitement to pass
through me I had done an honest piece of work—I went
weary and closed my eyes and nearly dozed, so that when
my mother brought up my orange juice and cereal I ate with
an unready mouth.

IX

ALONE he walked through the white width. His hooves
clattered, the fourth scraping (bone against bone), on
the limestone plateau, sunstruck from above. Was the dome
bronze or iron? From Sky to Earth, they said, an anvil would
fall nine days and nights; and from Earth again it would fall
nine days and nights and on the tenth day strike Tartaros. In
the first days, when Uranus nightly coupled with Gaia, the
distance must have been less. Perhaps now it was more, perhaps—the thought deepened his sickness—an anvil could fall
forever from Sky and never strike Earth. For indeed, was
not Mother Ge, who from her damp clefts had once freely
brought forth the Hundred-handed, the metal-wielding One-
eyed, deep-swirling Oceanus, Caeus and Crius and Hyper-
ion and Iapetus, Theia and Rhea, Themis and Mnemo-
syne and gold-crowned Phoebe and lovely Tethys the mother
of Philyra; Ge who when watered by the blood-drops of her
consort's mutilation brought forth the avenging Erinnyes and
the gentler Meliai, the shadows of ash-trees and the nurses of
Zeus; Ge who brought forth Pegasos from the drops of the
Gorgon's blood and who mating with Tartaros brought forth
her youngest and most terrible son Typhoeus, whose lower

body was two wrestling serpents and whose arms stretched from sunrise to sunset and who flung whole mountains daubed with his blood and for a time hid the sinews of Zeus himself in a bear's pelt—was not Mother Ge who had summoned easily from her brown belly such prodigies now tranced by a strange quietude? White, she was white, death's own color, sum of the spectrum, wherever the centaur's eye searched. He wondered, Had not the castration of Sky worked a terrible sterility upon Gaia, though she herself had cried aloud for rescue?

The plants by the side of the road he walked were bare of leaves and sparse in variety. Orchard grass the signature of Ceres, sumac the dermal poison, dogwood whose bark was a mild purge, mulberry and pin oak and choke cherry, staple of hedgerows. Sticks. In this season they were barren of virtue and the ground of blank snow made them calligraphic. He searched their scribble for a word and found none. There was no help. There was not one of the twelve he had not consulted and not one had given him the answer. Must he wander forever beneath the blank gaze of the gods? The pain in his tissues barked and tore like a penned pack of dogs. Set them free. *My Lord, set them free.* As if in fury at his prayer there poured through his mind like the foul congested breath of Hekate the monstrous tumble of aborted forms and raging giants that composed the sequence of creation: a ferment sucked from the lipless yawn of Chaos, the grisly All-father. *Brug.* His wise mind gaped helplessly ajar under this onrush of horror and he prayed now for only the blessing of ignorance, of forgetting. Politic, he had long ago made it his policy to ask of the gods only what he believed they could not help giving. The gates narrowed; he mercifully forgot a little of what he knew.

The scene he had left behind him came to trouble his mind. His child lying fevered. His heart moved in pity for Ocyrhoe, his one seedling, with her wealth of hair. Needed a haircut. Poor kid, needed everything. Poverty. His inheritance, deskful of debts and a Bible, he was passing it on. Poverty the true last child of Ge. Sky, emasculate, had flung himself far off raging in pain and left his progeny to parch upon a white waste that stretched its arms from sunrise to sunset.

Yet even in the dead of winter the sere twigs prepare their small dull buds. In the pit of the year a king was born. Not a leaf falls but leaves an amber root, a dainty hoof, a fleck of baggage to be unpacked in future time. Such flecks gave the black thatch of twigs a ruddy underglow. Dully the centaur's litmus eye absorbed this; slowly the chemistry of his thought altered. The intervals between the hedgerow trunks passed him like ragged doorways and he remembered walking on some church errand with his father down a dangerous street in Passaic; it was a Saturday and the men from the sulphur works were getting drunk. From within the double doors of a saloon there welled a poisonous laughter that seemed to distill all the cruelty and blasphemy in the world, and he wondered how such a noise could have a place under the sky of his father's God. In those days he customarily kept silent about what troubled him, but his worry must have made itself felt, for he remembered his father turning and listening in his backwards collar to the laughter from the saloon and then smiling down to his son, "All joy belongs to the Lord."

It was half a joke but the boy took it to heart. *All joy belongs to the Lord.* Wherever in the filth and confusion and misery, a soul felt joy, there the Lord came and claimed it as his own; into barrooms and brothels and classrooms and alleys slippery with spittle, no matter how dark and scabbed and remote, in China or Africa or Brazil, wherever a moment of joy was felt, there the Lord stole and added to His enduring domain. And all the rest, all that was not joy, fell away, precipitated, dross that had never been. He thought of his wife's joy in the land and Pop Kramer's joy in the newspaper and his son's joy in the future and was glad, grateful, that he was able to sustain these for yet a space more. The X-rays were clear. A white width of days stretched ahead. The time left him possessed a skyey breadth in which he swam like a true grandchild of Oceanus; he discovered that in giving his life to others he entered a total freedom. Mt. Ide and Mt. Dikte from opposite blue distances rushed toward him like clapping waves and in the upright of his body Sky and Gaia mated again. Only goodness lives. But it does live.

Now he came to the turn of the road. A hundred strides ahead of him he saw the Buick like a black mouth he must enter. It had been an undertaker's car. It made a black spot against the heaped snow, fifty-fifty he could get it out. Above the brow of the field on his left the Amishman's silo poked with its conical hat of corrugated iron; an abandoned windmill stood stark; a few grackles wheeled above the buried stubble.

Brutish landscape.

The invisible expanse the centaur had in an instant grasped

retreated from him with a pang; he focused forward at the car and his heart felt squeezed. An ache spread through his abdomen, where the hominoid and equine elements interlocked. Monsters are most vulnerable in their transitions.

Black.

They really put the shellac on those old pre-war Buicks. As Chiron drew nearer, the shattered grille looked astonished. He saw now that this was the mouth of a tunnel he must crawl through; the children he was committed to teach seemed in his brain's glare-struck eye the jiggling teeth of a grinder, a multi-colored chopper. He had been spoiled. In these last days he had been saying goodbye to everything, tidying up the books, readying himself for a change, a journey. There would be none. Atropos had opened her shears, thought twice, smiled, and permitted the thread to continue spinning.

Chiron bit back a belch and tried to muster his thoughts. A steep weariness mounted before him. The prospect of having again to maneuver among Zimmerman and Mrs. Herzog and all that overbearing unfathomable Olinger gang made him giddy, sick; how could his father's seed, exploding into an infinitude of possibilities, have been funnelled into this, this paralyzed patch of thankless alien land, these few cryptic faces, those certain four walls of Room 204?

Drawing closer to the car, close enough to see an elongated distortion of himself in the fender, he understood. This was a chariot Zimmerman had sent for him. His lessons. He must order his mind and prepare his lessons.

Why do we worship Zeus? Because there is none other.

Name me the five rivers of the dead. Styx, Acheron, Phlegethon, Kokytos, and Lethe.

Who were the daughters of Nereus? Agaue, Aktaia, Amphitrite, Autonoe, Doris, Doto, Dynamene, Eione, Erato, Euagore, Euarne, Eudora, Eukrante, Eulimene, Eunike, Eupompe, Galateia, Galene, Glauke, Glaukonome, Halia, Halimede, Hipponoe, Hippothoe, Kymo, Kymodoke, Kymothoe, Laomedeia, Leiagora, Lysianassa, Melite, Menippe, Nemertes, Nesaie, Neso, Panopeia, Pasithea, Pherousa, Ploto, Polynoe, Pontoporeia, Pronoe, Proto, Protomedeia, Psamathe, Sao, Speio, Themisto, Thetis, and Thoe.

What is a hero? A hero is a king sacrificed to Hera.

Chiron came to the edge of limestone; his hoof scratched. A bit of pale pebble rattled into the abyss. He cast his eyes upward to the dome of blue and perceived that it was indeed a great step. Yes, in seriousness, a very great step, for which all the walking in his life had not prepared him. Not an easy step nor an easy journey, it would take an eternity to get there, an eternity as the anvil ever fell. His strained bowels sagged; his hurt leg cursed; his head felt light. The whiteness of limestone pierced his eyes. A little breeze met his face at the cliff-edge. His will, a perfect diamond under the pressure of absolute fear, uttered the final word. *Now.* ἀνίατον δὲ ἔχων τὸ ἕλκος εἰς τὸ σπήλαιον ἀπαλλάσσεται. κἀκεῖ τελευτῆσαι βουλόμενος καὶ μὴ δυνάμενος ἐπείπερ ἀθάνατος ἦν, ἀντιδόντος Διὶ Προμηθέως αὐτὸν ἀντ' αὐτοῦ γενησόμενον ἀθάνατον, οὕτως ἀπέθανεν. Chiron accepted death.

EPILOGUE

ZEUS had loved his old friend, and lifted him up, and set him among the stars as the constellation Sagittarius. Here, in the Zodiac, now above, now below the horizon, he assists in the regulation of our destinies, though in this latter time few living mortals cast their eyes respectfully toward Heaven, and fewer still sit as students to the stars.

MYTHOLOGICAL INDEX

(Compiled at my wife's suggestion. Chiron and Prometheus, being ubiquitous, are omitted. Not all characters have a stable referent; Deifendorf, for example, is now a centaur, now a merman, and sometimes even Hercules.)